# Nine Candles

## of deepest black

Matthew S. Cox

# NINE CANDLES OF DEEPEST BLACK

## MATTHEW S. COX

DIVISION ZERO PRESS

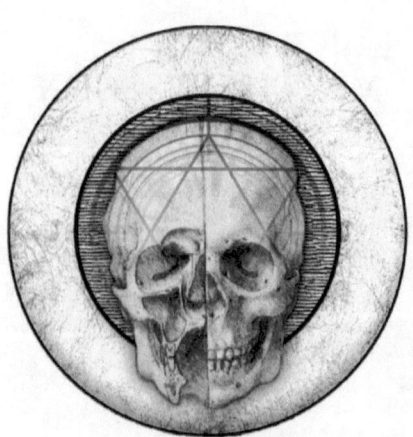

Nine Candles of Deepest Black
A Novel
© 2015 – Matthew S. Cox
All Rights Reserved

ISBN (ebook): 978-1-949174-62-5

ISBN (print): 978-1-949174-63-2

# CONTENTS

# THE PLEASURE OF EXISTING

Thursday October 8 - 6:22 a.m.

**S**orrow weighed down the lifeless morning sky and pressed heavy in the pit of Paige's stomach. Five dark toenails tipped a porcelain foot at the end of leggings the same shade of black as the polish. She scrunched her fingers into her second grey sock, not quite able to advance putting it on from concept to action. Cloud shadows crept across the wall in front of her, over posters of two bands she'd forgotten why she ever liked. Melissa's distant laughter at another one of Mom's lame jokes brought on a wave of *blah* that made Paige flop back on her bed. She didn't want to move. She didn't want to go to a new school. She didn't even want to leave her bedroom.

"You're gonna be late for school," said Amber.

Paige let gravity pull her head to the left and stared up through a tangle of jet hair at the sideways figure of her older sister and her Penn State sweatshirt. "So?"

"*So...* You're sixteen. You have to go to school." Amber walked around the corner of the bed, her jeans swooshing. "Come on. Don't do this to yourself."

"I don't like it here. Why did Dad have to move us to Shadesboro? I miss Ardmore." Paige let her grip on the sock loosen, and her arms flopped limp at her sides. "It's not fair."

"How can you miss Ardmore? I don't mean to sound harsh, but you didn't exactly have friends. You hung out with my friends."

Paige sighed. "Yeah. They didn't want me around after you left for college."

"Please. For me?" Amber leaned over the bed, her long brown hair draped free. "I hate seeing you like this."

"Whatever." Paige sat up and pulled the sock on before reaching for a pair of gothy black boots with extra buckles.

"Jesus... why did you get those?" Amber blinked.

Paige stuffed her feet into them. "Because Mom wouldn't let me get the thigh-highs."

"I mean... what's with all the"—Amber waved her hand around—"dark eyeliner and morbid stuff lately?"

"I dunno." Paige zipped the boots and let her head sag into her hands, hiding from the world behind a wall of dense black hair. "Why do they have to start school so damn early?"

From downstairs, Mom yelled, "You need to be out the door by six-thirty."

"Thank you alarm clock," muttered Paige. She sighed. "Mom won't let me dye my hair and I'm whiter than the damn Pepsi bear. Everyone thinks I'm Goth already; why not go all the way."

"It's not you." Amber reached to fuss with Paige's mane, but pulled back. "You're not this girl. And isn't the bear Coke's thing?"

"I am now." Paige looked up. "You see how Mom is... it's like it's only her and Melissa in the world, and Dad's a damn zombie. I can't believe they didn't take his gun away."

Amber folded her arms. "Dad's not the one who wanted to—"

"No!" yelled Paige. "Stop. Fine. All right, I'll go." She covered her mouth with one hand and cried. A few seconds later, she sniffled. "Dump the guilt trip already."

"I'm sorry." Amber stared at the beige carpet around her sneakers. "It's my fault Dad's being so distant and Mom's gone off the deep end with Mel. I wish I—"

"Will you stop?" Paige glared up at her. "It's not your fault. Not like you *wanted* to die."

The door squeaked open as Mom peered in. The small, glossy pink backpack in her hand provided the perfect accent for her beige sweater and black yoga pants. "Get off the phone, Paige. Good grief. Who are you screaming at this early in the morning? You don't have time. Get moving."

"Yeah, I'll get right on that." Paige scowled at the wall, wiping away tears. *Bet she'd notice Mel crying.*

Melissa appeared in the doorway, dolled up in a pink dress, purple leggings, frilly pink socks, and silver ballet flats. The girl's long, wavy red hair made her look like a tiny version of Mom, only with green eyes instead of blue.

*She doesn't even care we left our home.* Paige frowned off to the side so her little sister didn't see. *How can she be so... cheerful.*

Melissa crept up to the door until the tips of her shoes almost touched the color change in the rug. "I'm not in your room."

Paige drew in a breath to yell 'go away' or something similar like she always did, but swallowed it at a baleful stare from her older sister.

The little redhead bounced on her toes and swayed side to side. "Come on, Paige. We're gonna be late. Don't you wanna see the new school? Mom says my school is right next to yours. We can see each other at lunch." Pure glee radiated from her face.

"Yeah." Paige bent forward and raked both hands up through her hair. *Gotta deal with her at home* and *at school? Shoot me now.* "Great. Be right down."

Melissa darted off. Seconds later, the *thump thump thump* of soft shoes on carpeted stairs faded to silence.

"Don't say it," muttered Paige.

"You know Mel looks at you the same way you idolized me." Amber sat on the edge of the bed. Her arm settled like a cloud of cold mist around Paige's shoulders. "Don't take it out on her because Mom's not coping well. It's not Mel's fault. She's eight. She'll grow out of it. Every time you scream at her to get lost, she crawls under her bed and cries."

More tears rolled down Paige's face. "I'm sixteen and I still…" She tried to cling to Amber, but fell through her and wound up kneeling on the floor hugging the mattress.

"I made a bad choice." Amber let her arm drop. "I believed Eric when he said he was sober enough to drive. You tried to warn me, but I ignored you and… I'm sorry."

Paige sniffled and stood. "It's not fair."

"Hey, don't be like that. I'm here now, aren't I? Not away at school."

"It's not the same." Paige tried to put a hand atop Amber's, an intangible cloud of cold. "You're like icy mist."

"Paige?" yelled Mom from downstairs. "Enough with the stalling. You're going to be late. Move it, young lady. Right now."

Paige held two middle fingers at the floor, twisting them around like radio dials. "Ugh, the sound of her voice is like razors on glass."

Amber smiled. "Like the way she yelled when I got caught sneaking out for that party when I was seventeen."

Paige giggled despite tears. "Yeah. She was *so* pissed."

"Go on. I'll be here when you get home."

"Yeah." Paige sighed, grabbed her empty backpack, and trudged out into the hall.

She pulled her door closed before plodding down the stairs to the living room, hooked a hard left, and crossed the dining room to the kitchen. Despite the grey outside, the décor had enough white and yellow to seem almost bright. Dad perched at the far side of the basic wood Ikea table, lost in something on his laptop. A plain white tee shirt announced his probable freedom from work today.

"Morning." Paige flopped into the seat across from Melissa.

Her little sister attacked a bowl of Lucky Charms like a pink wood chipper. She paused a second to peer up at her with an adoring look while making an 'mmm' noise through a mouthful of cereal. The overabundance of cheer made Paige want to throw her into a closet.

*Amazing there isn't milk all over the wall.*

Mom leaned over the sink, pouring water in a flowerbox outside the kitchen window. Paige glanced from the blank table in front of her to Mom, and grumbled. Her pet black cloud popped out and hovered over her head. She let the backpack slip off her shoulder, stood, and went about collecting a bowl for herself. *You'd think a work-at-home Mom could spare ten damn minutes to make breakfast. She's up at the butt-crack of dawn.* A lump grew in her throat. Mom hadn't cooked breakfast for 'the family' since the accident. Every so often, Melissa got pancakes if she begged. *I can't even get a 'good morning.'*

Paige fell into the seat and set her bowl down. Melissa made funny faces at her. A tiny hint of a smile squeezed out from under the black cloud.

"I've decided that I'm willing to help you get your own car when you turn seventeen, but there's a condition." Dad looked up from the screen. "I don't want you riding in any car with a boy your age driving… If you can agree to that, we'll talk car on your birthday."

"Wow." Paige stared at him, frozen with a dripping spoon inches from her mouth. "That was… like actual conversation. To what do I owe the pleasure of existing today?"

Dad frowned. "I don't appreciate the snark."

She fumed. Melissa seemed to sense the mood in her eyes and shrank in on herself, staring at her cereal. Paige bit back the urge to shout for the second time that morning. "Snark? You've barely said six words to me over the past eleven months. Today I get a whole sentence. It's not attitude; it's shock."

Mom swooped around the table behind Melissa and fussed over her. "I forgot to do your hair… Oh, sweetie, it's all over the place." She set to the task of fiddling with every detail of her sister's outfit. "You're adorable. It will be nice when I have *two* daughters again, but your sister never much cared for pink… or frills."

Melissa un-shrank and glanced at Paige, as if asking for permission to smile.

"I've had a lot on my mind." Dad returned his attention to his computer. "We all have."

Paige stared at the pristine skin on the inside of her right wrist. *How much could it possibly hurt?*

"Maybe someday your sister will outgrow all that doom and gloom nonsense." Mom gasped. "Where are your earrings?"

"I'm right here, Mom. Stop talking about me like I don't exist." Paige stabbed her spoon into the cereal, scowling when it didn't cry out in pain.

Melissa shrugged before grabbing her earlobes. "I dunno."

Mom zoomed down the hall, headed for the stairs. Paige turned away so the dagger-eyed look chasing her mother off didn't stab her kid sister.

"Well?" asked Dad.

Paige munched three spoonfuls of Lucky Charms. "What if I don't like boys? Does your condition apply to girlfriends?"

"So you agree?" asked Dad.

*Wow. Not even a raised eyebrow.* Paige gave Melissa the 'just kidding' wink, setting off a milk-spraying giggle fit. "Would you even notice if I died too?"

Melissa went stone-still, staring, lip quivering.

Dad looked up from the screen. Paige had expected no reaction at all, or anger if anything, but he looked... broken. "That's not the kind of thing to ask, Paige. We've all suffered because of what happened. Can you please stop feeling so sorry for yourself? There's more than you in this family, you know."

"Yeah." She dropped her spoon in the cereal, no interest in finishing it. "I guess I'm being selfish for wanting, I dunno, maybe a 'good morning' once in a while... or a 'hi.' You should get the bolts on your neck checked soon. I think you need a recharge."

He grumbled and went back to whatever he was doing on the computer.

Melissa focused a stare on her that seemed to say 'please don't hate me.'

Mom glided in, her hair in a scrunchie she didn't have before. She helped Melissa put on two cheap, plain gold earrings. Paige thumped her left elbow on the table and braced her head in her hand while stirring at her cereal. Black draped over half her face, blocking one eye. She teased at her naked earlobe, replaying several screaming matches her twelve-year-old self had with Mom over hating being too 'girly.' Her hair hid the scowl she directed at Mom as the woman doted on her little sister. She'd been almost as clingy with Amber since she was 'the first,' and now Melissa got special attention for being the youngest. Paige... well, Paige just was. *At least Dad ignores Mel too.*

Melissa finished her cereal and Mom took the bowl to the sink, almost pulling it out of her grip before the child could slurp up all the milk. Paige forced herself to finish off the last of her breakfast, but didn't bother drinking the sugary mess at the bottom. She stood and grabbed her backpack.

"Don't leave your dishes on the table," said Mom.

"Oh, so I exist when it's nagging time." Paige fired off a spiteful look and started for the hallway, ignoring the bowl on the table. "I'm gonna be late, remember?"

"Give me a minute." Dad flipped the laptop closed. "I'll drive you two."

Melissa shivered. "I don't wanna go inna car. I don't wanna crash."

Mom rolled her eyes out of Melissa's view. "Oh, sweetie. Your father's a State Trooper. He's not going to crash."

Melissa sniveled, lapsing into a pattern of breathing that preceded crying.

"I was gonna walk, Dad. I can take her with me." Paige paused at the door. "It's not too far."

Melissa let out a squeal of glee. "Can I can I can I can I?"

"Is it safe?" asked Mom. "That's almost a half-mile of woods. She's only eight."

"Along a road," said Paige. "Dad moved us to East Bumblefart, but there's still roads."

Melissa zipped out of her chair, grinning from ear to ear, and took Paige's hand. "Mom? Please? Can we walk?" She bounced, causing her hair to fluff and fall.

"Better get going now then." Dad leaned back in the chair and stretched. "It should be safe, Andrea. The worst thing to happen in this place is a couple of kids spray-painting the stores downtown. That's why I picked it."

"That's exactly what I'm worried about." Mom grabbed Melissa by the backpack. "It's always the 'towns where nothing happens' where a little girl walking to school alone doesn't come home."

"Alone?" yelled Paige. "What is *wrong* with you? I guess I *am* invisible. Fine. Drive her. Maybe I'll disappear and you'll find me in a shallow grave next month. Not like Mom would notice."

"Paige…" Mom reached, but Paige ducked her shoulder away from the grasping hand and ran to the door.

She stopped at the bottom of the porch steps, where a gravel strip about fifteen feet long connected to a two-lane rural street. Dad's State Police car, a white Ford, tucked up so close to the blue family Suburban the push bars on the front touched it. *Walking alone?* "I don't *believe* you, Mom. Really? Say that right in front of me?" A quick glance back at the house revealed the animated silhouettes of a parental argument. Whatever they said, they kept too low for her to hear them outside.

Melissa ran out onto the porch behind her. "Pay…"

"What?" asked Paige, not looking back.

"Can I still walk with you? I don't wanna go in a car." She bounced down the steps. "Dad said it's okay." Melissa bared her teeth in an expression part hopeful grin, part fear.

*Now I know how sharks feel with those little fish clinging to their ass.* Paige looked away from the empty window. "Fine."

She took Melissa's hand and crunched down the driveway until gravel met paving. The road running past their house formed a veritable tunnel of trees; to the left, it led downhill toward Shadesboro downtown, the other direction held about three or four more miles of houses before hitting open farmland. Mom's worry something would happen to them precisely because this was the sort of town where 'that kind of thing didn't happen' made her hesitate. She stared at the wavering brown-orange leaves while listening to the faint hiss of the breeze. Maybe Dad had a good idea for once; the place *did* strike her as peaceful. She glanced up and back at a second story window—the parents' room—and made eye contact with Amber. Her older sister, her face half hidden behind a curtain, offered an encouraging smile, and faded away.

Paige took in a deep breath filled with the fragrance of damp woodlands, pulled her backpack up on her shoulder, and set off down the road.

# 2

# FITTING IN

Thursday October 8 - 7:03 a.m.

F allen leaves crunched under Paige's boots, disturbing the whisper of a breeze through the woods. She kept a tight grip on Melissa's hand and guided her younger sister across the street to the right. Every so often, the girl looked up with a broad smile brimming with adoration. *Did I give Amber that same face?* Her black cloud crawled out of the neckline of her jacket and hovered a few inches to her left.

For most of her life, Paige had worshipped the very ground Amber walked on. She'd spent more time trying to fit in with her older sister's friends than finding ones her own age. Not that her parents noticed, but Amber's death had gutted Paige. She hadn't paid much attention to anyone—least of all Melissa—for the first few months after that night. As best she could remember, the little one hadn't reacted much. For all she knew, her sister bawled her eyes out for weeks on end. It was hard to tell what went on when you're curled up in a ball trying to wish the world away.

Melissa shrieked and pulled back.

The sudden noise on top of Mom's suggestion of danger in the woods brought a yelp of fear from Paige before her brain shrugged out of her spiral of bleak. She looked around, seeing nothing threatening. "W-what?"

Melissa pointed at the ground, and burst into tears. "It's icky!"

About three feet in front of them, a dead deer lay covered in flies. Six or seven feet of smear continued in the direction a car had been going. Paige waved at a pair of buzzing black dots checking out her face.

"It's roadkill, Mel. It won't hurt you."

"It's eww!" Melissa writhed in an effort to escape Paige's grip on her hand. "It's got like *all* the bugs!"

Paige glanced back to make sure no cars approached, and strayed into the road to give the carcass a wider berth. Melissa continued squirming and making faces for a while after they'd passed it, until the trill of a distant bird distracted her attention into the trees.

The road between their house and downtown went a little over a half-mile, past six other houses. Two sat so far back in the woods at the end of long unpaved driveways she'd only guessed at their presence due to mailboxes next to the road. At the approximate halfway point between home and Shadesboro, the hill leveled off and the opening at the end of the tree tunnel filled in with signs of civilization: parked cars, streetlamps, and buildings.

"Are there snakes?" asked Melissa.

Paige shrugged. "I dunno. Maybe copperheads or something."

Melissa whined and tried to climb her.

"Get off." She stopped short of shoving her away.

Sniffles. "B-but Pay... snakes."

"Well, you wanted to walk. How long have you been afraid of cars?"

"Since before." Melissa kicked at an acorn. The pink ruffle around her ankle wobbled like a limp daisy.

"How much did they tell you?"

Melissa looked up, her gait slowed to a near standstill. "Amber got hurt inna car 'cause she was with Eric and let him drive."

Paige squatted, holding her sister's hand in both of hers. "Right. It wasn't the car. Eric had too much to drink. He blew through a light and they got hit."

"Why did he blow up a light?" Melissa tilted her head.

Paige couldn't help but smile. "I mean he didn't see it turn red. He drove right through it. Getting in a car isn't going to hurt you. It's alcohol that's the problem."

"Oh." Melissa looked down as they got underway again. "Daddy won't talk about it. Do you think he'll ever smile again?"

"I dunno." Paige decided to play kick-the-acorn as well. "I miss her too."

"Don't go away," whispered Melissa. "Please."

Paige cringed. *How much did she hear?* "I won't. I don't think I even wanna go to college."

"It's okay if you don't want me touching your stuff." Melissa jumped at a snap in the woods and let out a gasp.

A deer perked up, staring at them.

Paige's boot scuffed on the paving, echoing into the trees and spooking the critter into a sprint. Melissa squeezed her hand, looking around whenever a bird squawked or something made noise among the trees. A steady cascade of snaps, thumps, and rustling came from everywhere. It didn't seem scary, but it made her imagine an army of invisible gnomes working on wrestling moves. Every so often, a squirrel appeared and raced up the side of a tree, though they couldn't possibly have made the deeper thuds.

Her sister kept quiet for the remainder of the walk into town. Soon, forest gave way to a row of small shops, a McDonalds, and a coffee shop with green and white signs that looked like an attempt to trick tourists into mistaking it for a Starbucks. They passed a Hess station on the right corner, across the street from a small First Fidelity bank. Beyond the gas pumps, a strip mall with clothing and ski supply stores stretched northward.

Five blocks in, Paige felt like she stood in the center of the smallest town left in the US still large enough to have concrete buildings instead of something lame like log cabins. She kept waiting to see the creepy hillbillies or local cop who looked ninety-five years old, but most of the people running around appeared to be out-of-towners preparing to head south to go skiing. Not that Paige felt much like a 'local' yet.

Melissa's grip tightened on her hand as the pedestrian traffic thickened. Paige headed straight for the school grounds: four blocks in, left turn, three blocks down. She pulled her sister along a little too fast for small legs, but she wanted to beat the clock. Though she had only skimmed the paper Mom left on her bed, she remembered first period started at 8:00 a.m. According to her cell phone, she had about forty-two minutes.

She brushed among a scattering of high-school students on the sidewalk rimming an impressive slab of concrete bearing silver metal letters: Emmet G. Waterford Memorial High School. *Who the hell is that? Well, was...*

A channel of parking lot capped by a large grassy field divided a pair of buildings in the general shape of two Ls pointing their long ends at each other. The structure on the right was Shadesboro Elementary, as indicated by a smaller sign nearer the entrance. A pastoral spread of autumnal leaves shrouded the outer edges of both schools, rustling in a gentle breeze.

Clattering came up behind them. Paige glanced over her shoulder at a boy, probably in seventh or eighth grade, in a deep squat on a skateboard. He jumped a mild incline at the edge of the parking lot entrance and careened on a collision path with Melissa, who screamed.

The boy looked up, startled. He lunged forward and stomped the nose of his board, which flipped up behind him as his sneakers clomped hard on the asphalt. He caught the board at his side in what appeared to be a well-practiced maneuver, and came to a stumbling halt within arm's reach of them.

"Uhh, sorry." He flashed a cheesy smile and ran off with the board tucked under his arm.

Melissa seemed unable to decide if the near miss was worth an explosion of tears, and rendered a noncommittal sniffle. She kept quiet as Paige led her up the same steps the boy took.

The office, walled in glass with thin aluminum strips, sat on the far side of a large atrium filled with sports trophy cases and paintings of boring, stuffy-looking old men in suits. She trudged over a six-foot circle bearing a grimacing cartoony goat in a football helmet, and shoved open a door that scraped with a sound like tearing metal.

A pudgy, grandmotherly woman looked up from behind a counter tall enough to reach Paige's collarbones. The woman's glasses only half filled their frames and dangled on a beaded chain. She flashed an expression of mild disdain after her gaze darted between them.

Paige smirked. "What? We just moved here. First day."

"Oh. I was just wondering where your parents were." The woman's apprehension faded away to the sort of smile that could give someone diabetes. "Name?"

"Mine or hers?" Paige fidgeted.

"Well, why don't we start with hers? You look a bit old for this half of the school." The woman winked. "I'm Mrs. Reinhardt."

"Melissa Thomas. She was in third grade back home."

Two other older women crept up to get a look at the little one. The usual chorus of 'awws' followed.

Melissa tilted her head, grinned ear-to-ear and waved. "Hello. We're new here. I'm Melissa, and that's my sister Paige."

*Mel's gonna get carded when she's thirty.*

Mrs. Reinhardt handed Paige some papers Mom needed to sign. "You can take her down the hall to Miss. Phelps's class. It's the sixth door on the left side labeled 3B. I'll call ahead and let her know you're coming."

"Thanks," said Paige.

Melissa waved again to the office grandmothers and followed Paige down the hall to the indicated door. The roar from a sea of third-graders left to their own devices prior to the start of class rumbled from within. Her little sister seemed as unfazed at the thought of walking into a room full of strange kids as she had at leaving their home behind to go two hours away.

"You gonna be okay?"

"Thanks for walking me." Melissa raised her arms as if about to hug her, but flashed a sheepish smile instead. "Sorry."

Paige's voice echoed *'stop touching me!'* in the back of her mind. Okay, so calling Amber back from the dead wasn't her only special power. She could make little sisters burst into tears at will too. She gave her a one-armed mini-hug. "S'okay."

Melissa's pink dress flared as she spun to face the door and walked inside, glossy pink backpack gleaming in the overhead lights. Paige edged up and leaned on the doorjamb, smiling as quiet settled over the kids when they noticed a newcomer. Melissa marched up to a woman about Mom's age with mouse-brown hair, who tended to something on the computer at her desk. The teacher smiled at her before casting a warm look in Paige's direction.

Melissa twisted around to grin at her. "That's my sister, Paige."

Mrs. Phelps glanced at her watch and nodded in the direction of the high school.

"Yeah, yeah," mumbled Paige.

She waved at Melissa and trudged down the hall, deciding to head through the long strut of the L, which would open closer to the high school. After she crossed the central atrium, rooms for the sixth, seventh, and eighth grade classes went by on either side, as well as a few doors labeled 'Aux' or 'Music.' The older kids seemed far quieter than those in the other hallway. Paige stuffed her hands in her jacket pockets and marched to the door with her head down. *I guess I have been crappy to Mel.*

Sniffling echoed from somewhere nearby.

Paige stopped. She lifted her head and pulled her hair from her face, twisting side to side. The quiet whimpering seemed to be emanating from the lockers on the left. Her gaze ran down a row of narrow metal doors devoid of padlocks, stopping on the only spot that had one. She crept up to the door.

"Hello?" She leaned up to the vent slats. "Is… someone in there?"

Two eyes and a pale face appeared in the slits.

Paige gasped and jumped back. "Holy crap."

"Let me out," whined a tiny voice. The door rattled. "They tricked me."

"It's locked," said Paige.

"I know. I can't get out." The girl inside cried.

Paige glanced down the hall toward the office. "I'll get a teacher, hang on." She grumbled, grasping the padlock. *Who the hell puts a—*

A pall of dizziness swam around in her head. She braced her other hand on the lockers as her legs went to jelly. The wall of identical metal doors painted in pea green faded away to an enormous round combination dial, as if she'd held it up to her eye. The numbers rotated to thirty-eight, counterclockwise to nineteen, then clockwise again to eleven.

Paige blinked and shook off the daze. She stared at the lock draped in her fingers. *What the hell was that?* The sniffling on the other side of the door grew louder. She cocked her jaw at it. "I've got a ghost in my bedroom. Hallucinating shouldn't be this weird."

"What?" asked the girl.

"Uhh, nothing." Paige dialed in the sequence from the daydream. Her smirk evaporated to a startled gasp when the hasp popped free. *Whoa.*

The kid rattled the door. "Help!"

Paige twisted the lock and pulled it out. The door flew open, revealing a tween in a black dress and socks, black shoes, and long, straight black hair down to her waist. Red rimmed her brown eyes. She looked up at Paige as if seeing a ghost.

"Who are you? You're in high school, right? What are you doing over here?"

"First day in town." Paige took the girl's hand and helped her unfold herself from the otherwise empty locker. "My little sister's in third."

"Oh." The girl wiped her face. "Thanks. I'm Sofia. I, uhh, gotta go. I'm late." She started away, but stopped to check out Paige's head-to-toe black. "Nice outfit."

"You too." Paige chuckled and pocketed the lock. *Mine now.*

Sofia ran deeper into the building, heading for a door marked 8A.

Thirty-ish feet later, Paige pushed open a side door and went outside, squinting at a blast of autumn wind and leaf bits. By now, the parking lot had filled up, with the exception of a row of spaces nearest the street. Most of the cars looked like they belonged to kids taking auto shop, since no way would a responsible adult drive something in that condition further than walking distance from their house. Nearer the high school, a few looked newer. She jogged up another five-step concrete staircase littered with cigarette butts to a raised walkway that curved around a statue of some prig in an old-looking military uniform.

The front of the high school had three pairs of double doors where the grade school had one. A similar layout contained a big atrium crammed with trophies, but these held larger awards... and more of them. Rather than pictures of old dudes, the walls held a shrine to past quarterbacks of the Goats. Paige sighed in her throat. *Great. The whole place is football crazy.* Her pet cloud had grown wider than her shoulders by the time she walked straight into the glass door for the office.

A thin man in a grey tweed jacket with thick brown hair, glasses, and a dense moustache looked up from behind the desk and made a pulling gesture.

She yanked it open. The door went the opposite direction from its counterpart in the grade school, but emitted the same squeal of grinding metal. "Funny. What genius reversed it?"

"Sorry?" The man cocked an eyebrow.

The four women at desks behind him seemed half the age of the grade-school clerks. Not one of them looked up.

"Never mind... Uhh, I'm starting today. Do I have to, like, check in or something?"

He moved to a computer terminal. "Name?"

"Paige Thomas. I'm a sophomore."

The man typed for a few seconds. "Held back? Says here you're sixteen."

"No. July birthday." She sighed through her nose. "I was going to school in Philly, so I probably could jump right to junior year if you want in this place."

"Oh, here it is." He tapped the screen and a laser printer whirred to life. "Your schedule's already set. Looks like you've got a few minutes yet before the bell. Head to the cafeteria for now." He handed her two papers with a class schedule, teachers, and room numbers on it.

She glanced over the form:

---

Thomas, Paige E (SOP)
    Locker A158-4
    Period Subject Room Instructor
    8:00-8:45 Chemistry 204 Ruiz
    8:45-8:55 Travel - --- -
    8:55-9:40 Geometry 112 Pritchard
    9:40-9:50 Travel - --- -
    9:50-10:35 Art 131 Hollis
    10:35-10:45 Travel - --- -
    10:45-11:30 Gym Aud McDonnell
    11:30-11:40 Travel - --- -
    11:40-12:25 Lunch Caf - -
    12:25-12:35 Travel - --- -
    12:35-13:20 English 216 Martin
    13:20-13:30 Travel - --- -
    13:30-14:15 Soc Studies 118 Serrano

---

"What's SOP?" Paige flicked a fingernail over the corner. "Standard Operating—"

"Sophomore." He chuckled. "Do you have a parent outside? There's a few things we need signed."

"No, I walked. I can bring it home." She held out her hand.

"Sorry. I can't release the documents to a minor. A parent will need to come in." He seemed a little apologetic in his smile, or was it patronizing?

"Yeah, okay. I suppose you get a lot of kids forging their parents' signatures to *attend* school."

The man shook his head and sat back in his chair.

Paige fished her cell phone from her pocket on the way out of the office and swiped her finger around, tracing the password glyph. Three taps later, she held ringing to her ear.

"That was fast," said Dad. "What happened?"

"Nothing." Paige trudged toward the cafeteria. "Mr. Flanders at the office says you or Mom has to sign some stuff. They wouldn't let me bring it home."

"Oh." He exhaled. "I'll head on down there in a few minutes. Do you, uhh, need anything?"

A dozen different answers swirled around in her head, but all that came out of her mouth was—"nah. Mel's checked in. I got her paperwork for you."

"Okay. I might as well deal with that as well. I should be there in about ten minutes."

"'Kay. See ya." Paige hung up and shouldered through a pair of green flapping double doors.

The lower-grade hallway had nothing on the roar within the high-school cafeteria. Hundreds of students ranging from fourteen to some who looked nineteen crammed themselves into long row tables. Freshmen draped over book bags big enough to hide bodies in. Others appeared to be trying to sleep. The usual cliques: jocks, cheerleaders, misfits, and supernerds gathered here and there, interspersed among the invisible masses. Paige headed for the far end by a long window looking out on a narrow strip of parking lot behind the building, as well as the forest beyond.

She avoided making eye contact with anyone, kept her head down, her hands in her pockets, and shuffled toward an open spot at the last table by the windows. Paige flopped on the end of the bench seat, within a three-step of a green door bearing an 'emergency exit only' sign. Judging by the condition of the push bar, it saw regular non-emergency use. A clock hung to her left above an empty section of wall where she assumed a queue of teens would assemble come lunchtime. *About ten minutes to kill.*

The schedule printout included a basic map of the building, first and second floor, with room numbers. She plotted a route from the cafeteria to Room 204, where her day would start with chemistry. *Ugh. Science first period? I should've had coffee.*

"Hey," said a girl.

Paige straightened in her seat enough to get a look at the one who dared invade her aura of solitude. A slim dark-skinned girl with a puff of frizzy purple hair and a plain blue shift dress sat opposite her, bundling a heavy coat on top of a green backpack. She looked at least a junior, maybe even a senior.

"Mmm."

"New girl, right?"

"You the welcoming committee?"

"Ooh." The girl grinned. "One of *those* days? Wow, are those real?"

Paige stared.

"Your eyes." The other girl laughed. "I'm Renee, by the way. Wow, are they violet?"

"Yeah." Paige sighed. *Oh, boy. Gonna be a month of that in a new town.* "And yeah."

Renee reached for the schedule. "Mind if I see what they did to you?"

"You're gonna run off with it."

"No." The girl made a *pff* noise. "We outcasts gotta stick together."

"Outcasts?" Paige blinked. "You look like a model outta Macy's catalogue or something... well, okay, the purple hair."

"Thanks, but..." Renee gestured over her shoulder with a thumb. "Place isn't exactly a varied gradient."

Paige lifted her head and swept a gaze over the assembly. True enough, Renee seemed to be the only black person in the entire high school. "Wow, Dad really did bring us out to the sticks." She smiled. "I'm Paige. Sorry, that sucks. We just moved to Shadesboro on Monday."

"Eh, it's okay. For the most part the people here are cool... just, well, awkward sometimes." She seemed sad for a moment, but a smile sprang back onto her face. "I can't get over your eyes. Anyone else in your family have 'em?"

"Neither of my sisters do." *Did.* She looked down, flicking her thumbnails over the schedule.

"What's wro—"

"Hey, who's this?" Another girl took the chair to Renee's right.

Paige kept her head down.

"Paige?" asked Renee. "What's up? This is Santana, she's one of 'the guys.'"

"Where's Kenz?" asked the new arrival. "She's gonna get crap from Mrs. Weems if she's late again."

With the urge to cry swallowed, Paige looked up. The girl sitting next to Renee offered a curious look. A black tee shirt with a vampire Hello Kitty face peeked out from under a well-worn, long-sleeved blue flannel. She had dozens of bracelets on both arms, a mixture of cloth, plastic, and loose chains. Santana's straight brown hair looked even longer than Melissa's, down to her butt.

"Hey," said Paige.

Renee snatched the schedule. Two seconds later, her eyebrows shot up. "Oh, damn. Sant, she's got your dad first period." She flipped to the other page and back. "Lucky girl. She didn't get Powers for social studies. He's such a douche. Ouch, she's got Pritchard. That man's so boring he could put Richard Simmons to sleep in two minutes." She offered the schedule back.

"Who the hell is Richard Simmons?" asked Paige, folding the paper into her coat pocket.

"Powers isn't *that* bad." Santana pulled out a small compact and tweaked her dark eye shadow. "He's only a douche if you don't read and give him BS answers on quizzes. Oh, wow. Look at her eyes."

Paige crossed her arms on the table and let her head fall on them. "Ugh. Great. I get to have people freak out at me all year."

"Do you have to, uhh... You know." Santana suppressed a giggle. "I saw on the 'net that people with violet eyes don't gotta deal with feminine issues."

"That's *so* a lie." Paige muttered into the space between her arms and the table.

"Mackenzie should be here soon," said Renee. "And if you wanna stick around, you'll probably meet Sofia after school."

"Sofia?" Paige folded the schedule and tucked it in her jacket. "Weird."

"What is?" asked Santana.

"I found a kid named Sofia stuck in a locker this morning."

The other girls exchanged annoyed glances.

"Wait, you guys hang out with an eighth grader?" Paige scrunched up her face.

Renee nodded. "She don't fit in with kids her age. It was Kenzie's idea. I kinda feel bad for her. She's not at all weird and creepy."

Paige frowned at remembering herself three years ago. "Yeah."

A girl with shoulder-length blonde hair and model looks rounded the end of the table and swooped into the seat next to Paige like an eagle claiming the top branch. She set a paper carrier holding two cups of fake-o Starbucks on the table. Both had 'PSL' written in marker on the side. This girl had to be eighteen or close to it. Aside from the heavy black eyeshadow, overdone mascara, and spiked black leather choker, she looked like the homecoming queen, even down to a billowy white dress with a hem likely violating school policy.

"Hey," said the blonde. "New victim?"

Santana took one of the cups. "You're a lifesaver. Kenz, meet the new girl. Check out her eyes."

Paige wanted to implode into a tiny space. This girl was *way* too loud, and attracting stares from nearby tables.

Mackenzie leaned over like a mother hen trying to coax a chick out of the coop. "She's adorable. So Goth it hurts. You need a choker or something. Maybe some spiked bracelets, and someone needs to teach you how to put on makeup."

"I'm not wearing makeup." Paige glared. "I *am* this pale."

Mackenzie blinked. "Wow. Purple eyes... contacts?"

*Kill me.* "No."

The cafeteria hushed in an instant. Paige looked up. Dad walked in, in full Pennsylvania State Police uniform. Every eye in the room tracked him to the table of 'outcasts,' and a few whispers of 'that figures' or bets on who was about to get carted off circulated.

Paige pulled the papers from the grade school out of her jacket and held them up as he approached.

"Good morning, Hon." Dad smiled, taking the papers. He nodded to the others. "Ladies. Everything okay?"

"Yeah." *Oh, God. He's doing the peacock thing. Now everyone knows my Dad is a cop.*

He thwapped the papers into his left hand twice. "I just had a nice conversation with"—he cleared his throat—"*Mister Flanders* in the office."

Mackenzie burst into giggles.

Paige shrank. "You took that literally, didn't you?"

"Yep." Dad's expression remained neutral. "He didn't find it too funny."

"Uhh, sorry."

"All right. See you later." He saluted her with the folded papers and walked off.

Mackenzie leaned up in her chair, staring.

"Are you checking out my dad?" Paige grimaced at her.

"He's kinda cute for an old man. Gotta be the uniform."

"That's nasty," said Santana.

Renee gazed down, picking at her cup.

An electronic bell noise shredded the quiet, and the room erupted in chaos. Both Paige and Renee remained seated.

"Hey," said Mackenzie. "Meet up outside after school by the soccer field?"

"Maybe," said Paige.

Renee sighed and stood. She walked past Mackenzie and joined the throng filing through the main cafeteria entrance.

"Think about it." Mackenzie leaned over to whisper. "I think you'll fit right in with us."

Paige slung her backpack over one shoulder and stood as Kenz merged with the crowd. *Out the door, cross the space with bathrooms, down the hall, upstairs, left, four doors.* She traipsed along with the flow of students, gazing up at the drop ceiling tiles and three pencils someone had whipped into them like daggers. Her plans of dozing most of the day so she could rush home to stare at her bedroom walls rattled around her head. *What kind of losers hang out with an eighth grader?* The padlock weighing down her pocket made her think back to the strange episode in the hallway. While trudging up the stairs to the second floor, she took it out and held it, rubbing her thumb back and forth over the dial.

*The last time something weird happened...* She made a fist around the lock as a tornado of grief swelled up out of nowhere. Dad thought she was having 'separation anxiety' after Amber had gone off to school. No amount of begging had convinced him to call her and order her to come home. Her mind swam with images of her old bedroom ceiling, the night she couldn't sleep.

Two in the morning, they'd gotten 'the call.' Amber had been killed in a three-car accident on the way back to the dorms from a party. Of course, the police hadn't dropped the bad news on them until they got there in person. She drifted for a moment, feeling as though she'd gotten sucked back in time to that long, crappy ride in the middle of the night. Too tired to focus, too wound up in knots to dare sleep.

Paige snapped out of it, finding herself alone in a hall full of lockers and doors. Her boot heel squeaked as she turned and backtracked to the classroom she'd walked right past. An energetic discussion about alkali metals skidded to a halt as twenty or so kids and one late-thirties Hispanic man in a dingy olive suit jacket paused to look at her. She caught sight of an open desk near the back and slouched, hair over her face.

"Miss?" asked the teacher.

"Sorry I'm late. First day. I got lost." Paige hurried to the back of the room and slipped into the desk, clinging to the backpack in her lap.

The teacher walked over and set a chemistry textbook down in front of her. "Welcome to Shadesboro. I'm Mr. Ruiz. You'll be needing this." He gestured at a wall of square doors in the back of the class. "Cubby 25 is yours. Apron, gloves, goggles for when we start our project for world domination."

Chuckling spread through the room.

"Thanks." Paige kept her gaze locked on the desk.

Mr. Ruiz smiled, patted the textbook, and looked over the class. "I hated public speaking too at your age. Everyone, this is Paige. She's new in town. Not going to make her stand up and introduce herself, since she's probably going to have to do that five or six times today."

Some people muttered hi, some waved, and some ignored her.

"Okay," said Mr. Ruiz as he returned to the front. "Who can tell me what lithium, sodium, potassium, rubidium, cesium, and francium have in common?"

"They all big words," said a boy three desks to her right.

Subdued chuckling spread over the class.

*They're all boring.* Paige slumped to the side, leaned back, and tried not to make eye contact with anyone.

# 3

# MAGIC NUMBER

Thursday October 8 - 2:01 p.m.

Paige's pet black cloud had grown to the size of an adolescent elephant in Mr. Serrano's last period social studies class. The bearded, rotund man in green suspender slacks and round spectacles seemed jovial at first—she'd thought him a Puerto Rican Santa Claus—until she'd made the mistake of saying she didn't think it mattered who started World War I since it was already over. 'Archduke who?' hadn't gone over well either, and 'whatever' had brought full-on maraschino red to his face.

Of course, she'd made friends with her classmates at that point since he'd spent the last forty minutes rambling on and on about why 'young people' needed to care about the past, and politics, and civic responsibilities. A diatribe about unmotivated youth couldn't be put on a quiz.

With the teacher engaging some of the more responsive students in the front row, Paige sank back into the obscurity she adored, and turned her attention to the giant old-fashioned clock over the door. The thing had likely been part of the building since it was first built—in 1950-whatever. Another four minutes and freedom. Her gaze locked on to the orange second hand, which wobbled each time it leapt forward in quarter-inch steps, an arduous march in an endless circle. The ticking crashed onto her brain with the weight of a hammer on an iron cauldron.

*Bzz.*

Paige jumped as her left thigh vibrated. Once sure Mr. Serrano wasn't looking at her, she pulled her cell phone out and glanced at the screen.

Mom: what time do u get out?

*Wow. First Dad talks to me and now Mom realizes I exist.* She texted back '2 mins' and put the phone away.

When the bell rang, she stood and hauled her now-stuffed bag off the floor, swinging it up to her shoulder. It hit her back with almost enough force to knock her over, but she kept her balance on the way out into the hall. Mr. Serrano rambled on, hastily spouting off about the two chapters everyone needed to read for tomorrow. Paige started to get upset at getting even more homework on the first day, but this wasn't *the* first day, only *her* first day.

*Couldn't Dad have waited to move during the summer?*

After a brief stop at her locker to ditch the hardcover textbooks she didn't need to take home and put her new lock to use, she followed the swarm out the front doors. Twenty or so feet from the door, she stopped in the shadow of an armada of gleaming school buses. At some point during the day, the sun had come out.

Paige wandered across the grassy patch in front of the high school, avoiding the parking lot and eager seniors racing to get out of there. She held her phone, expecting it to ring any second.

"Hey," yelled Renee.

Bright purple hair made the girl easy to pick out of the crowd. She jogged over, trying to control her laden book bag with one hand. Santana followed close behind with a huge hockey-style sack on her shoulder.

"Damn, what's in there? Sofia?" asked Paige.

Santana rolled her eyes. "Books. If I wanna get into college, I need to get a scholarship."

"Wait, isn't your dad a teacher?" Paige blinked at her.

"Why do you think she can't afford college?" Renee laughed. "So you gonna come to Kenzie's?"

"I dunno. I'm supposed to take my stupid sister home." *Maybe I can pawn her off on Dad today.*

"You gotta babysit?" asked Santana.

"My sister is—" Paige's phone rang. "Hang on." She answered. "Speak."

"I'm picking Melissa up after school. You can probably see me at the end of the line. Good grief, this place needs a larger driveway. We're going to the mall so I can get her some things she needs for her classes."

Paige scanned the traffic, spotting the shape of Mom's navy Suburban about nine cars from the front of the grade school. *Guess I'm disinvited.* She scowled. "Whatever."

"Pay!" A missile of red hair and pink fabric zoomed across the parking lot and straight into her side. "You gotta see Miss. Peterson's classroom. There's *so many hamsters*! They're *adorable*. One's white and brown and his name is Hammy. I wanna take him home."

Renee and Santana made 'aww' faces at her.

"Is that Melissa?" asked Mom. "Where are you?"

"Look for the black cloud. I'm standing under it."

"Very funny, Paige. Oh, never mind. I see you."

The line dropped.

*Yeah, well, whatever. I didn't wanna go anyway.*

Melissa chattered on and on about her day. Paige forced a smile, eager for the high-pitched needles to stop jabbing her in the eardrums. Renee grinned at the red-haired sprite while Santana looked about ready to break out the duct tape. Mom pulled out of the line waiting to get into the curved driveway near the grade school and rounded into the central lot.

"Mom wants to take you to the mall," said Paige.

"We're going to the mall?" Melissa swiveled at the squeak of the Chevy's brakes.

"No. Just you and Mom."

Melissa thrust out her lower lip and sniffled. "You don't wanna go?"

Paige shot a dirty look through the reflection of clouds on the passenger door window, Mom's presence a dim silhouette inside. "I'm not wanted."

"Oh." Melissa sulked. She bit her lip and glanced at the truck. "Do you have a bad feeling?"

Paige scowled at her boots. "Nah. Not that kind of bad feeling. Mom just doesn't want me around."

Melissa reached up, but again aborted a hug with a fearful glance. She backed up for two steps and walked over to the Suburban, dragging her feet with her head down. Paige rubbed her stomach in an effort to dispel guilt while the little girl hesitated at the open door, as if terrified to get in.

"Guess you're off the hook," said Renee. "Your sister's totes adorable."

"Is she always that hyper?" Santana shivered. "My brother's easy. All it takes is an Xbox and he's quiet all damn day."

Melissa looked at Paige and bit her lip, her leg twitching. After a long stare, she climbed in.

Sofia trudged across the parking lot from the grade school. A smaller version of Paige's black cloud hovered over her head. Her book bag dangled from two fingers of her left hand, straps scraping the ground.

"What's up Sof? You look like you're going to kill someone." Santana raised an eyebrow.

A strange soapy-sweet smell clung to the eighth-grader.

"Brett"—she made air quotes—"'spilled' chocolate pudding on my head. And Brittany started a rumor that I dyed my hair black, so the assistant principal almost sent me home for being out of dress code. She didn't believe me. Said it was *too* black to be natural."

*What the heck god did this girl piss off in a former life?*

"Hey." Sofia's glare softened when she noticed Paige. "Thanks for this morning."

"You met already?" asked Renee.

Sofia's face flushed. "Uhh, yeah. Stupid Michelle Porter dared me I couldn't fit in a locker."

"That's yo' own damn fault for bein' stupid." Renee shook her head. "Locked you in, didn't they?"

"Yeah." Sofia stared down. "With an actual lock too. Paige let me out."

A little beige Kia Soul with dark brown trim whirred up to a stop nearby. Mackenzie leaned over the passenger seat to yell, "Sorry it took so long."

"Kenzie likes coffee so much she drives a cappuccino." Santana grinned.

"So, you coming?" asked Renee.

Paige shrugged. Going with them promised to be as boring and pointless as sitting at home. Nothing really seemed worth bothering with since the accident. Amber would probably want her to go... make friends... have fun. She always harped about how it pained her to watch Paige just 'give up' on everything. The out-in-the-sticks school only increased her feeling of isolation, even in a huge crowd. It bothered her how fast these people—well, okay, Renee—decided to be friendly. Granted, no one else seemed to be even looking at her. Tiny thunderbolts rumbled across her pet cloud.

"You're not, like, freaked by occult stuff are you?" asked Renee.

"She's a witch too," said Sofia, in a tone as calm as if she had pointed out Paige's hair was black. "She did magic on the lock."

*What?* Paige almost gasped, but managed to hide her surprise. "No idea what she means."

"Michelle said she put a new combination on it without even looking, so no one knew what it was. She said I'd be stuck in there all week until they had someone from the lock company come in to figure it out. They made jokes about having to cut food real small to pass it through the slots." Sofia shivered. "But you opened it."

"It wouldn't have been a damn week." Renee threw an arm around the smaller girl. "The maintenance guy would've cut the lock off. They were only trying to scare you."

"Come on," yelled Mackenzie. "Or you're buying me gas."

Renee smiled at Paige. "Well?"

"Sure. I guess it can't be any more boring than staring at my wall."

Santana ran to the little cube on wheels and claimed the passenger seat. Paige wound up behind her with Sofia sandwiched between her and Renee. Mackenzie let off a cheer and pulled out. Paige stared at a bundle of green plant matter dangling from a bit of twine off the rearview mirror. The mass resembled an enormous joint.

"Is that pot?" whispered Paige.

Sofia covered her face in her hands and giggled.

"Sage," said Renee. "It's for purification and cleansing."

"Wisdom too." Santana yawned. "So, what's this about the lock?"

"I dunno." Paige fidgeted at her hair. *These guys believe all that stuff. Maybe they'll think I'm cool... or nuts.* "When I touched it, I sorta got this, uhh, daydream. I saw the dial turning to the numbers."

"Wow." Sofia looked awestruck. "That's wicked. I think she's a scryer."

"Supposedly, witches have a specific area of magic they excel at," said Renee.

"Scryers see stuff," said Sofia. "Past, present but somewhere far away... sometimes even future."

Paige clutched the top loop of her backpack in both hands between her knees. "I didn't *do* anything but touch it. I've read a little about Wicca, but I didn't like... invoke or anything."

"Maybe she's like a clairvoyant or something?" asked Mackenzie. She leaned on the gas to beat a light.

Sofia rolled her eyes. "Clairvoyant is psychic stuff, not magic."

"Easy." Santana gestured over the seatback. "New girl's dad's a cop."

"Perfect. She's like a living get-out-of-tickets card then." Mackenzie sped up to seventy.

"Slow down," yelled Paige. "Please..."

Mackenzie's laughter lasted two seconds before the desperation in Paige's voice got through. She backed off to sixty. "Uhh, whoa. What's up with that? You sounded like Sofia."

"If a scryer tells your ass to slow down, you slow down," said Renee.

"Uhm." Paige shivered. "My older sister died in a car accident."

"Oh, crap." Renee grabbed her shoulder and squeezed. "I'm so sorry."

Santana mumbled something in Spanish. "Hope she's at peace."

*She's in my bedroom.* "Thanks."

Mackenzie drove north out of the main part of town and followed a street past about six blocks of relatively normal-looking suburbia before they once again rolled into a shrouded tunnel of trees. Paige jostled about, staring at the pattern of sunlight creeping across the seat in front of her, broken into random shapes by leaves. Ten or so minutes later, the Kia pulled into a long winding driveway composed of two dirt ruts separated by a raised channel of gravel. At least there, Mackenzie slowed to the car to a jog. Despite the crawl, every bump jostled the girls around.

A quarter mile or so later, the jarring ride ended in a wide grassy lot in front of a huge powder-blue house that seemed far too upscale and modern for this part of Pennsylvania. A long triangular peak stretched upward from the front door with a massive rectangular window offering a view into all three stories. A chill spread down Paige's back the instant she looked at the place.

Mackenzie hit a button over her head and the rightmost door of an attached three-car garage opened. She parked next to a hot-pink convertible so small it looked like a real-life version of a Barbie corvette. Paige cringed away from it.

"I agree," said Renee. "Whoever did that to a car oughta be slapped."

"Leave Linda alone," said Mackenzie. "She's in her own little world. I keep trying to talk her into ordering custom white tires for that thing."

Santana laughed.

Paige opened the door. The second her boot touched concrete, the same inexplicable coldness rose around her leg. She went still, barely suppressing a shiver as the sensation crept up and over her torso and shoulders. *Something bad happened here.*

"Hey. You okay?" Sofia, stuck in the Kia because Paige had stopped, pushed at her arm. "You seeing something else?"

"Uhh, no." She followed Santana around the front end, past the pink atrocity and the empty third parking space.

Sofia jumped down; her shoes striking the floor together made a *crack* like a small gunshot. Paige twitched. Two steps at the door led up to a hallway/chamber with a washer and dryer. Past a bathroom, it opened into an interior corridor connecting the front door atrium with both a stairwell going up and another corridor leading to a giant sunken living room with a grey sectional couch, fireplace, and television almost as big as the short wall of Paige's bedroom.

She paused in the atrium. Something upstairs didn't feel quite right. Far removed from the panicky dread of 'that night,' it burbled in her gut with simmering unease. Mackenzie gave her a conspiratorial wink and shifted her attention to Renee.

"I'm gonna go wash the school away. Be right back." Mackenzie jogged upstairs.

Renee, Santana, and Sofia bee-lined for the expansive couch. Feeling like the fifth wheel, Paige followed suit and sat on the near end by the recliner part. Left of the television, a cut stone fireplace stood dormant behind a black wire mesh shield. Wooden models of sailing ships adorned the mantle beneath a three-by-five-foot oil painting of similar vessels at sea. Sliding glass doors to her right offered a view of a deck big enough to play volleyball on, with an industrial-sized brushed steel grill tucked against the railing. Shimmery glow on a cedar fence in the distance hinted at a pool.

*Damn. Kenzie's parents must own this whole town.*

A slim blonde in a white turtleneck dress that clung to her hips like spray paint glided in from an archway behind Paige. She padded over, smiling at the girls, and set a tray with glasses, a huge pitcher of iced green tea, and plain brown cookies on the coffee table. Fluorescent neon pink toenail polish glowed when she stepped into a patch of sunlight.

Paige tried to melt into the sofa when the woman bent forward in front of her. *If her boobs were any bigger, they'd pop. Damn, her sleeves are longer than the skirt on that thing.*

"Hi girls," said the woman. "You planning on sticking around for dinner?"

"Not sure yet," said Santana. "Thanks for the snacks."

"You're welcome." The blonde smiled and waved with her fingers, clicking pink nail extensions. "Holler if you need anything, I'll be in the rec room."

Renee helped herself to some tea, as did Santana. Sofia grabbed three cookies.

"Wow. Kenzie's sister is, uhh…" Paige scooted forward on the couch to reach an empty glass.

Sofia giggled.

"That's her stepmom." Santana bit a cookie.

Paige covered her mouth. *Amber looks older than her… and she's nineteen.* The eerie feeling radiating from upstairs peaked and fell. She glanced at the ceiling.

"Kenzie's dad's a lawyer. He commutes to Philly, but only goes in three days a week." Renee rattled ice around in her glass.

"She's had work," muttered Sofia. "She's like old. Almost thirty."

"Naw, she's closer to twenty." Santana shrugged. "We shouldn't be talking about her like she isn't right in the next room. She *is* nice, even if it's beyond creepy to sleep with a dude old enough to be your father."

Paige shivered.

"Why do you keep looking at the ceiling?" Sofia's eyes widened. "Do you feel something?"

"I dunno." Paige sipped tea and grimaced at the realization it lacked sugar. "Gah!"

Renee tossed her a little squeeze bottle of stevia extract. "Easy with that stuff. Three drops is super sweet."

"What the hell is 'stevia?'" Paige held the bottle up and looked at the label.

"Kenzie's stepmom is all about the healthy and natural. Those cookies are probably made from hemp or wheat germ or something ridiculous." Renee smiled.

Santana grabbed another cookie, overacting her eagerness to swallow it whole.

"Not that kind of hemp." Renee chuckled.

Rapid thumping down the stairs preceded Mackenzie flying into the room in a knee-length pink tee shirt bearing a cartoon rabbit with diamond-studded sunglasses and a pimp cane rendered in tiny silver discs, which glimmered in the sun. Her black eyeliner hadn't survived the shower, but she'd added a pair of plastic skull earrings to compensate. She stopped to grab tea and two cookies before flopping on the left-most part of the couch with her bare feet up on the coffee table.

"So…" Kenzie shot a pointed look at Sofia. "You're up, kiddo."

Sofia shrank in on herself as if surrounded by bullies. "I dunno, Kenz. If I get caught, I'm gonna get grounded till I'm out of college."

"You didn't seem too worried when you agreed to it." Mackenzie bit a cookie in half. Her calm smile broke for a second as the flavor appeared not to be what she expected. "We're counting on you, Sofia."

The thirteen-year-old wrung her hands in her lap. "I know, but… I'm afraid of getting caught."

"You promised… and you do want to hang with us, right?" Mackenzie flashed the smile of a Christmas elf. "My dad'll smooth it over if anything happens."

"Promise?" Sofia looked up.

"Swear." Mackenzie drew an X over her chest.

"What are you asking her to do?" Paige sniffed at one of the brown discs. It smelled vaguely of 'sweet,' but beyond that nothing. It didn't taste bad, but it didn't taste like much of anything.

Mackenzie held her arms out, speaking like a fortuneteller. "All will be explained in due time." She grabbed a remote, flipped on the TV, and hopped channels before settling on a movie channel showing the DiCaprio version of *The Great Gatsby*.

Random snippets of conversation about the movie traded breaths with Santana and Renee grumbling about stuff they had to do for school— apparently they both had the same class schedule. Mackenzie, a senior, interrupted with comments here and there about tricks for passing Mrs. Wheeler's English III class. Apparently, all her test answers followed either an ACDAB or BBCAD repeating pattern.

"She hasn't figured out that people know that?" asked Paige.

"Well, I'm not saying you just run down the dots without reading the questions… but if you're stuck, and it looks like the pattern is there, why not?" Mackenzie refilled her glass.

Sofia's head had gone back, mouth agape. Apparently, *The Great Gatsby* struck her as The Great Snooze. Paige studied her, trying to figure out why people teased her. She wasn't too short or too tall. She looked on the thin side, and reasonably pretty for an eighth-grader. *Maybe it's the black?* Paige had suffered the occasional random jab about being 'Goth' before Amber died. After, she hadn't cared enough to listen to whatever they said behind her back.

"So... New Girl." Mackenzie put her feet down and leaned forward. "Tell me about the lock thing."

Paige rambled through the story again. At the mention of her name, Sofia woke up.

"That's pretty cool." Kenzie tapped a fingernail on her front teeth for three clicks, her eyes contemplative slits. "You religious? Freaked out by spooky stuff?"

"No, not really... to both."

"How do you feel about witchcraft?" Mackenzie refilled her tea.

Linda poked her nose in. "You girls need anything? More tea? I can order a pizza or something if you get hungry."

"Thanks, Linda." Mackenzie smiled. "I think we're okay for now."

"What flavor are these cookies," asked Sofia.

"Green tea. Like the ice cream from a Hibachi place. I found a recipe on Pinterest." Linda did the fingernail-clicking wave again and disappeared into the back of the house.

A few minutes passed where everyone but Sofia zoned in on the movie.

"Well?" asked Mackenzie.

"Uhh. I never thought much about it really. I mean, I read a little. Guess I figured if I went pagan it might get a rise outta my dad, but he didn't notice so I stopped."

"Not Wicca. I mean *real* witchcraft. Magic and spells and stuff." Mackenzie gestured with her glass.

"Uhh, aren't they the same?" asked Renee.

"What are you, Satanists or something?" Paige bit her lip.

"Naw." Kenzie waved dismissively. "No and no. Wicca's like the Halloween version of what we do. It's all new agey and like nature stuff."

"I know a couple of people back home who would seriously kick your ass for saying that." Paige chuckled. "They take it pretty seriously, and they '*do* spells.'"

"Well, whatever." Mackenzie smiled. "Since you're not looking at me like I'm nuts, I get the feeling your mind is at least open."

Paige shrugged. "I guess. I think there's stuff out there we don't understand yet." *Wow. They didn't think I was crazy when I told them about the lock.* Amber used to love to watch those ghost hunting shows with her. A bit of pre-accident Paige crept out, the little part of her fascinated by the paranormal. Maybe she could fit in here after all. She slid back on the couch and crossed her legs.

"Uhh, boots... couch... Linda will go all *Ghostbusters* librarian on you if she sees that." Mackenzie cringed. "Skin peeling off her face, mouth open like a snake. Ugly stuff."

"Sorry." Paige debated taking off her boots, but decided to leave them on and sit normally. "I've got a ghost in my house."

"Really?" Sofia leaned to her right and crawled around the bend in the sectional to kneel right next to her. Between her dress, socks, and leggings, black fabric covered every bit of her except face and hands. "Who were they? Were they killed in the house? Are they mean?"

Santana rolled her eyes until she got a good look at Paige's expression. "Whoa, you're serious?"

Mackenzie grinned like a meth head staring at a fifty-pound bag. "Spill. Speak all the things."

It was Paige's turn to knead her hands in her lap. "It's... I haven't told anyone yet 'cause I don't wanna get sent to a shrink. I'm not sure I believe it either."

"I believe you," said Sofia.

Renee's eyes widened. "Oh, crap. What happened?"

Mackenzie got up and moved to sit next to Paige, putting an arm around her shoulders. "It's okay. We believe you. If it's too hard, you don't gotta say anything, but sometimes talking about things helps."

A tickle on her cheek made her aware of a tear she hadn't noticed fall. Paige wiped it. "My older sister died in a car accident last November. She was nineteen... first year in college. We'd always been close." Paige sniffled and blushed. "I like worshipped everything she did. I hated it when she went across the state to school."

Mackenzie rubbed her back, making sad, consoling faces. Sofia looked down at her knees and squeezed her toes through her sock. Renee offered a comforting sigh. Santana muttered something in Spanish that sounded like a prayer.

"The night it happened... I was lying on my bed at, like, ten or so listening to one of her CDs, generally being pissed off that she'd moved out. Out of nowhere, I feel like this pressure on my chest." Paige grabbed her shirt and pushed in on her ribs. "I couldn't breathe. Then, all I could think about was Amber. I didn't see anything, but it kinda felt the way I'd feel if I was watching her running at a cliff and she was looking back at me so she didn't see she was about to fall and die. I freaked out and called her, but she said she was fine and had to go 'cause some people were waiting for her."

Mackenzie squeezed her. "Wow, you're shaking. You sure you're okay telling us this?"

Sofia reached over and held her hand. She seemed caught between an expression of sympathy and awe.

Paige put both hands over her mouth and nose. "Yeah." *Deep breaths. Take deep breaths.* She lowered her hands. "I remember running downstairs and asking my

Dad to call her and order her to come home right away. He didn't take me seriously. Thought I was just being melodramatic about her moving out. I think I even threw up. He carried me to bed like a little kid, but I couldn't sleep. I called her myself three more times, but after the first one, she shut her phone off."

Mackenzie sniffled.

"She *is* a scryer," whispered Sofia.

"I was still awake at 2:03 when the phone rang. State College police called. Eric, her boyfriend, had swerved into oncoming traffic. They hit another car head-on. Amber"—Paige crunched forward, crying. A few gasping breaths later, she got herself under control—"died instantly. So did Eric. Some other girl in the back seat survived, but she still walks with a cane."

"Oh my God," said Santana in a near-whisper. "That's awful..."

Paige blocked out her memories of the two or three months that followed. "I was real close to her. Everything she did, I wanted to do. I didn't have any friends my own age. I hung out with hers. I couldn't believe she was gone. And one day, there she was... only a ghost. She's been in my bedroom ever since."

"You like see her and talk to her and stuff?" asked Sofia.

"Yeah." Paige fidgeted with her sleeves.

"Is she an oracle?" Mackenzie's eyebrows went up. "Does she tell you stuff about the future or other people?"

"No. She's just my big sister. Says stuff a big sister would say. Talks me out of doing dumb crap."

Renee stared at her.

*She knows. Her too?*

"I didn't... I mean... I thought about it, but." Paige grabbed another cookie, trembling fingers pressing the bland treat to squeezed-shut lips.

The girls sat in awkward silence for a moment.

"What kinda spell are you trying to cast?" Paige nibbled on the cookie.

Mackenzie hugged her, touching heads. "I think we have our fifth."

"Spells?" said Santana. "We cast numb-ass and the curse of pins and needles mostly."

Paige quirked an eyebrow at her. "Huh?"

"She means we sit on the floor for two hours and nothing happens." Sofia smirked. "Her butt fell asleep last time. She could barely walk to the car."

A spray of crumbs flew from Renee's mouth as she laughed. Santana leaned over and punched her on the shoulder, which only made her laugh harder.

"That's why your part is important." Mackenzie pointed at Sofia before smiling at Paige. "My grandmother had this old book. I found it in the attic."

"What, like a spellbook?" asked Paige.

"Not exactly. It doesn't contain 'spells' per se, just the rules on how to construct them. Symbols, circles, names of entities and elemental associations. The words don't matter too much. It's all about belief and desire. You have to believe you can make what you desire affect the world around you."

"We been believing and desiring a lot of crap, but all that's happened has been us talkin' to the floor." Santana folded her arms.

Mackenzie clapped Paige on the shoulder. "That's because we've been trying to do things with four people. Now we have five... like the pentacle."

"Desire and belief?" Paige glanced up at the ceiling at another pang of unease. "I definitely wanted Amber back, but I didn't believe I could do anything about it."

"You probably did and didn't realize." Mackenzie gestured to Sofia. "Did you want to help her get out of the locker?"

Sofia's eager stare fell to a glower.

"Yeah. She sounded so... scared and small." Paige stared at her hands. "I did want to help, but I didn't believe I was gonna do anything but go get someone with bolt cutters."

"Interesting," said Santana.

Sofia blushed, refusing to make eye contact with anyone.

"I think we're gonna do something this time. You in?" Mackenzie grasped Paige by the shoulders, as if giving her a neck massage.

Paige thought back to the hokey 'druid priestess' from that one episode of *Ghost Investigations America*. At the time, she'd been really into Wicca, yet that woman seemed unbelievably lame. Amber's laughter at how ridiculous the televised 'ritual' looked echoed in her memories. Paige grinned. "Okay. Guess it's better than dealing with Zombie Dad and Invisomom. What do we do?"

"Oh, not here... and not now." Mackenzie smiled at Sofia. "We need some things first."

# 4

# WARM UP

Thursday October 8 - 6:22 p.m.

Paige took off her boots and squirmed into a more comfortable position on the sectional couch, with her feet tucked into the pocket between the cushions and the back. Sofia spent about twenty minutes edging closer and closer until she wound up leaning against her like a lost puppy. The movie ended, and Mackenzie switched channels to a haunted house film that looked older than Dad. It got off to a slow start... family moving into a new place with creepy little windows in the roof that made the building seem to have eyes. Through the patio glass at her right, the sky had become angry again, prematurely dark with a heavy downpour.

"This is boring," muttered Sofia.

"It gets better later." Renee stretched. "Be right back. Tea wants out."

Mackenzie got up a second after Renee. "Idea."

Paige sat in silence until the awkwardness grew too intense. "Santana, your dad seems cool."

She shrugged. "I guess. Don't let him fool you. He tries to be your friend, but if you don't do the work, he's not gonna stay so nice."

"I never really liked science at all, but his class is interesting."

Linda returned with a fresh pitcher of tea.

"Thanks, uhh, Mrs..." Paige flashed a helpless smile.

"Walsh." Linda tilted her head. "I don't remember you. Are you one of Kenzie's friends?"

"Uhh, I just met her today. We haven't traded IDs yet. Paige Thomas. Moved to Shadesboro Monday."

"Oh." Linda set the empty pitcher down long enough to hug her. Boobs like air-filled balloons pressed into her. "Welcome to the neighborhood!"

*Kenzie's stepmother is the six-million-dollar woman... and not for bionics.* "Thanks."

A moment after Linda walked out, Mackenzie trampled down the steps with a battered cardboard box like the ones board games come in. As soon as she dropped it on the sofa, Paige stared.

Ouija.

"Are you sure that's a good idea?" asked Sofia. "Mom thinks those things are evil."

Mackenzie rolled her eyes. "She probably believes in the Bible too, right? It's cardboard and plastic... made by Hasbro or whatever."

"But you expect it to do something?" Paige pointed at the box. "So you believe in it."

Sofia shrugged.

Paige glanced sideways at the girl tucked up to her. *Ugh. Having one cling-on was bad enough. Did Amber feel like this when I wouldn't leave her alone?* Melissa took it hard whenever Paige ditched her. She shot a sour look at the rain-pattered deck through the glass doors. *Maybe I shoulda gone with them. Mel's so scared in cars.* Renee strode back in looking much happier.

Mackenzie unboxed the Ouija and set the planchette in the middle.

"Again?" Renee plopped on the sofa.

"I wanted to try it with our new friend." Mackenzie winked. "Come on."

The girls took positions around the coffee table, most sitting back on their heels, though Sofia perched upright on her knees. Mackenzie directed Paige to the side of the table that aligned her with the top center of the board, facing it upside down. Santana took the left, Renee the right, while Mackenzie and Sofia shared the long side at the bottom.

"Okay, you know how this works, right?" asked Mackenzie.

"Duh." Paige reached out and touched her fingertips to the planchette.

Renee, Santana, Sofia, and Mackenzie followed suit.

"I call out to any spirits nearby." Mackenzie closed her eyes. "We want to talk to you. If you can hear me, come to the Ouija and speak to us."

They sat in silence for a few minutes. Paige stared at the upside down skull-faced sun in the corner by her right elbow. The wood grain seemed to come alive, the darker streaks pulsating like capillaries. A sudden presence overhead made the ceiling feel as if it pressed downward. Faint hissing seeped through the painted drywall, as though someone far off in another room struggled to breathe. The cookies Paige ate churned, and a hint of chocolate burbled up in her throat.

*Chocolate?* She grimaced and swallowed. *Those cookies weren't chocolate.*

"Is there a spirit with us?" asked Sofia.

The planchette crept an inch to the right, hovering in the dead space between QR and XY.

"That's you," said Santana. "Someone's twitching."

"Belief and desire," whispered Mackenzie. "Come, spirits."

Sofia poked Paige in the finger. When they made eye contact, the eighth-grader mouthed 'you try.'

Suppressing the urge to roll her eyes, Paige took in a deep breath. *Something might be upstairs... what was that feeling?* "If there are any spirits here, please come talk to us."

The planchette remained motionless. Four breaths later, she got a feeling as though someone had walked around behind her. Paige glanced over her shoulder, but nothing stood between her and the patio glass but empty carpet.

"Is there someone behind me?" asked Paige.

Sofia shook her head.

The muscles in Paige's back tensed; the sensation spread down over her butt and into her legs, turning them numb.

"I feel you." Paige closed her eyes. "I… think there's a spirit behind me."

A slight gasp in front of her had to have come from Sofia.

"Nice try," whispered Santana. "At least you're scaring the little one."

Sofia raspberried.

A shroud of thick, icy air wrapped around Paige. She trembled as though she'd gone out on a December day in a bikini. Her teeth chattered. Leaden weight burdened her arms and legs; a growing pressure pinned her to the carpet. She tried to say 'I can't move,' but only a weak wheeze came out of her throat. Frightened, she tried to scream, but wound up moaning.

"Whoa," whispered Sofia. "She looks different."

"She's faking it," muttered Santana.

The planchette moved.

"Hello," said Mackenzie, once it stopped.

"I'm here," wheezed Paige. *What the... I didn't say that.*

"Are you a ghost or a demon?" asked Renee.

The planchette moved back and forth. Paige tried to open her eyes, but couldn't.

"G… h… ghost," said Mackenzie.

Sofia huffed. "Oh, like it wouldn't lie if it was a demon."

Paige's hands slid back and forth, pulled about by the Planchette.

"L… I… A… R," said Mackenzie.

"I'm not lying." Sofia grumbled.

Inexplicable anger welled up inside Paige. Her arms got heavier.

"It's saying something else," said Santana. "Holy crap! Paige, your breath is fogging."

"Wow…" Sofia sucked in air. "That's so cool."

"Nnnnh," wheezed Paige. *Help. Make it stop!* "Mmmmngh!"

"Dude, knock that off." Santana sounded frightened. "That ain't funny."

"D… I… A… N… A," said Renee. "Oh my God, it's Princess Di!"

"Was it an accident?" asked Santana. "Did the government kill you?"

The planchette almost pulled Paige over to the left it moved so fast.

"No," said Mackenzie. She sounded hesitant. "T. Not… P. R. I… not princess."

"Aww." Sofia whined.

Paige's lips curled into a snarl. Dizziness joined the anger. No matter how hard she tried to open her lungs, she couldn't draw in any air. She struggled to move her arms, but they ignored her. Below the waist, her body had gone as numb and heavy as stone. Again, the planchette flew around. Paige forced her eyes open.

The pointer spelled out H E R E. Renee spoke the letters when it paused over each.

Mackenzie's suntan ran away from her face.

D E A T H.

"Nnngh," said Paige. Her heart slammed against her breastbone; fire burned in her stomach. *Stop. Let go of me. Who are you? Please let me breathe.*

The planchette spelled out Diana again.

"Diana?" asked Renee. "Are you a friendly ghost?"

D I S Q U I E T.

"Does that mean angry or worried?" asked Sofia.

"P-p-pissed," wheezed Paige. She scrunched her face and sipped air through her teeth.

"Why are you angry?" asked Santana.

Mackenzie stared down.

B E T R A Y E D.

Renee shivered. "What year did you die?"

"Do you see God?" asked Santana.

Sofia whispered, "Am I gonna get in trouble?"

The lights, the TV, and the central heat all cut out at once, plunging the room into darkness. Feeble light from the stormy sky provided only the hint of silhouettes and shapes. Heavy footsteps pounded across the ceiling.

Everyone but Paige screamed.

Silence.

"I-it's c-cold," whispered Sofia. "I'm scared."

Linda, elsewhere in the house, cried out seconds before a heavy *thump*. Metal clattered, and something crashed to the floor. The sudden noise startled another scream out of the group. A loud electric tone came from the TV, similar in tone to an emergency broadcast warning mixed with a buzz.

Paige strained to pull away from the planchette, but an invisible force held her fingers down, gripped by numbing cold. A low growl in her throat erupted into a roar of exertion. *Please stop!* The heaviness evaporated and she snapped free, landing flat on her back with her legs in the air. After a second of paralysis, she sat up, hands braced behind her.

Scraping passed across the ceiling, along with a chattering hiss. Plates and cupboard doors in the kitchen rattled. As soon as the clamor stopped, a soft fabric-like mass brushed past Paige.

"*Madre de Dios,*" muttered Santana.

"What just happened?" asked Renee.

"Something touched me!" yelled Mackenzie.

"That was me," whispered Sofia.

"I think there's a ghost here... She was in me, using my body." Paige gasped. "She's really angry."

"Kenzie?" yelled Linda, sounding a few rooms away. "Why are all the lights out? Did the breaker go?"

"I dunno," shouted Mackenzie.

Paige shifted forward onto her knees, pawing the air until she got a hand on the table.

The lights flickered on. Labored grinding from the central heating fan echoed from the vents in the floor near the wall. Mackenzie knelt on the opposite side of the table, grasping the edge. Sofia had backed away into the couch, curled into a ball with most of her face hidden behind her black legging-covered knees. Santana and Renee stayed perched at the long ends, stretched across to reach the board. They remained in contact with the planchette, which rotated among the letters D-E-A-D in a repeating cycle.

"Make it stop," whispered Santana. "I can't let go."

"Me neither." Renee's eyes looked about to pop out of her head.

Cream-colored silk hovered in the left corner of Paige's vision, wavering in a nonexistent breeze. Paige's throat tightened. She turned her head in a slow, hesitant motion despite not wanting to look.

A pallid fortyish woman with scraggly blonde hair down to the middle of her back stood in a cloud of frigidity, staring at Mackenzie with an expression of mournful sorrow. A mottle of light-brown vomit spattered the front of her almost transparent nightie. Paige slid a hand up, covering her throat. Renee stared through the spirit at Paige, as though she couldn't see it.

The apparition glided forward, into the table, and put a hand on Mackenzie's shoulder.

Mackenzie let off a shriek.

Darkness.

Everyone (except the ghost) screamed.

A moment of silence passed pierced only by rapid breathing before the central heating kicked on again. Seconds later, the lights flickered to life. Paige whirled around, searching, but no trace of the spirit remained. The air had gone warm... too warm for a jacket. She shrugged out of it and flapped her tee shirt to get air moving.

Renee and Santana had leapt away from the board during the blackout. Both sprawled on the rug looking freaked.

The planchette slid on its own—without a single finger touching it—to 'GOOD BYE.'

Sofia's eyes went wide. "Ohmigod ohmigod ohmigod." She jabbed her finger at it in a rapid stabbing motion. "Did you see that? It just moved."

Mackenzie shoved Sofia hard enough to knock her to the carpet. "That wasn't funny."

"What?" Sofia sniffled. "I didn't do anything."

"The ice cube on my back." Mackenzie pulled her tee shirt forward to study the fabric behind her right shoulder, unconcerned with who noticed her lack of a bra.

"I didn't touch you with an ice cube. Your shirt isn't wet." Sofia sat up.

*Wham!*

The girls jumped as the house shook from an impact to the ceiling.

Linda speed-walked into the room. "What's going on? Why are you girls screaming so much?" She set her hands on her hips and smirked at the television. Blood oozed from the walls in the movie. "Oh, you shouldn't be watching that stuff. It's obviously too much for you. Damn this storm. Every single time it rains, the power cuts out."

A door upstairs slammed.

Renee and Santana screamed again, flailing. Sofia darted around the table and pounced on Paige, clinging. Mackenzie stared up at the ceiling.

"Don?" yelled Linda, leaning toward the stairs. "Is that you?" When no answer came, the woman backed away, whispering, "Stay here. I'm going to call the police. Someone's in the house."

"I don't think so," said Mackenzie. "Had to be the wind."

Paige looked at the smoky grey carpet between her knees. *That woman looked like Mackenzie in twenty years.*

The doorbell rang.

Paige gasped; Sofia screamed; Santana's eyes shot wide open; Renee and Mackenzie jumped.

Linda gave them a confused look and hurried off to answer.

"That was intense," said Santana. "Did that really happen?"

"I think so." Renee hugged herself and shivered.

Mackenzie's look of flustered worry faded to a broad grin. "This is *so* gonna work now. Paige, you are the awesome."

"Sofia?" yelled Linda from the foyer. "Your Mom's here. Time to go home."

"Okay," Sofia yelled, got up, and stuck her feet into her shoes one after the next. "That was... cool. Scary as hell, but cool."

"Remember." Mackenzie pointed at her.

"Yeah..." Sofia looked down. "I'll try."

Paige glanced at Mackenzie as the eighth-grader headed for the door. "What did you ask her to do?"

Mackenzie picked at the carpet by her knee. "Nothing bad. Just borrowing some stuff no one needs anymore. Stuff that's already gonna be thrown out. It's not stealing."

Renee grabbed the remote and switched the TV until a *Buffy* rerun popped up. Santana hadn't moved from where she'd scooted away from the table, and had a look on her face as though one more loud noise would send her running for the door.

"So you want her to steal something?" Paige swallowed, trying to get the flavor of chalky chocolate out of her mouth. A twist lingered in her gut, though she couldn't tell if it meant something else was imminent or if it came from what she'd just seen.

"It's really nothing." Mackenzie grabbed at the sofa arm to pull herself upright, clinging as if afraid to fall over. She seemed to be working hard not to cry. "I don't think I'm gonna be sleeping tonight."

"No kidding," muttered Renee.

The mood melting down from the ceiling hadn't gotten any friendlier.

*Whoa... It's getting angrier.* Paige gulped down a few swigs of tea, which swept the last vestiges of chocolate out of her mouth. "I should probably go home."

Santana and Renee exchanged looks. Renee stuffed an entire cookie in her mouth at once while Santana kept fidgeting at her sleeves.

"Okay." Mackenzie padded to the wall near the door down to the garage, and took keys off a peg. "I'll drop you off. It's too nasty out to walk, and I need to get outta here for a bit."

"Uhh, you're not dressed?" Paige pulled her boots on, glancing at the girl's knee-length pink tee shirt. "Isn't it, like, illegal to drive with no pants?"

"I'm staying in the car. No one will notice." Mackenzie disappeared down the hall to the garage.

"What's up with her?" asked Paige.

Santana bit her lip, leaning to the side as if to make sure Mackenzie was out of earshot. "Her mother's name was Diana. She's rattled."

"She good to drive?" asked Renee.

Santana laughed. "Has she ever been?"

Renee's expression said 'good point.'

A little horn beeped.

Paige took a breath, held it, and let it out through her nose, worrying about the ride home. Whatever storm brewed upstairs frightened her more than the idea of Mackenzie's driving ability. She focused on the thought of getting in the car with her. Since no bizarre feelings of dread came on, she stood. "Later, guys."

# 5

# MIDDLE DAUGHTER

Thursday October 8 - 7:14 p.m.

**M**ackenzie pulled her cappuccino-colored Kia to a stop where driveway met road, and stared at the state police car. Rain pelted the roof in a sudden upsurge, turning the windshield into a blurry smear of road and trees. Mackenzie shifted into park and leaned forward to peer up at the sky.

"Wow. It's really coming down. If you wanna hang a minute till it lets up, I don't mind."

"Thanks for the ride," said Paige, fingers on the door handle.

"Wow. Is that a real cop car?"

"Yeah. My dad's. Well, he doesn't own it. I mean it's his to use." *It's not that far.* Paige pushed the door open. "See ya tomorrow."

"Figured." Mackenzie grasped Paige's shoulder as she went to slip outside. "Don't tell him about what happened... or what we do. Magic is for witches, not squares."

Paige rolled her eyes. "He wouldn't believe me if I did. I'd probably wind up dragged off to therapy or something... again."

Mackenzie gave her a look of condescending pity. "Aww. I'm so sorry about your sister. Maybe you can ask the spirits to bring her back?"

*That's got bad idea written all over it. I saw that movie with the pet graveyard.* "Uhh, maybe."

Paige pushed the door open and leapt out. She shoved it behind her and sprinted through sheets of rain. In less than a second, freezing water pierced her clothes and soaked her to the skin. Gravel crunched under her boots, loose rocks went flying. Her head-down run halted on the shallow porch. Safe under the cover of a roof, she fished in her pockets for the keys. Mackenzie tooted the horn, waved, and pulled a U-turn in the middle of the road. Paige hovered in the open door, watching the little beige Kia's taillights glide off in the rain.

"In or out," yelled Mom. "What are you, a cat?"

Paige closed the door behind her, perhaps a little too hard. A trace of food lingered in the air, pulling her along by the nose to the kitchen. No sign of a meal, in progress or cooking, existed. She checked the fridge for leftovers, but nothing inside looked quick or easy. Mom sat at the table, fiddling with little metal wires, beads, and strips of fabric.

"Uhh, what's for dinner?"

"Oh." Mom looked up. "Since you were out so late, I thought you were going to eat at your friend's."

*Thanks for calling to ask.* Paige glared at the stove, sighed, and flung open the freezer. The blast of cold hit her wet shirt and got her teeth chattering. Her gaze circled around boxes of white, orange, and yellow before settling on the giant wholesale-sized carton of Hot Pockets. She fished out two and slammed the door before banging the cabinet open and taking out a plate, which hit the countertop hard.

"If you break something, you're replacing it," muttered Mom.

*Whatever.* She popped the plastic wrap with the heel of her hand and stuffed the pockets into their 'crisping sleeves' before tossing them in the micro. After hitting 'minute up' four times, she ran upstairs to her room, ditched the backpack by the bed and traded her wet jeans for black pajama pants covered in a repeating pattern of quarter-sized cartoon skulls with pink bows. Her wet top and bra came off next into a bundle she threw at the pile on the floor. After a moment in the bathroom worrying at her hair with a towel, she slipped into a nice, *dry* (and somewhat too big) black tee shirt with a Type-O Negative album cover on it.

By the time she got back downstairs, the micro had stopped.

"Did you get any homework?" asked Mom.

Paige closed the microwave and walked out, carrying her food upstairs.

"Don't ignore me, young lady."

She tromped up the stairs to her room and closed the door hard. Melissa sat on the bed, in the same outfit she'd gone to school in minus shoes. Her broad smile fell to a worried look at the glower on Paige's face.

"I told you I don't want you in my room." Paige fumed.

Melissa's face reddened. She sniffled and dragged herself off the bed. Sniveling kicked in two steps later.

Paige caught her arm. Melissa cringed as if expecting a punch.

"Sorry." Paige sighed and set the plate on her desk. *She's up my butt just like I was to Amber.* "Forget what I said. I'm a bitch sometimes." *It's not her fault.* She picked Melissa up and deposited her back on the bed. "You can hang out... just don't break any of my stuff."

The redhead looked stunned for a second, then grinned.

Paige flipped her modest flat panel TV over to Netflix and waited for Melissa to pick a movie. She chose *Tangled* and flopped on her belly near the foot of the bed. Paige slumped over her desk, trying to force herself to read textbooks while munching on her pathetic dinner. Between what happened at Kenzie's and feeling like an unwanted houseguest in her own home, little of what she skimmed over stayed in her brain. Concentrating became even harder when Melissa decided to tell her all about the trip to the mall earlier. She'd gotten some notebooks and stuff to write with, a basic set of paints for the art class she had, a new outfit or three for school, and they stopped for ice cream.

Paige's pet black cloud popped out and grew four feet wide. *Mom never took me school shopping. Amber did.* The little girl's voice drowned into an indecipherable warble gnawing at her consciousness. It didn't take a genius to figure out Mom didn't really want her. They'd given her eight years to become the girly daughter Mom wanted before having Melissa, probably another chance to 'get it right.'

Melissa's ramble trailed off. "Pay? What's wrong?"

"Nothing. This crap is boring."

"Oh." Her little sister crossed and re-crossed her ankles, then tried to arch herself backwards and touch her toes to the top of her head.

Paige found a smile hiding under a couple blankets of gloom. The cloud shrank down to basketball size. She finished reading her assignments in the English book, shoved it aside, and pulled out her geometry work. Forty minutes and three pages of problems later, she trudged to the bathroom. Melissa waved at her, grinning, when she returned. Paige managed a weak smile at the overenthusiastic greeting, flopped back in her chair and grabbed the book for Serrano's social studies class. *Ugh. I can't believe I have to read twenty damn pages.*

"Mel, get ready for bed," yelled Mom from downstairs.

Melissa paused the movie and ran out. When she returned a few minutes later, she'd changed into a nightgown and had a pink-haired plush mermaid under her arm. She clambered back onto the bed and resumed the cartoon.

The story of John Brown at Harper's ferry dragged; having the movie on in the background didn't help her concentrate, and soon historical figures appeared in her thoughts as singing Disney characters. Her chair springs creaked when she leaned back and covered her eyes with her hands.

"Ugh." *Enough for one night.*

She moved to the bed and sat up with her back to the headboard. Melissa crawled around and tucked up close under her right arm.

When *Tangled* ended, Paige snagged the remote. "Okay. Time for old school." She put on the Pixar movie *Cars*.

"This is old," said Melissa.

"Have you seen it before?"

"No."

"I loved this one when I was… okay, younger than you."

Melissa grinned.

Amber peeked out of the closet and smiled at Paige. It took her right back to watching movies in her big sister's room. She choked up and squeezed Melissa tight without even thinking.

"I miss her too." Melissa stared down at her lap.

They watched the movie in relative silence for a little while. Rapid thumping passed in the hall as Mom walked by. A door squeaked, followed by an irritated sigh. Thumping returned and Paige's door opened.

Mom leaned in. "Paige. What are you doing keeping Melissa up past her bedtime? She should've been asleep over an hour ago. For crying out loud, if you won't be responsible for your own life, at least take care of your sister."

"Aww, but Mom!" Melissa whined. "Paige never hadda go to bed at eight. She never had a bed time."

"That's because Mom actually cares about you," muttered Paige.

Melissa took forever to get up and drop to the floor. Head down, she trudged toward Mom.

"I heard that missy." Mom scowled. "We can play that game if you want. How's 9 p.m. sound?"

Paige narrowed her eyes. "I'm not a little kid."

"Thought so." Mom slid her hand around behind Melissa's head and guided her out of the room.

The door closed with a soft *click*.

"Hey…" Amber walked out of the closet. "If it makes you feel any better, Mom never gave me a bedtime either."

Paige crossed her arms and looked to her left at the window, eyes red. "She didn't have to. You always went to bed so early. You were their first so they didn't have rules."

"And I woke up at like five." Amber meandered about, pulling at her sweatshirt. "Worst part about being a ghost is I'm stuck in this frumpy outfit."

Paige's scowl deepened. "You're still dead." She shut off the TV.

"You don't have to forgive me. I'm sorry I didn't listen to you."

"I had to sound like a crazy person." Paige wiped her eyes. "Hey… I saw another ghost today."

"Oh?" Amber stopped pacing. "The Amish guy across the street?"

"No." Paige took a breath to keep speaking, but stalled. "Wait, what? There's a dead guy across the street?"

"Yep." Amber walked through the bed to the window. "Dropped dead in the middle of his field sometime in the 1800s. Probably had a heart attack or something. He seemed nice enough, but apparently I'm not right with God for wearing men's clothes."

Paige sighed at the ceiling. "No, it wasn't him... I met this girl, Mackenzie..." She gave her an 'introduction' of the group of friends she'd run into. "... and she brought out this Ouija board. I got a strange feeling from upstairs, and this ghost woman appeared."

"Did she talk to you?"

"Nope." Paige leaned forward, put her feet together, and grabbed them with both hands, pressing her knees down with her elbows. "She didn't say or do much. Appeared, touched Kenz, disappeared. The whole time she was there, I just felt so... *angry*. Sad too. Like... It felt..."—she held up her hands, searching for the right words—"deep, and heavy. And *too much*. I couldn't breathe. Thought I was gonna pass out."

"Weird. Maybe she's still stuck in the other place. Sounds like you channeled her... like ghost writing only with the board instead of a pen and paper."

Paige stared at her older sister.

"Before you pulled me back, I was stuck around the area of the crash. If I wandered too far away, everything got foggy and weird like I was in a crappy video game where they only made a small map and a wall of smoke surrounded it. I could hear people but never saw anyone except this one fat woman. I think Eric's parents brought her to the crash site trying to make contact." Amber chuckled. "Maybe she felt me there."

"So you were trapped?" Paige shivered. "What, like because of the violent death?"

"I have no idea." Amber sat on the bed. "The two guys from the pickup truck were there for a little while, but they disappeared. I remember hovering over Annie telling her to hang on. Her ghost kept trying to sit up out of her body and I pushed her back. Do you know what happened to her?"

Paige couldn't stifle the wrack of grief that pulsed through her. A cold arm went around her shoulders as the tears came. It took her a moment to compose herself enough to speak. "She's alive. Still has a cane though." Sniffles. "So, wait... You think *I* pulled you out of there?"

"I believe that, yes." Amber smiled. "I heard you crying, begging me to come back and not be dead. You wanted me to be with you. A sort-of tunnel-like thing opened up and you got louder. I went through it and wound up in your old room."

"Sorry." Paige pawed at her ghostly sister, trying to hug air. "I didn't mean to."

"It's okay. I'm not upset. It's not like you dragged me back to Earth from paradise or anything. Besides, you needed the help."

Paige's emotions leveled off to a midnight black cloud of gloom. She stared at the dead TV, not caring at all about anything. "I don't think I would've done it. I couldn't even figure out how I'd do it." She rubbed her wrist. "Razor would've hurt too much. And I'm scared of pills."

"Don't lie to yourself." Amber frowned. "I walked in on you staring at Dad's gun. There's two kinds of people when it comes to suicide. Those who call for help, and those who really want to die. The ones who want to die rarely fail. They hide it from everyone until it's too late." Her voice dropped to a whisper. "I could feel which one you were, so I came to help."

"Staring at a Glock and killing myself aren't even the same thing." Paige scooted to the side of the bed. "I gotta pee."

Amber kept quiet as Paige walked by heading for her en suite bathroom.

She sat on the toilet, pajama pants still up, and tried to sob in silence. Amber glided through the closed door.

"I'm on the toilet," yelled Paige.

"Paige." Amber stopped an arm's length away. "You never were good at keeping things from me, and it's impossible now that I can feel what you're feeling. Please don't give up. Yes, Mom's being a shit to you and Dad's off in his own little world... but Melissa would be destroyed. You wouldn't fix your pain, but you'd give her so much more... and you *would* be around to watch it ruin her. You won't believe me, but you'd kill Mom and Dad too."

"I know... I know." Paige leaned her head back and blinked tears from her eyes. "I'm not gonna do it. I promise."

Amber's ethereal hand brushed frost over Paige's cheek and froze a tear. "I believe you. I'm not *gone*; I've just lost weight. That was really sweet of you to let Mel stay in here tonight. You gotta be the big sister now."

Paige sniffled and let out a sad chuckle. "It sucked being the middle kid."

"Go to sleep." Amber drifted through the wall.

"Easier said than done. This place still doesn't feel like home." She brushed her teeth, used the toilet, and crawled under her covers. White paint overhead tinted indigo in the moonlight. "Hi new ceiling. I'm Paige. We're gonna be best friends."

# 6

# THE ODD GIRL

Friday October 9 - 12:04 p.m.

**P**aige balanced a lunch tray in her left hand while navigating a narrow channel between two tables. Hundreds of conversations turned the air near tangible, pressing in on her from all sides. She ducked and scurried, hoping to avoid notice. Fortunately, most of the other students saw her much like her mother did—which is to say, not at all. She pulled her backpack up on her right shoulder and hooked a left at the end of the aisle, heading for the last row by the windows. She had no idea why the table nearest the back doors was always empty, but she didn't want to look that gift horse in the mouth.

The black cloud rode her shoulders heavy all morning. A dream of being a ghost watching her family react to finding her dead got stuck on repeat. Dad's 'oh, that sucks' reaction didn't bother her, nor did Mom simply nudging her body out of her way with a foot. Watching Melissa's complete breakdown and subsequent attempt to grab Dad's gun woke her up in the middle of the night.

Mr. Ruiz seemed to sense the gloom around her and somehow managed to elevate her mood from wherever it was to merely 'bad.' Whoever put together the class schedule had to be a genius. Ruiz could probably make the most boring subject in the world entertaining even in first period. The place Mackenzie got their coffee from tried hard to look like Starbucks, but it wasn't as high octane. One cup wouldn't do it for *those* kinds of mornings without two extra hits of espresso. Chemistry was at least interesting on top of that. He'd pulled her a few inches out of her shell, but Pritchard's second period monotone geometry class knocked her (and a third of the class) clean out.

After dropping her backpack on the table, she stepped over the bench and sat, staring at the sorry excuse for a cheese steak and fries the cafeteria produced. Every other Friday back at her old school, a local place brought in *real* cheese steaks. This thing looked like it came out of a freezer at a gas station convenience store. She grumbled and dug in anyway, even if the cheese smelled like molten plastic.

"Hey," said Renee. She took the opposite seat, having opted for the spaghetti. A plain black tee shirt and jeans made her the most normal looking of the 'outcasts.' Well, save for the purple hair.

"Hey." Paige stared down at her lacy black miniskirt. Even with the dark-violet leggings, Dad gave her the 'that's too skimpy' look, but didn't bother saying anything. Mom hadn't even looked up. A thin strip of bare stomach peeked out from her tee shirt. Two ankhs and a pentacle necklace dangled in front of her breasts. "Ugh. I don't have any drool on me do I? Pritchard's class is so damn boring."

Renee chuckled. "Oh, I remember him from last year. Couple of students complained about him if you can believe that. Assistant principal came in to 'monitor the class,' and you know *he* wound up snoring."

Paige smiled. A laugh started to climb up her windpipe but lost interest halfway there.

Santana swooped in on her left, also with a cheese steak. She seemed to be wearing the same clothes as yesterday. "'Sup girl? You okay? Looks like you didn't sleep at all. Love the black lipstick, but don't let McDonnell get a good look at it. She'll make you wipe it off."

"Crappy dreams." She lifted the sandwich to her mouth, but didn't bite it. "Your dad's pretty cool."

"Me too." Renee tried to twirl spaghetti onto a plastic fork. "That really happened, didn't it?"

*Ugh. I should walk across the street to the gas station. Their food's gotta be better than this, and an hour of detention would be worth it.*

"I guess. My dad likes having other people's kids over the house. A lot more fun when you only gotta deal with them for a few hours, and then they're someone else's problem." Santana picked up her cheese steak in both hands. "And yeah, it did."

Renee laughed.

Mackenzie breezed over, her springy blonde hair bouncing with her stride. Today she looked like the preppie her expensive house demanded: peach dress, light makeup, and no trace of spiked anything. She sat and tore into a brown paper bag containing a sandwich from a deli a few blocks away.

"It's bogus they don't let juniors go off school grounds for food." Renee scowled. "Wonder how much the lunch people paid the principal for that."

"If we could leave, no one would eat this crap," said Paige.

Santana, one end of the cheese steak in her mouth, looked insulted.

A flurry of laughter spread through a small patch of cafeteria ten tables away, where the seventh and eighth-graders shared space with the high school lunchroom. Sofia attempted to carry her tray down a row while avoiding other kids trying to bump it out of her hands. Some merely laughed at her, others added jeers. A blonde girl in a blue dress, patent leather shoes, and frilly white socks, stuck her leg out. Sofia stumbled and came close to flying face first into her lunch. Even though she saved herself from a fall, both tables erupted with laughter.

Sofia took three quick steps before another girl with chocolate-brown hair got up and stepped on her low-slung book bag. The stomp sent Sofia to her knees, jostling the lunch tray—but, again, she saved it. The brown-haired girl looked impressed, and clapped.

"Nice save, Wednesday."

Another round of laughs rang out.

Sofia glowered at the floor and made it another two steps before the girl stepped on her book bag again, making her stumble to her knees the exact same way. Sofia left the bag on the floor, still attached to her arm by a strap, and dragged it on her way to the table in a half-hunched loping walk.

Paige took a breath, half tempted to go over there and yell, but sighed it out. "Why do they pick on her? She's not fat or ugly. Did she do something mean?"

"Don't bother." Renee put a hand on hers. "They'll complain that high-school kids are bullying them and *we'll* be the ones in trouble."

Mackenzie took on that same mother-hen look she gave Paige yesterday. "Her parents run the Anderson Funeral Home. They all think she's like creepy and obsessed with dead people."

"No, that's you, Kenz." Santana winked.

Sofia, red eyed and sullen, sat next to Paige and kept her head down. The spaghetti *did* smell better than the pitiful cheese steak.

*Live and learn I guess.* Paige forced herself to eat another fry.

"Hey Sof." Renee smiled.

Sofia attempted a happier expression, but it didn't work. She pulled her book bag into her lap, opened it, and took out a white paper package, which she passed to Mackenzie before dropping her bag on the floor between her feet and reaching for her soda.

It exploded as soon as she pulled the tab, spraying her, Paige, and Renee with Coke foam. Sofia clamped napkins over the fizzling soda-grenade, and sat there dripping. Mackenzie stuffed the package into her Land's End backpack and zipped it.

The innocent-looking blonde girl who tried to trip Sofia cackled and giggled.

"I'm sorry." Sofia's eyes grew redder. Her lip quivered.

Paige helped wipe up soda. "Ignore them. That girl's probably pissed off that her parents dress her up like Cindy Brady."

Sofia smirked. "That's Brittany Kutzen. Her dad owns the car place downtown. She's been on TV."

Renee shook her head. "Local public access aired a commercial. Maybe fifty people saw it."

"Still." Sofia glared. "She acts like she's Angelina Jolie or something."

"Hey, you guys going tonight?" Santana grinned.

"I dunno." Renee cut a meatball in half with her fork.

"Aww you gotta go." Mackenzie grabbed Renee's shoulder and jostled her. "They've been planning this party for weeks. You're coming, right Paige?"

*Yeah right.* The suggestion of going to a party set off an explosion of butterflies in her gut. "Nah. I'm just a sophomore. No one's gonna want me around."

"It's fine. They won't notice. We might as well bring Sofia too."

"Bad idea," said Santana. "If the cops *do* show up and they find a twelve-year-old in the same house as beer... we're all screwed."

"No way." Sofia shook her head. "My parents would freak. If you want me to show up for the next circle, I can't get grounded." She reached around behind Paige and tried to punch Santana in the shoulder. "I'm thirteen."

Paige's smirk grew to a smile. "My dad's a cop. Maybe if I staggered home drunk and high he might notice me."

Renee glared at nothing in particular.

"What?" Paige looked at her. "You gave me that look when he showed up here, and now you look like you wanna rip someone's face off. Something wrong with cops?"

Mackenzie stifled a snicker.

"Nah." Renee picked at her fingernails. "I ain't seen my dad since I was like three. He left. I'm just being a jealous bitch."

"Oh." Paige huffed, the upward breath lifting her hair for a second. "I might as well not have one. He ignores me. Ever since Amber died, he's different. He barely even talks to Mom."

"People get weird when they lose someone. I see all kinds of random things at the home." Sofia stuffed a forkful of spaghetti in her mouth.

"I bet," said Santana.

"This one guy tried to climb into the coffin with his dead wife." Sofia dabbed sauce from her face with a napkin. "I've even seen fights."

"I heard some people even laugh there." Mackenzie snickered.

Sofia, mouth full, nodded.

"So you two are coming?" Mackenzie looked back and forth between Renee and Paige.

"Not a party sorta girl. Thanks but... nah." Paige gnawed on the now-hard cheese steak.

Mackenzie rolled her eyes. "It's not *that* kind of party. It's a school tradition. Even the nerds are going. It should be fun. Nee?"

Renee looked about as enthused as Paige felt. "I got stuff to do. Maybe if Paige goes."

"Awesome, so you'll both want a ride, right?" Mackenzie grinned.

*Ugh.* The mere thought of being in a house full of so many other people made her skin crawl. She looked up at Renee, making eye contact in an effort to read if she wanted to use Paige as an excuse not to go or really tried to talk Paige into going. The cafeteria lights and violet hair made her face even darker, and hard to analyze. Cold pressure in her gut came out of nowhere, knocking the wind out of her. She grabbed her stomach and stifled a burp.

Sofia giggled.

"You okay?" asked Renee. "Look like you just got punched."

"Uhh." She glanced at Mackenzie's massive smile. "I guess I'll go. Mom's taking Melissa somewhere again." As soon as she'd decided to go, the discomfort in her belly faded. *Oh, shit.*

"Great!" Mackenzie rolled up the bag her lunch came in, leaving it resembling a cartoony cigar. "I'll pick you up like seven-thirty or so."

"Great." Paige poked at the remaining third of a now-fossilized cheese steak. "Can't wait."

# 7

# PENALTY PLAY

Friday October 9 - 8:27 p.m.

Wind hissed through the treetops overhead, sending an occasional orange-brown leaf dancing in a spiral whorl to the ground. Paige sat on her porch steps, frowning at the empty driveway. Dad at work, Mom still off with Melissa, having fun. Jealousy burned like a coal in her gut, but it wasn't Melissa's fault. She fidgeted with her baggy black pants, bunched up where they tucked into her boots. Three thin belts studded with chrome pyramids circled her waist under a black half-shirt and mesh jacket. Two ping-pong-ball-sized skull earrings wobbled against her neck. She reached up and picked at her spiked leather choker. Going to a senior party with a bare stomach seemed a lot like chumming shark-infested waters, but she didn't feel approachable. She'd find a corner to haunt until it ended.

*Why am I bothering?* She scratched at her belly, trying to figure out what the strange cold feeling meant. *Was that Amber poking me and saying go?* "Amb? Is that you?"

No response came.

A few seconds after the whirr of a small engine emerged from the quiet rustle of trees, Mackenzie's Kia pulled into the driveway, Renee and Santana already inside. She considered bailing and going back to her room, but the sick feeling returned, making her dizzy again. The essence of beer rode a vurp into the back of her throat and she gagged. *Okay... Okay...* Paige shoved herself upright and stuffed her hands in the pockets of her black outer coat.

By the time she reached the Kia, she felt fine again. She got in behind Mackenzie and pulled the door closed with a *whump*.

"Hey," said Renee, also in the back seat. She all but vanished in a dark blue pullover shirt and jeans.

"'Sup." Santana grinned. "Ready for your proper welcome to Shadesboro?"

"This isn't some kinda setup is it?" Paige gripped the door handle.

"Nope." Santana smiled. "Just the monthly ridiculous. You drink?"

"'Course." Paige smirked at the window.

"You're such a bad liar," said Mackenzie. "It's okay, sweetie. You can be a good girl if you want."

"More for me." Santana put bare feet up on the dash.

"I've had beer before." *Over a year ago.* Paige grumbled. "Got sick, but I had it."

"Oh." Renee grabbed her hand. "Don't be so insensitive, Sant... Her sister... drunk driver."

The car got quiet save for the rumble of the road.

Mackenzie smacked her lips. "Oops. Well. I'll let you hold my keys then. Heck, you can drive us home if you want... if you're not gonna get oblitificated."

"She doesn't have a license." Renee swatted the headrest on Mackenzie's seat.

"Or a permit." Paige chuckled. "Course, not like I'd get a ticket. It would probably be my dad pulling us over. There's only like six Staties in this area, and they gotta cover forty-something miles in every direction on the highways too."

"Settled." Mackenzie laughed and swerved into a left turn.

They left the downtown behind and zipped along a side street amid an area that reminded Paige of Philly suburbs, only with more trees. After a right turn three blocks deep, a large cluster of cars came into view. One house on the left glowed from every window. Mackenzie parked in the nearest open spot more than a block away, killed the engine, and handed the keys over her shoulder to Paige.

"Here. You'll be driving us all home later. Sure you don't wanna drink?"

Paige took the keys. "Uhh, yeah I'm sure." She flicked at the keys, uncertain if her hesitation came from what happened to Amber or some part of her still trying to be 'the good girl' for Dad. It hadn't worked so far—he still didn't seem to care about her.

"Too much bad energy." Santana relaxed her attitude with a sympathetic smile and pulled on black flats. She tugged at the neckline of a clingy coral pink dress that barely kept her decent from breasts to thighs.

Mackenzie hopped out, sporting a lime-green miniskirt, black stockings, high-heeled boots, and an oversized sweater top hung off one shoulder. She spread her arms wide as if to hug the distant house.

"Kenz is here. All your beer are belong to us."

Paige trudged after the three older girls, head down, a dense wall of hair between her and the world. Five cars crammed into the driveway of a house pulsating with loud music, and three sat on the front lawn. The living room throbbed with green light, courtesy of colored saran wrap on the lamps as well as novelty bulbs. Seniors packed it wall-to-wall, most holding plastic cups of soda or beer. A few girls sat in a few boys' laps on the sofa. Partiers extended down the hall to the kitchen, where a handful of less socially adept guys raided the fridge.

Mackenzie elbowed the others and pointed at a senior boy with short dark hair and a cute nose. He had a varsity jacket, one elbow on the fireplace mantle, and the other arm around an auburn-haired girl in a basic white dress and kitten heels. The two seemed completely enamored with each other. Paige instinctively disliked him at the sight of the varsity jacket, thinking back to the entitled rich kids who'd ruled over her last school, but his clothes underneath had a scruffiness to them that suggested otherwise. She watched him for a moment; the way he smiled at the girl seemed genuine in a way she'd only seen on TV before. *Okay, maybe he's not a douche.*

"That's Cole. He's mine, but he doesn't know it yet." Mackenzie prodded her in the shoulder. "I see the way you're looking at him. I got dibs."

"Doubt it, Kenz." Santana winked. "He's allergic to bitchiness."

"I'm not *looking at him*," Paige rolled her eyes.

Renee flashed a mischievous grin. "Emily's not even human. Real people aren't that *nice.*"

A lanky guy with a day or four worth of stubble and unkempt brown hair slipped out of the crowd and stopped in front of them. His denim jacket bore a number of patches for bands Paige liked: Beseech, Metallica, Type-O, Sisters of Mercy, Candlemass, and a mix of local (she assumed) metal and Goth groups. A smoldering handmade cigarette—pot from the smell of it—dangled from between two fingers on his left hand.

"You're so damn hot," yelled the boy to Renee. "Want a drink?"

*That dude looks like he's old enough to buy beer. What's he doing here?* Paige gave him the up-and-down glance. At the instant she made eye contact, a powerful sense of vertigo came over her. The room disappeared as her vision went black. Amid the nothingness, a hand dumped powder into a plastic cup of beer, which foamed. Renee's face appeared, eyes half-closed. She swooned on her feet and fell away from view. Pressure like fingers digging into her breasts drew forth a gasp.

The horrible pop music and noise of the crowd surged back to the now with a rush as though she'd come up from being underwater. Paige gazed up at the ceiling, finding herself flat on her back

"Holy crap, Paige." Santana stooped to help her up. "What was that? You just collapsed."

She accepted the pull back to her feet and tugged Renee against the wall at the foot of the stairs. The boy winked at Renee, nodded to the crowd, and disappeared into the throng.

"What's up?" Renee glanced at the hand on her arm.

"This is gonna sound stupid, but stay away from him." Paige shivered. "I got a really bad feeling about that kid. He's... I think he's gonna put something in your beer."

"Better listen to her." Santana clucked her tongue. "Our little scryer seen your voodoo."

Renee fidgeted. Her mood darkened as a male voice came out of the crowd, telling the metalhead he was wasting his time.

The kid from chemistry class who made the 'they're all big words' crack pointed at Renee. "She ain't into guys, man."

The metalhead gave him a playful shove and wiggled an empty red Solo cup at Renee.

Santana cheered and hurled herself among the dancing mass, lost in seconds. Paige paused at a white post connected to a bannister beside the stairway up, not quite six feet from the door. Renee stayed next to her, though Mackenzie followed Santana into the fray. An archway on the right side of the living room led to a dining room, the apparent home base of a trio of five-gallon Heineken mini-kegs, a dozen bottles of soda, and a mountain of chips, pretzels, and Cheetos.

The top-forty music tweaked Paige's nerves, but she tried to ignore the prepubescent singer's squealing voice as he attempted to set a record for the number of times he could cram the word 'baby' into a chorus. *If Melissa winds up liking this crap in a couple years, I'm going to shoot myself.* Paige clenched her fists hard enough to leave nail gouges in her palms. *Yeah, I probably shouldn't joke about that considering...* The memory of gazing down the barrel of a 9mm Glock came on, vanishing under Amber's horrified scream of "Don't!"

Paige looked up at Renee and yelled, "I'm gonna get a soda. You want one?"

"Yeah sure. Any cola is fine." Renee leaned on the wall. "Just don't give me any of that diet shit. That nutra-crap goes right to your brain stem and eats it."

"Where'd you hear that?" Paige blinked.

"I saw it on Facebook."

"Oh." Paige exaggerated a nod. "So it's *definitely* true."

Renee laughed.

Paige turned her body sideways to slip among other students. Few bothered to pay attention to her, as though her very nature was so at odds with the energy of the party she didn't exist to them. Already, two boys lay passed out on the floor. She stepped around and over them, hurrying through the arch to the somewhat quieter dining room. A thick-bodied senior in a denim vest with *Dimmu Borgir* back paint and jeans held a yellow Rubbermaid pitcher under one of the mini-keg spouts, running beer into it. Something about his half-aware expression gave her the impression he was on the shallower end of the gene pool.

*Bubba's gonna have a job with his name on his shirt, probably inside a white oval.*

He turned his square-jawed head toward her, grinned, and... shimmied. "Hey."

*Who does this dude think he is, Jack Black? This guy's a hot mess.* She went for a bottle of diet cherry Coke and didn't look at him. "Uhh, hi."

"I'm Todd. You sure you don't want something a little, uhh, stiffer?" He winked.

She stared at him under furrowed brows. "Seriously? Uhh, no thanks." *Crap 'Nee doesn't want diet.*

Todd took a step closer, eyeing her ass.

Paige sighed. "I'm sixteen and my dad's a state trooper. He'll believe whatever I say happened."

"Uhh." The man—he looked older than eighteen—backed up, more angry than worried. "You got the wrong idea. What the hell you come here for if you don't wanna have a good time?"

She tamped down the urge to run like hell, acting calm. "We have different ideas of what fun is."

"Yo, Todd," yelled another older-looking boy, even bigger, ruddy and ginger with a goatee. "What takes so damn long to procure? We need the suds man. Bong is ready to go." He noticed Paige and smiled. "Hey."

While she glanced up at Redbeard, Todd traced a finger across her bare stomach.

Paige yelped and jumped back, bumping the table and knocking over a stack of potato chip bags. "Don't touch me!"

Redbeard grabbed Todd's hand. "Hey man. Girl don't look interested. Give her some space, dude."

Her shriek drew notice of a couple juniors and seniors in Goats Football varsity jackets. Four of them walked in behind the two older teens.

"Problem?" asked a boy that could've been a stunt double for *Smallville.*

"Naw," said Redbeard. "We're just talking. *Right* Todd?"

"Uhh. Yeah." Todd gave her a 'what's your problem?' look before shaking his head and filling a couple plastic cups with beer.

A muscular Hispanic kid reached toward Paige with a beckoning gesture. She slipped out from between Todd and the table, letting the football player grasp her shoulder and usher her behind a wall of varsity jackets.

"Dude. Jail bait." Redbeard patted Todd on the shoulder. "Say it with me, man. Jail. Bait."

Todd shrugged his friend's hand off his shoulder. "Chill out, I's just tryin' a be friendly and shit. She didn't look like them stuck up bitches."

The two denim-clad seniors wandered deeper into the house. Redbeard glanced over his shoulder at her with an almost apologetic 'don't mind this idiot' look.

"Y'awright?" asked the muscular kid.

"Yeah. Thanks... umm... Whoever you are. The fat one thought I wanted to be touched." She filled a second cup (with non-diet) for Renee.

"I'm Joe," said the boy with his hand on her shoulder.

"What the hell are those two doing here anyway?" One of the other players leaned as if to go after them. "Didn't Pete get arrested and expelled last year?"

"You look a little young." Joe raised an eyebrow. "Not like a senior."

Paige grumbled. "Sophomore. Mackenzie said it wouldn't be a problem."

The blond jock gestured at her soda. "Looks like it won't be."

"You're worried about *me*? There's no one here old enough to drink and that one guy's got a joint."

"Crap. Sweeney's here too?" A third player, Cortez according to his jacket, pinched the bridge of his nose. "You know tonight's gonna end with cops in the house."

"Hey, check it out," said Joe, elbowing the blond boy. "Kenzie's circling Cole like a shark."

"Man. Why do girls always go after the dude who's got a chick already?" Cortez refilled his beer.

"Chirp chirp," muttered Paige. *I hate that word.* "We're not baby chickens."

"What, you want her?" asked Joe.

"Hell no." Cortez waved him off. "Girl ain't got no ass."

"Uhh, thanks for getting rid of those losers." Paige smiled. "Gonna find my friends."

The players moved to let her get by, but lingered by the kegs.

Paige hurried into the living room. Four boys and two girls crammed onto the couch, the girls sitting on the armrests, passing a peace pipe of marijuana back and forth. She coughed on the cloud, held her breath, and trotted to the bottom of the stairwell, where Renee wasn't.

With her back to the wall, Paige looked around at the crowd. The only familiar face she found belonged to Mackenzie, leaning on the wall next to that Cole kid. The auburn-haired girl laughed and chatted with them. The daggers flying from Kenzie's smile bounced off his girlfriend, as though she remained blithely unaware of them.

"Renee?" yelled Paige.

She scanned the sea of faces again with no luck before darting to her left along the side of the stairway. In a closet beneath the steps, she found two seniors making out—but Renee wasn't one of them. The hallway passed an empty bathroom and brought her to a kitchen where two boys slow danced by the sink. Four senior girls sat around the kitchen table chatting about random, meaningless things. Upcoming Halloween dance, bands, boys, clothes. *Ugh.* Paige rolled her eyes.

After crossing the kitchen, Paige poked her head out the door to the backyard deck. Nine boys stood around with cups as one kid did a handstand and slurped beer from a hose connected to a giant funnel. Redbeard raised it high while Todd held the upside-down kid's ankles. No sign of Renee or the man with the joint. Paige ducked inside before either of the two metalheads saw her. She returned to the dining room and scurried farther down the hall to a den where a group of boys sat around on a small leather sofa and individual chairs. Based on their general appearance and clothing, she figured she'd found the geek squad. A movie involving dragons on the TV eliminated any doubt.

A lanky kid with curly black hair and a large nose smiled and sauntered over, can of Mountain Dew in one cheeto-stained hand. "Hey there. I just failed my saving throw against charm. I'm yours to command."

"What?" Paige blinked. "I have no idea what that means."

"Looks like a critical failure on seduction, Lundberg," said a kid with a ginger version of an afro.

"Uhh, have any of you guys seen Renee?"

A mixture of shrugs and confused looks came back.

"Purple hair, black girl?" Paige sighed.

"Nope," said Lundberg. "I'm Steve. Haven't seen you before."

"Oh, I've seen her at school... didn't know she was here tonight," said a new voice.

"Hi, Steve. Uhh, I gotta find her." She handed him both sodas.

He gazed at the one with black lipstick prints on it as though she'd given him the Holy Grail.

*Oh, no.* Paige ran to the stairs. After what she'd seen—or hallucinated—worst case scenario led to the bedrooms. She hauled ass upstairs and tore open the first door she found: a blue bedroom, from the looks of model fighter jets and posters of cartoon superheroes, it belonged to a prepubescent boy. She slammed the door and opened a linen closet on the left, bathroom on the right, an older teen boy's bedroom on the left where a couple made out with their shirts off.

"Sorry," whispered Paige, backing up and closing the door.

Another closet on the right held no Renee.

She grabbed the knob of a white door with pink trim, and it rattled —locked.

"In use," said a man.

Paige thumped on it. "Who's in there?"

When no answer came, she banged her shoulder into the door and rattled the knob again. "Renee?"

*Crap!*

Paige ran downstairs and plowed into a mass of unfamiliar people. Her shouts for Santana or Mackenzie drowned under the horrendous music. Most of the partiers in the living room seemed too drunk or high to notice who grabbed and shoved them out of the way. She sent two guys spilling over the back of the couch, and a cluster of girls she rammed into all went down at once. An eternity of unfamiliar faces passed before she spotted Santana sitting on the floor in the corner next to a small marble-topped table with a Victorian-themed lamp on it. Her friend had a mostly-gone beer in one hand, the peace pipe in the other, and stared at the ember as if it spoke to her.

"Sant!" Paige ran over. "Need you. Renee's in deep shit."

"What's up?" Santana raised bleary eyes at her. "Renee?"

Paige grabbed the pipe and tossed it to one of the seniors on the sofa. She took Santana's hand and dragged her upright and toward the stairs.

"Hang on." Santana dug her heels in and drained the rest of the beer. "What's going on?"

"You're wrecked." Paige wanted to scream in anger and cry from frustration, but did neither. "Renee is in trouble."

"I am not wrecked." Santana set her hands on her hips. "I'll have you know I can handle my shit. I've only had two."

"You're swaying on your feet and you look ready to pass out. Shit. Come on." She dragged Santana up the stairs to the door she couldn't open and worried at the knob again. "Help me open this."

Santana pushed her. "What, you think the Puerto Rican bitch can pick locks?"

Paige pounded on the door, stopped, and whispered, "What was the name of that kid that hit on Renee?"

"When you fainted?" Santana stifled a burp. "He isn't that hot."

"Yes him." Paige shook her by the shoulders. "Hurry."

"Jason... Jeremy..." Santana stared into space for a second. "Jared!"

Paige whomped on the door. "Jared! Open the damn door. Don't you dare touch Renee. I know you slipped her a roofie or something in a beer."

*Wham.*

The floor shuddered under her boots. Something banged again, followed by stomping noises.

"Sant, help me!" Paige flung her body into the door.

Santana joined in on the third try. Both girls rammed shoulder-first against the door twice more before it gave out with a small spray of splinters. They stumbled into a chilly bedroom done up in pink and white. Renee sprawled out cold atop a puffy queen-sized bed that looked like something you'd find in a dollhouse. Her shirt lay on the rug and her bra was half off. To the left of the bed, a tall window let in the outside air, open as far as it could. Two lavender curtains billowed in a steady breeze.

"Nee!" yelled Paige. She ran over and jumped on the bed, shaking Renee.

Santana grumbled and cursed before pushing the door closed. "You think Jared slipped her something?"

Paige felt Renee's neck for a pulse, then fixed her bra back in place. "Yeah, but I can't like tell anyone. No one will believe me. I... uhh... had a vision. I didn't actually *see* it. Shit she's out. Where are we?"

"In a bedroom." Santana gazed at the wall. "Everything's *sooo* pink."

"Don't be a bitch. What's the address here?"

Santana shrugged, waving her arms around and grinning. "We're... somewhere in Shadesboro."

Paige pulled out her phone. A couple taps to a GPS app spat out 1145 Monroe Court, Shadesboro, PA. Contacts. Dad. Call.

Santana swayed on her feet. "What are you doing?"

"Calling my dad." Paige looked at her. "Find Kenzie and get out of here."

"Paige?" asked Dad. "You know I'm on duty right now."

"Yes, Dad. I know. I'm at a party and this guy slipped a roofie or something to Renee. She's out cold. I can't wake her up and I'm afraid she's gonna like overdose or something."

He took a few seconds to answer. "Are you clean?"

"Yes. I didn't touch anything but soda." She gave him the address. "I interrupted before he got her pants off."

"Stay with her. I'm on the way. How many kids are there? You sure you're clear?"

"I swear, Dad. Only a half-cup of Cherry Coke."

A smile shone through his voice. "Good girl. What's the situation like in the house?"

"Like a hundred people here. Mostly seniors. Beer. I think I smell pot. I'm upstairs in a girl's bedroom with Renee."

"We'll talk later about what you're doing there. I, uhh..." He sighed.

"Okay." Paige hung up.

"You got this?" Santana shivered.

"Yeah. How smashed is Kenz?"

Santana opened the door. "No idea. I haven't seen her in a while. She was with Cole for a bit, and then *poof.*"

Paige picked up Renee's shirt and draped it over her chest before sitting on the side of the bed, holding her hand. Santana ran off. Within minutes, suppressed yells of 'crap' and 'oh shit' echoed from the open window amid the clatter of patio furniture knocking around and bodies scrambling over chain link fencing. Paige squeezed and rubbed Renee's hand.

"Come on, Nee. Wake up."

A flurry of red and blue lights lit up the houses outside. Paige kept her vigil for another few minutes. The music downstairs cut out. A deep male voice barked, ordering people to sit still, get down, move over there, and so on.

Heavy tromping approached in the hall. Dad, and another Trooper walked in. Paige looked up at them, unaware she'd been crying until the glower on Dad's face collapsed at the sight of her. They approached. The other cop took Renee's hand and felt for a pulse at the wrist.

"What did he give her?" asked Dad.

"He dumped some kind of white powder in a beer. I dunno what it was."

"You saw him do it?" asked Dad.

*Technically, I did.* "Yeah."

"Who?" The other cop grabbed his shoulder mic. "Need an ambulance at eleven-forty-five Monroe Court. Female, late teens. Unknown intoxicant. Unresponsive."

"I haven't seen him before tonight. Someone said his name is Jared."

"Sweeney." The other cop frowned at Dad. "We know him rather well. Nineteen, dropped out last year. Bunch of petty pops."

"Great." Dad shook his head. "Paige…"

She hung her head. "They said he wasn't supposed to be here. He just showed up."

Dad moved to the gaping window and beamed his flashlight around the sill and sashes, then pointed it out into the yard. "Back porch roof. Looks like he jumped. Did you see him with her?"

Paige bit her lip. Dad was *really* good at sniffing out lies. "No. I saw him pour the stuff in the beer, but I didn't actually see him give it *to* Renee or her drink it. I lost track of her when I went to get soda. I couldn't find Renee anywhere, and this door was locked. When I knocked, Jared said 'in use,' so I assumed he was gonna… uhh… you know… We banged and pounded on it, but he didn't open up and Renee wasn't answering. I got scared so we crashed the door in, but he was gone. Half her bra was off."

The other cop scowled. "I don't think we can do much with that. We'll have to see what Miss. Morris remembers when she wakes up."

"I didn't drink, Dad. I… can't. Not after…" She bit her lip. "I'll blow in the thingee if you want."

His jaw clenched. "It's okay, Paige. I believe you."

A siren wailed outside as an ambulance arrived. Paige backed away from the bed. Soon, a paramedic crew entered with a stretcher, loaded Renee up, and wheeled her out. Dad guided Paige downstairs and out the front door. Three other State Troopers took down names from a line of teens too disoriented or lazy to have fled through the backyard. Everyone got grilled about who provided the alcohol and stood in a queue while another cop attempted to contact parents. The presence of eight other officers in dark blue startled her. *Wow, I didn't think this place had locals.*

"Not arresting them?" Paige snuck a peek at the seniors as Dad walked her to his patrol car.

"Too many of them, not enough of us... small town can't handle it, and they're not going to want to pay to bus them out to a larger facility for something like beer. We'll let the parents deal with it for now. Whoever is responsible for there being alcohol at a high-school party isn't going to be having a good day though." He stopped and pulled her around to look her in the eye. "That's not permission to drink because it's a slap on the wrist."

"Okay. Look. I know you don't trust me after what happened at Meredith's place, but I got sick as hell from that... and... Amber. I wanna throw up even thinking about beer."

He squeezed her shoulder. "I'm proud of you, Paige. I look pissed off, but it's because we can't nail the son of a bitch who tried to take advantage of your friend."

"Is she gonna be okay?" Paige slipped into the passenger seat when he opened the door.

"I'm no doctor, but more than likely. There can be memory loss associated with those drugs. Let's hope he was stupid and threw out the baggie in the house and we can get a print. They're going to do bloodwork. If they identify the drug and we can find it on him, it should be enough for a warrant. We might need you to testify to the prosecutor that you saw Jared dose the beer. Are you willing to do that?"

*Damn. It's my fault she was even here.* "Yeah, sure."

Cole and his auburn-haired girlfriend walked out of the house followed by a cop. He shook hands with the officer before putting his arm around the girl and wandering off to a '90-something Camaro. Neither of them looked the least bit intoxicated.

A voice came from the radio on Dad's belt, requesting another ambulance for an unresponsive eighteen-year-old female with suspected alcohol poisoning.

Paige glanced at the house. "Guess they found Kenzie."

# 8

# FIVE, NINE, AND ONE

Monday October 12 - 7:02 a.m.

Paige stumbled out of the shower and tripped over the thick black bathmat. Her foot slid out from under her on the cold tile; she flailed and grabbed at the wall, but wound up on all fours in her bedroom. The idea of remaining on the floor half-covered by a towel for a few more minutes of sleep almost gained purchase in her brain. She grumbled and forced herself upright, dried off, and got dressed in a black babydoll over a tank top with black jeans. Again, she sat on the edge of her bed holding plush grey socks and lacking the motivation to put them on. Out in the hall, Melissa whined about Dad 'destroying' the bathroom, while coughing and gagging for effect.

"What's bothering you?" asked Amber, appearing out of thin air at the foot of the bed.

"Renee." Paige mushed her sock through her fingers as she explained what happened at the party. "It's my fault. She wouldn't have even gone if I hadn't agreed to."

Amber pressed her insubstantial fist into Paige's shoulder. The playful 'punch' left a weak cold spot on her damp skin and she shivered. "You don't know that. She might've changed her mind anyway without you, and then you wouldn't have been there to watch her back."

"I guess." Paige pulled one leg up and worked the sock over her toes. "You think that guy is gonna come after me?"

"Does anyone know who called the police to the house?" Amber attempted to fuss with Paige's hair.

"Only Santana… and she wouldn't tell anyone. She was pretty high though, might not remember it. People might assume it was my Dad tracking me down." She put on her other sock and yawned. "Don't suppose I can convince you to let me stay home today?"

"You can't dwell on stuff." Amber sat next to her. "Don't give up."

"It's not that. I'm not depressed… well, I mean." Paige sighed. "Not because of that. I got like three hours of sleep."

Amber gave her a mischievous grin.

Ice ran down Paige's back; she leapt to her feet, back arched, and squealed. "Awake now?"

Teeth chattering, Paige tried to rub feeling into a cold spot she couldn't reach. Playful anger took over and she leapt at Amber, but tackled only the mattress. Melissa ran past the door, heading downstairs.

Paige grumbled. "Well, I'm awake."

After repacking a few stray textbooks, she dragged her backpack downstairs and left it at the front door. In the kitchen, Melissa worked on an omelet. Two cartoon mermaids on her pink long-sleeved sweater seemed to stare at the food with rapt interest. Pink frill socks peeked out from under her jeans, and she swung her silver ballet flats back and forth. Paige frowned at the blank table where she usually sat and trudged to the cabinet to grab cereal.

"Mom, why don't you make eggs for Paige too?" Melissa seemed to regret the question as soon as it happened, and cringed.

"Mom's got one daughter, Dad *had* one daughter, and I just take up space." Paige slapped the cereal onto the counter.

Her mother set the pan she'd been washing down hard in the sink and faced her. "Will you stop with the melodrama, Paige? You're not being fair here."

Paige glanced at the table. "I'm not? Where are my eggs then? You're already washing the pots."

"Did you forget that time you told me I couldn't get a job cooking for White Castle?" Mom set her fists on her hips. "I distinctly remember you telling me you could do better, and that starving third-world children would send back my cooking."

A screaming fit bubbled up in the back of Paige's throat, but exhaustion sucked the vitriol right out of it. She sighed. "So? I was upset about Amber… I hated everything."

Mom blinked, seemingly caught off guard by the lack of shouting.

Paige poured Fruity Pebbles in a bowl and stuffed the box back in the cabinet. "Don't worry; I'll be out as soon as I'm eighteen and then you won't have to worry about me and my attitude."

"No," yelled Melissa. She lapsed into pre-cry breathing. "Please don't leave."

Mom turned away, bracing her hands on the counter, head bowed. Paige took the bowl to the table, sat facing her little sister, and dumped milk into the multicolored flakes. Melissa tried to swap breakfasts with her, but Paige smiled.

"Thanks. You already ate most of it anyway." Paige winked.

Dad breezed in from the hall, kissed Mom, and started to walk out. He stopped, backed up, and patted Paige on the head before ruffling Melissa's hair. "You two have fun at school today and stay out of trouble."

"Okay," said Melissa, still staring pleas at Paige.

Paige gazed into the rainbow morass in her bowl. *Dad noticed me.*

He tromped out. A few seconds later, the front door clattered closed, followed by the rev of his car and the grind of rubber on gravel. Melissa's emerald eyes widened at Paige in surprise.

"Yeah, I know," whispered Paige.

Mom drifted out, heading for the dining room and whatever project she had on her table. Paige finished her cereal and rinsed out the bowl. Melissa waited for her at the front door, struggling to hold Paige's backpack up. She snagged it, tossed it over one shoulder, and led Melissa by the hand down the road toward town.

Clear sky glowed bright blue above a spread of yellows, browns, and golds. The wind jostled the trees in a continuous wavering motion and kept flinging her hair in her face. Melissa seemed happier and tried to catch a few stray leaves whirling by. A hint of pumpkin pie broke through the fragrance of the woods for a few seconds as they passed the third house, where an elderly woman set about hanging cloth 'ghosts' from her porch.

Melissa leaned around her to stare. "Ooh. I bet she's gonna give out lots of candy on Halloween. You gonna go treating?"

*Ugh. Lame.* "I'm too old for that, but I'll walk you around."

"Aww." Melissa jumped up and down. "You gotta dress up! It's in the rules."

Paige pulled her hair out of her eyes again. *I could pass for Halloween any day.* "Maybe."

Melissa raised her arms to the sides and walked heel to toe on the yellow stripe as if it were a balance beam. "What are you gonna go as?"

"I dunno. Maybe a witch."

"Oh. *Everyone's* a witch." Melissa rolled her eyes. "Or a black cat... or a vampire. It's not scary. You should do something different."

"It's not about scary. It's about candy." Paige laughed.

Melissa poked her in the side. "You're doing it wrong."

They laughed and discussed potential costume ideas the rest of the way along the tree-tunnel road to downtown, and eventually the school. Paige kept her head down both in gesture and in concept, hoping no one connected her to the appearance of police at the party last night. She walked her sister up the steps into the crowded hallway of the elementary school, letting go of her hand once inside. Melissa gave her a quick hug and ran off, dragging her pink backpack. Paige watched her go until she disappeared into her classroom. She headed down the long corridor, turning sideways at times to squeeze among the sixth-to-eighth-graders sifting through their lockers. A few kids gave her 'what's she doing here' looks while a handful of others seemed afraid of her.

An ear-piercing scream silenced everyone.

All eyes turned to Sofia, standing by her locker. She crept backwards, hands clamped over her mouth as a mound of six or seven dead birds fell out to the floor. Other kids backed away, holding their noses.

"You can take them home, Wednesday," said Brittany Kutzen, still dressed up like some creepy porcelain doll in a pastel yellow dress.

Sofia cried, edging another step backwards. "Eww. That's horrible! Why!"

Brittany put on an imperious smile. "Found them at my dad's lot. Your family takes care of dead things, don't they, *Wednesday?*"

Paige glared and stomped over. "Hey, Cindy Brady." She punted one of the starlings, almost landing it on the blonde girl's chest. "You *do* know what Wednesday Addams does to people who piss her off right?"

The laughing eighth-graders got quiet.

"Is there a problem here?" asked a man in the most hideous brown suit Paige had ever laid eyes on.

"No, Mr. Rice," chanted about six kids.

"Sofia?" The teacher approached and peered over his glasses at the pile of dead birds.

"I didn't..." Sofia hung her head and wept. "They're not mine. I swear."

"Whoever did this should go to the nurse's office right away. Handling dead birds is dangerous. You could get very sick." He eyed the pack, and snagged the three who looked most worried. "Kutzen, Smith, Connor... with me, now."

They whined.

Sofia gave Paige a grateful look and wiped her tears.

The teacher glanced over. "Aren't you in the wrong building?"

"I was dropping off my sister. She's in third."

"Oh." He nodded at her before patting Sofia on the shoulder. "Don't touch them. I'll send a custodian over."

Sofia sniffled, but smiled at him.

Paige pulled her backpack up on her shoulder and crossed the parking lot. She went around behind the building and ducked through the 'emergency doors' directly to the high-school cafeteria, staring at her boots the whole way. If anyone gave her dirty looks, she didn't notice. Once more in her usual spot, she plunked down on the bench and hugged her backpack on the table, face buried in it.

She almost got to sleep before the table bounced with the arrival of Santana and Renee.

"Nee!" Paige lifted her head. "What are you doing here? Shouldn't you be home sick?"

Renee grasped Paige's arms and squeezed. "I owe you one, girl. I don't remember much, but they told me what they think happened."

"Did Jared give you a beer?"

She shrugged. "I don't know. The whole party's a blur."

"It's gotta be him." Santana scowled. She looked around and leaned forward to whisper, "No one knows who called the cops. Paulie's parents are mega pissed off. They took his car away and he's like grounded till he moves out to college."

"Who?" Paige sat up and yawned.

"That was his house." Santana leaned her head right and left fast, causing a faint *pop* from her neck. "His 'rents were away. They took his kid sister and brother to visit the grands."

"Hey all," droned Mackenzie. She glided over and settled in next to Paige, since Renee and Santana had taken the facing bench. Today, her coffee carrier had three cups. Her half-closed eyes suggested she could pass out at any moment. "Why is it so damn loud in here?"

"Damn girl," said Renee. "F'I was you, I'da called my butt out sick."

Mackenzie yawned. "I'm okay. Slept most of the weekend."

"There's a legitimate difference between 'asleep' and 'passed out,'" muttered Renee.

"Oh, I could kiss you." Paige grabbed the one nearest her.

"Kenz likes girls," said Santana in deadpan. "She'd be up for it."

"I do not." Mackenzie sipped her pumpkin spice coffee. "Though I've considered experimenting."

Renee's expression remained neutral with a touch of bashful while Santana failed to suppress a mild cringe.

"What about you Paige?" Mackenzie threw an arm around her.

Paige shrugged. "Never really thought about it much. I had a couple of boyfriends, but after Amber died... I dunno. I guess I'm not interested in anyone at all right now."

"Sounds like you're depressed." Mackenzie rubbed her back. "Can't say I blame you. Hey if you ever wanna talk, I'm taking an intro to psych class. Maybe I could use your situation for my paper... names changed of course."

*Ugh. I need a button to jump the day to 2 p.m.* "Great. Paige the lab rat."

"Okay." Mackenzie removed her arm and leaned forward over her bag. "Serious time. Everything's ready. I want to do the circle today after school."

"You look like a zombie," said Paige. "Are you sure?"

"Absolutely." Mackenzie took a long gulp from her coffee. "I'll be fine by the end of the day. Plenty of time to sleep between now and two."

Nervous eagerness glimmered in Renee's expression. She offered a curt nod.

Santana rolled her eyes. "There's a lot more I can do with the two hours that'll take than talking to the floor."

"You *were* at my place the other day when the lights did that freaky on off thing, weren't you?" Mackenzie gestured at Paige. "We have the magic number now. Five. You're coming, right, Paige?"

"I gotta walk my sister home after school, but... yeah I guess."

"I'll drive you two."

Something made her want to keep Melissa as far away from this as possible. Paige shook her head. "No. Melissa's terrified of cars. The whole drive up here from Philly, she sobbed and every time another car passed us, she screamed. She thinks she's going to die in an accident like Amber."

Renee made a sympathetic face. "Aww."

"Oh, no." Santana cringed. "I hope she's not a scryer too."

"Nah." Paige fidgeted with one of her backpack's straps. "She's just eight, and dealing with it in her own way."

"Okay... so I'll pick you up." Mackenzie patted her on the back. "Think about what you want to ask the spirits to do for you."

*Beep. Beep. Beep.*

A few hundred students stood up all at once.

"Ugh, loud bell is loud." Mackenzie grumbled. "Today is gonna take *forever!* See you at like two-thirty."

"Right." Paige followed the crowd into the hall and made her way upstairs to chemistry.

MACKENZIE'S KIA SOUL ZIPPED ALONG A SEMI-PAVED ROAD NORTHWEST OUT OF Shadesboro. Paige gazed at the passing smear of yellow-orange-brown trees, broken every so often by stretches of grassy fields with the occasional horse or three. Santana zoned in the passenger seat, listening to Mp3s on her phone. Sofia, sandwiched between Paige and Renee, kept smoothing her black pleated dress over her legs. She looked like a collision of doom, gloom, and faerie princess. Renee twirled a strand of frizzy violet hair around her fingers while staring out the right-side window. She seemed somewhere between angry and determined. Mackenzie drove a little fast for comfort, though not to the point Paige demanded she slow down.

*She's like a six-year-old running to the Christmas tree in the morning.*

Sofia glanced up at Paige. "Nice choker."

Paige shrugged. "It's okay."

"Can I try it on? My mom won't let me wear things like that."

"Sure." She removed it and held it out.

Sofia put it on and fussed with it. The spiked leather band almost worked with her Wednesday Addams dress and black knee socks. If the girl wore her hair in braids, she'd earn the nickname.

"What do you think?" Sofia smiled.

"That dress is a little plain for it, but it's not a bad look for you."

The younger girl frowned. "Mom hates the whole 'punk' thing. If I'm not going to bed, she wants to me to dress 'nice' all the time."

"You're dressed like one of them creepy-ass dolls," muttered Santana.

"Ugh," said Renee. "Your dad's in on it too?"

Sofia huffed. "He treats me like I'm still six. 'Course, it's not all bad. I can get him to buy me stuff with this face." She widened her eyes and let her lower lip stick out a little.

"Don't overuse that," said Renee. "Remember, with great power…"

"So where is this place?" asked Paige.

"My dad's got some land a ways out of town. We have a cabin there. Used to go camping when my mom was still around. Dad never goes there anymore."

Paige picked at the crinkle of denim at her knee. "Did your parents not get along? Maybe your mom is still at the cabin?"

The Kia wobbled.

"Uhh." Mackenzie stared at her via the inside mirror. "What do you mean?"

"Your mom's name is Diana, right? I think she's the spirit who showed up on the Ouija."

Mackenzie slowed and leaned forward. "Did everyone figure out what they want to ask the spirits for?"

Paige narrowed her eyes at the headrest in front of her.

"Yeah," said Sofia.

"Yup." Renee stopped playing with her hair.

"Kinda." Paige shifted her weight. "I'll come up with something."

Mackenzie turned left onto an all-dirt path. The Kia wobbled and rocked, forcing Santana, Renee, and Paige to grab handles at the roof. Sofia clung to Paige. After a short distance that felt like a downhill grade, the little SUV splashed through a puddled basin and ascended a stiff incline. The road on the far side didn't throw them around as much, and the girls sat normally.

Seven minutes later, the trees parted to reveal a clearing where a rectangular one-room cabin perched near a small creek, separated from the forest by about forty yards. Pale grey slats looked as though someone had gone over the boards with watery whitewash that failed to conceal the grain. A porch held a pair of ancient rocking chairs flanking the only door. Peeling white paint revealed dark wood underneath, and a long rust scar bled down from the knob.

"Wow." Paige felt less comfortable getting out of the car. "This is like straight out of some B-grade slasher movie."

Mackenzie brought the car to a halt about fifteen feet from the door and shut it off. "It needs some work. Dad kinda ignores the place."

Paige's pet black cloud came out to play. "Yeah. Dads are good at ignoring stuff."

"I haven't seen your dad in a while, Kenz." Santana opened her door.

"He says he's busy with trial prep or lawsuits or whatever. I'm surprised Linda hasn't left him since he's never home. Hope she doesn't. She's nice, but a bit dim. At least she signed the pre-nup."

"What's that?" asked Sofia.

"Like a marriage contract." Mackenzie got out and took a huge breath. "Basically, if they get divorced, she agreed not to seek alimony or half his assets. She goes out with the same $38.50 in tips she had in her waitress apron."

"Burn," said Renee.

"Though I bet she gets to keep her $40,000 tits." Mackenzie took a large brown leather satchel out of the Kia's back end and headed to the door, fumbling with her keyring.

"Yeah. Giving them back would be kinda messy." Santana cradled her breasts. "No one's ever coming near my girls with a knife."

"You don't even *have* 'girls,'" said Renee. "Sofia's are bigger."

"Sofia's flatter than the cafeteria soda." Mackenzie grinned.

The youngest girl blushed.

Santana whirled about, walking backwards. She cupped them at Renee. "Sure I do. Just not ones that'll give me black eyes when I run."

Paige pulled her jacket closed, feeling conspicuous. She had more than Santana, but Mackenzie's were bigger.

"Go to hell." Renee laughed. She had them both beat.

Mackenzie opened the door and walked inside. The 'porch'—basically a patch of boards set right on the dirt—clonked and clumped under their shoes. Paige brought up the rear, hesitating at the door. The inside seemed colder than it should be and sent a static electric tingle down her back. Aside from a full-length mirror in a tilt frame at the back right corner and a threadbare red throw rug, not a scrap of furniture remained. Tattered gauzy curtains hung dead on either side of the four windows. The wall opposite the door had no windows, but a fireplace sat long dormant at its center, packed with cobwebs and old mulch. A scattering of withered leaves and acorns covered the floor, gathered in thicker piles at the corners.

Tingles spread over Paige's hands. "Whoa. There's some strange energy here."

Mackenzie set the satchel down, squatted, and rolled the rug up to expose a circumscribed five-foot-wide pentacle painted on the floor in silver. Scuff marks both inside the star as well as along the perimeter gave away where less-permanent inscriptions had once been.

"Wow." Paige tilted her head and walked around it. "That's pretty cool."

"There's real silver dust in the paint." Mackenzie seemed particularly proud of herself. "Okay… umm. Let's see." She rummaged a notebook out of her satchel and flipped through it. "Right. Paige… You have the top point. I'm giving you the Element of Spirit since you have the whole ghost thing going. Santana, upper-left point, you're still Elemental Air. Sofia, water." Mackenzie pointed at the upper right point. "Renee, you're Earth as usual."

Renee stood at the lower-left tip.

Mackenzie, already at the lower right arm of the pentacle, smiled. "I'm channeling Fire."

Paige sat cross-legged near the 'top' point of the star.

Mackenzie pulled a bunch of wax-paper-wrapped black candles and a single white one out of the satchel. After creating a pile, she unwrapped them one at a time and set each candle down on its base. The sight of them stirred an odd feeling in the pit of Paige's gut. Rather than normal black-colored objects, they seemed to *absorb* light, appearing to be candle-shaped holes in reality.

Paige reached over and picked one up, finding it cold to the touch. No matter how she turned or tilted it, the surface never shined. "Whoa. Sick."

"Careful," said Mackenzie, taking the candle back like a mother pulling something breakable away from a toddler. "These aren't easy to replace."

"What did you do with the blood?" asked Sofia.

"In the candles." Mackenzie smiled.

"What blood?" Paige wiped her hand on her jeans.

"Sofia was kind enough to help us out with one of the reagents. Blood from a corpse that had been dead less than three days."

Paige grabbed her stomach. "Ugh. Seriously?"

"They suck it out into this big tank when they do the embalming." Sofia shrugged. "It's like filling a cup from one of those machines in the cafeteria. I didn't touch the body. They're gonna cremate it anyway."

"What the hell." Paige blinked. "You had her steal blood from her funeral home?"

Mackenzie rolled her eyes. "It's not stealing. They're going to burn it. There's a reason people who do real magic are rare. Some parts of magic are… unpleasant. Not everyone's willing to do the things."

"This one spell…" Santana shivered. "Supposed to be for invisibility, right? You take three beans and put them in the mouth of a severed head then bury it at the base of a tree near a graveyard and water it with red wine every day at midnight for thirty days. Then you dig it up and if you eat the beans you turn invisible."

Paige gagged. "Or get sick and die."

Sofia put her sleeve-covered hands over her mouth and mumbled, "Eww."

Mackenzie set black candles at each of the outermost points of the pentacle. She placed the white candle where the two lower star arms met in the middle of the bottom. At the other four interior corners, she placed black candles. Paige stared at the corpse-blood candle in front of her. The wick resembled string dipped in silver paint. Mackenzie took a wooden bowl and a Ziploc bag of feathers out and handed them to Santana along with some incense cones. She set a mason jar of water and another bowl in front of Sofia. Renee got a bowl of dirt and two acorns, and Paige a short length of white rope. Mackenzie placed a squat red candle on the ground next to the black candle at her star point. Last, she withdrew a giant leather-bound book and arranged it on the ground by her knees.

Mackenzie stretched. "Okay. We're going to do a ritual to summon and focus the energy of the elements and the cosmos to our desires." She handed out scraps of paper to everyone. "Those are your key points. The exact words don't matter though. Focus on what you want to happen. Once we close the circle, we'll go around and say our parts."

Santana smiled. "Shouldn't we be doing this out in the woods at night? Dancing naked around a big ass fire?"

Sofia turned bright red. "You didn't say we'd have to do that."

Paige stared at Mackenzie. *No way.*

Mackenzie rolled her eyes. "That's Paganism. We're doing Witchcraft."

"What we're doing is killing a Monday afternoon." Santana smirked.

"Wicca *is* Paganism," said Sofia in a tiny voice. "I don't want to take my clothes off. Are you gonna kick me out if I say no?"

"Damn sure that ain't happening." Renee folded her arms. "That's some Alistair-Crowley-level shit right there, and it ain't gonna be my bare ass prancing around the forest."

"Okay, fine. Druidy whatever." Mackenzie eyed Santana. "No one's taking anything off. Relax. We're doing *magic*, not primitive tribal hoodoo. If you don't believe it's going to work, there's no point in even trying it."

Sofia exhaled, relief clear on her face.

Paige relaxed. *Okay. She's completely clueless. This is creepy, but fun.*

"Fine… Fine." Santana looked at Paige. "I dunno. After that freak show at your house, I'm not so sure."

"It's real," said Mackenzie. She took off her baggy brown leather high-heeled boots and set them near the satchel.

"Do we haveta be barefoot?" asked Sofia.

"Only if you want to." Mackenzie winked. "Those are kid leather, five grand. I'm not sitting cross-legged in here with them on and scuffing the crap out of them. Now gimme a minute to set the rest of this up."

Mackenzie hunted through the big book and stopped at a page full of strange symbols. She studied it for a little while before she took a brush and black ink from the satchel and painted some of them on the floor within the pentacle.

Paige looked over the paper in her hands:

---

*Spirit/Aether. The element of living things and spirits. Invoke 'The Lady' or 'The Horned God' while holding the cord symbol in the air. Say something like 'I call upon the aspect of spirits and invite The Lady to our circle. Hear our pleas and answer.' Then say something about what you want to happen. When we open the circle, I will ask how you enter. Say (and mean) 'In perfect love and trust.'*

---

*I could ask for Amber to come back.* Paige cringed at a sudden press of dread. *Uhh, maybe not. That'll probably turn out bad.* She sighed. *Yeah right.* Doubt that anything would happen crumbled under the reality of having spent the past three months talking to Amber's ghost, not to mention what happened at Mackenzie's the other day.

Sofia gasped.

Paige looked up from the paper. Mackenzie held a small bottle of blood, adding to her painted symbols with an eyedropper. Renee fidgeted, as if worried or guilty. Sofia looked sick. Santana seemed on the verge of curling up on the floor and going to sleep from boredom.

Mackenzie fiddled with a few more runic symbols and pictograms, taking small bottles of various colored powders, herbs and ground up who-knows-what from the satchel.

"Geez, Kenz, where did you get all that stuff?" Paige blinked.

"New Hope's like an hour and a half drive away. Awesome stores there." She finished off a symbol and smiled. "We're good." She gestured for everyone to stand and took a ten-inch dagger out of the satchel. "This is going to work this time since we have all five people. Plus, Paige is our channeler to the spirit world."

Paige gasped.

"Relax. I know you're a virgin, but there's no sacrificing here. This is an athame. It's not for cutting anything. It's a focusing implement."

"I know…" Paige fought back her embarrassment. "I did read a little bit about this stuff online a while ago."

Mackenzie held the knife in both hands and pointed it at the floor. "Everyone hold hands. Sofia, you and Renee put your hands on my shoulders to make the circle."

The girls did so.

"We're going to walk around in a complete circle three times, then sit," said Mackenzie. "Air starts. Then we go around, and end with Paige." She stared at the Celtic knot engravings along the flat of the knife, seeming lost in her thoughts. "Picture a circle existing between our world and the spirit world. Picture it existing where the silver paint cuts through reality and bridges the worlds together. Visualize the spirit energy welling up from the earth, powered by the air and fire, and guided by water."

Mackenzie lifted her left foot, and the girls moved in unison, walking in a sideways shuffle clockwise around the pentacle. A glimmer raced over the paint on the floor, startling a twitch in Paige's back. *Did I imagine that?* None of the others seemed to react to the flash. Leaves and twigs crunched. Mackenzie stepped on a few, but showed no reaction to a rock that should've hurt her bare foot. She kept the knife pointed at the circle, lost to her focus.

After the third rotation, they stopped.

Mackenzie held the athame toward Sofia, point aimed down. "Sofia Anderson, I invite you to this circle. How do you enter?"

Sofia stood tall. "In perfect love and trust."

Mackenzie shifted left a few degrees. "Paige Thomas, I invite you to this circle. How do you enter?"

Paige felt a little cheesy, but said, "In perfect love and trust."

"Santana Ruiz, I invite you to this circle. How do you enter?"

"In perfect love and trust." Santana didn't sound too enthused.

"Renee Morris, I invite you to this circle. How do you enter?"

"In perfect love and trust." Renee bowed her head.

Mackenzie waved the athame as though she re-drew the pentacle with a laser beam projecting from the point. She sat cross-legged at her star tip, and the others followed suit. After using a match to light the stubby red candle, she held it out to Santana.

Santana stuck the tip of an incense cone into the flames and waved it around. "I call upon the Element of Air to aid our circle." She grasped a few feathers and tossed them over her shoulder.

Renee cradled the acorn in two hands and held it up. She lowered it with reverence, placed it in the bowl of dirt, and buried it. "Element of Earth, empower our circle. Stabilize and ground us. Give us strength."

Mackenzie reached in to her oversized white angora top and pulled a folded-up piece of notebook paper scribbled with ballpoint pen ink from her bra. She held it to the red candle's flame until it caught, and dropped it in a small metal bowl. "I beseech the Element of Fire to come and aid us. Passion, Love, and change." She raised her hands over her head. "The symbol of pure magic, infuse our circle."

Sofia poured the water from the mason jar into her bowl, dipped her fingers in it, and spritzed droplets onto the pentacle, and at each one of the girls. "I call upon the Element of Water to purify us."

Paige took a deep breath at the pregnant silence indicating it her turn. She grasped the white rope and held it out. "Spirits, we call on you to hear us, to bring us balance." Taking the rope in her other hand as well, she tugged on it. "The Aether binds us to each other and to the world. Empower our circle."

Something in the room changed. An alteration of light, an increase in the fragrance of woodlands, a drop in temperature. A sense of presence filled in, exuding from every wall.

Paige swallowed the last of her doubts. *Whoa.*

Mackenzie used the red candle to light all the black ones, saving the white one for last. The paper she'd burned sputtered out to a wisp, a slender thread pulled by the breeze to the door, but it welled up against a faint curve in line with the circle around the pentacle. Paige stared at the smoke behaving as if it hit a cylinder of glass.

Sofia gasped at a creak in the floor behind them, where no one stood.

After a moment, the black candles crackled as they burned.

"Why are the candles so loud?" whispered Santana.

"I put a strand of my hair in each wick." Mackenzie smiled and raised her arms, palms up. "Hold."

The girls reached up and grasped hands again, all sitting cross-legged by their respective star points.

Flames upon the black candles fluttered a few times and went still, stretching tall, immune to the breeze. Mackenzie looked at Sofia and nodded.

Sofia glanced at the paper on the floor in front of her. "Hear me, Aphrodite, Lady Marianne, and Yemaha. I call upon your ancient wisdom and power." She closed her eyes and breathed in and out twice. "Please stop the others from teasing me. I want them to be my friends. By the power of the spirits, nymphs and pond faeries, grant my request."

Mackenzie's expression drifted toward the 'aww'/patronizing spectrum, until a smirk from Santana dispelled it.

"Brigid and Vesta, Vulcan and Agni, hear me." Mackenzie leaned back, staring at the ceiling. After a few seconds, she took a small stick figure from the bag and plucked a strand of her hair, which she wound about the doll's chest. "I call upon your power. I lay claim to Cole Harris. I wish his heart to be mine. Stir within him the unquenchable fire. I wish his love to echo that which I hold for him. Grant us each magic, knowledge, and wisdom." She removed another folded paper from her sweater and burned it.

Renee dropped her note and sifted dirt between her fingers. "I invoke the Goddess Gaea and Rhea. Ceres and Demeter. Hear me Athos, Cernunnos and Mardyk." She concentrated in silence at the bowl. "Guide my father back to us. Make my family whole again. Unite us." She strained the soil back over the acorn.

Santana's blasé demeanor appeared to have dissipated at the palpable change in atmosphere. Her hands trembled as she lit the second incense cone from the black candle nearest her and held it aloft. "I speak to the Goddess Nuit, and the Gods Thoth and Shu." She glanced at the notes Mackenzie gave her. "If you're listening, please help my family. We're struggling to pay our bills and eat." She blushed, unable to make eye contact with her friends. "It's making us fight all the time. Please send us a financial boon, so we do not struggle. I ask not for great wealth, but for security."

Mackenzie made a face that said 'money, nice. I can understand that.'

*Something is going to happen. Whatever I say here is really going to do something.* The want to hug a physical Amber again grew painful. Paige's heart pounded against her chest. *No. I can't risk anything happening to her. They buried that cat and it came back all crappy and evil.* Breathe in. Breathe out. She held up the length of white rope, which seemed to attract the smoke wisp. "I channel the energy of the spirits to the north point. I am the focus through which the source flows. I provide the connection for all elements to exist with each other. I call upon The Lady and the Horned God to hear us and bless us with their boon." Her mind raced. She squeezed Sofia's hand. "Ever since my sister died eleven months ago, my Dad, Drew Thomas, has been lost to grief. By your power, please give him the strength to break his burden. Please let him be free from his grieving funk."

"Aww, that's *so* selfless of you." Mackenzie smiled. "Aren't you going to ask them to do something for *you*?"

Paige bit her lip and looked around at the others. "I'm not really that bad off. My life's okay. Dad needs help more than I do."

"Okay." Mackenzie shook her head with a mild eye roll. "Everyone picture your wants and requests." She closed her eyes and made faces as if imagining herself with Cole.

The girls set down the ritual objects and clasped hands in a circle once again.

Paige thought about how Dad was before. It had been a long time since he smiled. Since he *lived*. She wanted her Dad back, not the hollow shell in his skin. She imagined him smiling, able to sleep, able to work, without the constant weight of loss dragging down his heart.

Sofia squirmed, her eyes closed in deep concentration.

Santana, eyes closed, mumbled a repetitious phrase in Spanish.

Renee gazed sullenly at the bowl. Tears slipped down her face and fell into the dirt.

Mackenzie raised her arms, which caused the other girls to follow suit as they still held hands in a ring. "Our spell is cast. Our wishes true. Spirits of the past, I call to you. Hear the words which I chant, our boons I charge you grant. Help us now I ask of thee. Answer our call; so mote it be."

The nine black candle flames darkened to blood red and grew, stretching ten inches tall.

"Uhh." Paige leaned back. "Are they supposed to do that?"

# 9

# IT WATCHES

Monday October 12 - 4:13 p.m.

The girls gazed in silence, mesmerized by tall crimson flames standing motionless upon their wicks. Above the lone white candle, the burn remained ordinary and orange. Paige's throat tightened; shadow silhouettes of her friends moved along the walls, erratic, and not matching the pose or gestures of the person casting them. Every tiny pebble or scrap of leaf on the warped floorboards sent long daggers of shade outward from the pentacle. Mackenzie's grin tinged manic. Snaps and thuds echoed in the forest outside, drawing forth gasps and worried whines from Sofia. Paige's heart skipped at the sight of the windows—dark as a midnight sky. Her nose wrinkled at a building smell in the air, a trace of smoldering corpse.

"Holy shit, look outside." She tried to point, but Santana wouldn't let go of her hand.

"Don't break the chain," said Santana.

Sofia trembled, wide-eyed. "It's dark out!"

"The spirits are here. They have heard us." Mackenzie swayed side to side. "Focus on your desires."

Sofia mumbled a series of names, her expression alternating from wounded to angry and back again. Renee whispered as if speaking to her father, asking him to come home. Santana stared mute at the pentacle.

Crackling from the black candles increased in volume, building into a crescendo that sounded more like a raging bonfire. The flames shrank to less than an inch and exuded dark trails of foul smoke. Nine wisps threaded around each other in a spiral, collecting at the center of the pentacle. Paige's heart continued hammering at her breastbone as a cloud of opaque ebon vapor formed from the interwoven trails.

The upper part took on the silhouette of a man's head, with sharp ridges accenting the shape of the eyes. Four small horns grew, two per side. A suggestion of a lipless mouth formed, as did arms. The apparition rose to the ceiling, though in place of legs, threads of candle smoke intertwined like spun rope. Except for the five-foot disc inside the pentacle, the floorboards rattled and bounced as if a legion of hands pounded up from below.

Sofia teetered on the verge of screaming. She tugged away, trapped in place by Mackenzie's iron grip. Paige held on too, though more out of fear.

"T-that doesn't l-look friendly," whispered Santana.

Mackenzie leaned forward, closer to it. "The ancient spirits do not look as we do. They are from another place, another time. We do not fear the powers we beckon. The false religions stole the imagery from the spirits to make their devils and demons, to frighten people from true power."

The entity swirled about, regarding each girl in turn. It faced Mackenzie the longest, and didn't stop—barely slowing—as it rotated past Paige. *Figures. Invisible girl strikes again.* When it gazed down at Sofia, the entity emitted a low noise part breath, part chuckle. The girl trembled, seeming too frightened to make a sound. Santana shrank away from its piercing stare. It bowed its head toward her before facing Renee for a little longer than it had given Paige. The shadow rotated back to lock stares with Mackenzie, who looked upon it with manic adoration.

A second later, the mass of smoke exploded in a rush of energy that knocked the girls apart, sending them sliding into the nearest wall at the end of trails of clean floor. Paige smacked headfirst into old wood, legs and ass in the air. Sofia screamed and wailed. Incoherent cries traded back and forth with random shouts of 'Daddy!'

Paige flung her arm around as a counterweight and rolled to sit upright. Sofia ran to the door and rattled the knob. When it didn't open, she panicked and pounded on the wall while shrieking out sobs.

Mackenzie righted herself. Her blonde hair swirled in all directions like she'd gone for a dive through a hedgerow, but she smiled. After a grateful look at Paige, she crawled on all fours back to the circle and gazed into the candle flames, mesmerized.

Thumping in the ground and loud *cracks* surrounded the cabin, as though an army of grizzly bears cavorted in a drunken dance. Sofia cried to the point of choking on her own tears. She gave up pulling on the door and ran over to Paige, clinging and sniveling like a girl half her age. Santana curled up against the wall where she'd hit. Renee, the only one of them standing, had a distant look in her eye as though she gazed into some other reality than the cabin. She didn't react when Sofia almost knocked her over.

Paige hugged Sofia, patting her on the back and trying to calm her down. A sucking noise drew her attention to the tall mirror. It no longer reflected the interior of the cabin; the glass held an image like a painting of a creepy forest in a freestanding wooden frame.

"What's out there?" Sofia hid her face against Paige's shoulder. "Something's out there."

Branches snapped and heavy footfalls pounded into the earth. The clattering of a tremendous hailstorm fell upon the roof, gaining and ebbing in surges.

Mackenzie blew out the candles one after the next. She grasped the nearest black one and recoiled with a yelp, waving her hand as if burned. Despite her sudden motion, the candle stood rigid, seeming nailed to the floor. The cabin rumbled and shook; floorboards clapped, and the windows rattled in their frames. Outside, the chaos grew louder and louder, a clamor like a great army thundered across the grassy field toward them.

Sofia screamed, caught her breath, and shot Paige a pleading stare. "I wanna go home."

An ear-splitting roar exploded in the room. Paige twisted around, shielding Sofia from the expected pelting of shattering glass and wood fragments, but only noise hit them.

"I'm out," yelled Renee.

Paige unwound herself from cringing against the wall. Sunlight once more filtered in through unbroken windows. The woods fell silent. Mackenzie sat a few feet away from the circle, curled in a ball with a terrified expression. Paige braced a hand on the wall and stood, still holding on to Sofia. The air didn't quite feel the same as it had when they first arrived, but the oppressive weight of presence no longer thickened the atmosphere.

"I think it's gone," said Paige.

Renee tried the door, and it opened. She walked outside.

"Wait," yelled Santana. "We have to open the circle."

Mackenzie sniffled and nodded. "Y-yeah. She's right. We need to finish."

"Noooo," whined Sofia. "I wanna go home right *now*."

"We have to." Mackenzie stood at her point of the star. "We must respect them. Bad things will happen if we don't."

Paige had to drag Sofia to her place, but the girl didn't run away when she let go.

Mackenzie, a faint tremble in her limbs, bowed at each of them. "Farewell and merry part."

The girls echoed the phrase back to her.

"Our thanks to the Element of Water. We thank you for your purity," said

Mackenzie. "Blessed be."

Sofia poured the bowl through a gap in the floorboards.

"Our thanks to the Element of Fire. We thank you for your energy." Mackenzie blew out the stubby red candle. "Blessed be." She shifted to face Renee. "Our thanks to the element of Earth. We thank you for your protection. Blessed be."

Renee scurried to the door and tossed the dirt onto the grass.

"Our thanks to the Element of Air. We thank you for your wisdom," said Mackenzie. "Blessed be."

Santana squished out the incense cones and hurled the feathers out the front door, giving them to the wind.

"Our thanks to the Element of Spirit," said Mackenzie. "Blessed be."

Paige glanced down at the white cord, unsure what to do with it. An icy feeling manifested inside her, as though she'd gulped down a cup of frigid water and it swished around her stomach.

Mackenzie took the cord and tied it around Paige's right wrist. "In twenty-four hours, take it off outside and throw it backwards over your shoulder. Don't look at where it goes. Now, widdershins."

At Mackenzie's urging, they joined hands and circled the pentacle counterclockwise. She muttered names of various gods and goddesses, thanking them for their power and presence. At the instant her toes lined up with her star point on the third rotation, a tremendous *boom* echoed in the woods and the black candles flared to life.

Thick, inky ether swelled out of the mirror in the corner, washed over the girls, and raced outside. A half-second later, a rush of freezing cold flooded the cabin.

Sofia screamed and ran. Paige followed without thinking. The thirteen-year-old rocked the Kia Soul from her effort to rip the locked door open. Santana trotted up behind them. Renee sprinted around to the other side. Crashing and snapping in the woods on the distant bank of the stream thundered louder, as though some monstrous being came for them.

"Kenz!" screamed Renee. "Get your ass moving!"

Sofia kept shaking the car, screaming for the two minutes it took for Mackenzie to appear. She strolled out, having put her boots on and claimed her satchel. As soon as the Kia beeped, Sofia jumped inside and took her spot in the middle of the back seat, shaking. Paige got in, and the girl clamped on to her arm.

Santana jumped into the passenger seat and yelled, "Go. Go. Go!"

After depositing her bag in the rear, Mackenzie closed the back door and stopped in place. She gawked at the woods, turned pale, and scrambled in, shivering and muttering.

"S-something's coming," whispered Mackenzie while fumbling with her keys.

"No shit, Sherlock." Renee stared through the windshield at the cabin. "It's watching us."

"Come on. Come on." Santana shook Mackenzie by the shoulder. "Start this bitch up."

Paige flashed a crooked grin. "This is the part in the movie where the car won't start and the monster picks us off one by one as we try to run away in the woods."

Sofia wailed, tears streaming out of her eyes.

Renee shoved Paige. "Don't say shit like that."

Santana squealed. "Ohmigod! There's glowing friggin' eyes in the trees."

"Mommy!" Sofia hid her face in her hands. "I wanna go home."

The keys hit the floor.

"Clumsy bitch," yelled Santana. She lunged over, headfirst into the space below the wheel. A second later she pushed herself up, holding up the ignition key. "That ain't hard to find."

Mackenzie swiped the key from her, jammed it in, and started the engine.

A collective gasp of relief filled the car. Mackenzie slammed the shifter in reverse and stomped on the gas pedal, sending dirt spraying. She peeled around in a donut, shifting again and flooring it once they faced the bouncy dirt road. Paige held on to Sofia, who continued sobbing against her shoulder, and peered out the back window at the retreating cabin. Two pale spots hovered in the darkness among the trees overhead, as if the eyes of a beast large enough to devour the little building in one bite. Mounting dread got her shivering and a knot of sick wrenched her insides.

Sofia reined in her emotion and looked at her. "You're shaking."

"I..." *Haven't felt this sick since the night Amber...* "Really bad feeling. Please drive carefully... I think we're going to get into an accident."

"You saw us get hit?" asked Sofia.

"Not exactly." Paige gulped. "I just got this feeling like something horrible is gonna happen."

Mackenzie seemed to relax once they got off the dirt trail and back onto the semi-paved road. The girls remained quiet for about ten minutes before Paige couldn't resist looking out the rear window again at the nagging itch they weren't alone on the road. Trees and empty paving stretched back as far as she could see. As much as it *felt* like something ran along behind them, the road appeared empty. She shifted forward in the seat and grasped her knees. Sofia took the choker off and handed it back to her.

"What did we do?" whispered Paige as another pang of doom settled in her gut.

Mackenzie grinned at her via the rearview mirror. "Everything we wanted."

# 10

## TOO QUIET

Monday October 12 - 4:49 p.m.

Paige snugged her choker back on and hopped out of the Kia. Her boots hit the gravel together with a loud *crunch*. She leaned back into the car and waved at Mackenzie and Renee. They'd dropped the others off on the way to her house. Anderson Funeral Home didn't look half as creepy as Paige thought it would, though it did seem odd that they lived there, on the second floor above the mortuary. If not for the big sign, she might've mistaken it for a small mansion.

Mackenzie offered a gleeful wave and drove away. Paige trudged up the driveway past the State Police car. The family Suburban was missing. She glanced at the road. *Guess Mom took Melissa somewhere.* She stood under her pet black cloud grumbling and again watching Mackenzie drive away. Once the Kia vanished, she went inside. The television murmured from the left, some sci-fi show Dad seemed to be only half watching. She lurked in the archway between hall and living room for a little while before walking upstairs to her room. Her jacket sailed into the corner, boots went flying, and she shirked off her jeans. After tossing her bra in the general direction of the dirty laundry mound, she slipped into a thigh-length sweatshirt and ditched her now-damp socks as well as the choker.

Being alone in her room lasted a hair less than five minutes before she couldn't take it. That sense of something circling around her and sniffing hadn't let up since the ride home. She frowned at the backpack. *I'll do it later.* Her closet door creaked. She sucked in air and held it, staring at the strip of darkness. Amber didn't appear. Three seconds later, mounting dread that a being far less cordial than her ghostly sister had come to play forced her out of the room. She padded down the stairs and ran to the living room. Dad still had his uniform pants on with a white tee shirt and socks, and typed on his laptop.

Paige walked between him and the TV, and flopped on the couch an arm's length away. Guys in grey jumpsuits traded purple laser blasts with silly-looking aliens that reminded her of bipedal snails with shells obviously made of plastic.

"How was your day," asked Dad. His tone made it sound like a reflex reaction to her presence more than an actual question.

"Had a quiz in geometry I probably bombed. Aced a chem quiz, almost got into a fight with eighth-graders, oh, and we opened a portal to hell after school."

"Cool," said Dad, tapping away on the keyboard.

*Invisible Paige.* She sat like a lump for a while, too unmotivated to change the channel to something less stupid. "So, you're just gonna watch TV all night?"

"Did you want to do something else?" He clicked something that darkened the reflected light from his screen on his face.

Paige glanced sideways at him, hating the way he tuned out the world since her sister's death. Where was the Dad she'd grown up with? *I could tell him Amber's upstairs, offer to play translator.* She crossed her ankles, heels up on the coffee table, and teased at the cord bracelet. *Yeah, sure. And I'll get carted off to a mental hospital. Mom would be all for that. Get me out of her hair.* "I dunno." *Not even a comment that I'm out of my room.*

"Well, if you think of something." He typed a few more words.

She leaned up, trying to see. "What'cha doing?"

"Work. Reports and stuff."

"About the party?" She slumped into the cushions.

"Nope. Nothing even that exciting. Logging mileage, couple tickets."

*Wow. That's more talking than he's given me in weeks.* She edged closer. *Maybe the magic did something?* "You eat yet? Wanna go like grab a burger or something?"

"I need to finish this stuff before tomorrow." He frowned at the screen. "Probably don't have time to go anywhere."

*Or not.* She leaned forward and grabbed the remote. "Right. Four tickets and an expired registration looks like hours of paperwork. Are you watching this?"

"Change it if you want." He hesitated, but kept typing.

"Amber's ups..." *What am I doing?*

"What's that?" He glanced over.

"Nothing. I… Amber's up in heaven. She's like watching us or something."

"I guess." He tapped his finger on the computer case a few beats. "But that wasn't what you were going to say, was it?"

"I—"

*Thud. Thud. Thud. Thud. Thud.*

Footsteps passed overhead. Paige looked at the ceiling. "What was that?" *Amber's not that heavy.*

Dad eased the laptop onto the sofa between them and took his Glock from the utility belt on the end table. "Stay here."

Paige tucked her feet up and pulled the Eagles comforter draped over the back around her.

Dad raised the gun and moved to the hall, training the weapon up the stairs. "State Police. Show yourself. I hear you up there."

Paige huddled against the couch back, peering over it as Dad went up the stairs a step every few seconds. China rattled from the dining room. She turned toward the noise. A flash of cream fabric drifted through the doorway at the far end, heading for the kitchen. Her throat tightened. *Is… that Kenzie's mother?* She pushed herself up on her knees, leaning forward to peer further into the kitchen, but saw nothing.

The lights faltered.

"Great," muttered Dad. "Whoever's in my house better show themselves. If you're one of Paige's friends, no harm done. Don't make me shoot you."

"Diana?" whispered Paige. "Uhh, Mrs. Walsh?"

A pat of cold, as if a single raindrop landed on her right shoulder.

Paige spun to the right.

Mrs. Walsh stood two feet behind her in a sheer nightie. Her skin had taken on a deathly pallor and the odor of spoiled milk and cheap chocolate surrounded her, emanating from the spatter of brownish vomit down her front. The woman's expression seemed… pleased, but fell short of smiling.

Paige screamed and ducked under the comforter. A heavy *thud* overhead preceded banging and thumping down the stairs.

"Paige?" yelled Dad. "What happened?"

She shivered in place until he pulled the green fabric away from her face. Mrs. Walsh was gone. Paige sniffled, all attempts at speaking came out as babble.

"Did you see someone?" Dad scanned the living room over his weapon.

"I'm not crazy." Paige pulled her knees up to her chin. "You heard the footsteps too, right?"

"I did." He lowered the Glock and exhaled. "No one is upstairs."

"Yeah." Paige bit her lip. "It's a ghost."

He started to give her that 'oh here we go' expression, but froze at another *bang* from the back door. As Dad rushed off toward the sound, Paige stretched her legs to the floor. The eerie quality upstairs had departed. The house felt normal again.

"Ghost huh?" Dad returned three minutes later. He walked by, put the gun on the end table, and flopped on the couch.

"Unless we have some really fat squirrels in the attic." She giggled despite her fear. *She didn't look like she was mad at me, but gah, she felt so pissed off the other day.*

"Amber's death hasn't been easy on any of us. If you're trying to get attention, there are better ways."

She slouched. "Okay. Go find what I set up to make the footsteps then if you don't believe me."

Headlights washed over the front windows. Car doors *clunked* shut, and a few seconds later, rapid soft thumps traversed the porch. Melissa ran in, flip flops popping, and halted at the edge of the couch clutching a square foam box with a TGI Friday's logo pressed into it. Her pink dress had a black tutu skirt covered in pink and white dots, and sauce stains dribbled down her white leggings. Red rimmed her eyes, a little snot gathered at her nose, and her trembling hadn't quite ceased. Despite her evident fear, she forced a hopeful smile.

*Guess she's not totally over the car thing yet.* Paige reached out and ruffled Melissa's hair. The child's grin nudged toward genuine.

Paige smirked at Mom. "I guess I'll make hot pockets again."

"Oh." Mom sighed. "I couldn't find you."

"And you thought I was going to eat with my friends. Yeah... I get it."

Mom shook her head. "You know they have these things called phones. Would it kill you to ask instead of just hope I'm psychic?"

Paige's pet cloud popped out. She glared at the rug.

Melissa held up the box.

"Aww." Paige smoothed her sister's hair back. "That's really sweet of you, but that's your food. I don't wanna take it. I'll find something."

Melissa's radiant smile shattered to a lip-quivering pre-cry. From thrilled to devastated in one-point-two seconds. "But, Pay... I brought it home for you."

Guilt punched her in the stomach. "Okay... hey. It's okay. Thank you." Paige accepted the offering.

Melissa's mood reset to grinning. She darted out of her flip flops and climbed up on the sofa next to her. Paige switched the TV over to Netflix, went to the Disney section, and gave Melissa the remote. Serenaded by the *ping ping ping* of the child scrolling through movies, Paige opened the carton. Half a chicken breast sandwich almost as big as Melissa's head sat on a bed of lettuce next to a portion of steak fries.

Paige munched. Melissa settled on *The Rescuers*, and Mom went to the dining room where she resumed working on some crystal and bead necklaces someone from Virginia had ordered a dozen of. Dad worked on his tickets. Aside from Melissa's occasional giggle, cheer, or effort to sing along with the movie, no one spoke. *Did I drive Amber crazy?* Page shifted, letting her arm slide around Melissa's shoulders. The girl peeled her attention away from the movie long enough to give her a shocked, but worshipful look. *No... Amber wasn't a bitch.* She held on as Melissa snuggled up against her side.

At eight on the dot, Mom walked back in and gave Melissa 'the look.' She whined, but got up and went upstairs. Mom started for the dining room, but stopped. "Paige?"

"What?" She hadn't had much luck using chicken sandwich juices as a divining tool, but tilting the box back and forth to make the liquid run around the grooves wound up being entertaining.

"Do you have homework tonight?"

Paige stopped moving the box. *Whoa.* "Uhh, yeah."

"Have you done it yet?"

*I'm a little tapped out after summoning the essence of pure evil into our world.* She shuddered at the memory of the *thing* that appeared. "Not yet."

Mom drifted around behind the couch and put a hand on Paige's shoulder with a light prodding push. "Well, unless you're planning to fail... why don't you go upstairs and do it?"

"Okay." She shrugged out of the comforter and stood.

Dad glanced over with a raised eyebrow.

Paige hit the stairs by way of the kitchen to throw out the empty container. Once in her room, she flopped at her desk and pulled out her chem book. 'Fill in the electron' charts took her mind off ghosts and spooky things for a while.

Melissa ran in wearing a pink nightdress with a white daisy-shaped collar and a mermaid holding a flower to its chest. "Good night." She rushed into a hug, held on for a moment, and scampered out.

Mom lingered at the doorway.

"What?" asked Paige.

"I've noticed you're not being a snot to Melissa lately." Mom fidgeted. "I'm worried you might be gearing up to do something... drastic."

Paige let the pen fall out of her fingers and roll onto the desk. A sound like a shotgun racking echoed in her brain. "I was gearing up to kill myself four months ago, Mom. You didn't notice. Obviously, I didn't do it. I'm not gonna do it."

Mom put a hand over her mouth.

*Blam. Direct hit.*

"Really, I'm fine. I was a shit to Melissa because I was jealous of the way you worship her when you treat me like I'm not even here. If you want me to talk to a shrink, whatever... but I'm not gonna do anything. It would kill Melissa if something happened to me, and I can't do that."

"Paige..." Mom walked over. "I wish you would've said something."

"I did. Like *all the time.*" Paige picked her pen up. "Maybe in a bitchy way, but I did."

"Look at me."

Paige filled in one more electron and glanced up at her mother.

"You're not still thinking about harming yourself, are you?"

Solid eye contact. "No, Mom. I promise."

Mom relaxed.

Paige returned her attention to the paper.

"Hey," said Mom.

"Hmm?" Paige looked up again.

Mom's face shifted into that of Mrs. Walsh. Not-mom's voice came out of her. "Thank you."

Paige shrieked and leapt back off the chair, crashing to the floor in a cascade of textbooks and Goth-cessories that spilled from a falling Tupperware basin.

"Gah!" Mom clutched her chest. "That's not funny."

"I..." Paige gasped for breath, flat on her back, one leg over her chair. "I..."

Mom looked behind her. "What the devil are you screaming about?"

"N-nothing. Just... I didn't sleep well last night. I think I'm going to bed early tonight."

"Are you okay?" Mom helped her up.

"Yeah. Whacked my elbow on the desk, but"—she rubbed it— "nothing major."

"We'll talk, okay?"

"Okay, Mom."

Paige stared at the doorway long after her mother walked out. *What did we do?* Once the adrenaline faded, she slogged through the rest of her homework. Fortunately, for a Monday, the teachers had gone easy on her and assigned a light load. Mr. Martin for English class wanted her to read *Fahrenheit 451*, something she'd had to do last year in her other school.

At 9:58 p.m. she repacked her books and stood. After closing her bedroom door, she slipped her underpants off, kicked them onto the pile of dirty laundry, and grabbed a clean set of flannel pajamas from the dresser. She carried them to the bathroom, closed the inner door, and pulled off her long sweatshirt. Soon, a relaxing spray of hot water cascaded down her chest. She stood for a while in the blast from the shower, envisioning worry, fear, depression, panic, and thoughts of suicide leeching out of her and following the water swirling down the drain.

A bath would've been better, but she wanted to sleep more than soak. She hurried washing herself before lathering her hair up with shampoo. Eyes closed, she leaned her head into the stream to rinse off...

And felt watched.

Soap burned her eyes when they snapped open. She threw water over her face and blinked at the darkened space between the shower curtain and the tile-covered wall. The first thought she had blamed Melissa for sneaking into her room and turning off the lights, but her little sister had never been a prankster. She stood in the tub, water running, gazing at the iridescent blue glow of moonlight on white porcelain. Her skin blended invisibly, taking on the same eerie color.

"Hello?"

Wet hair slid up her back as she leaned forward and pulled the shower curtain away from the tiles—and peered out at gnarled forest. Leafless trees of stark pale grey ran in jagged lines over a field of blackness. Icy wind made her yelp and wrench the curtain shut. She recoiled, back pressed to the interior wall in an effort to get as far away as possible from the shower curtain and *woods*.

"What the shit?"

The water petered out to a trickle, then stopped. A droplet gathered at the showerhead, swelled, and fell in slow motion. It landed on the drain with a noise like a metal spoon striking a giant cauldron. Paige shivered, wrapping her arms around herself.

*I'm asleep at my desk. This is a dream.*

She reached over with a shaking hand and pulled back the plastic curtain again. October wind flooded the once-warm bathtub, almost turning the water on her skin to ice. She stuck her head out, peering left and right. The area around her bathtub seemed to have been lifted out of her home and dropped in the woods near Mackenzie's cabin. Hundreds of malevolent yellow eyes flickered in the darkness.

Her bathroom, and her pajamas, towel, rug, sink, parents, and sister were nowhere close.

*What the f...* She contemplated going to the cabin, but couldn't bring herself to move. *Even if this is a dream, I'm not streaking through the woods.* She covered herself as best she could with her arms and stood in place, shivering. Paige craved the safety of her own bedroom, her inner sanctum.

"Amber?" she yelled. "Is this a dream?"

Creaks and crackling echoed amidst the trees, a racing sound that drew closer, faster, and louder. The grass swelled up in four distinct trails zigzagging toward her.

She backed into the wall again. The tiles broke apart as though they'd been stacked on end, without mortar or drywall behind them. Paige screamed as the shower curtain collapsed with the loose tiles, leaving her exposed. She dropped to sit, and tucked up against the tub wall.

"What's going on? Is this a vision? Am I supposed to go to the cabin?" *No damn way.* The cold hit her like needles. *I'm going to die of exposure.*

The splintering became deafening; a clamor of snapping twigs and fracturing branches sounded inches away, but nothing moved in the dark. She took a few breaths.

*This is a dream. There is no way I teleported out to the woods from my bedroom.* With her hands still clamped over her body in a poor attempt to cover herself, she wobbled upright. *Okay. It's my dream. No one can see me, right?*

She lifted her right leg over the side, searching for the ground with her toes.

As soon as cold twigs touched her sole, jet black roots ran in venous streaks up her leg. Screaming, Paige abandoned modesty and tried to grab them. Thousands of roots and vines erupted from all around her, whipping over her skin and striking the porcelain in a fusillade of clanking. Jet-black vines devoured the tub in a thickening bird's nest of jagged kindling. Scratchy, piercing nails raked down her flesh, dragging her to the bottom of the tub. Sharp wooden crone hands tightened around her arms, legs, body, and throat. She screamed; rational thought lost to utter blind panic as the knotwork of narrow branches fused together above her and blotted out the sky. No matter how hard she struggled, she couldn't move. A finger-sized branch forced its way past her teeth and slid down her throat.

Paige snapped awake, gagging, curled fetal on the bottom of her bathtub under a freezing shower spray. Her bathroom glowed near blinding in contrast to the nightmare forest. Trembling from the fading sensation of narrow branches constricting around her unprotected skin, she sat up and jerked the water dials to the off position. Her teeth chattered. She grasped the edge of the tub and got to her feet, a task complicated by cold-stiffened muscles and shivering.

"A dream." She exhaled. "Just a damn dream."

She stepped out onto the fluffy black bathmat. Pain like a bee sting shot up from her foot. "Aaah!" She almost fell over the tub rim, but steadied herself on the shower curtain bar. Paige lifted her leg to look at what hurt her. A six-inch black vine stuck to her sole, which bled from where two thorns had pierced.

With a grunt, she pulled it free. A cursory glance found no more surprises on the plush bathmat. She hobbled to sit on the carpet-covered toilet lid and rubbed the sore spot until the burning subsided, all the while staring at the inexplicable length of wood on the floor. Her skin showed no other cuts or bruises. After toweling off, she jumped into her pajamas, ran out of the bathroom, and hid under her covers like a five-year-old.

# 11

# A NIGHT DISQUIET

Tuesday October 13 - 12:40 a.m.

Sleep decided it wasn't on speaking terms with Paige that night. After hiding in a ball for some hours, she risked a peek at the darkness. Nothing looked wrong. Nothing *felt* wrong. She reached up and turned on the little lamp on her nightstand, then pulled her foot up and looked. Two red dots proved the thorns weren't a dream.

"Amber?" She looked around. "Are you here? Did we mess up? Did we do something bad?"

The crickets outside grew deafening.

Whispering came from the bathroom. Paige gathered blankets at her chin and shrank down.

"Who's there?"

Rasps and titters continued, unchanged by her voice. Of course, the thought of the bathroom made her acutely aware of the need to use it. *Figures.* Paige stared at it for a while, unwilling to leave the 'safety' of the blankets. *Ugh. What am I, six? My bed isn't gonna stop a demon.* She peeled the blankets away and stood, hands balled to fists at her sides. Step by step, she crept to the door between her bedroom and its attached bathroom, favoring her right foot. The two-inch gap offered a view of whispery darkness. The voices grew louder as she got closer.

"Something's going to jump out at me." Paige grasped the edge of the door. *It doesn't matter how much I expect it; I'm going to scream.* She braced herself and whipped the door open.

The whispers ceased.

Paige stared at the strip of light leaking in from her bedroom, stretched over the white tile floor and shaggy bathmat. Her gaze settled on the empty spot where she'd left the thorn. *Of course it's gone.* She allowed herself to breathe again and fumbled for the light switch. Eerie became bright, clean, and normal. Paige avoided stepping on the bathmat on the way to the toilet.

Not two seconds after the stream stopped, a creak came from the bedroom. She shot upright where she sat and pulled her pajamas as far up her thighs as she could without standing. "Who's there?"

Silence.

She finished up and moved to the door, peering around the corner at an empty bedroom dark in comparison to the mostly white bathroom. *I'm either losing my grip or I've pissed something off.* She thought about what Mackenzie said… New Hope. *Maybe I can find an old witch there who can fix this.*

Nothing felt off, so she swiped at the bathroom light switch and scurried back to bed. The warm cocoon of blankets embraced her with the prospect of a rapid fall to sleep. Paige reached up, switched off the nightstand light, and snuggled into the pillow.

Seconds later, she sensed a presence and opened her eyes.

Melissa's face hovered inches from hers, staring into her soul.

Paige shot upright, screaming. Melissa backpedaled and fell on her butt.

"Holy crap." Paige grabbed her chest. "You scared me half to death."

Melissa looked down. A mermaid doll dangled by one arm from her left hand.

"What's wrong?"

"I'm scared too." Melissa crawled to the bed and grasped the edge, peering over it. "Can I sleep here tonight? Someone was talking in my closet."

Paige swallowed hard. "Okay." She held up the covers.

Melissa crawled in and cuddled close. Paige lowered her arm and wrapped her little sister in a blanket hug. A nose full of strawberry-tinted red hair wasn't the worst way to spend the night. She tried not to think about anything, especially not about the shadowy figure hovering over the candles. Melissa's breathing changed, indicating sleep within two minutes. Mildly jealous, Paige closed her eyes.

## Tuesday October 13 - 2:18 AM

Paige started awake. She leaned up and glanced at the clock. *Ugh. I should've asked the spirits for the ability to sleep through the night.* Melissa had shifted to lay flat on her back, arms at her sides as if posed for an autopsy.

Paige began to settle down, but stopped at the notice of the odd pallor in her sister's cheeks.

She nudged the girl. "Mel?"

No reaction.

Paige reached over and flicked the light on, and gasped. Melissa's skin had turned a shade of grey impossible for a living person. With panic nipping at her heels, she pressed a hand to the girl's chest, but felt no breath. Had the dark energies she'd beckoned taken a blood tithe? The thought that whatever had been whispering in her bathroom—and Melissa's closet—had come to take a life as payment summoned instant tears.

"Melissa!" Paige shook her, but she didn't move.

She leaned over and pressed her ear to Melissa's chest. Dry scratching came from within her chest instead of a heartbeat. Paige shot up, seconds from screaming in anguish.

The girl's cheek moved.

Paige froze. "Mel?"

A tiny swollen lump rose near the child's left shoulder and glided down her arm to the wrist, where it receded.

Paige stared for a few seconds, and poked her in the side.

Melissa's left cheek rose upward in the distinct shape of a spider crawling beneath the skin. Paige jumped back, blinking.

"No... no... I'm still sleeping." She slapped herself hard enough to see spots dancing.

Another small lump appeared at Melissa's collarbone and glided down the length of her nightdress. At the hem, a gloss black spider with a body the size of a fat blueberry emerged and crawled down her shin. Paige let off a yelp and swatted the creature off into the dark end of the room.

Thin black arachnid legs poked out of the eight-year-old's nostril. Another spider pulled itself out; in place of fangs, the creature bore the shriveled ash-white face of a tiny old man. Manic eyes stared at Paige above a leering grin. A mass of legs emerged from Melissa's lips. Three more spiders climbed out, forcing the dead jaw open. Her sister's face bubbled and roiled as spider after spider crawled under her skin to the nearest orifice. They squeezed out of her ears, nostrils, mouth, eyelids. A flood of blackness surged from the end of her nightgown, engulfing her legs, swarming over her feet, and spilling over the side of the bed.

Paige shrieked and fell off the mattress, landing flat on her back. Something tickled over her hand. She swatted and flailed, shrieking and howling while she scrambled upright. Sheets of spiders formed a diaphanous, shadowy gauze that slid up the walls all around her and covered the windows. Melissa continued erupting, her body moving only by virtue of the massive amount of arachnids teeming within her, writhing beneath her skin. Paige backed into the corner, seeing nowhere to run without plunging into millions of tiny chittering faces.

Her closet door swung open. Amber appeared in the mirror as though on the other side of a window. She pressed one palm to the glass. "What did you do? What's happening?"

A curtain of tingling arachnids hemmed her in and climbed her legs. Another clump distended from the ceiling, about to fall on her head. Screaming, Paige shoved away from the wall and danced among the endless mass of spiders. Anywhere she put her bare feet, a legion of prickling legs crawled all over her. She shrieked and kicked, trying to fling them away before anything could bite her. Three times on the way to the door, she fell and swatted the needle-crawlers from her arms. Two made it halfway up her thigh under her pajama pants, but died in sickening squishes when she crushed her hand down on them.

She jumped through the door to the hallway and slammed it.

"Paige," said Dad.

She jumped back against the wall. "D-Dad…"

He stood outside the master bedroom in full uniform, holding a shotgun. Her father shook his head and looked down. The kind of look a farmer might make before they put a lame horse out of its misery. "Why couldn't it have been you instead of Amber? She had such potential… Why couldn't it have been you that died?"

"No!" Paige yelled. "You're not real!"

She darted away before he had the chance to raise the weapon, taking the carpeted stairs down in a half-falling sprint. Hissing and white light came from the living room. No tromping followed; Dad seemed content to stay where he was.

Panting for breath, Paige crept down the hall. Mom's bronze wall hanging of metal flowers cast sinister shadows on the plaster. Dad's mounted swordfish (probably fake) seemed to be staring at her with sentience behind its plastic eyes. She edged around the archway to the living room.

Her mother sat on the tip of the couch cushion, ramrod straight, a vacant stare aimed at a television screen full of snow. White noise came from her mouth rather than the speakers.

"Mom?" Paige sidestepped to get a better look at her mother's face, but she didn't react at all. "Mom!"

She waved a hand back and forth in front of Mom's eyes. The woman's gaze remained nailed to the TV. Paige slapped her, but she may as well have hit a granite statue. She recoiled cradling her hand. "Ow. Damn."

Scratchy skittering crossed the room behind her, as if something outside dragged claws against the house.

"Mom! Wake up!" Paige cried as she yelled. Desperation kicked in. She shouted the F bomb. The C word. Several variations of both of them put together. Mom didn't move. Still, she sat with white noise pouring from her gaping mouth.

"It should've been you," said Dad.

Paige jumped at his sudden appearance behind her, and raised her hands as if they'd catch shotgun pellets. "Dad. Don't. I'm still your daughter. Please don't."

"I'm not going to hurt you. I'm just disappointed." His weapon remained sideways, aimed at nothing. He bowed his head. A lone tear gathered in the corner of his right eye. "Why is it always the brightest star that gets extinguished? It doesn't matter what you do, Paige. You'll never be as good as Amber."

Fear and sorrow exploded to anger. "This isn't real."

Since Dad blocked the front door, she ran the other way through the hall to the kitchen and crossed the freezing linoleum to the back exit. A flash of cream-hued light flickered in the yard. Paige flung the door open and ran out into the grass. Frozen dew chilled her toes and dampened the pajamas around her ankles.

"Leave Melissa alone!" shouted Paige at a sky of infinite black. "If this isn't a dream, stop. I command you back to wherever you came from."

"Hello, Paige," said a woman.

She whirled, face to face with Mrs. Walsh.

"Thank you for opening the door." The apparition smiled. "I've been waiting quite a while for this."

Paige screamed.

Mrs. Walsh evaporated into a cloud of silvery fog.

A light upstairs—her bedroom—clicked on.

She raced back into the house, wet feet sliding on the kitchen floor. After catching a near wipeout against the doorjamb to the hall, she zoomed over carpet to the stairs. The TV was off. No Mom in the living room, no golem of a father with a shotgun. Her heart surged, thrumming in her eardrums as she took the stairs two at a time. The wonderful sound of a very much alive Melissa crying filled the upstairs hallway.

Paige ran to her room. Melissa sat in the middle of the bed, sobbing and hyperventilating. Paige leapt up and gathered her in a hug. The girl clamped on, sniveling.

"I had a bad dream."

"Me too." Paige bowed her head, face in the crook of her sister's neck. "It's okay. It's over."

Melissa dug her fingers in, holding on. Her little body trembled and shook with coughs and erratic breaths.

"Only a dream." Paige patted her on the back.

Melissa coughed, sucked in air, convulsed, and coughed again. A wet *splat* hit the mattress. Melissa doubled over in Paige's lap, gagging. Paige twisted to look behind her, aghast at a black spider mired in a blob of phlegm. Its tiny old man face grinned at her, and giggled in a pixie's voice.

She swatted the little horror off the bed and stomped on it before realizing she had no shoes on. *Eww.* Cold slime spread across her sole, as though she'd stepped on a used tissue. Paige cringed. *At least it's not moving.*

Her door creaked open. Dad in his boxers. One eye open. "You girls okay? What's wrong?"

"Dad?"

He squinted and wiped his face. "Screaming. Woke me up. What happened?"

"I had a nightmare," said Paige, sounding quite a bit younger than she intended.

"Me too," whispered Melissa.

He lumbered over to the bed and sat on the edge. Paige cradled Melissa in one arm and clung to him with the other as he stroked her hair.

"Whoa, damn," said Dad with a hint of a smile. "That was a big spider. I think I might've screamed too."

# WHEN A SECRET FALLS

Tuesday October 13 - 3:41 p.m.

A burp brought a mixture of café mocha and chicken parmesan into the back of Paige's throat. She sat up on Mackenzie's sofa, gagging. The shape of her body vanished in a baggy black sweatshirt and sweat pants. School that day had been a blur. Mr. Ruiz managed to keep her attention enough to ward off sleep. Pritchard's geometry class felt like it took four seconds. She'd slept hard, but he either didn't notice or care. Her Facebook wall blew up with pictures of her open-mouthed and snoring at her desk.

Art with Mrs. Hollis wasn't too bad. Volleyball in Mrs. McDonnell's gym period had kicked her ass. Fortunately, one of the boys on the other side of the room had decided to elevate the game to a contact sport about halfway through, and took down the net. McDonnell and the other PE teacher killed fifteen minutes yelling at him, letting Paige catnap on the bleachers. For a smallish woman with a short black bob, McDonnell seemed to have no trouble putting the boys in their place.

Lunch had passed without incident. By Martin's English class at 1:10 p.m., she'd found enough juice to stay awake. At least until Mr. Serrano's lecture on the political climate preceding the American Civil War knocked her out again. Unfortunately, unlike geometry, *he* noticed. He did, however, buy a story of a little sister emotionally traumatized by the untimely death of their older sibling keeping her awake all night with screaming nightmares.

Paige sat up holding her gut. "Ugh. I'm either sensing impending cataclysm, or there was something wrong with the chicken parm."

Renee gnawed on Mackenzie's stepmother's attempt at 'all natural' brownies. "Did you hear some kid got run over by their dad this morning?"

Paige gasped.

"Yeah. Kelly Parker." Sofia, cross-legged on the floor by the coffee table, picked at the rug. "She's in my class. Her father backed over her in the driveway. It's only her foot. Broke it though."

"Sorry about your friend," said Renee.

Sofia offered a noncommittal shrug. "I wouldn't call her my friend."

"You don't look all that upset," said Santana. She stretched flat on her back, powder-pink sweatshirt lifting to expose a bit of her belly. Her navy-blue parachute pants swished as she raised her legs, pointing her toes at the ceiling. "This yoga stuff is weird."

"Kelly's the girl that kept stepping on my bag and making me fall." Sofia traced lines in the carpet pile with one finger. "I can't say I'm sorry she got run over. She also helped Michelle trick me into the locker. She got in first and they let her out, then told me I was too fat to fit. They always call me Wednesday, and I *hate* it."

"You're not even close to fat," said Paige. "You look like you eat once a month."

Sofia gave her a hurt glance.

"Oh, I don't mean it like that. You're pretty. You have nothing to be ashamed of." Paige smiled.

"Maybe you might not wanna wear so much black." Santana rolled over and put her ass in the air.

"What the hell are you doing?" Mackenzie drifted in from the kitchen in a huge beige shirt/dress down to her shins that bared one shoulder and almost the breast on that side.

"The pose is called downward facing dog," said Santana.

Mackenzie set a pitcher of iced green tea on the coffee table. "Looks more like 'Need Man Now.'"

Santana couldn't sit up fast enough. "That's not funny."

"I think it's hilarious." Mackenzie winked. "So, Sofia's wish is taking shape. Anyone else have anything happen yet?"

"Kenz," said Santana. "The 1980s called. They want their clothes back."

"My dad noticed me last night." Paige untied and retied the string on her sweat pants.

"Cool." Sofia smiled.

"Not really." Paige let her arms slide limp off her lap. "I had this wicked nightmare. Scared me so bad I wanted to suck my thumb like a little kid. I cried so loud he came to my room to see what was wrong."

"Aww, who's so adorbs?" Mackenzie winked. "Spirits do things in odd ways sometimes."

Paige sat up. "You don't understand. That was like… heart-attack scary." Her breathing picked up at the mere thought of it. "Check this out." She pulled her right boot off, peeled away the sock, and held her foot up.

"Eww," said Santana. "Put that thing away."

"Look." Paige pointed out the two red dots. She explained the bathtub nightmare… then how she found a thorn vine for real in her bathroom.

Sofia shivered.

"You probably stepped on something else and your brain made it look like that vine when you woke up. Real cut, wrong explanation." Santana flipped her hair back off her shoulders. "You still got the stick?"

"No, it disappeared." Paige put her sock on.

"See?" Santana shook her head. "All in your head."

Renee poured herself a glass, scowling at the deck.

"What's wrong?" asked Sofia.

"Nothing's happened. No sign of Dad. Nothing going on at all. At least your stuff is coming true. The people you're mad at are getting their karma back."

Sofia shied away. "I asked the spell for friends, not to hurt people."

Paige zipped her boot. "But what did you *want?* Did you say friends but think about how angry you were with them?"

Sofia made faces at her lap and poked the carpet.

Santana giggled, but covered her mouth.

"What?" asked Mackenzie.

"No… no." Santana shot an apologetic look at the rug. "I can't say it. I don't wanna hurt Sofia's feelings."

The thirteen-year-old looked up. "It's okay. I get picked on all the time anyway."

Santana's mirth faded to a sad stare. "It just hit me as ironic. They always call you Wednesday, and she does awful things to people that make her mad."

Paige found a neutral direction to look at.

"That *is* kinda funny." Mackenzie plucked a brownie off the tray. She took one bite, cringed, and set it aside. "I need to talk Linda out of this organic thing. These aren't brownies. I think I'll call them UCOs. Unidentified Cake-like Objects."

"She forgot to sweeten it. Baker's chocolate." Santana took another bite. "They're not that bad once you get used to it."

"Damn, girl." Mackenzie laughed. "You must really be starving at home if you're eating these things. You guys wanna get pizza or something? I'll buy."

"Lemme ask," said Sofia. She took out a phone and got to texting.

"Me too." Paige felt a little weird, but shot a text to Mom: *'Is it ok 2 eat at Kenzie's?'*

Mom: *you sire?*

Mom: *\*sure*

Paige grinned, and replied: *not big deal. Will w8 for home if u want.*

Mom: *Only if you walrus tits.*

Mom: *Darn ohine. Want to\**

Mom: *Phone\**

*I kinda do.* She stared at the screen for a few breaths before typing a reply. *K I'll b home 4 food.*

"I got commanded to eat at home tonight." Paige stuffed the phone in her pocket.

Renee, Santana, and Sofia all agreed on pizza.

"You sure you can't weasel out?" asked Mackenzie.

Paige bit her lip. "I got a feeling I should do it. I asked for my Dad to snap out of his fog, right? Mom's been ignoring me lately... and she like asked me to have dinner at home. Maybe that's the spell working."

"Oh... good point." Mackenzie widened her eyes. "You better go then. Bad things happen if you work against your own spell."

"What about you, Kenz?" Renee cocked an eyebrow. "I don't see Cole in your bedroom."

Mackenzie smiled. "Things take time. I'm patient."

"*You?* Patient?" Renee raised an eyebrow. "Wow. We did do magic."

Paige's cell phone beeped. She pulled it out and peered at the screen: *Toss cord—4:10 p.m.* She stood and walked to the patio door.

"What's up?" asked Mackenzie.

"It's time." Paige held her wrist up and shook the cord. "Gotta toss it, right? You said twenty-four hours."

"Oh. Yeah... right. Uhh, if you don't mind, go all the way to the end of the yard and chuck it over the fence. Just so it's not on the property, 'kay?"

"Sure, whatever."

The sliding glass door was heavier than it looked, requiring both hands to pull open. Paige jogged over the huge deck and down the stairs at the far side. She ran around a massive pool shaped like a peanut with a tumor (hot tub) midway along the top curve of the left end. Twelve-foot red cedar fencing surrounded the yard, mixing its fragrance with that of recently cut grass. Waning afternoon sunlight, muted by a half-stormy sky wavered on the surface of the water. An inexplicable sense of dread came on at the sight of the deep end. She shied to her right, walking over a bed of egg-sized grey stones at the base of the fence, unable to take her eyes away from the mesmerizing blue tiles thirteen feet down.

Scratching leaves spun in whorls across the concrete pad around the pool.

She put her back to the fence and moved sideways, feeling as though to move one inch closer would pull her in and drown her. A hint of chlorine crept up her nostrils. The overwhelming urge to get away from the pool came on, but she couldn't find the will to move, needing all her concentration to keep breathing through the heaviness pressing in on her chest. After swallowing a mouthful of dryness, Paige broke away from the fence and ran to the back corner almost a hundred-and-fifty yards from the house. She wormed between a pair of conical evergreen bushes and faced away from the fence.

"Elemental Spirit, we thank you for blessing our circle."

Paige tugged at the knot, unable to budge it. She bit the cord and gnawed for a little while. Nascent fear faded away as the rope loosened and dangled limp through her fingers. Lapping water sounded unnaturally loud. Again, she stared at the water, which seemed to churn as if someone struggled to keep their head above the surface, though the pool was empty.

*I'm seeing things.*

She thought of gratitude and directed it toward the Element of Spirit, then hurled the rope high to the rear. *Hope that went over the fence.* Without looking behind her, Paige walked back to the house, again skirting the pool with one shoulder brushing the fence for twenty yards until she was sure she couldn't slip and fall in.

The grass between the pool area and the deck passed in a blur. She rushed in and pulled the patio door closed hard enough to startle the other girls.

"Whoa," said Renee. She leapt up and ran over, grabbing Paige by the shoulders. "You okay? You look like you need to change your panties."

"Girl *is* that pale," said Mackenzie with a wry smile.

"Did you see something?" Sofia perked up, interested.

Santana stared without a word while Mackenzie smiled.

"Uhh… I had the craziest feeling near the pool. I couldn't stop staring at the water." She approached the coffee table and downed her tea in one long series of gulps. After a gasp or two for air, she coughed. "It felt like it wanted me to fall in and drown… or maybe someone did drown there already, or it'll happen in the near future."

Mackenzie nibbled on her brownie, and made a face as if forgetting how bad it tasted. "A guy from the landscaper service drowned in it when I was fourteen."

Sofia wrapped her arms around her legs, wide-eyed.

"Don't most people cover pools by this time of year?" asked Renee.

"Uhh, it *is* covered," said Mackenzie. "That happened like halfway through September."

Paige twisted around; sure enough, a heavy-duty black pool cover concealed the water she'd seen moments before. She pressed a hand to the side of her face, feeling woozy.

Santana glanced at the patio doors. "You never told us your Dad killed the guy your mom cheated with."

Mackenzie laughed. "That's because I'm messing with you guys... no one drowned out there. Jeez! Do you think I'd go near that pool if someone died in it?"

*Thump.*

Paige looked up at the ceiling. No one else reacted to the noise. She stood. "Mind if I use the bathroom?"

Mackenzie waved at her in a 'knock yourself out' gesture and poured herself more tea before channel surfing. She reached for another UCO, but thought better of it. Paige headed for the stairs, heeding a pull she didn't notice until the halfway point. She hesitated. Renee started a discussion about the shadow apparition, wondering if anyone else remembered seeing it. Sofia ignored the question while Mackenzie and Santana admitted they saw it too.

Paige hurried the rest of the way up before anyone tried to ask her. She found the bathroom halfway down the hall on the left, still full of the warm soap-scented fog of Mackenzie's post-school shower. *Who showers three times a day? That can't be good for the skin.*

She skipped over the steamy pink and white room. The door at the end of the hall seemed to want her. Whatever feeling dwelled there didn't radiate malice, so she let her legs keep moving and snuck into the master bedroom. Various chintzy exercise items littered a port-wine-colored rug: a thigh master, some shake weights, jump rope, and other devices she couldn't imagine how anyone would use to work out. A shrine to home shopping networks filled the near corner on the left, several of the items looked as though they'd never even been opened.

The air felt twenty degrees cooler than the rest of the house. Her breath fogged.

A king-sized bed shrouded in black sheets sat between a pair of matching black wardrobe closets with an overbed cabinet crossing above the pillows. Between the wardrobes and the bed, nestled a pair of small nightstands. On the left one, as she faced from the foot end, a tall glass contained about an inch of chocolate milkshake. No sooner did Paige stare at it than her insides twisted up. She held her stomach, cringing from stabbing pains shooting through her guts. Her muscles refused to move.

"What are you doing in here?" said Mackenzie.

Paige gasped and spun around. "I... uhh..."

"Wow, are you okay? You look even paler than usual... and for you, that's saying a lot."

"Sorry." The pain receded. "I had a really weird feeling and... I'm not sure why I walked in to this room. I just kinda did. Something was pulling me."

"Hmm." Mackenzie looked around.

"I didn't steal anything." Paige held her arms up. "Go ahead, check my pockets."

"Oh, knock it off. I'm not accusing you of being a thief." Mackenzie backed up. "C'mon. You might see something nasty in here. Dad takes, uhh, pictures with Linda."

"Eww." Paige glanced back as she started to leave, but froze. "Whoa. The shake is gone."

"Huh?" Mackenzie's tan faded from her cheeks. "Did you say 'shake?'"

"Yeah. On the nightstand." She walked over to where it had been. "Right here. A glass with about"—she pinched her fingers an inch apart—"this much left in it. Looked like a chocolate milkshake. As soon as I looked at it, I felt like two clawed hands mashed my guts into meatloaf."

A glimmer of fear in Mackenzie's eyes faded to red-eyed crying. She collapsed to her knees. "My mom died in this room. She killed herself with one of those slender-quick diet shake things. Put a bunch of pills in it." She clamped a hand over her mouth to hold in a few sobs. "They'd been fighting for months. A couple days before she did it, Dad said it was a mistake to have ever fallen in love with her. He didn't mean it." Mackenzie covered her mouth and nose with her hands, sniffling. "Just things people say when they fight, ya know?"

"Oh my God." Paige dropped to her knees and put a hand on Mackenzie's shoulder. "I'm so sorry."

Mackenzie sniveled and wiped tears on her sleeve. "Three years ago when I was fifteen. Sorry for yelling at you. I hate this room. I... don't like it when people come in here. Wow. You're the real deal. No one but Dad and the police know about the milkshake." She narrowed her eyes. "Wait, you didn't find that on like one of your father's files did you?"

"No. We haven't even been in Shadesboro two weeks yet. And Dad's a state trooper. He wouldn't have any reason to have files on a local suicide investigation. All he usually does is write traffic tickets and stuff. They call it 'deer hunting,' but the 'deer' are really New Yorkers."

"Yeah, that makes sense." Mackenzie stood. "Sorry for falling to pieces. It's still hard. I have nightmares about finding her still."

Paige gasped into the hand she clamped over her mouth. "*You* found her?"

Mackenzie nodded, lip quivering again as if she might explode into full-on bawling any second. "Yeah. She was already cold. I never even got to say goodbye."

A computer at the far right blared to life, flooding the air with a haunting minor key harpsichord. Both girls jumped and screamed as an ethereal female vocalist sang of secrets and honey. Five seconds later, the PC shut down.

Something crashed downstairs with a heavy *slam*, drawing shrieks from the others. The impact rattled up through the wall and popped open one of the doors in the headboard cabinet; a handful of DVD cases tumbled out like dominoes. One slipped to the floor, bounced, and landed face up at Mackenzie's knees.

Season One of *Pretty Little Liars*.

Paige pretended not to look at it. "Something broke downstairs."

Mackenzie threw the DVD onto the bed before standing and running out. Paige followed her down the hall to the stairs. Santana, Renee, and Sofia sat on the floor around the coffee table, gawking up at the Ouija board stuck to the ceiling.

The instant Mackenzie's foot hit carpet at the bottom, the board fell to the table with a *slap, and the girls around it jumped.*

"What's happening?" asked Sofia in a wavering voice. "Did we do this?"

"No." Mackenzie picked the board up. The closet it came from hung open, boxes, a vacuum, and coats spilled out. "It's an angry ghost."

Santana muttered in Spanish. "Who's it pissed at?"

"No one here." Mackenzie padded back to the group. She flashed a wide smile, though her hands clenched in fists. "So, what toppings do you guys want?"

Paige hooked her thumbs in the waistband of her sweat pants. "I, uhh, should go home."

# 13

# DIRE INFLUENCE

Tuesday October 13 - 5:16 p.m.

Walking home from Mackenzie's house seemed better in idea than practice. The reality of walking something like three miles sucked, as did the sore muscles in her legs. For at least a half-mile, Paige followed a winding wooded road with no sign of another person. She passed the occasional driveway, but they all twisted into the trees, leading to houses too far removed from the road to spot. Snaps, cracks like wooden boards clapping together, and random hoof tramples burst out of the underbrush without warning. A chill ran down her back accompanied by the sense of being hunted.

Out of nowhere, all sound ceased, even the rustle of wind in the trees.

She hastened up to a jog. Foreboding followed her all the way to the downtown part of Shadesboro. Surrounded by buildings, paved streets, and the activity of others, her dread waned. Paige leaned on a telephone pole to catch her breath. An older woman and a boy of about twelve stopped to ask if she was okay a few minutes apart. They accepted a lame excuse about being from the city and not used to hiking. Once she had her wind back, she set off at a brisk walk toward home.

The school passed on her right, and soon she found herself in the tree-tunnel between town and home. Here, the houses sat close enough to the road to see. *I guess she doesn't want to follow me this far. I wonder if she's angry with me for not saying anything?* Paige shivered. *Dammit Kenz, what did you do? Did you kill your own mother?*

She tried to reconcile the movie-star perfect smiling blonde who tried to console and go all motherly on her with the idea of a fifteen-year-old poisoning her mom. *It doesn't make any sense. She seemed real when she cried. She's not that good an actress, is she?*

Paige jogged up the steps to her porch and inside; the door couldn't close fast enough. "Mom?"

"In the kitchen."

She hurried down the hall, finding Mom with her head in the fridge, making disappointed clucking noises. Without a second thought, she ran up behind her and clamped on.

"Paige?" Mom twisted around, returning the hug. "What's gotten into you?"

"I found out Kenzie's mom died a few years ago. I…"

"Oh." Mom squeezed her. "And your head's running off with guilt."

"Something like that."

The hug intensified for a few seconds, then released.

"I'm looking at what we've got in the fridge and it's not going to cut it for anything. Looks like I've got enough to get started on a base for spaghetti sauce. Would you mind running to the store while I get started?"

"Uhh. I guess…"

"Melissa's not feeling well and you know how she is about cars." Mom looked up at the ceiling. "Though she's screaming less lately."

"I kinda had a talk with her about it." Paige cringed at the thought of having a spider in her throat. "W-what happened to Mel?"

"Oh, she had a really bad dream last night. She's frightened of her own shadow today."

"Yeah. I had a doozy too. Guess Dad didn't tell you."

Mom looked worried. "What are the odds you both have a nightmare?"

"Well, we *are* sisters and we slept in the same bed last night. Maybe we're like psychic or something. Hey, can I take the Sub?"

"Paige… You don't even have your permit yet and your father's a State Trooper. Do you really think I'm going to let you drive?"

Something pulled her attention to the front door. A desire to feel the wind in her hair and smell the trees blossomed, irresistible. She stared, wordless.

"What's wrong?" Mom peeked over her shoulder. "Did you hear something?"

"No. I… you're right. I should walk."

She peered through the windows flanking the front door, trying to decipher the sudden onrush of *wanting* to walk instead of explaining she might've talked Melissa down from her fear of cars. Mom worked up a list on a small pad and handed her the paper plus a debit card.

"Pin's 0819, right?"

"Yep."

Paige stuffed the list and card into her sweatshirt pocket and started to walk out, but Mom whirled and grabbed her arm. "Paige."

"Hmm?"

"I… I'm sorry for making you think I ignored you. You're right. I was shutting out everything but Melissa. She's the baby. You're older. You can take care of stuff she can't. I… was scared."

Paige hugged her mother again. "Amber's death put me in a bad headspace for a while too. Truce?"

Mom offered a fist bump.

"Really?" Paige laughed and returned it. "I think you're over the minimum age limit for that."

"Truce," said Mom.

With a huge grin on her face, Paige trotted to the door and headed off down the road to town. *Is this the spell, or just Mom?* She batted the idea around. So far, the effect of the magic—provided she wasn't simply nuts and hallucinating—had been strong, negative, and dark. It didn't seem plausible for the same energy to be responsible for Mom's change in attitude. *It scared me so bad Dad wanted to protect me.* She stopped in the middle of the road. "Oh, shit. Kenz said it works in weird ways. It's gonna give me both barrels till Dad snaps out."

The forest radiated the quiet serenity of an autumn afternoon. Birds sang, the wind brushed leaves about, and the little old lady seemed to be baking again. Paige got hungry at the smell and picked up her pace.

About forty yards ahead, an auburn-haired girl in a boys' varsity jacket with white pseudo-leather sleeves and a red back emerged from a side street and turned right, walking in the same direction as Paige. The growling goat logo of Waterford High's 'Goats' football team stared at Paige, daring her to challenge it.

*Emily… That girl from the party.* She shrugged and tucked her hands in the center pocket of her sweatshirt. *It's kinda lame Kenz is trying to steal her boyfriend.* An unsettling feeling teased at the underside of Paige's stomach. She raised her head, watching Emily walk. She looked pretty in tight jeans, and had a girl next-door vibe going. *She's not Mackenzie-hot, but not every guy wants Barbie on his arm. Right?* She glanced at the trees as if they'd answer.

Her hunger had evaporated. Now the scent of Mrs. Old Lady's pie made her sick. *Am I picking up on something? Crap.* Paige hustled up to a jog, leaving her hands in her pockets. Emily turned at the hollow scuffing of boots on the road. Up close, the girl looked perhaps an inch taller than her.

"Emily?"

"Oh, hi. You're that new kid, right? You're in Pritchard second period."

"Yeah. I'm Paige." She kicked a rock off the paving into the brush. "That dude is so damn boring. They should record his class and sell it as a sleeping aid."

Emily laughed.

"Sorry. I know we haven't met, but I got a creepy feeling from the trees like someone was watching me. Mind if we walk together?"

"Of course not." Emily smiled, pulled buds out of her ears and let them drape around her neck. "Rude to listen to this when I have someone to talk to. I hate walking alone too! You look nervous."

"Thanks. I'm not great with meeting new people. It's awkward."

"It's okay. Moving to a new town can be scary. I can't really understand it since I've been here my whole life." Emily stuffed her hands in the pockets of her jacket, walking with no great hurry. "It must be difficult to leave everything you know behind."

"I didn't really have many friends. I have more here already than I did back home." Paige chuckled. *Assuming they're genuine.*

"Doing anything fun?"

"Nah. Mom sent me to the store to grab some stuff for dinner."

"Sucks not having a car."

Paige shrugged. "I don't even have a permit yet."

Emily let off an exasperated noise. "I want one so bad, but my parents can't afford it. It's cool though. I'm gonna work next summer and get an old clunker."

"You're a junior, right? What are you doing in Pritchard's class?"

"I'm not awesome at math. In fact, I am the exact inverse of awesome at math." Emily raspberried at the trees. "As soon as they throw letters into the mix... I just can't."

Paige laughed. "Wait, didn't you work last summer?"

"I did. Saved up about $1600."

"So... doing it again for a nicer car?"

Emily smiled. "No. I gave it to my Mom to help out with some repairs on the house. I don't really need a car here. Everything's so close I can walk."

*Wow. Renee is right. This girl's way too sweet to be human.* "That's... nice of you."

The edge of the downtown emerged at the end of the tree-shrouded road. A glint of sunlight passed over the grille of a large blue sedan as it turned onto the road, facing toward them. Paige wheezed, unable to breathe. The more she stared at the car, the worse she felt. Dread burbled up from the pit of her soul and turned her blood to ice. Not since the night Amber died did she feel so terrified for no good reason.

"Paige?" Emily grasped her arm. "Are you all right? You look like you're going to pass out."

She peeled her gaze off the approaching car. "Yeah. I..."

"It's okay if you have panic attacks. My cousin gets them after their house burned down. It's nothing to be ashamed of." Emily offered a reassuring smile. "You're safe. Think about breathing. Look at me."

"I'm fine. It's not that." Paige hovered close to the girl and hurried up to a brisk stride. "I think I'm starving. Maybe low blood sugar or something."

"Oh. Diabetic?"

"No." Paige gazed upward. "Just haven't eaten since lunch. Trying to make a joke."

Engine noise revved. The car picked up speed, probably doing close to fifty. Stray pieces of gravel sailed away from its tires.

"That guy's going too fast," said Emily.

The car teleported forward thirty yards in an instant and swerved right at them. Paige screamed and braced for impact, but the car snapped back to where it was.

A vision.

Paige shouted and dove at Emily, tackling her off the road. A horn blared and something huge brushed by close enough to clink the zipper on Emily's borrowed jacket. Paige landed on top of Emily in a shallow ditch beside the road. Sand and small stones rained over them.

*Wham.*

After a great crunch of metal, the horn continued blaring. Seconds later, a subdued *bang* echoed inside the car.

"What the hell?" Emily rolled over and helped her stand; a second later, she screamed.

Paige whirled to look. A Mercury Grand Marquis had landed some twenty feet off the road at the end of a trail of demolished saplings and scrub, crumpled nose first into a thick tree. A limp, bloody airbag draped from the wheel, beneath a man in a suit.

Emily gasped for breath and ran to the car. Paige took two steps, but hesitated.

"Emily, wait. It might explode. Get back."

"Hey, mister?" yelled Emily. She pulled at the door, which wouldn't open. "Hey! Are you awake?" She kicked at the glass. "He's trapped!"

The woods around the car seemed to drift closer to her. *Mackenzie... It's gonna kill her so she can have Cole.* Paige felt like throwing up. *No. No. No.*

"Paige!" yelled Emily. "Call for help!" She kicked the door twice more, then ran around and opened the passenger side.

Paige pulled out her phone. Before she could swipe through the password lock, police lights flashed on the trees. "Uhh, they're already here. Guess they saw it."

A local police car pulled to a stop by where the Mercury went off the road.

A blonde woman in dark blue got out, took one look at the car, and grabbed her radio. A few seconds later, she hurried over.

"Are either of you injured."

Paige shook her head.

"No," said Emily.

"You two wait up by the road."

"Okay," said Paige.

"Yes, ma'am," said Emily. She grabbed Paige by the arm and dragged her up the shallow hill to the street.

The officer broke the window with a tool from her belt and reached in to check on the driver. She backed up with a grim look on her face and muttered something else into her shoulder mic.

Emily shifted gears from 'gotta help' to 'holy crap we almost died.' She clung and shivered.

"This is gonna sound stupid," said Paige. "But—"

"Girls," said the cop.

Paige bit her lip.

She and Emily looked up.

"Did either of you see what happened?"

"Not really." Emily's teeth chattered. "We were just kinda walking to town and Paige jumped on me. I… think she saved us."

The cop looked at Paige.

"Uhh. I saw the car coming up the road. He was bouncing around… had to be doing like sixty. I just had this really bad feeling and then he swerved right at us."

"You're a damn lucky kid." The officer pointed her pen at Paige's sweatpants leg, where a dust smudge covered her right outer calf.

Paige gawked at the car. A matching clean smear ran along the driver's side from front door to rear fender. She dry heaved. Emily put an arm around her and helped her sit on the side of the paving.

"Are you certain that neither of you are hurt? Do you need an ambulance?"

"No, ma'am." Emily rubbed Paige's back.

*I just need new underpants.* She forced a smile. "No. It missed. Is he…?"

"The driver didn't make it." The officer collected their ID cards. "Oh, you're the new Statie's kid." She smiled.

"Yeah," said Paige. "That crash didn't look hard enough to kill the driver, especially with an airbag." *Would've smeared us though.* She stared into the car, at the bloody steering wheel. *The airbag went off late…*

"Good eye." The officer jotted down their info and returned the cards. "I think he probably had a coronary or something before he went off the road. Course, that's just a guess. I'm no ME."

Sirens approached.

Despite shaking and generally freaking out about almost becoming a hood ornament, Emily squeezed and comforted Paige.

The officer moved to meet another patrol car and an ambulance. She waved at the paramedics. "I called it in DOA. You guys are late to the party."

The police murmured too far away to hear.

Paige hunkered over and grabbed Emily's hand. "Hey, this is gonna sound crazy, but you gotta trust me. I think something is trying to hurt you."

"What? Me? Why?" Emily gasped.

Paige exhaled. "Do you believe in, like, ghosts and stuff?"

"I dunno. Maybe."

"What about magic?"

Emily tilted her head. "Like card tricks? It's an illusion."

"You're not going to believe me, but I think there's a dark energy out there that's trying to hurt you. Someone's jealous of you and it's gone off the leash."

"Oh." Emily's hazel eyes shimmered with concern. Not a single trace of near-death panic remained. "You must be so terrified at almost getting run over. Are you sure you're okay? If... I don't wanna sound patronizing or anything, but I hear you Goth kids experiment with like drugs and stuff. Did you take something?"

*Figures.* "No. I'm not high. Yeah. Okay, maybe I'm just freaking out." *Mackenzie couldn't really want to kill someone like Emily? She's so damn sweet.* Paige grabbed her throat and shivered. *Oh... wait. What if it wasn't meant for her? Maybe the thing is trying to scare the crap out of Dad by half-killing me?* She let a whine slip out of her nose while staring at the smudge of dirt on her pant leg.

The female cop approached. "If you girls are not stating an injury and refuse medical attention, you're free to go. I've got your info. If the investigators need to contact you, they might pay a visit."

"That's fine, ma'am." Emily stood. "I'll walk you home, Paige."

"Thanks." She didn't look at the car. "Still need to hit the store."

Emily held her hand. "Not a problem. I was just going to sleep over a friend's house and watch movies. She won't mind if I'm a little late."

As they entered downtown, Paige glanced back up the road. *Maybe the nightmare got under my skin. That could've just been a man having a heart attack.*

Tuesday October 13 - 8:04 p.m.

Forearm-deep in sudsy dishwater, Paige frowned through her beleaguered reflection in the window over the kitchen sink at the patch of dark where a backyard should be. The corner of a neighbor's house shone yellow in the glow of an old light bulb, so far away it looked more like a will-o-wisp among the dense trees. Mom almost fainted at her offer of cleaning up, but accepted seeing as how she had to finish an order of sixty charm bracelets someone placed Friday and wanted by the coming Wednesday.

Dinner had passed in relative calm once Dad had finished asking his thousand-and-one questions about the accident. Mom seemed far more frazzled at the thought of the Thomas clan almost being minus one more daughter than Paige expected.

She looked down past her night-tee at her legs, bare from the knees down, and pictured the smear of dirt on her pants. *That car didn't 'almost' hit me, it made contact...* She lost her grip on a saucepan, which slid into the water with a muted *thump* against the steel sink, and grabbed the front of the sink to keep her balance. *Oh God... I almost died.* The urge to run into the living room and cling to Dad surged and subsided, along with her shivering. *It's giving me nightmares to rattle me. That car had Emily's name on it.*

She exhaled, refreshed the sponge with hot water, and hunted under the lemon-scented foam for the saucepan handle. Her fingers brushed aside some forks and found an unidentifiable glop of slime that had been considered food twenty minutes ago. *Eww.* She cringed. Glasses and a serving bowl clattered amid the rummaging. The instant she started to withdraw the saucepan from the sink, a pallid arm burst upward in a splash of suds, clamping around her wrist with a loud clap.

Paige shrieked.

Water went flying as she abandoned the sponge and struggled. She grabbed the sink edge and strained to pull away, but the frigid limb held her fast. Her feet slipped in soapy water on the linoleum, ramming her toes into the baseboard. Fear became terror and her muscles locked as a keening whimper leaked through her teeth. She stared at the ghastly grey hand, trying to twist her arm out of its clammy hold. Its fingernails darkened; soon, thin lines branched upward across its corpselike skin, tree roots drawn in jet pulsated. Her wrist went numb. Two rubbery veins peeled away, wavering like blind worms sniffing the air. They curved downward and stabbed into her forearm, sliding under the surface, slithering between muscle and skin.

"Daddy!" she screamed and burst into sobbing wails.

Driven by panic, Paige thrashed to the point of losing her balance. She dangled by the unrelenting grip, her hip banging the cabinet door. Bulges crept down her arm, accompanied by the nauseating sensation of vein-worms sliding back and forth inside her, forcing their way toward her shoulder.

The instant Dad called her name, the phantom limb let go, and the rubbery tendrils snapped free. Her butt hit the floor a second before he ran in, with Mom close behind. Paige curled up where she landed, sobbing into her knees. He rushed to the window and peered out for two seconds before taking a knee at her side.

"Paige?"

Mom hovered in the doorway between the kitchen and the hall.

She looked up at him, blinked, and flung her arms around him, bawling.

Dad patted her back and rubbed her shoulders, making soothing noises. Once she stopped weeping aloud, he leaned back enough to make eye contact. "What happened?"

"I..." She looked up at the rim of the sink while rubbing her forearm to get that awful feeling out of her mind. *What am I gonna say? They'll take me straight to the hospital.* Paige stared at him, dying to tell him the truth, but terrified of doing so. Three breaths later, she forced her terror into the box her little black cloud lived in. "I, uhh..." She wiped her eyes and ran her hands over her hair. "Wow. Umm. I guess I haven't been getting enough sleep. I just had this really wicked nightmare I guess." A nervous giggle leapt out of her throat. "Must've fallen asleep on my feet. I thought a hand came outta the water and grabbed me."

"It's those movies she watches." Mom drifted closer.

Paige un-hid her arm from where she cradled it, expecting to see finger-bruises and two holes, but her porcelain skin bore no marks. As Mom neared, she cringed, bracing for the sarcastic remark.

"Maybe you should go to sleep early tonight?" asked Mom. "Want me to finish this?"

"I'm okay." Paige grabbed the counter overhead and pulled herself upright. "I'll go to bed right after. Sorry for scaring you guys."

Dad gave her the 'I'm not sure if you're lying' look.

"It felt so real..." She swiped at suds, exposing a 'window' in the dishwater. The intact—and quite solid—bottom of the sink wavered six inches below. No hole, no hand, no trace of anything unusual. The fear in her eyes rang genuine enough; his expression softened.

"That's a good idea, Hon." He hugged her before walking to the dining room where Mom had resumed her work. "She almost got hit by a car today, Andrea. That would rattle anyone. She probably had a little anxiety attack. Give her a couple days."

Paige grabbed paper towels and squatted to sop up the water on the floor.

"Do you think we should take her to see someone?" asked Mom.

Dad sighed. "You're worried she's like your mother?"

"Well... okay, perhaps the thought had crossed my mind." Mom's nails tapped out a rhythm on the table. "I don't want to take chances."

"You know I can hear you guys, right?" Paige stood and made a three-point shot with the wad of wet towels into the trashcan. "I'm not nuts. Sorry... 'eccentric.'" She eyed the dishwater. *I hope.*

# 14

# FEEDING THE DARKNESS

Wednesday October 14 - 7:53 a.m.

P aige hugged her backpack atop the cafeteria table, head down, and tried to sneak a few minutes of sleep. Her thin leggings, vertical black and white stripes on the right, stars on the left, didn't do much to shield her butt from the cold metal of the bench. Eyes still closed, she reached up and pulled her jacket tighter, already regretting her choice of shirt, cut to bare her left shoulder down to the elbow and let her bra strap show. She couldn't resist the MC Escher inspired pattern of interlinked grinning skulls down the front, even given the day's chill.

Her teeth chattered. *Okay, maybe this was a bad idea.*

"Hey." Renee landed on the bench at her left hard enough to bounce her cheek an inch off her backpack. "You look beat."

"Mmm." Paige sat up and wiped at her eyes.

"Damn, girl. Do you own anything other than black nail polish?"

"Yeah." Paige yawned. "Hot pink, electric violet, and bone white."

Renee made an appraising face with a protruding lower lip. "I could get down with some violet."

Against her will, Paige remained upright. She yawned again, finding amusement in Renee's olive-drab dress, black stockings and Uggs. "You look like you walked off the page of LL Bean."

Renee examined her fingernails. "Needed a change from Macy's."

They laughed.

Mackenzie appeared at the double doors at the cafeteria's main entrance, and came breezing down the outer space between table ends and the wall. She'd opted for a white shift that left both shoulders bare over pale pink leggings and white versions of those expensive kid leather boots. Almost every male head, and a few girls, stared at her until she sat opposite Paige and set down a cardboard tray of fake-o Starbucks and a paper bag.

No one seemed to notice Santana trailing behind her in a dingy green flannel long-sleeved top and black yoga pants.

*Geez. Santana can barely afford food and Kenz has* two *pairs of five-thousand-dollar boots.*

"Morning." Mackenzie grinned at everyone as she worked open the bag and retrieved two paper-wrapped egg sandwiches. She handed one to Santana and opened the other. "Sorry. You didn't reply to my text."

"You sent a text?" Paige yawned and pawed at her pocket to get her phone.

"Oh that shirt's *adorable,*" said Mackenzie. "Ugh. It's making me dizzy too." She tilted her head far to the left. "The cute little skulls are... Ooh, I love how the eye sockets have like an infinite spiral of skulls in them."

"It's 'art.'" Paige smirked at her phone. Sure enough, Kenz *did* ask if she wanted food. "Ugh. I must've been out of it. I never noticed. S'okay, I ate at home."

"Wanna catch a movie later?" Renee cradled her coffee to her chest for warmth.

"What's playing?" asked Mackenzie. "There's more on our Dish than the theater."

Renee sipped her drink. "Yeah, but the Dish doesn't get new releases for a couple months. I wanna see that new one with the angel/demon war thing."

"Who's in it?" asked Paige.

"Uhh, no one famous. Everyone's new. The director was trying to do something 'artsy' I guess. I think it's called like *The Hour of Acheron* or whatever."

"Oh!" Mackenzie's eyes lit up. "I saw a preview for that. The angel guy is super hot. I heard they show a full frontal too."

Santana made embarrassed-interested-bashful noises.

"So it's decided." Mackenzie nodded. She put a hand on Santana's arm and winked.

"Kenz... it's okay. You don't have to keep paying for me."

"I want to. It's not your fault they don't pay teachers enough. Maybe I'll ask my dad to whine to his senator friend," Mackenzie said. "Okay, so meet up in the lot after last bell?"

"I gotta walk my sister home." Paige held her coffee cup back and stared at it. "What the hell flavor is this?"

"Supposed to be a caramel latte." Mackenzie reached for it.

Paige handed the cup over.

The blonde sniffed at it, peeled the plastic lid up, and drank a little. "Bleh. That explains the odd look. I think he mixed caramel and raspberry syrup."

"No wonder the raspberry tastes funky." Santana took another sip of hers. "I think I got coconut."

"Whatever." Paige accepted her cup back. "It's caffeine."

"Coffee guy, you had *one job!*" called Renee at the ceiling, before laughing.

"Oh crap, Paige. Your bra strap is showing." Santana pointed. "Don't let a teacher see that or they'll send you home."

Paige scrunched her eyebrows. "Huh?"

"We're not allowed to be too distracting to boys you know." Mackenzie rolled her eyes. "School's really for them, they only let girls come so they don't get sued."

"Conspiracy much?" Renee laughed.

"When was the last time you saw a boy sent home because his clothes 'distracted girls?' I've got a right to my education as much as he does." Mackenzie examined her fingernails.

"Is that why you never do homework?" Renee smirked. "Or sleep in physics?"

"Beside the point." Mackenzie drank. "So, Paige, you coming?"

"I gotta walk Mel home."

Mackenzie smiled. "Bring her with us."

Santana sputtered coffee. "What is she, like, seven? They're not gonna let her in to see a movie with that much skin... not to mention demons tearing people apart and eating their guts."

"I'm eighteen," said Mackenzie. "I can 'give permission' to get her in."

Paige grabbed her cheek at a tickle that made her remember the spiders. "No way. I'm not bringing her in to see a movie like that. She's eight... and she's already having nightmares about"—she leaned down over her bag and whispered—"whatever we did."

A scraping outside the window morphed into the drag of skateboard wheels on pavement as it approached. Paige glanced over her shoulder at the same boy who almost ran Melissa over on their first day. He stomped his right foot on the road for speed, clearly in a hurry to make it over to the grade school before the bell. The boy kicked his board in an attempt to jump one of the concrete stops at the end of a parking space. His skateboard leapt into the air in a rapid lateral roll, threading around his legs in a trick jump. At the last second, the end dipped—and he landed crotch-first on the point, with the other end on the asphalt. For a second, all his weight seemed supported by the board in his nuts before his feet touched down.

He fell forward and smacked his face on the pavement. Half the cafeteria erupted in applause. A number of boys chanted 'dick' over and over. Some gasped. Two of the teachers rushed out the back door. The boy didn't move until one of the teachers got to him. He sat up howling, with both arms braced through his crotch. Blood streamed out of his mouth and nose; one of his front teeth was gone.

*Beep. Beep. Beep.*

"And that's bell." Mackenzie stood, gathering her book bag. "Ugh that poor kid."

"I don't even have balls and that hurt to watch." Renee squirmed.

Paige stared at him. The boy wailed like a four-year-old with a skinned knee as the frumpy middle-aged Mrs. Collins dabbed a napkin at the blood on his face.

"Paige. Bell." Renee jostled her with a grip on the shoulder.

"He's an eighth-grader, isn't he?" asked Paige in monotone.

"No idea." Renee pulled her standing.

Mackenzie bounced the wadded-up paper bag off Paige's forehead. "Walk your sister home and meet us at the theater? We'll wait for you."

"Okay." Paige stumbled around the table, following the crowd. She couldn't peel her gaze from the injured boy. She stopped at the doors of the cafeteria to watch until they carried him out of sight. "I don't like where this is going."

Wednesday October 14 - 2:27 p.m.

"How was school?" yelled Mom from the dining room.

Paige set her backpack down to the left of the door. Melissa ran in, trailing a mass of long, red hair. "Fine, Mom. I'm gonna… uhh, can I go to the movies with the guys?"

Mom and Melissa chattered at each other for a few seconds before Mom poked her head in the arch. "Guys?"

"Not actual guys. Santana, Renee, Kenz…"

"Oh. What movie?"

Paige shrugged. "Something about angels. Not sure."

"Oh, that sounds cute." Mom smiled. "You've got your phone, right? Call if you need anything."

"Okay. Uhh, need me to grab anything while I'm downtown?"

"We're good tonight. Why don't the three of us go shopping Saturday?" Mom smiled.

Paige wandered to the arch and smiled at Melissa, who'd gone elbow-deep sorting Mom's box of crafting miscellany, the carpet around her littered with spilt beads and feathers. "'Kay."

"Enjoy the movie." Mom sat by her workspace and put on a headband-mounted magnifying lens.

*Be careful, forces of evil are on the way to our house.* Paige sighed. *Yeah. I'm one verbal slip away from a strait jacket and a padded room.* "I'll come back right after."

"Okay." Mom smiled.

Paige headed outside and down the windy rural road. The palette of autumn looked well on its way to vanishing and leaving behind a field of skeletal trees. Leaves spiraled about the road, gathering in clumps. Giant piles adorned front yards, between wide swaths of untended woods separating properties. Nothing seemed to be watching from the forest today, so she kept her head down and walked until she spotted tire gouges in the dirt at the side of the road.

She refused to look at the impact point: the smashed tree. The man hadn't died there... he passed away on the road, but that didn't make her feel better. It could've been her and/or Emily pinned between the front bumper and the giant oak. Her mind teased her with a momentary image of sliding off the car, her body severed at the waist, unable to get a grip on the blood-soaked hood.

Fortunately, a panic-inspired daydream didn't have the vividness of her strange visions.

Her pace quickened until she reached downtown and an actual sidewalk. The presence of the city calmed her for the first block, but a chill ran down her back when she rounded the corner, setting off trembling she couldn't contain. Paige fell squatting under a wave of dizziness and nausea that made jumping in front of a moving car seem like a good idea. She squatted in place, arms wrapped around her knees, and shuddered. "Ugh. Now what?"

"Are you okay, kid?" A pudgy forty-something guy in a Transformers tee shirt and camo shorts emerged from a tiny comic store.

"I..." Paige took a couple breaths. The feeling receded, and she stood. "Yeah. Thanks. Lunch isn't going down without a fight."

He chuckled. "Okay."

She got up to a walk again. Nine steps later, the feeling returned. Weaker this time, it didn't force her down, but the pervasive sense of dread hung around her shoulders like a cloak. Paige looked around for another errant vehicle. Three visible cars all drove slow and normal, not one over twenty-five. The handful of people walking around gave no indication of threat either. She continued past four more buildings. A random urge made her glance to the left.

A reflection in the window of a hardware store revealed Jared shadowing her about a half-block behind. He kept fidgeting with his large denim jacket, cradling something under his left arm. Paige walked as fast as she could go without looking too much like running away. Glimpses in passing windows showed Jared keeping pace with her. When she turned right at the next corner, he followed fourteen seconds later.

*Daddy!* Paige sniffled. Her heart thudded in her head. Her palms broke out in a cold sweat. *If he's got a gun... Wait, what if it's one of those rags with that sleepy stuff?* Thoughts of being shot or abducted and assaulted got her up to a full-on run. A thread of worry at everyone labeling her insane stopped her from screaming for help. All he'd done so far was walk in the same direction.

Green caught her eye. Paige crossed the street and ducked into the fake-o Starbucks, which turned out to be named 'Shades-brew-o.' She got in line behind a woman pushing two babies in a tandem stroller. In front of her waited three men she didn't recognize and a boy about ten making contemplative faces at the sign over the barista, who watched him with thinly veiled impatience.

Paige pulled out her phone, intending to call Dad. She stifled a scream when Jared appeared right outside the coffee shop; no one reacted to the whine leaking from her nose. Jared didn't make eye contact. He stared off at the distance as if transfixed on something other than Paige. Dark rings under his eyes made him seem older, well into his twenties, as did a few days' worth of not shaving.

The feeling of something being *wrong* intensified. Rather than nausea, it triggered shivering. Without a doubt, she knew he was going to do something *bad*. Her shaking hand clenched around her phone. An undirected sense of urgency frustrated her to the point of growling. She *had* to do something, but no idea what. *That* night, figuring it out was easy—tell Dad to order Amber home.

*Beep.*

*Ringing.*

"Hey sweetie." The rumble of a passing truck went by in the background. "Working radar, so I might need to go in a hurry."

"Dad. You gotta come to town right away. Something bad's gonna happen."

"Whoa. Slow down, Paige. Are you okay? You had a close call the other day. Do you want a ride home from school?"

"No, Dad. I already went home and... look you need to get here fast. He's gonna do something." Paige slipped out of the coffee shop and followed Jared past a few people walking the opposite direction. "The guy who drugged Renee is here. I thought he was gonna attack me, but he walked right by like a zombie."

Dad kept quiet for ten seconds, probably thinking. "Where is he? They got a pick up warrant for him. Don't go near him, hon. He might be on something if he's acting spacey."

"He's downtown. We're on Main Street and we just crossed Emmet Avenue."

"Okay, I'll call it in to the locals."

"Dad. You gotta get here. I'm scared."

Jared made a sudden left and walked into traffic as if he couldn't see the cars. Paige waited for a battered pickup to trundle by and hurried across the street after him, gagging on exhaust fumes.

"Paige. You had a nightmare and then a car almost hit you." He breathed in and out. "Find somewhere quiet to wait and I'll get there as soon as I can. You don't need to get yourself all emotional."

Jared paused near the door of a bar and stared at the First National Bank another block and change down the street. The instant Paige spotted the green-lettered sign, her nerves screamed. She seized up, feeling as though she watched Melissa in the path of a speeding tractor-trailer and couldn't do a damn thing to save her.

"Paige!" yelled Dad. From the sound of him, he'd been yelling her name over and over, but she'd only heard one. "Paige? What's going on?"

She sniffled, realizing she'd burst into tears. "Daddy… He's going to the bank. I think he's got a gun."

"You saw him with a weapon?"

"No, Dad. I feel like—"

"Oh, Jesus Paige." He sighed. "Look, I'm sorry for putting you through hell. We'll find a therapist or something and—"

"Dad!" she yelled. "I'm not being emotional. You said the same thing the night Amber died! I feel almost that bad now. The same out-of-nowhere dread. Something is going to happen. You didn't believe me then and look what happened." She wiped her tears on the back of her jacket sleeve and rushed after Jared.

"I… don't know what to say to that. Okay. I'll be right there, but if this is some cockamamie fantasy gone out of control, we are going to get professional help for you."

Paige dug in her back pocket and pulled out the earbuds for her phone. She plugged in and stuffed the device into her inner jacket pocket, out of sight. "Please hurry. Don't hang up."

"I won't."

The subdued presence of a siren came over the line from Dad's end.

*Wow. He's going code three. He either believes me or thinks I'm the one that needs to be taken off the street.*

Jared loped up the walkway to the bank door and went in. Paige waited with her back to the brick wall of a vape store on the opposite side of the street. A minute or so later, a flurry of silhouettes in the bank windows scrambled about and dropped out of sight.

"Oh, shit, Dad. He's robbing the damn bank."

"Are you sure?" Dad's voice sounded distant, like his phone sat on the passenger seat in speaker mode.

"Uhh. Everyone inside the bank just dove to the floor. What do you think that means?" She swallowed a glob of fear and pushed off the brick wall.

"I'm a minute away."

She strained to listen; the weakest trace of a siren in the distance met her ears. "Okay."

Paige ran across the street and up the walkway to the tinted doors. *What the hell am I doing?* She shrouded her hands over her eyes and leaned up to the glass.

Jared waved a handgun at two old men, one chubby guy, three women, and two little girls, shooing them away. They crawled to the back end of the bank and lay on their stomachs. A sixty-something man with snowy hair in a white security guard shirt sprawled face down and bleeding from the temple inside another set of doors on the far end of an alcove with an ATM.

"Dad," whispered Paige. "Ohmigod. He's got a gun. There's people crawling. Two kids. He maybe killed the security guy."

"Where are you, Paige?"

"At the door."

"Get out of there, now!"

Jared pointed his gun at a Hispanic woman behind the counter who looked like an older version of Santana. The woman grabbed money and stuffed it in a cloth bag. Time seemed to freeze around Paige. Amid another vision, Jared laughed, shot the woman square in the forehead, and walked out without even taking the bag of cash.

Reality returned in a rush of wind and screaming hostages. A woman's voice begged him to let her daughters go.

"Everyone stay on the goddamned ground," yelled Jared.

When he swung around to yell, he faced Paige for a second but his hollow stare passed over her without notice.

*What the hell?*

Paige pulled the door open and ducked in. The space between two sets of glass doors housing the ATM trapped warm air in a small greenhouse effect. The children inside screamed and sobbed. She opened the inner door. Jared didn't twitch.

"Paige. God dammit. I can hear the... what the hell are you doing? Get out!" Dad shouted over the phone.

She eased the door wider and slipped in.

Jared swiveled to his left, brandishing his handgun in the general direction of the customers lined up on the floor like sausages on a grill. The two kids—*they're younger than Mel*—huddled against their mother, sobbing. Jared's eyes had gone onyx black from corner to corner. Dark smoke seeped through his teeth and drew back in with each breath.

The security guard moaned. Jared whipped around and aimed at him. Paige scooted to her left as he came stomping over to the older man. He disregarded her, despite being less than five feet away, and took a revolver off the guard's belt. With a gun in each hand, he returned to the teller window, grinning.

"Jared?" asked Paige.

"What are you doing," hissed the chubby customer. "Get on the floor kid. You're gonna make him shoot us."

"Shut up!" Jared fired the revolver from his left hand, shattering a flowerpot near the heavyset man.

The hostages all screamed.

"Jared," said Paige, louder.

He ignored her.

Paige stood. "You're Santana's mom, right? I don't know why he can't hear me, but you gotta believe me. He's going to kill you when you're done packing that bag. Go as slow as you can. Cops are already on the way."

The woman shivered, her gaze darting between her and Jared as she tried to stuff cash into a white canvas bag. Paige walked up behind Jared as the hostages hissed and made noises at her. She established eye contact with an athletic-looking man among the bank customers. He nodded and moved his hands as if about to do a push up.

"Three... two..." Paige dove into Jared in an attempt to tackle him.

A painful jolt rocked her, as though she'd been shot full of icicles. Seconds later, a blast knocked her flat and sliding across the floor, paralyzed by coiling scratchy pinpricks. A feeling too much like the black vines from the bathtub surrounded her. She'd have screamed, but her jaw refused to open.

Jared twitched and convulsed in place, a grand mal seizure in fast forward. The effect lasted only three seconds before he again had the gun pointed at Santana's mother. The athletic customer blinked at her, but remained flat on the floor.

"Well... that didn't work," whispered Paige. "Ow."

"What the hell?" whispered one of the older men.

"I said no talking!" Jared swung his gun over, but didn't shoot again.

Paige stood, hesitated a second or two, and walked over to the mother and girls when Jared continued to ignore her.

*Okay, for once I'm happy to be the invisible girl. This is messed up.*

She grabbed the kids' hands. "Stay quiet and follow me."

The mother started to protest, but wound up staring at Jared, mute.

"They'll be okay." Paige pulled the kids upright.

Their mother covered her mouth to stifle sobs, and nodded. The other hostages quieted at the wail of sirens outside.

Paige led the two girls to the door, concentrating on the want for Jared not to see them. Whether it mattered or not, she didn't care. Dad's patrol car squealed to a halt at the curb, joined seconds later by three local cruisers. She hurried through the ATM chamber with the kids.

Dad sprinted to her, but Paige waved him at the door.

Five local officers ran up as her father drew his weapon and advanced. One took the little kids; another grabbed Paige around the back and hurried her toward the street.

"Jared Sweeney!" yelled Dad. "Police. Drop the weapons and get on the ground."

Two gunshots went off back to back. A woman screamed.

Paige twisted around. Jared's body had taken on a pose of Michael Jackson proportion: up on his toes, arms swaying like a marionette run by a drunken puppetmaster, head thrown back. Dense black vapor welled out of his back where a bullet had pierced him. Churning mist peeled out in a spiraling trail that flattened across the floor and rushed in a mass of three-inch-deep fog past her father. A random twist raised the revolver arm. Dad fired a second bullet, which struck Jared between the shoulder blades.

Jared's gun discharged again, a wild, uncoordinated shot into the ceiling. He whirled in a dead man's pirouette and collapsed in place.

The cop with his arm around Paige lifted her off her feet and ran down the walkway. He stashed her behind a police car with her back to the door. She wrapped her arms around her legs, shaking. A *boop* indicated the call to Dad's cell phone dropped. A half-hearted tug pulled her earbuds out. She rolled up the wire and stuffed it in her coat pocket with the phone.

TWENTY MINUTES LATER, PAIGE SAT ON THE REAR BUMPER OF AN AMBULANCE with Dad on her right, a local cop on her left, and a plain-clothes detective in front of her.

"I was walking to the movie theater and I saw the guy. I thought he was following me at first." Paige recounted the party and the drugging of Renee. "But when I hid in the coffee place, he went past. I saw a gun in his coat so I called Dad and followed him to the bank. He gave me a look like he wanted me to take the little kids and get out, so I did."

The detective took notes. "The other witnesses had quite a story. They said he didn't seem to notice you were even there."

Paige shrugged. "Maybe they're in shock."

"The cameras too?" The detective raised an eyebrow.

At the mention of cameras, two of the local officers broke out in a sweat.

The detective raised an eyebrow. "You were walking around speaking and he didn't react. Even when you recklessly tried to tackle him, he miraculously decided not to shoot you or anyone else."

"I dunno." Paige looked at her boots. "He looked high. I don't know why he was ignoring me. You don't think I was like helping him or anything?"

"Well, usually when there's a guy waving a gun around a bank the other person standing next to him and not getting shot, hit, or shoved to the ground is his accomplice... but, none of the witnesses said anything to implicate you had anything to do with it." He tapped his pen on the pad. "I do have one more question."

"Okay." Paige looked up.

"Several people mentioned you told Mrs. Ruiz that Jared was going to kill her. When your father made entry, Jared tried to do just that. Did you have any advanced knowledge of any plot to harm Mrs. Ruiz?"

"No, sir. I just saw the look in his eyes. It seemed like he wanted to kill someone and she was the most conspicuous target."

The detective nodded. He spent a few minutes talking to Dad a few feet away, about availability for interviewing if needed. Dad returned, took her hand, and led her to his car. She flopped in the passenger seat, pulling his phone out from under her ass a second later and dumping it in a cup holder.

Dad got in and closed the door. "Okay, now tell me what really happened."

"I'm not crazy."

"I didn't say you were." He reached over and took her hand. "You've had two brushes with death in one week. What's going on? Are you trying to give me a heart attack?"

"You know how I had that feeling that night..."

He sighed. "Yes. You were out of your mind."

"It happened again when I saw him, only it didn't like *hurt* as much. I guess 'cause it wasn't about someone I loved. At first, I thought he was going to kill me for calling you to the house. When I looked at him, I... *saw* him shooting Mrs. Ruiz. I just knew he was going to do it. He wasn't really there to rob the bank." *That's the spell making it look coincidental.*

Dad kept quiet.

"You okay, Dad?"

"Yeah."

"Ever shoot someone before?"

"Not fatally."

She reached over and grabbed his hand. "If you didn't, he would've killed her."

"I know." He started the car. "The whole thing is on camera. It's a clean shoot, but I'm still going to be on desk duty pending the investigation. Hmf."

He chuckled. "You're the one seeing visions and I'm going to have to see the shrink." He shut off the roof lights and pulled out into traffic, headed for home.

"So, do you think I'm nuts? If you want me to pee in a cup, I will. I'm not on drugs."

"No, Paige. That's what I'm afraid of." He flicked his thumbs on the wheel. "Two nights ago, I could've sworn I heard Amber's voice telling me she's okay and to let go."

"She's worried about you." Paige sniffled. "So am I."

"Paige?"

"Hmm?" She looked up.

"You saw Jared die."

"Yes."

Dad glanced at her, his face ashen. "Did you see that black stuff too?"

Her throat tightened. "Yeah."

He pursed his lips. "I'm not going to mention that to the shrink."

"Good plan." Paige exhaled into her hands to warm her fingers.

# 15

# SET IN MOTION

Thursday October 15 - 12:12 p.m.

C lear blue sky overhead and unseasonable warmth brought many of the students out to have lunch among the tables on the grassy field between the high school and elementary building. Sunlight shimmered from the windows of cars in the adjacent lot and danced in a dapple pattern on the grass amid the shadows of leaves. The trees stood serene; the wind had taken the day off. High-pitched voices pierced the low din every so often whenever a grade-schooler across the field laughed or yelled at someone.

Paige sat next to Renee, who also had a plate of turkey-in-gravy, mashed potatoes, and peas. The cafeteria's version of 'pumpkin pie' looked as though it had been summoned from the same place as the shadow-being. *Nah, this stuff is more evil.* Mackenzie worked on a salad from a clear plastic carton with a Friday's logo. At the jealous look it earned, Mackenzie laughed.

"I snuck out of Physics early to pick it up. Perks of having a car." Mackenzie winked. "Thursdays always suck at the cafeteria."

"You hear anything about Santana?" asked Renee.

"Nope." Paige used her plastic fork to cut two quarter-inch-thick slabs of turkey into bite-sized pieces. "Mr. Ruiz is out too. We had some sub who made us read the whole period. I don't think he even knows what an atom *is.*"

"The guy with the green bow tie?" asked Renee. At Paige's nod, she laughed. "Copeland or something... he's like the grade-school music teacher."

"Warm body at a desk. Probably cheaper than hiring a real sub."

Mackenzie stabbed a wad of salad. "I'm not surprised they're out. Her mother was almost shot. I heard the bullet passed like two inches away from her head. Your dad startled that asshole and made him miss."

"Not even two inches. She has a cut on her ear." Paige stared down past her black tee at her blue jeans. "It's our fault."

"How is anything that piece of shit did our fault?" Renee glared.

"Think about it." Paige looked up. "What did we ask for? Santana wanted money. Financial security, right? You and I were both pissed off at Jared."

Renee wagged her finger. "'Pissed off' don't even begin to describe where I was at with him."

"Mmm!" Mackenzie's eyes flared. Once she finished chewing, she gasped. "Wow. Yeah. It used that. The spirits sensed our animosity toward Jared and fed off it to give Santana the money her family needed."

"What like rob the bank and let them find it?" asked Renee.

"No. Life insurance or something... or maybe her dad sues the bank." Mackenzie stabbed a cherry tomato and held it up. "Twisting circumstances to bring about what we desired." She popped the tomato in her mouth and crushed it.

"Having her mother die isn't what she asked for." Paige fumed. "I don't know about this. Maybe we should send it back. I'm sure that car that almost hit me was part of the magic too."

Renee grabbed her. "You almost got hit?"

Paige recounted the story. "It was either trying to scare my dad by almost losing me... or it was really going for Emily." She hesitated. *If it was gonna miss me anyway, I wouldn't have felt it coming... or maybe the spirits knew that and did it anyway so it felt right?*

"What the heck did Emily do?" asked Renee.

"She's dating Cole." Paige kept her gaze on her food, stirring peas with her fork. "Get rid of her and he's available."

Mackenzie bit her lip. "Ouch. Uhh. Not what I was hoping for, but..."

"But what? Acceptable?" Paige stared at her. "You *can't* let it kill her. She's like a bigger version of my kid sister. So innocent and nice. It's not fair to her."

"Umm." Mackenzie grimaced. "I'm not sure how to stop it, but maybe I can cast another circle later tonight and try to give it more explicit directions."

"Hey Wednesday," yelled a girl.

Paige looked over.

Sofia hurried up the grassy field from the direction of the cafeteria doors, carrying a tray. Brittany Kutzen, perfect blonde curls and all, chased close behind. They were too far away to make out words below shouting, but the patronizing sing-song tone of the other girl left little doubt as to the nature of the conversation. Sofia walked faster, dodging Brittany trying to swat the lunch tray out of her hands.

An eighth-grade boy at a nearby picnic table let off a hoarse wheeze and grabbed his throat. He choked, banging his fist on his chest as his face went blue. Brittany, and everyone else except Sofia, glanced in his direction. A few kids shouted for help. Another boy attempted the Heimlich maneuver.

Brittany screamed and went down, landing awkwardly on her right arm, breaking it halfway between wrist and elbow. Incoherent howls of pain came from the living doll as she dragged herself forward, freeing her foot from a gopher hole or whatever she'd stepped in. The way her leg dangled suggested it had fractured at the shin.

Sofia hesitated and looked back at the awful screaming. She set her lunch down in the grass and ran over to Brittany, trying to calm her. Three teachers sprinted over to the choking boy. His classmate's efforts at the Heimlich proved futile. A huge teacher, bald with a long goatee, pulled him aside and wrapped the kid in a bear hug. He hauled the boy off his feet and squeezed until a hunk of carrot went flying. The boy gagged, threw up a little, and lapsed into tears.

The other two, Mrs. McDonnell from Paige's gym class and a dweeby-nerdy man she didn't recognize, hurried to Brittany. McDonnell checked her out and got her laying straight and flat on the grass before pulling out a little walkie-talkie.

Paige, Mackenzie, and Renee ate in silence for several minutes. Everyone glanced up at an approaching siren, which cut out as an ambulance arrived and drove right onto the grass at the end of the parking lot. Once they loaded Brittany, Sofia got up, retrieved her cold lunch, and joined them at the table, still crying.

"Things are working for you, Sof." Mackenzie smiled.

Sofia got more upset, but calmed herself fast. "I don't wanna hurt them. That was awful. Did you hear how she was screaming?"

Mackenzie nodded. "Yeah, that sounded like it hurt. But, you like held her hand and stuff. When she gets better, she's going to remember you were nice to her. It's going to work out. For all the crap she's done to you, she deserved a little payback."

Sofia pouted at her food.

"Aw crap. Trouble incoming," said Renee.

Paige pulled her hair off her eyes and sat up out of the 'world-go-away' slouch she'd fallen into. Redbeard and the thick guy who'd hit on her at the party stormed out of the woods at the end of the field, heading right for their table. At a quick glance, no weapons appeared to lurk anywhere in their overabundance of denim. Several holes marred Redbeard's Guns 'N Roses shirt, while Todd's white tee had a decade of random stains over his bulging belly.

They came to a stop close enough to loom over Renee. Paige didn't like having her back to them, so she slipped off the bench and stood. One of Todd's thighs was as thick as both of hers. He'd been scary at the party, but now he looked angry—which made him much more frightening.

"Hey, bitches." Todd pointed at Renee. "You think you're slick, don't you? We know exactly what you did."

Mackenzie held up her fork with an impaled cucumber. "Oh? What did we do?" She put it in her mouth.

"You bitches set him up." Redbeard glared at Paige. "Your old man's a cop. He's probably on the take, and Miss. Richie over there bribed him to kill Jared and make it look justified."

Todd reached for Renee, but seemed to think better of it and held back. "You didn't have to kill him, dammit! He was only trying to impress you."

"He tried to rape me!" said Renee, barely suppressing the urge to shout.

"Oh, sure." Paige set her hands on her hips. "We somehow tricked Jared into getting a gun and going to a bank to rob it only so we could kill him. No wonder you guys dropped out of school. You couldn't find your asses with both hands, a compass, and an Andean Sherpa."

Mackenzie sprayed salad on a laugh.

Todd looked confused.

"He wouldn't have had to do that if you talked to him, bitch." Redbeard glared at Renee. "Guess you really are a lesbian."

Renee's anger grew to the point she appeared calm. "If by that you mean a person who's sexually attracted to people who aren't idiots and criminals, you got me."

Todd's simmering fury erupted. He lunged and grabbed a fistful of Paige's shirt and jacket, pulling her up on tiptoe. Despite being about to wet her pants, Paige kept an outward calm.

Sofia belted out a loud, clear, long, scream. The tone of it seemed less frightened and more as though she beaconed for help. Once her lungs emptied, she opened her eyes and stared at Todd.

"You two!" yelled a bookish male teacher in a cardigan. "You're not supposed to be on school grounds. Hey, Brian!"

The same muscular teacher who'd carried the choking boy inside looked up from a cluster of faculty by the parking lot lingering where the ambulance had been. Once he spotted the dimwitted duo, he charged up the field. The other teacher fell in step at his side.

"You really should leave us alone," said Mackenzie, sounding cold. "We're not the sort of girls to be messed with. You saw what happened to Jared." Another cherry tomato exploded between her teeth.

Todd flung Paige back onto the table and pointed at her as he backed up. "Keep one eye over your shoulder, freak."

The two dropouts ran into the trees a few seconds before the teacher arrived. Paige sat up on the table and rubbed her chest where Todd's knuckles had dug in.

"You girls all right?" asked the teacher.

"Mr. Lane," said Sofia. "Those two boys threatened us."

Paige slid to her feet, rubbing her butt where she'd landed on something painful.

"He assaulted this girl." The bookish teacher indicated Paige. "Sofia, please come to the principal's office when you're done eating. Miss…"

"Thomas." Paige fixed her shirt and jacket back to rights.

"Miss. Thomas, I'm Mr. Lloyd, if you need to send the police over to collect a statement."

Sofia looked worried. "I… I didn't do anything."

The thinner teacher raised a reassuring hand. "Only to fill out an incident report. You aren't in trouble."

"I'll wait with them," said Mr. Lane. "Mackenzie… did you cut my class to go off campus for lunch?"

"Sorry, Mr. Lane." Mackenzie looked genuinely contrite until he wasn't watching her.

*That guy teaches physics?* Paige, only as tall as the man's chest, looked up in awe.

"Of course you don't *have* to file a police report, but the school will be." Mr. Lane squinted at the trees. "Those two always did seem to have problems following after them."

"I… think they're going to do something." Paige picked up her tray. "We should get the police involved." *Before Mackenzie decides to make things worse…*

Mr. Lane gestured at the building. Paige walked on ahead with him close behind. She clenched her jaw to keep from giggling at the memory of Todd's face at the sight of the bald, goateed Viking teacher stomping up the grassy hillside. She almost wished Todd hadn't run off.

# 16

# CAN'T LET GO

Friday October 16 - 2:04 a.m.

**M**urmured conversations filtered up through the floor of Paige's bedroom. She grumbled and rolled over, annoyed at her parents for having people over when she tried to sleep. Minutes passed as she tossed and turned, unable to get comfortable. Mom's voice rose over the din in sobs.

Paige pushed herself onto her back and sat up. One look at the clock made her want to flop down again, but Mom continued wailing. Her half-awake brain cooked up only one plausible explanation for activity and crying at that hour, the fear every relative of a police officer lived with:

*Something happened to Dad!*

She flew out of bed barely remembering to hold on to the waistband of her pajama pants to keep them from falling, and sprinted down the hall to the stairs. The sheer number of different voices made the idea of a couple of cops bringing horrible news seem less likely. Paige slowed to a creep, letting her feet roll off the front end of each carpeted step. She clung to the bannister with both hands, sliding down inch by inch.

A living room full of formal wear gradually unveiled from beneath the rim of the upstairs floor. Men in suits stood in clusters. Women in black dresses sat on the sofa and on extra folding chairs she didn't remember her parents ever owning. Paige stopped on the last step, frozen in place at the sight of a small white coffin at the innermost corner, to the right of the TV.

Mom sat in the middle of the sofa, flanked by two older women Paige recognized but couldn't place. Relatives, but distant ones she hadn't seen since she was little. Each woman held one of Mom's hands, trying to comfort her as she wailed.

*A wake... this is a friggin' wake in our house.* She stared in horror at the white coffin.

She held on to the bannister to keep from falling over. Forty or fifty people chattered away about how tragic it was for Andrea to find her daughter dead against a tree out front, hit by a driver who hadn't stopped.

"Only eight years old... such a shame," said a woman.

Another elderly woman sniffled and dabbed at her eyes with a tissue. "She was so adorable. Precious. There's no justice in this world."

Paige slumped to her knees on the stairs, bawling. She'd wanted her dad to notice her, but not this way. Once the wave of sorrow lifted enough for her to move, she pulled herself upright with the bannister. Her foot landed on the ground-floor carpet with a *squish*. Cold, viscous blood welled up out of the pile through her toes. The muscles in her legs and back tensed. Forcing herself to ignore the disgusting feeling, she crept into the room.

Another elder gasped at her. "Paige Thomas, how dare you wear pajamas to your sister's funeral! What is wrong with you?"

Dad came out of nowhere and grabbed her, sobbing into her shoulder. "Oh, Paige... Precious Paige. I won't let anything happen to my last daughter. No one's going to hurt you."

She wheezed as he crushed the breath out of her. The carpet mushed and squidged around her feet; if not for him holding her, her legs would've shot right out from under her. Blood sprayed as she kicked and struggled to get her balance back. The old women didn't seem to notice the crimson flecks staining their white dresses or glowering faces.

"Dad." Paige cried. "This isn't real. I'm dreaming again. This is a nightmare."

He rocked her side-to-side, the way she remembered him doing when she was three and he would sing her to sleep.

An old crone pulled at her pajama top. "Disgraceful! Go upstairs and change. Show some damn respect."

Paige grunted and pushed at her father's chest. "Dad, let go."

"I'm not going to let you go. You don't have to go to school anymore, Paige. Stay in your room where it's safe. I'll lock all the doors. They won't get you. No one will ever get you."

Prison style bars slammed into the house outside, covering all the windows. Loud *clicks* came from the doors. A serpentine hiss from the ground emanated from a pair of leg irons slithering around to attack her ankles.

Paige yelled and pushed Dad away. She ran, waving her arms to keep balance on the saturated carpet, and crashed into the side of Melissa's closed casket. The well-wishers fell silent, and the weight of their stares drilled into her back. The woman who had been berating her for pajamas went ballistic, screaming at her for ruining her sister's ceremony. Paige dug her fingers into the gap under the lid, feeling around for a way to open it. Hissing and the soft rattle of chain came up behind her.

"You'll be safe, Paige," said Dad. "I promise."

The coffin lid gave way and she shoved it open. Upon pink satin padding lay nine black candles in a neat row, leaking blood.

No Melissa.

Paige shot upright in bed, covered in sweat. She stared at the tents her feet made in the covers, terrified that she'd find blood all over them. Silence in the house pressed down on her with tangible weight, broken only by the rasp of her rapid breathing. She gulped and pushed the covers aside, light-headed from fear. At the sight of her feet dry and clean, she slumped over sideways.

*Holy crap.* She shivered, wanting to run to her dad and cry. *Damn this spell.*

After a moment to gather herself, Paige walked out into the hall and headed to Melissa's room. Her little sister slept peacefully. She held the back of her hand to Melissa's nose until she felt breath and released a long sigh alongside it. She patted her sister on the head before trudging downstairs. The memory of the wake caused her to freeze on the stairs. She summoned her nerve and proceeded to the last step. Empty and dark, the living room held no wake, no angry old lady, and no little white casket.

*Yet.* Paige stared at the rug. *If I step in squish, I'm going to freak.*

Dry.

"Whew." She slouched.

Whispering from the kitchen got her hackles up again. With one hand on the wall, she edged down the corridor past the living room where Mom's current project, a bunch of vinyl window stickers for cars, lay strewn on the table. The raspy chattering increased in tempo.

"Amber?" She tiptoed forward. "Dad? Mom?"

She gasped at stepping on a kitchen floor colder than the dream blood. She glanced down at her toes in a patch of moonlight, half expecting something to well up out of the linoleum and grab her.

"You okay?" asked Dad, behind her.

Paige gathered her hands at her chin and screamed. Dad grabbed her before she could finish fainting, and held on as she surrendered to crying. He moved to a chair and pulled her into his lap.

"Bad dream?"

She sniffled. "Yeah. I don't know why I'm bawling like a little kid. I feel like such a baby."

"No shame in it." He patted her back. "You've been through a lot lately. Too much."

The bizarre urge to cry ebbed over the course of minutes. She tucked her hair behind her ears. "You know the feeling I got the night... umm, yeah. I've been getting them more often lately. I had one before that car almost hit us. I got it when I saw Jared in town." She bit her lip. "I... at the party. I didn't actually physically *see* him drug the beer. It was like a flash daydream."

He exhaled. "Visions now? What am I supposed to do with you?"

"Dad?"

"Yeah?"

"Is it or is it not true that they found GHB in Renee's system?"

"True." He stroked her hair.

"Do you think Jared slipped it to her?"

He let his hand slide to her shoulder. "They found some on him in the bank, but it's circumstantial at best."

"See. I'm not crazy."

"You've been a mess ever since Amber died. You were her little shadow. Always together."

Paige leaned her head on his shoulder. "Yeah."

"I can see why you'd think I played favorite. First kid, you know." He frowned. "You never seemed to need as much attention since you glommed on to whatever she did."

Paige started at a shadow moving past the kitchen window outside, as big as a large man—or Todd.

"What?"

"Thought I saw someone in the yard."

He eased her to her feet and crept over to the window. "Nothing out there."

"I don't know why I get these... uhh, premonitions." Paige sank into the chair. "I'm not trying to cry out for attention with that."

"No?" He almost smiled.

"That's what the black clothes, spiked choker, and attitude are for." She grinned for a second before frowning. "I feel invisible. You shut down when she died."

He turned away from the sink a half-second before the shadow whipped past the other way.

Paige gasped.

Dad whirled, leaned up to the window, and looked around.

"I'm probably seeing stuff since I haven't been sleeping." Paige yawned.

He dragged another chair closer, sitting so their knees almost touched. "I know I've been having a hard time coping with the accident. Our last conversation wasn't too pleasant. Amber called, asking for more money. I thought she wanted to piss it away on nothing."

"I was so angry with her for moving out to go dorm at Penn."

"I know." He leaned back and yawned. "That's why we thought you were acting out when you had that panic attack."

"Some belief systems give a lot of weight to the power of wanting. I couldn't let go of her either." Paige grabbed the chair on either side of her legs. "That's probably why she's still here. You, umm, could still talk to her if you want."

Dad's expression hardened. "Paige. That's not funny. You're too old to have imaginary friends, much less act like Amber's ghost is somehow still around. It's not healthy." He took her hand. "I'm getting more and more worried about you, sweetie. Do you really think Amber's spirit is in the house?"

Paige mashed her toes together and looked down. "Uhh. I... probably imagined it. 'Course, then you did too. Didn't you say you thought you heard her talking to you?"

He studied her, quiet for a short while. "You should go back to bed. You've got school in a few hours."

"Yeah. Good luck with that." She stood. "I've been having such twisted dreams lately."

Dad pulled her into a brief hug. "I'll be right down the hall. Hey... I'm sorry for being so out of it."

"I love you, Dad." She squeezed him.

"Love you too, kiddo. Now get to bed."

She walked back through the darkened dining and living rooms to the stairs, keeping her head down. The silence had weight, as though a presence lurked at the edge of her periphery, following... watching.

Paige ran up the stairs without looking back and dove under her blankets. She peeked out from a tiny gap in the fabric, whimpering as a long shadow stretched over the rug by her door. An instant shy of screaming, she made a faint squeak when Dad peered in.

"Night, sweetie." He pulled her door to.

"Ugh. Night, Dad." She exhaled and rolled on her back. "Hey, ceiling. How've you been?"

# 17

# REPERCUSSIONS

Friday October 16 - 7:38 a.m.

P aige dropped Melissa off at the doors to the grade school and headed across the parking lot. Mackenzie, Renee, and Santana sat in leaf mulch a short distance off the sidewalk leading to the front doors, beneath a tree. The cafeteria staff must've gotten an early start, as the siren song of bacon lofted on the breeze. Paige diverted toward her friends and flopped on the ground in the empty spot they'd left, forming an approximate circle.

Renee bounced, a broad grin on her face from ear to ear.

Santana looked like she'd had about as much luck sleeping as Paige.

Paige offered her hand. "Sant, you okay?"

"Not really."

Mackenzie flashed a game show hostess smile. "Score two. 'Nee's dad showed up yesterday."

"I can't believe it." Renee hugged her Land's End backpack. "He brought Mom roses and everything. I thought she was gonna rip his head off, but she didn't. Dad kept saying how sorry he was for ditching us and he wanted to spend the rest of his life making it up."

"Aww, that's so romantic." Mackenzie swooned.

Santana glared at the ground.

Paige leaned forward, head tilted, trying to make eye contact. "Is your Mom doing all right?"

"The bank gave her a week off, but it's unpaid so she can't take it." Santana picked at the spot where a button once existed on the left cuff of her flannel shirt. "She sees that kid die every time she closes her eyes."

"Bastards," said Renee. "Your Mom almost took a goddamned bullet and they won't give her comp?"

Mackenzie plucked fuzz from her cream angora sweater. "Hey, uhh... I can maybe ask my father if there's any openings at the firm. Can your mom do like receptionist stuff or whatever?"

Santana grumbled. "She's got a bachelor's degree in accounting and finance. She's working at the bank because it's the only thing she can find."

"I'll ask." Mackenzie sipped her pumpkin spice coffee, making a face of ecstasy. "If you want."

"Sure, why not. Guess we can't be too proud to take charity." Santana eyed Paige for a second before staring down and jabbing her finger at the leaves between her legs. "Mom wants me to invite you over so she can say thanks."

Paige pulled her fingers through her hair, and twirled a strand. "'Kay."

"What for?" asked Mackenzie.

"Paige was at the bank. She told Mom not to finish packing the bag 'cause Jared was going to shoot her anyway. Gave the police enough time to get there." Santana shivered.

Mackenzie's gaze sharpened to needles pointed at Paige. "You should be careful."

"What's that supposed to mean?" asked Renee. "She saved Sant's mom's life."

Mackenzie spoke in a whispery shout. "We shouldn't interf—"

Screeching tires preceded a dull thud and a wailing child.

Paige snapped her head up.

At the entrance to the parking lot, a beat-up land-yacht of a car wobbled on its suspension after coming to a hard stop. A brown-haired boy lay on the ground a short distance in front of it. He let off a yowl of pain and bit down on his right forearm. Blood seeped into the legs of his khaki pants.

The driver, a senior in a varsity football jacket, hopped out and ran over to him in a panic. He repeated 'I never even saw him' in an endless loop as he fumbled for a cell phone.

Teachers swarmed over to the scene. A few seconds later, the voice of Principal Hollister came over the PA, ordering all students to go inside the building.

"Sofia's going to be upset." Santana threw her enormous book bag over her shoulder, crumpling the same flannel shirt she'd worn three days in a row.

"Why?" asked Paige.

Mackenzie and Renee stood, neither in any great hurry.

Santana fell in step at Paige's side on the way into the high school. "That's

Keith, I think. She confessed to having a crush on him, but he thought she was 'creepy' since her parents owned the funeral home."

Paige glanced back at the injured boy surrounded by faculty. The senior looked ready to throw up. *We're losing control.* She tried to get Mackenzie's attention, intent on demanding they cancel the spell somehow, but the girl had already vanished into the crowd. *Maybe we never really had it.*

Friday October 16 - 1:40 p.m.

STUDENTS SNICKERED AS MR. SERRANO WROTE NOTES ABOUT GENERALS LEE and Grant on the whiteboard. His red sweater vest, protruding upon a rounded belly, swiped away the dry erase marker in his wake. Paige glared at the assignment sheet on her desk. He wanted a thousand-word essay on one or the other, explaining why the student chose whom they did, and rendering their opinion on the general's strengths and flaws.

Mr. Serrano noticed the smear of clean across the notes, and chuckled at himself. He swung his arms to the side in a bemused attempt at a shrug. "Ah, well. At least I wore red to match the marker."

A few students laughed.

He called Katie Eames over, a tiny blonde who looked like a seventh-grader, and handed her his notes. "Since you lack 'life experience'"—he patted his belly with both hands—"would you mind fixing that?"

"Okay."

The little teen's writing stood out in sharp contrast to the teacher's scribble, rounded letters with little hearts dotting each 'i'.

"Robert E. Lee graduated from the US Military Academy near the top of his class. He declined an offer of a senior command position in the Union army and—"

A siren outside stalled the words in Mr. Serrano's mouth.

*Not again.*

An ambulance took the turn into the parking lot, swung around, and backed up as close as it could get to the grade-school entrance.

Paige's entire class left their desks and swarmed to the windows. She pushed her way to the glass as paramedics ran inside with a stretcher. A few minutes later, the doors opened and they wheeled out a brown-haired girl. The most horrible, continuous screams of agony Paige had ever heard came from the slender figure on the stretcher. A teacher and a paramedic struggled to hold the girl's arms down at her sides. The tween stopped shrieking only long enough to refill her lungs and do it again.

The class stood in somber silence as the crew rushed her to the ambulance. Even the closed doors failed to contain the baleful shrieking. Paige shivered, brought to tears by the tone of the girl's anguish as well as guilt at being at least one-fifth complicit in causing it. She shuffled back to her desk while everyone else remained pinned to the window. The screaming echoed in her head, so loud and raw her throat ached in sympathy.

"Okay, everyone," said Mr. Serrano. "Back to your seats please."

A heavyset kid in the third row with an orange curly mop raised his hand.

"Yes, James?"

"Mr. Serrano, do you think the school was built on an Indian burial ground or something? Another kid got hit this morning too. People are saying there's a curse on the school."

"Well." Mr. Serrano chuckled. "Throughout our history, humankind has searched for ways to explain things we couldn't understand. Curses, demons, ghosts... They used to think certain plants were magical for curative properties. Modern science led to understanding their mechanism of action. Whenever something happens that seems to defy common sense, it's in our nature to imagine correlation or causation where there isn't any."

"Uhh, okay." James's hair wobbled like a sea anemone with his nod. "That means 'no,' right?"

"Miss Thomas," asked Mr. Serrano. "Are you all right? That wasn't your sister was it?"

Paige swallowed and wiped her tears. "No. If it was Melissa, I wouldn't be sitting here. Just... that screaming."

He bowed his head. "If anyone feels the need to talk to a counselor, you're free to head to the office."

"I'm okay." Paige sat up and tried to push that awful sound from her thoughts.

Friday October 16 - 2:09 p.m.

FOUR MINUTES AFTER PAIGE ARRIVED BY THE GRADE-SCHOOL DOORS, A SPLASH of red hair over a plum dress and black leggings emerged from the steady stream of children racing to a trio of buses, parents' cars, or heading off on foot. Melissa bee-lined over and took her hand.

Paige grabbed her in a hug. *Please don't let whatever we did hurt her.*

"Ow." Melissa squirmed. Silver ballet flats slid on the sidewalk as she tried to escape.

"Sorry." Paige relaxed the suffocating embrace, but refused to let go of her hand.

They walked to the end of the school property and paused at a cross street to wait for the light to change.

"A eighth-grader got hit by a light." Melissa looked up. "We're not gonna have gym for a while."

"A light?" Paige shivered at the memory of the haunting screams.

"Uh huh." Melissa's hair bounced about as she nodded. "A light fell off the gym ceiling and hit her."

On green, Paige did an overcautious side-to-side look for approaching cars driven by men with too much cholesterol, but nothing stood out. She rushed across at a pace Melissa struggled to match, making her whine.

"Is it the same bad thing from our house doing it?" Melissa pumped her legs to keep up. "Don't walk so fast."

Paige squeezed her hand. "Yeah. I think it is. Don't worry. It's not after you."

"What is it?" Melissa looked up at her. "Why is it in our house?"

"It's magic that a bunch of stupid people should never have messed with."

Melissa kept quiet for a few paces, staring at the ground. "I don't think you're stupid."

Paige bit her lip. "I'm not gonna let it hurt you."

"Pay?" Melissa set her heels until they stopped.

"What?" Paige looked down.

Her sister's eyes brimmed with tears. "You're not gonna go away, are you?"

*Sigh.* "I've still got three years of high school left."

"No." Melissa bit her lip. "I mean *go away*." Her voice fell to a whisper. "Like Amber."

Her heart fluttered. *That look in her eyes... she knows...* Paige took a knee and wrapped Melissa in a tight embrace, tears gathering. "No, Mel. I promise."

Melissa squeezed her, but didn't say anything more than a sniffled "'Kay."

After wiping at her eyes, Paige stood, took Melissa's hand again, and resumed her trek home, kicking the occasional rock or branch on the pavement back into the woods. In a few minutes, Melissa's smile returned. A few *snaps* in the woods made her look around.

"Pay? I see a deer!" Melissa pointed.

Cold scraped down her back, a side edge of a knife from shoulder to kidney. Paige whipped around with a yelp, but no one was there. She stood still, gulping air, looking in all directions. Melissa tilted her head. Paige squinted at alleys, at traffic, at the sky. Worry had sunk its fangs into her neck and wouldn't let go. A flash of dizziness came and went, laced with anticipation and bloodlust. Sweat trickled down her ribs under her shirt. Someone or something hunted her, and it felt close.

Another three-sixty failed to spot anything or anyone giving her the evil eye. *Maybe it's not here yet. I should call Dad. No, he's going to definitely think I'm nuts.* She tugged Melissa to the end of the block, crossed the street forward, and then cut right to the other side. Two doors from the corner, she went into a mom-and-pop ice cream parlor. Sugar-scented air flooded her nostrils, a blend of vanilla and fruit.

Melissa smiled. "Ooh!"

She took a booth seat facing the entrance. A thin man in a white uniform with a pink bowtie walked over.

"Good afternoon, ladies." He smiled, setting a laminated menu on the table.

Paige ordered a small vanilla sundae with hot fudge and crushed peanuts. Melissa picked strawberry with strawberry sauce. The man smiled, collected the little menu, and hurried around the counter to prepare the treats. Silence lasted about forty seconds.

"Did you know the girl who got hit?"

Melissa shook her head. "No. I'm in third grade, dork."

Paige smiled. "So, no gym for a while huh?"

"Yeah. Miss. Phelps said they gotta inspect so nothing else breaks."

The clerk dropped off their ice cream and left a check.

Paige dug a ten out of her pocket and handed it over. "Thanks."

"Thank you," chirped Melissa.

"You're quite welcome. Let me know if you want anything else." He retreated to the register near two huge canisters of multicolored sprinkles.

Melissa proceeded to incise her portion of ice cream, removing surgical spoonfuls with a dainty touch. Paige kept her attention on the sidewalk outside, suppressing the urge to twitch whenever a person walked by.

"Your ice cream is melting," said Melissa.

Paige sighed. *Maybe I'm imagining this.* "Yeah."

She scooped a huge spoonful into her mouth. Chocolate syrup and vanilla smoothed away the worry storming in her mind. Cold slid down inside, settling in her empty stomach. Her moment of peace ended at a *thump.* She tensed and stared at the door, but when the noise repeated, it became apparent as Melissa swinging her feet. Her heel hit a panel below the seat with another *thump.*

"Sorry." Melissa went still, looking frightened.

Paige leaned forward. "What's wrong?"

"Are you mad at me?" She sniffled.

"No, Mel. What makes you think I'm mad at you?"

"'Cause the way you just looked at me." Her sister hung her head. "You always used to yell at me and say mean stuff. I don't want you to stop being nice. Dad said you're 'stressed.' Are you gonna go back to being mad at me?"

"No." Paige smiled through a pang of guilt. "I was upset over Amber and mad at everything. It wasn't you. I'm not gonna treat you like that anymore."

Melissa beamed.

Paige grinned back at her for about four seconds before motion in an alley across the street made her lips fall flat. Todd and Redbeard huddled behind a dumpster, watching the ice cream shop. Vertigo pulled her down through the seat, as though she fell out of her body. Seconds passed with her vision flying inches over a field of grass. Her point of view slowed and pulled up to about her standing height.

Police searchlights illuminated a pale girl laying in the grass, her black jacket, ruffled black skirt, and black leggings disheveled and pulled apart, but intact enough to suggest the assault was limited to a beating. Blood pooled atop a porcelain stomach. Disorientation at the strange vision subsided, leaving her aware she observed herself on the ground—the victim wore the same outfit she had on now.

"Paige!" screamed Dad. He rushed over, skidding to a halt on his knees and taking her hand.

Other-Paige wheezed and lifted her head. She reached out to her left. "M-Mel..."

Dad swiveled his flashlight to a spot about six feet away, and wailed.

Melissa lay face down, bleeding from the mouth and nose. Her jaw looked broken and her eye had gone purple. Paige couldn't tell if her sister was alive or dead, but the amount of blood terrified her. Her father collapsed over Other-Paige, sobbing.

Paige sat up in the booth seat out of a sideways slump. Melissa startled and coughed. Trails of pink strawberry ice cream leaked out of her nostrils. The clerk gave Paige a concerned glance. She grabbed a napkin and dabbed at her sister's face, unable to forget the smashed jaw, loose teeth, and puffy eye. By the time Melissa stopped choking on ice cream, Paige's hand trembled.

"Come sit over here," said Paige.

Melissa ducked under the table and took the spot between her and the wall. "Okay."

Paige wrapped her left arm around Melissa and took out her phone. Two thumb swipes called her father.

"I really hope this is just a hello," said Dad.

"Daddy." Paige choked up. "Can you please come pick me and Mel up? We're at Donny's ice cream."

Her sister shivered.

"What's happened? You sound terrified."

"Melissa is here. We're okay."

"Something's wrong and you don't want to say it in front of her?"

"Yeah, Dad. You're right. That would be great."

He mumbled. "Can it wait five or six minutes? I'm in the middle of ticketing some idiot from New York."

"I think so. We'll stay inside."

"I'll be there as soon as I can."

"Thanks, Dad." Paige sniffled, hung up, and pocketed the phone. "I need you to be brave, Mel. We have to go for a ride with Dad, okay?"

Melissa nodded. "I'm not scared. Police cars don't have accidents."

*Oh, if only.* Paige hugged her close. *Get out of my head. Damn you for making me see her like that.* She glared at the alley. Redbeard peered over the dumpster while Todd tossed and caught a tire iron. Every time it slapped into his hand, she felt it pat against her cheek. Paige looked away, put her other arm around Melissa, and held on.

*I speak to the spirit we summoned. I forbid you from touching her. I call upon the Horned God and the Lady. Please grant your protection to Melissa. May no harm come to her. I accept whatever return I deserve, but she is not part of this. So mote it be.* She dipped three fingers in her glass of water and dripped it on Melissa's head. After an indignant glare, Melissa did the same back at her.

"Are you scared of the car too?" Melissa squirmed to look her in the eye. "You're shivering."

"No, Mel. Right now, I really, *really* want to be inside a car." *Especially one with Dad driving.*

A sudden inspiration came on. She pulled her phone out, opened the camera app, and aimed it at the two older boys with murder in their eyes. *He can use this to arrest them.* When the screen adjusted to focus, she zoomed in on the alley. Rather than Todd and Redbeard, a pair of black shadowy figures stared back at her. She took the picture anyway, but... Dad wouldn't be seeing it.

Melissa trembled. "I'm scared."

"Why?"

"Because you're scared. You keep looking outside like there's a monster waiting for us."

Paige took a deep breath and let it out through her nose. "There is."

Melissa made an 'eep' noise.

"It's okay. Dad's coming. It can't get us in here." *I hope.*

Her sister threaded one arm out of the tangle of limbs and took another spoonful of ice cream. Paige adjusted her grip so Melissa could finish the treat she'd bought her to take her mind off what happened at the school. Every time the tire iron spiraled in the air and landed in Todd's hand, Paige shivered.

*Come on, Dad. Hurry up.*

# 18

# UNINVITED

Saturday October 17 - 12:10 p.m.

Paige sat cross-legged on the couch with a pillow in her lap, still wearing the giant blue tee shirt she'd slept in as well as fuzzy black socks. Melissa sprawled on her stomach over the cushions at her left, feet scissoring in the air, simultaneously doodling in a pad while watching a cartoon. Paige picked fuzzies from the back of Melissa's cotton nightgown and flicked them onto the rug. Gloomy skies threatened rain, but she didn't care. She wasn't going out today. Paige spent a moment watching the low flame of a cinnamon-scented candle flutter before frowning at her sister's clothes.

*This girl likes pink way too much.*

Mom wandered by, smiled at them, and disappeared into the dining room. A few minutes later, she returned with a coat on. "I'm going downtown to pick up some stuff for another commission. Do you girls want to go?"

"I'd rather stay inside today, Mom." Paige absentmindedly rubbed Melissa's back.

"Are you two going to spend all day in your pajamas?"

"Yep," said Melissa without looking up.

"Probably." Paige smiled.

"I'm really happy to see you and Melissa together. It's sudden and weird but I'm not going to—" Mom's gaze dropped straight down. "What's that?"

She didn't look at Dad's .38 revolver tucked between the armrest and the seat cushion. "It is what it looks like it is."

"Paige Thomas…" Mom leaned over, grasped the weapon in a way that kept it out of Melissa's sight, and stood. "Can I see you for a minute?"

"Yes, Mom." Paige stood and followed her.

Mom whirled on her as soon as they reached the kitchen. "I thought you were more responsible than this. Do you have any idea what your father would do if he found out you took this out of the lockbox? You're supposed to know better."

"Mom, yesterday on the way home from school, these two guys followed me and Mel. One had a tire iron. They'd already threatened to 'get me back' for that guy at the bank. I… You know how grandma sometimes had… uhh, visions?"

Anger receded from the edges of Mom's eyes. "You used to make fun of her for that."

"Did you believe her?"

Mom folded her arms after dropping the gun in her purse. "I won't say yes or no. Some of the things she said were damn hard to explain."

Paige put a hand on her mother's arm. She forced herself to recount the vision of Dad finding them in a field, Melissa probably dead and her not far from it. Tendons on the side of Mom's neck swelled and red appeared around her eyes. "I know it sounds crazy, but it felt *so* real. They threatened me. A teacher, uhh, Mr. Lloyd, at the school, witnessed it. They think Mackenzie bribed Dad and I asked him to kill their friend at the bank. They would've attacked us if I'd walked home."

"Did you tell Drew, uhh… your father?"

"Yes. He knows."

"I should stay with you." Mom set her bag on the table.

Paige tried to clear her mind. "I don't feel anything. You can probably go. Your internet business is barely hanging on. No sense ticking off a customer. We'll be okay."

"You have to admit you've been erratic lately."

"Yeah." Paige frowned at her socks. "I thought you hated me. I thought I didn't matter. Amber was gone and no one cared about me." She sighed. "I'm trying to deal with it now instead of just hating everything."

Mom took the gun out of her bag. "I'm going to put this back upstairs in the lockbox. I don't like leaving it out and about with Melissa."

"She's not stupid. She won't touch it."

"Everyone who's had an incident says that. I don't expect her to be foolish, but it's also a chance I don't want to take." Mom headed down the hall. "The doors are tough. If anything happens, you should have enough time to get upstairs." She stopped. "I'm not wholly comfortable with you handling a firearm, but I understand. *If* something happens, you are to find a hiding place, *not* go hunting. Do you understand me?"

"Yes, Mom."

"How'd you figure out the combination anyway?"

"I didn't figure it out." Paige fidgeted with her sweater while biting her lip. "Dad gave it to me."

"That's a conversation I'll need to have with him later, but I guess he trusts you. I still don't want it lying out in the open. Accidents happen."

Her mind filled with that night in her old room, back home in Ardmore. Moonlight glinted from the yawning barrel of his Glock. She'd been staring at it for almost twenty minutes when Amber appeared. *Dad trusts me with a gun...* She clenched her eyes shut, sick with guilt. *I'm not gonna hurt myself.*

Paige walked behind Mom, diverting to the living room while Mom went upstairs. "Okay."

As soon as Paige sat, Melissa rolled over on her back and used her thigh for a pillow. She'd filled the sketchpad page with balloon-like unicorns and stick-figure faeries with pie-plate faces. Mom breezed down the stairs, collected her bag, and stopped at the archway between hall and living room.

"I'll be about an hour or so." She started away, but leaned back. "You sure you don't want me to stay home?"

Paige smiled. "Yeah. It's cool."

"Ok then. Remember, your dad and I have our phones on us, so call if"— her eyes focused on Melissa—"you can call us. I'll be back soon."

"'Kay, Mom."

Her mother grasped her by the shoulders, forcing eye contact. "You're sure you're okay? You seem nervous."

*If we're with you, maybe it'll make someone hit us.* She swallowed hard and forced a smile. "Yeah. Just a lot going on right now, ya know? Feels like it's safe here. Drive careful, okay?"

Mom hesitated, eyeing the door. "Did you...?"

"No... just saying. It's gonna rain and. Uhh. Yeah." Warmth spread through Paige's cheeks.

"All right." Mom hugged her.

Paige clung as if she didn't expect to see her again. A sniffle escaped.

"Oh, that's it Paige. I'm staying. You're a wreck."

She took two deep breaths. "Really, it's fine. I'm just... nightmares, those idiots, the shooting at the bank. Dad doesn't think they'll come to the house. You gotta make that stuff, right?"

Mom stared into her eyes for a long few minutes.

"Hey, you could've been there and back already." Paige pulled hair from her face and smiled.

It took Mom a minute and change to relent, shaking her head. "Okay. I'll be back as soon as I can."

As Mom started to walk off, Paige put a hand on her arm. "Mom. Don't rush. Maybe drive a little slow."

"Did you see something?"

Paige grimaced. *Okay, maybe I was pissed off at you when we did the ritual and maybe it picked up on that.* "Not exactly, but... nervous and rain and... Just be careful."

"Okay, hon." Mom leaned in and gave her a peck on the cheek. "Keep your phone near you and call me if anything happens."

"'Kay."

Mom headed outside amid the rustle of coat and handbag. Paige jumped at the oddly loud *whump* of the front door closing. Her mother hadn't slammed it, but something had amplified the sound. Her little sister didn't seem to notice. She hurried back to the sofa and flopped next to her.

Melissa introduced each unicorn and faerie by name. Paige asked about them, starting a conversation about their royalty that meandered for a while. Eventually, Melissa suggested a game and they both sprawled on the floor, Xbox controllers in hand, playing *Mermaid's Journey*. The co-op play was a bit cheesy, with the second player assuming a re-colored version of the mermaid princess. All the dialogue cutscenes reacted like only one princess existed. Of course, it didn't bother Melissa. *As if that kid would complain about* more *mermaids.*

An hour melted away before she knew it. *Is this how Amber felt with me?* She grinned. *It's kind of like having a daughter without all the annoying responsibility parts.*

Darkness. The underwater-echo music from the video game died. Only the patter of rain against the windows pierced the subsequent silence.

"Aaah!" Melissa sat up. "What happened?"

"The power went out." Paige grumbled. "Same thing that happened back home. Every damn time it rains."

*No, those two idiots didn't 'cut the power' before kicking in the door.* Paige got up and walked to the bay window. Most of the view consisted of near-skeletal trees wavering in the storm wind. Spots where she knew houses should be held blackness.

"Looks like the whole area's out."

"Is it the monster?" Melissa shifted onto her knees.

Paige glanced at the ceiling. "No, it's a crappy power grid."

"You sound like Daddy."

Melissa got up and ran to the downstairs bathroom. Paige rummaged the hall closet until she found Dad's electric lantern. "Who in their right mind made this thing camo? If you dropped it out in the woods at night you'd never find it." She plucked a rechargeable battery off the wall-mounted charger and turned the light on.

After a toilet flush, Melissa emerged from the sliding door near the closet. She pulled Paige along by the hand to the kitchen. Lantern held high, Paige smirked. *I feel like that girl they always have in movies roaming a haunted castle. All I need is a big, puffy medieval nightgown.*

Melissa grabbed a Clue board game from the kitchen closet and set it on the table. "This doesn't need electricity."

"Okay." Paige set the lantern down nearby and opened the box.

After helping set up the board, Melissa pulled her foot up on the chair and rested her head on her knee. They exchanged grins for a little while as the game got underway.

Paige glanced over at pink glitter nail polish. "That's a cute color."

"I got it last week." Melissa flexed her toes and curled them over the front of the chair. "It's called pixie fart. You can't see it now, but the glitter is purple."

"Really?" Paige giggled.

"Yeah." Melissa moved her game piece. "The store mostly had the stuff you like. Goth."

"I'm surprised Mom let you anywhere near that place. I think she'd go postal if you started dressing like me too."

Melissa shook her head. "Nope. I am the cute. No gloom for me. I'd love to see Mom's face if you did girly once."

Paige laughed.

"You want a pixie to fart on your toes?" Melissa wobbled her head back and forth making a silly face and emitting a *thbpbpbt* noise.

"Maybe. Black *is* getting a bit old."

*Whump.*

Melissa's smile ran off. Paige looked up.

"What was that?" asked Melissa.

"A creepy bang on the ceiling in a house that we're supposed to be alone in."

"Not funny." Melissa lowered her foot to the floor.

*Wham.*

"Maybe it's the wind?" Paige bit her lip. *Those guys didn't come in through a second floor window.*

Melissa rounded the corner and clung to her. "It's the monster that brings scary dreams."

"Stay quiet." Paige picked up the lantern and stood.

Melissa grabbed her left hand in both of hers.

*Whump.*

Both girls jumped.

Paige held the lantern out in front and crept to the bottom of the stairs.

The second-floor hallway wavered in feeble moonlight sliced apart by tree branches. She froze; that did *not* feel like home.

"Don't go up there," whispered Melissa.

Gloom and driving rain filled the tall, narrow windows on either side of the front door. Paige stood mesmerized by the storm until another heavy slam rocked the ceiling overhead.

*Uhh...* She doubted the usefulness of a pistol against spirits, but on the off chance Todd and Redbeard showed up, she didn't want to be helpless. "Wait here."

"No," whined Melissa.

"I gotta get something. I'll be right back."

"I'm going." Melissa trembled. "I don't wanna be alone."

Paige climbed the stairs, e-lantern held high. A wall of cold air hovered at the level of the second story floor. She shivered from the temperature shift and shined the lantern left and right. Thickness permeated the corridor, imbued with a definite sense of an entity watching them. She hurried through puffs of her breath to her parents' room where she set the lantern on the nightstand and knelt to pull a brick-shaped dark blue lockbox out from under the bed.

"That's Dad's gun box." Melissa shook her by the arm. "We're not supposed to touch it."

"Dad gave me permission." Paige keyed in the combination and popped the lid. She withdrew the .38.

"You're gonna get in so much trouble if you're lying."

"I'm not." Paige took the lantern in her left. "Back downstairs."

Her sister gripped the rug with her toes, an unsure look on her face. "Do guns work on closet monsters?"

*Wham.*

Melissa screamed and jumped behind her. The noise sounded as though it hit the wall right in front of them.

Paige scurried back. She aimed at the wall, but thought better of it and let her arm drop. "You have no purpose here. Begone whatever you are."

Melissa pulled on her arm. "I don't think it's scared of you."

"Come on."

Paige led her sister back downstairs and they hid in the large dining room closet. Melissa sat on the floor with the lantern between her feet. Paige concentrated on the boundaries of the closet and turned in place three times clockwise before sitting. Melissa hugged her from behind and rested her chin on her left shoulder.

"Don't shoot me," whispered Melissa.

"I won't."

Melissa seemed to grow increasingly frightened as the minutes of silence ticked by. Paige put her hand over her sister's arms where they crossed her stomach. Random bangs and knocks continued, some distant while others rattled the closet door. Melissa whimpered at a loud series of booming footsteps thundering overhead.

"Why is it mad?" a little voice whispered at her ear.

*It's trying to terrify me until I fall to pieces so Dad babies me.* She swallowed. *Or it's pissed at me for interfering with the car hitting Emily, or for messing up its attack on Santana's mom.* Paige trembled. *Crap. Kenz said it would go off the rails if we worked against our own spell.*

"Pay?" Melissa squeezed her.

"I don't know why it's mad. I won't let it hurt you."

*Bang.*

The closet door shook.

Paige's scream drowned out Melissa's shriek. She scooted back into a mass of coats, until they hit the wall. She leveled the .38 at the door, but her hand trembled so much she doubted she could even hit the wall.

*Wham!*

The closet door shuddered hard enough to knock paint flakes from around the door.

Paige took her finger off the trigger. *This thing isn't going to care about a bullet. Damn. What if it causes an accident? Dammit! I never should've taken this thing out of the box.* Paige opened the cylinder and let the six bullets fall out.

"What are you doing?" whispered Melissa.

"It's a monster, right?"

"A shadow monster," said Melissa.

"Bullets aren't gonna hurt it. I don't want it to cause an accident."

"Okay."

*Wham.*

The entire closet rumbled. Scratching came from the dark gap under the door. Spiders seeped through, gloss black in the stark white light of the electric lantern. Endless legs, so many they became a sheet of fluid, pressed in.

Melissa screamed. Paige scrambled to get up. Her sister jumped on her like a human backpack, desperate to get away from the floor. Once on her feet, Paige backed into the corner on tiptoe. The spiders welled up, stopping inches from the tips of her socks. Each about the size of a golf ball, the arachnids gazed up at her, tiny wrinkled faces grinning and snapping their too-human teeth at her. The closet door creaked and warped inward, inflating as if under the weight of billions of spiders.

The steady shrieking coming from Melissa's lungs could've shattered glass.

All at once, the spiders surged forward, climbing her legs, a tide of needlepoints over her calves, knees, thighs. She screamed and swatted, hoisting Melissa onto a shelf over the coat rack. Shoeboxes, folded tablecloths, candlesticks, and other junk fell as her sister stepped on her shoulder and leapt up and away. Each spider she smashed burst into a cloud of black fog. Paige stomped and swatted, screamed and thrashed.

"Go away!" she yelled. "I forbid you to do harm here."

The jumble of arachnids dissipated into an ebon morass, whispering and chattering in an icicle-down-the-spine cacophony. A tarlike mass congealed and withdrew under the door, which shrank back to being flat. It looked as though nothing had happened, aside from the scattering of paint chips. Melissa covered her mouth in her hands and bawled. Paige looked up at her, curled in a ball above the coats. The terror in her little sister's eyes filled her with such guilt she fell to her knees.

"I'm sorry... We shouldn't have done it." Paige scowled. "We have to send it back."

"Done what?" whimpered Melissa.

The doorbell rang.

Paige snapped her head up. When the bell rang a second time, followed by heavy knocking, she grabbed at the bullets on the floor and loaded four. More rapid knocking preceded the bell ringing twice more.

"Someone coming to kill me wouldn't knock." Paige clenched and released the gun handle. "Mel. Stay here. I'm going to see who it is."

"Don't go. It's trying to trick you."

"You're probably right." Paige grabbed the knob. "But I'm not afraid of it."

"Liar," whispered Melissa.

Rapid knocking accompanied a feminine yell.

She turned the knob and pushed the door. No spiders. A few inches farther, and she peered around it at the front door, raising the .38.

Renee pressed her face up to the glass, and screamed at the sight of Paige with a gun.

"Ack!" Paige let her arm fall and ran to the front door. She undid the deadbolt and pulled the door open. "Nee?"

Renee, soaked to the skin, backed up. "W-what's with the gun?"

"Are you real?"

"The hell kind of question is that?" Renee wiped a hand through her purple frizzy hair. "Of course I'm real."

"C'mon in." Paige backed away, and closed the door once Renee darted inside. "Jared's friends followed me yesterday. That's why the gun."

"Oh wow." Renee exhaled. "Sorry for just coming over, but you weren't answering the phone."

"It's in the living room. I didn't hear it."

"Thanks. I had to get out of the house." She might've been crying; the rain made it difficult to tell. "My parents were fighting bad. Dad accused Mom of having me to chain him down. They started throwing crap at each other."

"Sorry." Paige went to hug her, but stopped. "Uhh, you wanna towel or something? Maybe dry clothes?"

"That would rule. Sorry for drippin' all over your rug."

"Mel?" Paige looked at the no-longer-banging ceiling. "I think it's over."

Renee raised a brow. "What happened?"

"That thing we set loose has spent the past hour scaring the crap out of us." Paige explained the spiders, the banging, the freezing cold upstairs.

"Whoa." Renee shivered. "We definitely losin' control of this thing."

"Mel?" Paige walked back to the closet and pulled the door open. Empty shelf. No little sister. "Melissa?"

Silence.

Two bullets stood on end in the middle of the floor, balanced on their rounded points. Paige stared.

"Whoa," said Renee. She stooped and picked them up. "That was freaky." She tried to get them to stand on tip again, but they fell over every time.

Paige put them back in the gun. She ran up the stairs, calling out for Melissa. Long shadows stretched from the electric lantern; nothing but the echo of her voice answered. She jogged to her parents' room and put the .38 back in the safe, slapped it closed, and stuffed it under the bed. Renee's voice echoed in the hall, calling for Melissa as well. Paige crossed to her sister's pink-and-white bedroom, packed with dolls, stuffed animals, and a frilly white bedspread. Mermaid-themed posters, stickers, and crafts littered every available surface.

"Melissa? Please stop if you're messing with me."

Nine dolls spontaneously emitted recorded 'ma-ma's,' gurgles, or lines from whatever movie the character came from. Paige shrieked. A spring-mounted rocking horse Melissa hadn't used since she was six came to life, wobbling to and fro faster than any child could ride it. The creak-squeal of overstressed springs invaded her mind. Paige jumped away and pressed her back to the wall. Paralytic fear lasted two seconds.

"Go away!" Paige shouted. "This is not your house!"

The horse went still.

She ran to her bedroom, finding it quiet. Paige pulled her closet open and stared at herself in the full-length mirror mounted to the inside face of the door. One second, she looked normal. In the blink of an eye, all the bruises and bleeding from the girl lying in the field appeared. The reflection of her room behind her showed Melissa dead on the rug by the bed, her skull caved in.

Paige cringed away from the awful sight, comforted by the empty floor in the real world. She slammed her closet in disgust and stomped to her attached bathroom, half expecting to see trees. White tile, black rug, no Melissa.

Renee popped in. "I can't find her anywhere. Nothing."

"No..." Tears started, but Paige ran downstairs in a room-to-room search.

Every closet and cabinet got opened. Fortunately, the house had no basement. The back door remained locked and secured. She slid the nub of a small chain back and forth in its groove. If Melissa had gone out that way, she couldn't possibly have re-latched the chain from the outside. Paige raced to the closet where they'd hidden, but it remained empty.

After another search of the upstairs with Renee at her side, she collapsed on her knees by the dining room closet, dropped the electric lantern, and sobbed into her hands.

Renee knelt behind her and held her shoulders. "We'll find her. Mackenzie might know some way to help."

"It's her fault." Paige sniffled. "She tried to kill Emily, and I stopped it. I went against the spell, so it's gotten away from us."

"What?" Renee shook her.

"Kenz... she wants Cole right? How else is she gonna get him when he's so in love with Emily. If she's dead, Kenz can play the sympathetic shoulder and manipulate him into loving her."

"Oh, my God." Renee shivered. "That car..."

"Yeah." Paige wiped her eyes but it didn't help; the tears kept coming. "Now my sister is gone. It's lashing out at me for interfering."

A childish giggle echoed upstairs.

"Mel!" Paige bolted upright and ran to the stairs. Her hand clapped on the post at the bottom of the banister as she held on to avoid wiping out on the 180-degree turn. "Mel!"

Another giggle came from overhead.

She slid into the doorjamb of her bedroom and raised the electric lantern. Her closet door touched the wall, open as wide as possible. Melissa stood in front of it, hands flat on either side of the glass, smiling at her utter lack of reflection as if mesmerized.

Paige dropped the lantern and rushed over. She skidded on her knees and clamped her arms around her sister. Melissa glanced back with a pleasant smile.

"Mel!" Paige kissed her on the head and held her tight. "Where were you?"

Melissa tried to point, but Paige's hug pinned her arms at her sides. "Talking to Amber."

Paige let go. "What?"

"Talking to Amber." Melissa pointed at the mirror. "Oh. She's gone."

When she looked up, the mirror held a normal reflection of her kneeling behind Melissa.

*Wham.* The front door closed hard.

Melissa gurgled as Paige's hug crushed her again. "Ow."

"Paige? Melissa?" yelled Mom. "Sorry I'm late. I had to stop because of an accident. Idiot in an Acura almost hit me. Raced straight through a red light."

Bile rose in Paige's throat.

Renee stared at Paige. "You think?"

The lights flickered on.

"Yay!" Melissa bounced. "Mermaids!"

"Hey," said Renee. "Mind if I use your shower?"

Paige plucked a tee shirt and grey sweat pants from her dresser, along with a towel from her linen closet. "Go for it. I'm gonna go help Mel save the ocean kingdom."

Melissa ran ahead to the living room. Paige stopped in the hall by the front door where Mom unburdened herself of her coat and scarf. They exchanged a meaningful look.

"I was doing thirty-five," whispered Mom.

Paige fidgeted. "You never drive that slow."

Mom pulled her into a trembling embrace. "I couldn't get the look on your face out of my head. If... If I'd been doing ten more, that guy would've t-boned me."

"Mom." Paige sniffled, burying her face against her mother's shoulder. The want to tell her everything grew painful, but slammed into a wall of fear at the worst case scenario: straitjackets, padded cells, doctors, and being alone.

"Pay?" yelled Melissa from the living room. "You coming?"

"I don't know what's gotten into this town. It was supposed to be quiet." Mom released the crushing hug, and smiled.

"Yeah. Weird huh?" Paige folded her arms to hide her shaking hands.

*And as soon as I see Kenz, this shit is gonna stop.*

# 19

# COVENANT

Monday October 19 - 7:45 a.m.

All of Sunday, Paige felt normal. She'd spent the day with her family. All four of them went to the mall, caught a movie, and hung out at home playing video games. After Melissa went to bed, she watched a spy movie with her parents before going to sleep as well. The first few minutes of her dreams consisted of Matt Damon coming out of nowhere to save her from bombs, assassins, and a car with a cut brake line.

Two Shadesboro Police cars flanked the front of the school parking lot Monday morning. The officers stood by the doors outside, offering pleasant waves at any student who looked their way. Paige smiled, recognizing the woman who'd shown up where the Grand Marquis almost pasted her. All the high-school kids in sight seemed morose, as if the entire population of Shadesboro between fourteen and eighteen had been grounded indefinitely.

She headed to her usual spot in the cafeteria, finding the crew already there. She plopped her bag down on the table and climbed over the bench. "Wow, you guys are early today."

"Mmm," said Renee.

Sofia lifted her head from her book bag. "Hey." She let her face plop back down.

"Are you hung over?" Paige chuckled. "You're what, thirteen?"

"The light smashed Michelle Porter's left arm, a couple ribs, and broke her leg. She's gonna be in casts for months. They had her on so much pain medicine she can't even talk."

"Ouch," said Mackenzie. "What did she do to you?"

Sofia sniffled. "She's the one who tricked me into getting in the locker and then padlocked it. I visited her, but she didn't know I was there."

Paige shivered.

"Kyle broke both legs when the car hit him." Sofia sniffled up to crying. "It's my fault. He wasn't mean to me. He just thought I was creepy. I didn't want him to get hurt."

Santana looked down. "There's a two-hour thing for juniors and seniors today about drunk driving. Everyone's gotta go."

"But Jeremy wasn't drunk," said Renee. "He's way more upset over the accident than Kyle."

Brittany Kutzen, in a powder-blue dress, one leg and one arm in casts, hobbled in on crutches and made her way to a table. Sofia established eye contact with her, and the blonde returned an embarrassed smile before sitting.

"Is that why everyone's so quiet?" Paige accepted a coffee cup from Mackenzie. "We need to talk later."

Santana pulled her hair out of her face and hooked it behind her right ear. "Todd and Peter were killed last night."

"Who?" Paige slurped mocha latte.

"Those two lumps that came after us outside. Peter Beckett and Todd Miller." Renee fidgeted with her cup. "Word is they were drag racing with a couple of the football players and crashed head-on with a tractor-trailer at like a hundred. Killed the trucker too. Good thing it happened around midnight or there would've been a lot of people hurt."

Mackenzie pursed her lips. "I heard they found the guy who was driving the semi in the bed of the pickup truck."

Paige cringed. *They were gonna kill Melissa, but that other man was innocent.* She thought back to Redbeard telling Todd to leave her alone. *They weren't even really that bad... what did we do?*

"I told them to leave us alone." Mackenzie unwrapped wax paper from a scone. "Guess they decided not to listen."

Renee gawked. "How can you be that cold?"

"They did it to themselves. If they would have left us alone, their 'luck' wouldn't have been so bad." Mackenzie nibbled on her scone.

Paige gazed into nowhere. "They were going to kill my sister and beat me half to death."

"See." Mackenzie smiled. "Karma, accelerated." Her expression said 'you're welcome.'

"The magic made them. The one guy wasn't like that before. We're losing control." Paige fixed Mackenzie with a stare. "*It* was in my house Saturday."

"I got a bad feelin' about my Dad too." Renee slid the cardboard heat sleeve up and down her coffee. "When I got home Sunday morning, they were all smiles, like the fight never happened. I don't trust it. I'm scared to be in the house. He's... not right."

"What do you mean 'not right?'" asked Sofia.

"Creepy eyes." Renee drank a little coffee. "He looks at me weird, like he's high or something and just can't stop smiling even though he's really angry."

"We're not losing control." Paige took a long three-gulp swig. "We already lost it."

Mackenzie broke a large piece off her scone and ate it. "Don't chicken out now. The circle of perfect love and perfect trust. No turning back until the spell is done."

A sudden urge caused Paige to look out over the cafeteria and zero in on a gangly fifty-plus teacher in a too-large blazer and yellow straight tie. He departed the cashier station with a giant plastic mug and an even bigger smile. Long, spindly legs propelled him at a brusque pace while he greeted his way past a table of freshmen. His foot snagged the loop of a backpack someone left on the floor behind the bench seats and he lurched forward. His mug, and all the coffee in it, leapt out of his hand and streamed in a too-perfect arc, splattering over the chest and lap of a twig-thin eighth-grade girl in a frilly white top and white jeans.

The teacher flailed and landed on his chest.

The blonde girl shrieked. She jumped to her feet, flung her top off, and ripped her pants down around her shins while trying to scream, cry, and fan herself all at once. In seconds, red blotches appeared on her skin. The teacher shuffled onto his knees and removed his enormous brown blazer, which he wrapped around the scalded girl. After kicking his foot free of the backpack straps, he cradled the shrieking student in his arms and carried her out. Mrs. Hollis, Paige's art teacher, ran after them.

Mackenzie twisted around to face forward again and flashed a wry grin. "So what did she do to you, Sof?"

Sofia blushed. "Taylor snuck up behind me and pulled my pants down in the locker room."

"Gotta love karma." Mackenzie's smile grew to a grin.

"What's wrong with you?" Paige glared. "That girl's like twelve. She might have permanent scars from that burn, and her parents might sue that teacher... or the school."

"The cafeteria doesn't serve Mickey Dee's coffee." Mackenzie finished off the scone and dusted her hands free of crumbs. "It's not *that* hot. She was overacting."

"And the car that hit Keith wasn't going fast enough to break both of his legs. I asked my dad about it. He said the skid marks proved the kid was only driving like eighteen miles an hour." Paige stared into the fabric pattern of her book bag, picking at it. "Brittany shouldn't have broken both her arm and leg from that fall either. Gopher hole like that should've been a sprained ankle at worst. She wasn't even running."

Sofia cried. "I don't wanna do this anymore. I was like right next to Michelle when the light fell on her. I keep having nightmares about her screaming."

Paige shuddered. *I'll never forget that.*

"We can't stop now." Mackenzie wadded the wax paper into the bag the scone came in. "We made a covenant with the spirits. It will only get worse if we try to stop it. This isn't like a negotiation."

"We gotta do something!" yelled Santana. "My mother was almost shot. What has to happen before you stop giving us that stupid smug-ass smile?"

Paige put a hand on Sofia's arm. The girl abandoned her backpack to cling and sob into her shoulder instead.

"What about if we do another ritual?" asked Renee. "Go back to the cabin and be like 'hey, sorry, we messed up.' Or something?"

Paige gestured at Sofia while glaring at Mackenzie. "This has to stop before anyone else dies."

Mackenzie sighed. "Okay. Fine. I'll check the book when I get home and see if I can find a safe way to dismiss or redirect the spell. This stuff isn't a game you know. We pushed a boulder down a hill and it's gonna roll to the bottom or crush anything that gets in its way, including us."

*Beep. Beep. Beep.*

"Attention students, this is Principal Hollister. All juniors and seniors should report to the auditorium at this time. Freshmen and sophomores should proceed to their regular first period classes."

Paige stood, threw her backpack over her shoulder, and frowned at Mackenzie. "After school, we're gonna do something."

Sofia, Renee, and Santana edged up behind Paige. Under the combined stares of four on one, Mackenzie raised her hands. "Fine. If I can find a safe way out that won't kill us, we'll cast a counterspell."

Everyone nodded. Sofia ran off to the eighth-graders, and wound up carrying Brittany's book bag. Paige watched the girls talk, trying to understand what the hell was going on. *Maybe if she stops hating them, that portion of the spell would end.*

"That's it. Once it does what it needs to do, it'll stop." Paige turned, but the others had left. She grumbled, and hurried off to chemistry class.

# 20

# VOLATILE MAGIC

Monday October 19 - 8:31 a.m.

The class busied themselves reading chapter fourteen in the textbook, an introduction to alkali metals, as indicated by the dry-erase board. Mr. Ruiz had popped in at ten after eight for long enough to take roll, apologized, and darted out. A few students whispered about the unusual number of accidents going on. Someone observed it had only been eighth-graders and tried to resurrect the 'curse' theory.

Mr. Ruiz walked in carrying a white plastic case that resembled a half-size beer cooler. He set it on the large worktable at the front of the class, where he conducted demonstrations. Excitement swept through the students, most of whom lost interest in reading to watch him.

"Good morning, everyone." He smiled. "Sorry for the delay. Had to deal with some extra paperwork this morning. Anyway." He patted the box. "Today we're going to take a look at alkali metals. These are highly reactive substances that often have energetic interactions with other elements." He filled a twelve-inch flask halfway with water and set it in the middle of the table. "In this box, I have some sodium."

"Salt?" asked a boy in the front.

"Not quite. Can anyone help Kenny out?" Mr. Ruiz looked around before pointing at a brown-haired girl two desks away from Paige. "Allie?"

"Table salt is only partially composed of sodium, Na. It's sodium chloride, NaCl."

"Correct," said Mr. Ruiz with a grin. "Sodium is a silvery-white metal in its pure state. However, it is too reactive and therefore does not occur in nature as a metal. It only exists in this state if we manufacture it." He put on a pair of thin cloth gloves followed by a second pair of blue latex over them. After opening the white box, he extracted a clear flask containing a block that resembled lead, but with a bit more luster, in fluid. The chunk had a perfect rectangular edge on one side while the other looked like a stick of butter that someone had been scraping at. "If exposed to air, sodium will turn greyish-white due to oxidation. Immersing it in anhydrous mineral oil protects it."

Mr. Ruiz walked around, allowing students to get a closer look at the block. He returned to the front after passing each row, and leaned his hands on the desk. "I'm going to demonstrate the reactivity of sodium by dropping a small piece into this water. For safety's sake, everyone please retrieve your goggles from the storage cubbies."

Paige, and the rest of the class, headed to the right side of the room, grabbed eye protection, and returned to their worktables.

Mr. Ruiz used tongs to extract the sodium block from the oil and set it on a tray. He held up a standard butter knife.

Dread fell on Paige like ice water. She clamped a hand over her mouth to avoid spewing coffee and cereal all over. The walls spun in a disorienting blur and she found herself held up by the boy who shared her station... Charlie something...

"You okay?"

"No!" Paige reached toward Mr. Ruiz. "Stop! Don't do it."

"Oh, you're absolutely right, Miss. Thomas." Mr. Ruiz biffed himself in the forehead.

She exhaled and slumped over her worktable.

"I forgot the blast shield." He crouched down out of sight and opened a sliding door.

Paige whined and grabbed at her chest, struggling to breathe. Her heart pounded. Only Charlie seemed to take notice of her attack. As horrible as she felt, why wasn't everyone running over to check on her?

Mr. Ruiz stood holding a huge folding transparent barrier, about an inch thick. "Polycarbonate resin." He arranged it around the beaker and put on his eye protection. "Now..." A smile like a little boy about to play with a toy truck spread over his face.

He sliced a fragment off the block with the butter knife, grinning at the class's reaction to how easily the sodium cut. Mr. Ruiz held a wafer about the size of a thumbnail up so everyone could watch it turn from silvery grey, to dark, to white.

"In the air, sodium tarnishes at an extreme rate. The white coating is a mixture of sodium hydroxide and sodium carbonate. When exposed to water, however..."

"No!" yelled Paige.

With a vapid smile, Mr. Ruiz held up the tiny sliver between his thumb and index finger. "Oh. I should put this back in the oil before it all turns." He dropped the little sliver in the mineral oil and picked up the large block.

"Mr. Ruiz, no!" screamed Paige. She shoved Charlie on his ass and started to run for the teacher.

Before she cleared the corner of the desk, Mr. Ruiz dropped the brick into the water. She cringed and dove to the floor a split second before a tremendous explosion went off at the front of the classroom. The air filled with screams and odd-scented smoke. Paige uncrossed her arms from her face and looked up. Mr. Ruiz lay flat on his back on the far side of the desk, with several jagged spears of glass sticking out of his face. Two went straight through his goggles. The blast shield lay on the floor in front of the teacher's worktable with several shards stuck in it as well. Students nearest the front howled; at least six kids bled from dozens of small lacerations.

Paige screamed, and broke down in sobs. "No! Mr. Ruiz! No..."

A mass of panicking sophomores ran out of the classroom. One or two grabbed on to friends, unable to see with blood in their eyes and smoke in the air. Paige couldn't look away from the twitching body of her favorite teacher —and Santana's dad. Sniffling, she crawled forward until she spotted a sliver of glass on the floor. She sat back on her heels and checked her palms for cuts. Finding none, she pulled herself upright with the edge of another worktable.

She leaned forward, peering around the teacher's workstation. Mr. Ruiz stared with vacant eyes at the ceiling. Red saturated his chest and face, like he'd bore the brunt of a glass-filled shotgun blast. He gurgled, forcing more blood from the corner of his mouth.

"I'm sorry," she whispered. "It's... our fault."

"Paige!" yelled Mr. Lane.

The physics teacher ran over. Paige continued staring at Mr. Ruiz. Strong arms wrapped around and scooped her off her feet. She snapped out of a fog and looked up at him. He carried her straight to the medical station and set her on a small bed before approaching the nurse.

"I think she's in shock," said Mr. Lane.

Paige rolled on her side and curled up.

*What did we do...?*

# 21

# THREEFOLD RETURN

Monday October 19 - 9:29 a.m.

A steady, chilly breeze whisked across the grounds of Emmet G. Waterford Memorial High School. Paige stood at the side door, staring at a mass of meaningless blobs of color shifting about at the edge of the property. After a few seconds, she recognized them as people, and a moment later as people she knew. With the gait of an automaton, she trudged down the four concrete steps to the parking lot and wandered into the grassy field. It seemed silly that they also evacuated the grade school, considering it was a separate building over a hundred yards away, but evacuate it they had. Over there, kids clustered in groups sorted by classrooms. The high-school students formed an irregular swath, delineated primarily by friends and cliques. Teachers patrolled the space between the students and the school building, speaking into walkie-talkies every so often.

She floated in a daze, refusing to believe the day had been real. A patch of white on the lawn near the road drew her attention to the high school's sign. She frowned at the tall block lettering, especially the word 'memorial.'

*They're going to need to add a few more names to that title.*

Paige spotted Renee's purple hair and headed for her friends. Unsurprisingly, Santana wasn't there.

Renee pounced and hugged all the air out of her. "Are you okay? They said you were at the nurse's station."

Mackenzie put an arm around her too. Her motherly expression might've even been genuine.

"I couldn't stop it." Paige stared through Renee. "He was right in front of me, twitching."

Time blurred, becoming a haze of pats, comforting words, and squeezes. Paige threw her arms around Renee, not caring if anyone thought them lovers. In time, the tears abated and she stood on her own, trying to make sense of it.

"We killed him," whispered Paige.

"No we didn't." Mackenzie shook her head. "We made a request and the spirits manipulate circumstances in the most direct way possible to fulfill that request. They *could* have caused an armored truck to overturn in Santana's front yard, but that's too far removed from anything likely to really happen."

The rumble of conversation around them died down all at once.

Paige looked up. An ambulance pulled in without siren, only a few of the red lights snapping in camera flashes from the corners of the boxy vehicle. That one girl's continuous screaming replayed in her head as the paramedics dragged an empty stretcher inside.

"This is us. This is our fault. We set it loose and we have to put it back." Paige grabbed Mackenzie's hand. "Please Kenz. This is wrong."

"Somethin' bad's gonna happen at home," said Renee. "I got this feeling. Not like Paige here, but I just got this feeling."

Mackenzie smirked. "I already agreed to check the book later. You have to understand. Magic isn't like a light switch you can turn on and off. There are rules. The universe gets pissed off when we break those rules. I know you're all freaking out about this, but believe me... it can get *way* worse if we mess it up. We asked for this. Time for the big-girl pants. You know. Can't make omelets without breaking eggs and stuff."

Paige gawked at her.

The *clonk* of opening doors preceded Santana being brought out on the gurney. She seemed unconscious.

"Oh, no." Paige choked up. "What happened?"

Mackenzie folded her arms. "She couldn't handle it. She completely lost her shit when they told her what happened. They had to sedate her. He probably had life insurance or something, or maybe they're going to sue the school now. Either way, they won't have to worry about money anymore."

Renee grabbed Paige by the hips and whispered, "Needin' ta do something with my hands so I don't slap this bitch." She took a breath, and raised her voice. "How the hell can you say that?"

"It's true, isn't it?" Mackenzie shrugged. "I mean it's awful that her father's dead, but it's what she asked for."

"No it isn't," yelled Paige. "She's got a little brother who doesn't have a dad anymore. Her mother was almost killed a couple days ago... how... how is that anything even close to what she wanted? We have to stop this right now."

"I don't think so." Mackenzie narrowed her eyes. "You're in this as much as any of us. We're all going to get what we want."

"No." Paige pointed at the blonde. "You're going to get what you *deserve.* Law of Threefold Return. We send out bad, we get triple it back."

Mackenzie rolled her eyes. "That's new age Wicca nonsense. It's something for the tree huggers to feel at one with nature. We're doing *magic.*"

Sofia ran across the parking lot. Her long-sleeved black sweater, dark-grey pleated skirt, and black stockings made her look like a catholic schoolgirl from a Tim Burton movie. She grabbed on to Paige's left arm, wide eyed. "What happened?"

"Em?" Cole approached in a rapid walk, looking around. "Emily?"

"Hi, Cole." Mackenzie glided out in front of him. "Is something wrong?" She stuck her finger in her mouth, and put on a demure, innocent pose.

"Kenz... have you seen Em? I haven't been able to find her since the evacuation."

Paige's heart slammed against her sternum. "S... Santana's father was... killed."

Sofia gasped.

"Oh, no." Mackenzie looked horrified. "Maybe she's in the nurse's station. She's such a sweetheart; she was probably trying to comfort Santana Ruiz or something. Do you need a hand finding her? I'd love to help."

He frowned and shot her an impatient glance. "Uhh, I got it. Thanks."

Mackenzie's expression of worry became a fume after he hurried off.

"What happened?" asked Sofia.

Paige explained the sodium explosion. "He had the mother of all brain farts and threw the wrong piece in the water."

"No." Renee shook her head. "He wasn't that careless. That was the spell makin' it look like an accident."

Mackenzie lost a bit of her anger and gestured at Renee. "She's right. Not to be a bitch, but Sant didn't specify *how* she wanted money."

"You did *not* just blame her for this," said Renee. "Saying 'not to be a bitch' don't make you not a bitch when you say crap like that."

"I'm just being blunt." Mackenzie scanned the crowd again. "Spells find their own ways to do things without explicit instructions."

"It's dark," whispered Paige. "That dead blood made it dark..."

Sofia gurgled as if about to vomit.

Mackenzie rolled her eyes. "What do you think magic is, Paige? Star-capped wands and faerie dust? It's dealing with primal energies that have been around longer than humans."

"Find a counterspell," said Paige. "This isn't what we asked for. We opened a gate and let something out that doesn't belong here."

"Yeah." Sofia sniveled. "I don't want any more kids to get hurt. Please, Kenz. Pleeeease…"

"Oh, don't be such a little girl. If you want to hang out with us, you gotta suck it up." Mackenzie scowled at Cole's back as he picked through the assembly. "If we break the contract, we'll get it worse."

"So you're not going to look for a way out?" asked Renee. She let go of Paige's hips and made fists.

"I didn't say that. I don't expect to find one, but I will try."

"I saw your mom, Kenz." Paige got in her face. "She showed up at my house. You know what she said? She said 'thanks for opening the door.' And she smiled at me."

Mackenzie's face paled. "Uhh."

"She knows what you did." Paige glared. "Better look real hard for that counterspell before mama ghost gets enough strength up for payback."

"What did you do Kenz?" asked Renee.

"Attention students," said Principal Hollister via the PA. "We have decided to close down the School for the remainder of the day. All students under the age of eighteen are to remain on school grounds and await a parent or guardian to come retrieve them. Seniors who are eighteen must check in at the main office prior to leaving."

Mackenzie ran off.

Sofia looked up at Paige. "What did she do?"

Renee leaned closer on the other side.

Paige folded her arms and squinted at the swish of blonde hair racing to the office door. "I don't really know. I thought she might've poisoned her mother, but the ghost didn't seem pissed at her… more sad."

"Whatever it is, she's guilty as hell about something." Renee clucked her tongue. "No way do I believe she killed her mom though. Kenzie's not like that. She's a little shallow and manipulative, but she's no killer."

*A little?*

"Yeah." Sofia looked down, and started crying again.

Paige's cell phone rang.

"Hi, Mom."

"What's going on? I just got a recorded message from the school saying I had to come pick you and Melissa up."

"I'm fine. There was an accident. A teacher got killed. They won't let us leave without a parent." Paige turned away from her friends and sniffled, trembling as she whispered, "He was right in front of me, Mom."

"Paaaaay!" Melissa ran over and jumped on her, giggling. "We got the day off!"

"Oh, God. Okay. I'm on my way."

"Thanks, Mom."

Paige kept an arm around Melissa's back, tolerating the excited bouncing of a child who had no idea why they had the day off. Renee sat on the lawn and attempted to call home. Sofia's cell phone went off. She said 'yes' and 'okay' a few times before hanging up. Paige watched the street, waiting for Mom's blue Suburban to arrive.

Cole walked out of the crowd some hundred-and-fifty yards to the left and jogged toward the office doors. Mackenzie, most of the way across the lot, glanced toward him and smiled. Not watching where she was going, she collided with the broadside of a huge ancient convertible with the top down. Her runway-model body flipped up and over the door, dumping her headfirst into the back seat, legs in the air.

Ripples of laughter came from the crowd. Cole went right past her, attention focused on Emily as she bounced down the steps from the school office. Mackenzie popped up looking disoriented, her hair a tangled mess. As soon as she saw Emily and Cole embrace, she shuddered with palpable anger.

Relief at seeing Emily alive and well almost took Paige's legs out from under her.

Mackenzie lost her balance climbing out of the car and wiped out on the parking lot. Emily ran to her, reaching as if to help her up, but Mackenzie crawled away and stood on her own. Emily looked bewildered. Cole came up behind her and put a hand on her shoulder. She gestured at the departing blonde. Emily's 'what did I do?' expression left an uneasy feeling in Paige's stomach. He shook his head and waved at Emily as if saying 'ignore that girl,' then guided her into a kiss with a finger on her chin.

"What's wrong now?" asked Renee.

"Emily... she's okay." Paige pointed.

"Why wouldn't she be?" asked Sofia.

Paige stood behind Melissa and rested her hands on the girl's shoulders. She made a 'don't wanna say it out loud' face and indicated her sister with a nod. "Umm. Love spell with a sharpened point."

Renee and Sofia both looked horrified.

A black Cadillac pulled in and stopped near the grade school.

"Gotta go." Sofia ran down the sloping grassy field, across the lot, and up to the Caddy.

A man and a woman in their mid-thirties got out and met her with hugs. The woman looked like Sofia's twin sister aged up twenty years. Her father's eyes lurked under an overhang of thick, black curls. Both parents' clothes would've been appropriate for a funeral or wake. Her father appeared confused when Sofia burst into tears as soon as she reached them, and her mother seemed to inherit her daughter's mood and cried along with her. They spent a few minutes holding and doting over her before guiding her into the back seat.

Renee scowled.

Paige pushed her. "Hey. Don't be jealous."

"I know." Renee hung her head. "Ain't her fault my dad's an ass."

"Come over whenever, you can borrow mine." Paige winked. She looked at the sky. "I mean that in a playful sense. That was not an amendment."

"You sound like a witch's advocate." Renee smirked. "What do you think this is? Law?"

Paige closed her eyes. Mr. Ruiz's gurgle replayed in her thoughts. "No. If it was, we'd all be in deep shit."

"Ooh." Melissa poked her. "You said a bad."

"Yeah." Paige thought back to her fist holding the white cord during the ritual. "I said a real bad."

# 22

# UNBURDENED

Tuesday October 20 - 11:20 a.m.

Quiet pervaded the waiting area in the guidance office. Paige bundled her jacket in her lap and fussed with her lacy black skirt. It hadn't occurred to her that morning—or maybe she didn't care—that the violet and black corset baring her shoulders might violate dress code. She spent a moment picking dryer fuzzies from her black tights while debating if she should take the choker off before she spoke to the counselor.

Paige used her dark phone screen as a mirror, making sure her eyeshadow hadn't run. For the first three periods, she couldn't get the image of Mr. Ruiz's face out of her mind. At least she hadn't suffered another nightmare. Melissa asked to share the bed again last night, and Paige had spent most of the night clinging to her like a doll. *She didn't seem freaked enough for a bad dream. Maybe she thought I was the one who needed comforting?*

"Miss. Thomas?" asked a female voice on the deeper side.

She looked up at a dark-skinned woman in a grey skirt suit, her hair in a bun.

"Paige?" The woman tilted her head.

"Yeah." She uncrossed her legs. "I'm only here 'cause they said I had to come."

"Well, I promise I don't bite. You don't have to tell me anything you don't feel comfortable with." The woman gestured at a hallway.

Paige stood, and followed the counselor to an office. She slumped in a cushioned metal seat with rubber armrests facing a tidy desk. She kept her head down as the woman closed the door and walked around to her seat.

"I'm Trudy Jones. You're welcome to call me Trudy if you like. Miss. Jones if you prefer the formality."

"'Kay."

"Is there anything you'd like to get off your chest? I can tell you're carrying some extra weight on your shoulders."

"Why? You think everyone who dresses like this and wears black lipstick is a head case?"

Trudy smiled. "No, Paige. It's all over your face—pun not intended. I'm only here to help if you want it."

"I'm not wearing white face paint." She grumbled. "I *am* this pale. Then why did they *make* me talk to you."

"According to your file, you didn't leave the room with the rest of the class. Brian... Umm, the physics teacher, Mr. Lane, said he found you staring into space like you were in shock."

"First time seeing a dead person up close." Paige flicked the zipper dangling from the corner of her jacket. "I liked Mr. Ruiz. He was a great teacher... and Santana's father. Mr. Pritchard is so damn boring. Hollis is okay, but she's like spacy as hell. Sometimes she'll spend twenty minutes with one student helping them with their brush strokes... other times she rambles on like some little old woman with dementia, talking to no one at all while we're all painting."

Trudy typed on her computer. "What is she talking about?"

"Art stuff. Like how light defines shape. She's on topic in a general sense, but she just keeps going and switching at random."

"I see. You'd say that the accident was uncharacteristic of Mr. Ruiz?"

Paige stared at her boots. Guilt kept her voice hidden.

"Miss. Thomas?"

"Yeah. He was always so safety conscious."

"I understand you suffered a personal loss not too long ago. Do you want to talk about it?"

"I dunno." Paige sniffled.

Trudy leaned forward, lowering her voice to a soothing tone. "You can talk to me, Paige. With certain exceptions, anything you tell me I have to keep confidential."

"Like a doctor?" Paige looked up. "Exceptions?"

"If I become concerned a student presents an imminent threat to another person, they admit to certain crimes, or tell me about sexual abuse, I'm required to report about it."

"Okay." *I wonder if summoning demons is on that list of 'certain crimes.'* She held her gut.

Trudy laced her fingers together. "You don't have to answer these next few questions if you don't want to. Your answers will stay in this room for these. Are you experimenting with drugs, do you drink alcohol, and are you sexually active?"

"Wow, blunt much?" Paige fidgeted. "Haven't tried drugs. I drank myself sick *once* back home like a year ago. Now I can't even look at beer without wanting to chuck, and does taking it in the butt from fate count as being sexually active?"

"From fate?" Trudy typed a single letter at a time, trying to cock an eyebrow at her while recording notes.

"Bad luck. Feels like I ruin everything around me. Some guy almost runs me over, Jared robs a bank while I'm right there and I get to watch my Dad shoot him."

The counselor seemed to mull, tapping her fingers on the desk. "You don't feel responsible for what's going on around the school, do you?"

"Uhh." *I gotta say something or I'm gonna spill it all and get put away.* "My older sister died last year. A drunk driver hit her."

"I see. How did you feel about that?"

Paige lifted her head and glared through her bangs. "How the hell do you *think* I feel about that?"

"I'm sorry." Trudy cringed. "I didn't mean to imply anything. I'm trying to get you to explore your emotions."

Paige picked her nails. "I didn't have friends. I was that annoying kid sister who followed her around everywhere. I couldn't stand not being with her. We were like inseparable. She always made me feel better whenever I got teased. No matter how annoying and clingy I got, she never yelled at me or seemed like it bothered her." *Yeah, I'm a bitch.* The thought of how she'd been with Melissa lodged a lump in her throat.

"What would someone tease you for?"

"In like third grade, I..." *Whoa, slow down girl. You can't tell her about Mrs. Tibbett's ghost.* "Had an imaginary friend. I told people she was this old lady who died on the school grounds in like the 1820s."

"A little dark, but why would that get people to make fun of you?"

Paige looked to the side and smirked. "I was still talking to her in seventh grade."

"Oh. Well, that's not completely unheard of for students with social anxiety." Trudy read something on her screen. "Your transcripts are pretty clean except for a couple of fights during your freshman year, and a dip in your grades. Do you want to talk about what happened?"

"Take a wild guess."

"Paige, I'm—"

"Only trying to help, yeah..." She huffed. "My sister moved out to go to

Penn State. I was angry and not dealing. I told my parents I was gonna stop doing anything at school until they made her come home." Tingles pricked at the corners of her eyes. "A couple days after I actually did it, Amber called and begged me not to screw up my academic career."

"Go on."

"I did my work, but I guess I took it out on my little sister." Paige's face twisted sour, a mixture of anger and guilt directed inward. "The way I was with Amber, Melissa's up my ass the same way all the time. I used to scream at her, physically throw her out of my room... slam the door in her face."

"Why do you think you were so hostile to her?"

"Melissa is like *super* girly. Pink everything." Paige stuck her tongue out. "Loves mermaids, dolls, unicorns, faeries... Mom always wanted a girly-girl, and neither Amber nor I were anything like that. Amber was closer than me though. I guess I was jealous how Mom ignored me and Mel could get away with anything she wanted."

Trudy tapped a few more keys. "You're using past tense. Did something change?"

"Yeah. I thought about how I'd feel if Amber had treated me like that. Mel's on me worse than I was with Amb. She's like... *so* needy. Hates being alone. It's not her fault Mom ignored me. I... I'm like really worried about her now, ya know?" Paige stopped slouching and sat up. "She's so innocent. She doesn't know..."

"You want to protect her now."

Paige nodded. "Yeah."

"Do you think witnessing the accident with Mr. Ruiz brought you back to how you felt when you lost your sister?"

"No." Paige slumped forward, elbows on her knees. Her voice warped with emotion. "Don't make me cry. It took me like an hour to blend purple and black eye shadow."

"Anything you want to say, go ahead. If you want to change the subject. Talk about whatever's on your mind."

*Anything that won't get me a padded cell.* "I thought about killing myself after Amber died."

Trudy fumbled her mug. Streams of light brown dripped over blue porcelain. "Go on."

"A couple months after the accident. Mom didn't pay any attention to me at all. She spent all her time on Mel, and I felt like a ghost. Amber's death hit Dad as hard as me, but he shut down. I felt more and more alone and didn't care about anything. All I wanted was to be with Amber again."

"I can see how feeling invisible made you look for a way out, a way to be noticed. Do you still think about hurting yourself?"

Paige made eye contact. "No. I had a, uhh, dream that Amber came back to tell me not to do it. She said there's two kinds of people who contemplate suicide. Some are calling out for help. That wasn't me. I wanted dead. One night, Dad left his duty weapon out. I took it to my room and sat there staring at it for like an hour." *And Amber's ghost appeared.* "I, uhh, guess I fell asleep, 'cause I dreamed Amber was there and screaming at me, 'don't you dare do it.'"

Trudy moved around the desk and took the seat next to her, offering a hand. "I don't think you really wanted to end it all. You were hurt deeply, and trying to deal with things no child your age should ever have to deal with."

Paige squirmed. *I did stare at that thing for like... ever.* "Yeah maybe... I dunno."

"They say dreams are the subconscious talking to us. Inside, you knew your sister would never have wanted you to hurt yourself." Trudy's chocolate-brown eyes fixed on hers, tiny glowing dots from reflected overhead lights wobbled with the intensity of her stare.

"Uhh." Paige wanted to look away, crawl under the desk, or teleport home and sit in that little space between her bed and the wall. For some reason, she couldn't bring herself to retreat from this woman's searching gaze. "I'm not in that headspace anymore. Amber told me it would destroy Mel... the way her death destroyed me... and Mel's only eight, so she wouldn't even handle it as well." She let Trudy hold her hand. "I definitely don't want to die now. If anything, what happened to Mr. Ruiz made me feel worse for even thinking about it."

"How is your sister coping with everything? Amber's accident, Mr. Ruiz?"

"She's home sick today. Nightmares have been keeping her up late, and I think she's maybe getting a cold now too. She threw up twice this morning, so Mom kept her home."

"Do you think she's having a delayed reaction to the accident?"

"Nah. She doesn't really know what happened, just a teacher got hurt." Paige ground her boot soles together. "She got it out of her system in the first couple of months when I was in full zombie mode. I didn't really notice it then. Couple of my new friends have been reading a bunch of stuff about occultism and she might've found one of the books." She let off a half-hearted chuckle while staring at the floor. "It's fake... but I guess a little kid believed it enough to get nightmares."

"There's rumors going around the school... even in the elementary side." Trudy tapped her foot. "All the injuries lately. The deaths of those three seniors..."

"They weren't seniors." Paige surprised herself with the coldness in her voice. "They dropped out. One of them assaulted my friend, and the other two threatened to 'get me back' because my Dad shot the one who robbed the bank."

"You don't seem very concerned that three young men died. Are you pleased what happened to them?"

Paige took in a breath, held it, and let it out. "No. I wish none of it ever happened... but, they threatened to beat Melissa to death and force me to watch. I'm not happy that they died, but I like knowing I don't have to worry about them hurting us." She looked down. "Is that wrong?"

Trudy gasped. "I had no idea they threatened you like that. Did you report it?"

"No. I... wasn't sure if they were just being jerks."

"That could be." Trudy gave her hand a squeeze. "I'd like to talk with you again in a week or two."

"You're not gonna make them put me in a hospital or something, are you? I mean it. I'm not gonna hurt myself."

"I'm inclined to believe you." Trudy's smile filled Paige with warmth. "I'm not going to send you into the system, but I do have to put notes in your file about it. And I'd like you to come back so we can talk more, say once or twice a month."

Paige tensed.

"No one can read it without a court order aside from my immediate supervisor. I believe you." Trudy winked. "You came alive whenever you talked about your little sister, even under all that gloomy make up."

Paige chuckled. "I guess."

"I'm not sure those contacts are healthy."

*Ugh.* "They're not contacts. They *are* this color."

"I've never seen someone with violet eyes before." Trudy leaned in close. "Sorry for staring."

"My grandmom had them too."

Trudy returned to her chair and handed over a business card. "If you ever want to talk. You call me any time, day or night. Four in the morning if it's important. I'll sketch you in for Thursday week after next."

"Okay." Paige took the card and turned it over in her fingers. "I haven't been suicidal for at least six months, but thanks."

"No problem. You got a little sis to look out for, and I know you may not see it now, but your parents wouldn't know what to do with themselves if anything happened to you."

"Yeah." She slid the card into her backpack. "If I die, it's not gonna be suicide."

"What's that supposed to mean?" Trudy froze. "Are you involved in something dangerous?"

*Hah.* "Just all the crap going on..."

"Oh." She relaxed. "Don't let all those rumors get under your skin. There's no curse on this school."

*No curse, just an ancient demon running around.* Paige stood. "I don't believe in that stuff."

As she started to walk away, Trudy waved. "Wait." She scribbled something on a little yellow pad. "You'll need this to get excused for being late to your next class."

"Thanks." She took the guidance pass and walked out.

# 23

# COUNTERMAGIC

Tuesday October 20 - 2:17 p.m.

L eaves swirled around in mini cyclones, a skittering ballet across the road. More sky showed through the woods; the shedding trees no longer shrouded the street into a tunnel. Paige hurried along, battling back the worry Melissa's sickness might be more than a simple cold. What if her part of the spell attempted to shock Dad out of his funk by scaring him with the near-death of his remaining kids? She gazed up at the cloudless sky, squinting into the wind. As much mental effort as she could summon went into the *want* to protect Melissa.

"Leave her alone. Take me."

She let her head hang and trudged on. At the rushing noise of an approaching car, nerves pushed her off the street. Paige hid behind a tree until the Toyota went by. A few seconds after she climbed back onto the road, thoughts of Emily popped at random into her head. With each step she took, the urgency built. Her brain refused to let go of the other girl. She *had* to talk to her.

Paige took out her phone and stared at it, feeling like an idiot. Emily had never traded phone numbers with her, and she didn't even have it programmed in. She couldn't remember what her last name was, or if she'd ever even heard it. The 'slide to unlock' bar flashed at her, calling her, drawing her in. She traced one fingertip over it. Icons appeared. Her hand moved as if on its own, poking the green-and-white call icon before dialing a number on autopilot.

Ringing.

"Hello?" asked Emily.

She held the phone to her head. "Uhh, hi. It's Paige."

"Oh, Hi!" A smile sounded in her voice. "What's up?"

"I… had to talk to you about—"

Emily shrieked. She let out a series of yelps and rapid 'ohmigods' before she got quiet except for rapid breathing.

"Emily? Emily! Are you okay?"

A faint buzzing crackle came over the phone.

Paige broke out in a sweat. "Emily? Please say something. Are you okay?"

"P-Paige… I'm"—she gasped for air—"okay. Oh gosh. That almost hit me."

"What?" Paige sank to a squat on the side of the road. "What happened?"

Emily gasped. "A power line fell and almost landed right on me." She muffled the phone and said something like 'I'm okay' to someone nearby.

"No…" Paige pressed a hand into her stomach and bit back the urge to throw up.

"Oh my God!" screamed Emily.

Paige's head snapped up. *No… now what?* "Em?"

"If you didn't call me right at that second… I stopped to fish my phone out." Shivering affected her voice. "I would've walked right into it. Wow… what are the odds you'd have called me right at that second?"

"Remember what I said at the crash? I just got this intense feeling of worry about you and *had* to call. I don't even know how I dialed your number. You never gave it to me. I just started typing numbers."

"I… Y-you were right." Emily sobbed. "I think someone's watching me. I… gotta go."

The line dropped.

"Damn, Kenz, what are you doing?"

Paige tried to call Mackenzie, but it went straight to voicemail. She didn't want to bother Santana, and Renee didn't answer. Sofia's voicemail prompt said she was at the hospital visiting someone and couldn't use her phone.

Worry drove her to a run. She raced up the driveway of her house and rushed inside. Melissa lay on the couch, only her head visible from a cocoon of pink blankets. Paige dropped her backpack by the door and walked over. Melissa grinned at her.

"Hey, Mel. Feeling better?"

"Yeah." She frowned. "Mom says I gotta go to school tomorrow."

Paige ruffled her hair. "Good. I was worried."

Melissa sat up. "Did the monster make me sick?"

"I don't know. I have no idea what's going on anymore." Paige sniffled. "I don't know if we can stop it."

"Don't cry." Melissa crawled into her lap and hugged her, no hesitation at all in touching her. "Amber said you didn't do it."

"What?" Paige held her by the shoulders. "Amber?"

"Yep." Melissa nodded. "She said you asked for something nice so the monster can't take your wish and turn it black." Green eyes gleamed with worry. "Are all your friends nice?"

"Not exactly." Relief flooded Paige, but guilt chased it away in seconds. *So what if it wasn't my wish, I still took part in the whole thing. If it wasn't for me, they wouldn't have had enough people...* She fidgeted with her skirt once Melissa slid off her lap. "Where's Mom?"

"Working on necklaces and stuff." Melissa stuck her foot almost up Paige's nose to show off a wood-bead anklet. "She made this for me today."

Paige grabbed the leg and tickled Melissa's sole until she squealed for mercy. Mom came running in at the screaming, but smiled once she took in the scene. Winded, Melissa flopped across her lap and stretched.

"Pay... movie or *Mermaid's Journey?*"

"You pick." Paige tickled her belly through the thin nightgown.

Melissa curled up in a ball, giggling. "Mermaids!"

"Are you in for dinner tonight?" asked Mom.

"Yeah." Paige's sense of warmth and safety drained as soon as she glanced at the front bay window. "I'm not going anywhere." She hesitated a second before looking up at Mom. "You uhh, want any help cooking?"

Mom smiled at them both. "I think Melissa needs you right now... I'll try to make something worthy of White Castle."

Paige grimaced. "I deserved that."

Her mother lingered in the archway behind the couch for a little while before departing with a contented look.

*Whoa. I didn't ask for anything to affect Mom... That's real.* She squeezed Melissa for comfort like an overgrown ragdoll. Having her mother 'back' only made it feel more likely she'd lose it all.

Tuesday October 20 - 11:02 p.m.

PAIGE STOOD BY HER BEDROOM CLOSET, SMIRKING AT HER REFLECTION IN THE long mirror attached to the door. The off-white frilly nightgown was *so* not her style, but Melissa insisted she wear it at least once. *I feel like an enormous eight-year-old.* She'd spent the rest of the evening after dinner in it, hanging out with Melissa and helping a pair of mermaid twins save the oceanic kingdom. She didn't bother changing to do homework. It might've been girly and hideous, but it *was* comfortable.

With a final sigh at feeling ridiculous, she headed to her desk. Perched on her chair, she grabbed the bottle of black nail polish and twisted the cap off. The instant the brush cleared the top, spider legs poked out of the little opening. Paige jumped hard enough to knock the chair over backward and tumble to the floor. When she scrambled upright, the bottle looked normal. She stared at it for a few minutes before risking touching it. Nothing moved or felt strange. She redid her nails and spent the next few minutes waving her hands and feet around to dry them.

*Click.*

Paige jumped.

*Click.*

The noise seemed to come from her window.

*Click.* A small pebble glinted in the moonlight as it bounced away.

Paige almost clenched her hands into fists but stopped herself. Tacky nail polish plus fists equaled *argh!* She crept over to the window. *Okay, WTF. I don't have a boyfriend.*

She stood on tiptoe to peer over the windowsill a 'safe distance' back from the glass. Another rock, and three steps later, the shadowy figure of Emily in her backyard emerged from the dark. Paige relaxed. She opened the window and peered out. The auburn-haired girl shivered and cried, her face covered by streams of ruined makeup.

"Emily?" whispered Paige. "What are you doing in my yard?"

"Can I come in?" Emily bounced in place.

"Okay." Paige started to walk out, but turned around. "Are you real?"

"Huh?" Emily sniffled. "What do you mean?"

"Weird crap is going on. Are you a spirit messing with me and trying to trick me into opening the door, or are you really Emily Something."

"Weiss." Emily sniffled. "It's really me."

Paige scrutinized her, but no sense of inexplicable foreboding came on. "Okay."

She hurried down the steps, careful not to make noise. A quick peek through one of the narrow windows flanking the front door confirmed Emily Weiss—and not a shadowy demon—seemed to be on the porch. Again, no sudden feelings warned her off or churned her stomach. Paige opened the door.

Emily ran in and grabbed her in a hug, lost right away to a sobbing fit.

Paige did her best to hold on, shivering at the press of cold jacket on her nightgown. She nudged the door closed with her foot and broke the grip long enough to flip the deadbolt and main lock.

"Shh. My parents and sister are sleeping."

"Sorry." Emily covered her mouth.

She led the girl upstairs to her room, and closed the door. Emily took off her jacket, exposing a pale-grey Penn State sweatshirt and blue jeans. Paige gawked.

"W-what?" Emily looked behind her. "What's wrong?"

"Uhh. You're kinda dressed exactly like my other sister was when she died. Same sweatshirt and jeans."

"Oh." Emily sniffled. "I'm sorry. I didn't know."

"You had no way to. Not your fault. I haven't seen her in a while and I'm worried."

Emily blinked a few times. "Uhh, what? Didn't you say she was dead?"

Paige dug her thumbnail into her palm. *Crap.* "Umm, yeah. Go ahead call me crazy. Her ghost is here."

"Really?" Emily looked around. "Right now?"

"No, that's the problem." Paige sat on the edge of the bed. "I haven't seen her in a couple of days. She's been hiding or something since all this stuff started happening."

"All what stuff?" Emily flopped on the corner of the bed. "Sorry for showing up this late… Things were getting odd."

"Odd?" Paige felt almost as embarrassed at being seen in such a girly nightie as if she'd streaked the school.

"Cole came over and he was acting all kinds of weird. He's always been so charming and sweet. Tonight he was like… I dunno. Like really angry with something. He didn't seem upset with me, but everything I said only made him angrier. He couldn't tell me what put him in a bad mood, but he had this look in his eyes like he wanted to hit someone. I was afraid if I did the slightest wrong thing he'd lash out at me. He looked like Cole. He even sounded like Cole, but that wasn't him." Emily cried into her hands. "What's happening?"

"Uhh." Paige couldn't bear to look into such frightened, innocent eyes, and stared down at her toes vanishing into the carpet. "You wouldn't believe me if I told you the truth."

"I didn't believe you about the car… but that wire snapped today. You knew to call me, didn't you?" Emily grasped the blankets; her knuckles whitened. "Please tell me."

"Something made me think of you. I don't want you to get hurt. It's not right."

"*What's* not right?" Emily shook the bed. "Please. I'm really scared."

"Okay." Paige looked up. "I'll understand if you get pissed at me, but I had no idea."

Emily sniffled.

Paige explained about the ritual, how she'd gone there thinking it was silly and nothing would happen. "… Santana wanted money so her family didn't have to fight and struggle so much. Renee wanted her father to come home. Sofia asked it to make the bullies stop. I wanted my Dad to heal from Amber's loss." She hesitated, quiet for a little while, scooting her feet back and forth. "Mackenzie, umm." She sighed. "She asked the spirits to make Cole love her."

Emily looked horrified.

"When we were leaving, I felt this presence in the woods watching us."

"No way." Emily glared. "He'd never love her. She's so selfish and superficial. I've only ever tried to be nice to her, but she's as plastic as Barbie. Not like surgery, I mean fake."

Paige nodded. "Yeah. I fell for it too. Whatever we set loose isn't Witch Hazel. It's some next-level demonic dark crap. It's giving us what we asked for, but taking the worst way there. I think that shadow entity is trying to kill you so Kenz can jump in and be all comforting for Cole and then he'll fall in love with her. That car..."

Emily gurgled, turning green.

"I, umm, still don't know if she meant it to happen *that* way, or if she's as freaked out as I am about this. None of us knew what we were messing with." *She didn't seem happy when Emily turned up at the evacuation.*

"Oh, no. That's why all those kids are getting hurt... that one poor girl they always tease is mad at them."

"At first. She's right next to me in the 'oh shit' boat now." Paige shuffled her feet back and forth on the rug faster to warm them.

"Oh, God. Mr. Ruiz." Emily wept. "No wonder Santana had to be sedated. She couldn't have wanted that."

"No, she didn't."

*Wham.*

Paige gasped and looked up.

"What was that?"

"It wasn't an asteroid landing on the roof." Paige gulped. "The thing followed you here."

Emily whined. "Please do something."

Paige's mind raced. "Hang on."

She leapt into her desk chair and flipped open her laptop. A few minutes later, she skimmed over several new age websites devoted to Wicca and witchcraft. *Protection spells... cleansing... There!*

"Be right back."

Emily nodded.

Paige hiked up her nightgown and ran downstairs to the dining room where she rummaged Mom's stock of craft supplies. All the windows on the ground floor looked *too* black. Her hands trembled, but she fought the building fear clawing at her soul. Something outside stared malevolence into the house. The room seemed to shrink, the walls twisting and pushing inward. *It's pissed.* She found an agate arrowhead in one of Mom's plastic boxes and grabbed a length of leather cord.

The kitchen floor numbed her feet on contact, far too cold to be natural. She skidded to a stop with a grip on the kitchen counter, and sifted through the utility drawer.

*Eeeeeeekrrrrr.*

Paige cringed. Black talons as long as table knives scraped across the window over the sink. Muscles in her back seized at the grating screech. Her body went rigid, and she locked eyes with two pale white spots in the infinite nothingness outside where a yard should've been.

She clutched the counter, not trusting her legs to hold her up.

"S-spirit. I respect you and I know we called you into our world. There is nothing for you here. Please go back whence you came."

A hand grasped her ankle and jerked her feet out from under her.

Paige screamed and hit the floor on her chest. She flipped over and scooted back against the cabinets, alone in the kitchen. She started and whipped her head to the left at a scratch on the back door. Her breathing seemed as loud as a roaring bonfire.

"What am I doing? Move." She pulled herself up by the counter. "Candles... white... where?" Pot holders, rubber jar-openers, a mountain of old twist ties, and a few small screwdrivers went flying as she dug among junk in the drawer. At the bottom, she found a pack of six plain candles and matches. On the way out of the kitchen, she snagged a small bowl, salt, and the jar of ground sage. "Best I got."

Paige ran upstairs with her supplies, feeling like a little girl afraid of the dark. Dining room, living room, and hallway flooded with a malicious presence. Whispering caressed the silence behind her, but she didn't stop to try and decipher it. The stairs thumped under her rapid ascent, and she had to catch herself to keep from slamming her bedroom door.

Emily remained seated as she'd been before Paige ran out. "Did you hear that?"

"Candles on the rug is a really bad idea." She cleared textbooks from her desk and scooted the laptop as far to the left as she could. "Hop up here and take your sweatshirt off."

"What did you do to your leg?" Emily removed the sweatshirt, revealing a white tee with a yellow smiley face.

Paige looked down at a bruised handprint around her right ankle. The sight chilled her mute.

"Or do I not want to know."

"Probably not." Paige set a candle at each corner of the desk and sprinkled a line of salt around Emily once she sat cross-legged in the middle. "I'm gonna draw a little symbol on your chest, okay?"

"Is it gonna help?"

Paige shrugged. "No idea. According to this website, it's a ward against malignant spirits. This too." She held up the agate and the leather band. "Here, put these together into an amulet."

While Emily wound the cord around the stone chip, Paige lit the candles. She dumped some of the sage in the bowl and tried to set it on fire. When it didn't catch, she grabbed incense from on top of her dresser and nestled it into the pile of herb before lighting it.

"That'll have to work."

"Here." Emily handed over a passable amulet.

Paige pulled down the neck of the smiley shirt, and sharpie-markered the symbol from the Wicca website above Emily's breastbone. She scratched the same mark (more or less) on the agate with her house key, dropped it in Emily's hands, and closed her fingers over it. "Hold that."

"Did you read all this or are you making it up?"

"Yes."

Emily looked worried. "Better than nothing, right? Fight stuff that shouldn't exist with stuff that shouldn't work?"

Paige snickered. "Yeah, let's hope." She held her arms out and concentrated on the ring of salt, envisioning it as a tangible barrier between the realm of spirits and the realm of the living. *Desire* for it to be so gathered in her heart. "I surround Emily Weiss, and myself, with this shield of protective energy. I call on Gaea and Cernunnos for protection."

Emily squeezed her hands tight around the amulet.

"I freely accept and acknowledge that we drew forth the energies of the Elements and the Spirits. I know you are here at our request. I humbly ask that you do no harm to this innocent before you. You may not harm this girl to sate the selfish desires of another."

*Wham.*

The entire house shook.

"Whatever you're doing, keep doing it." Emily swallowed.

"Spirits we call, from the night. Breach not this wall, and do what is right." Paige grimaced, feeling lame as soon as she said it. "This protection I charge you grant. Do this, I ask of thee. To this girl bring no harm, so mote it be."

The incense cone flared up and consumed itself in seconds while the four candle flames at the desk corners pulled inward, all pointing at Emily.

She tried to look down at herself and squirmed. "I swear that thing you drew feels like it's getting warm."

Paige raised her hand and spun counterclockwise. "Thank you spirits for granting me your boon. Thank you for visiting us in our time of need."

After another moment concentrating on her desire to stop the entity from hurting Emily, she puffed out the candles.

"Is that it?" asked Emily.

"Put the amulet on now. I'm not sure if it'll work, but—" Paige stalled when she caught sight of the window. Stars and moonlight shimmered through the crone-fingers of naked branches. The infinite blackness had receded. "I... wow."

Emily draped the leather cord over her head and hopped down from the desk. "Hey, I'm feeling a little freaked out. Mind if I sleep over?"

"My sister has been having nightmares lately, she might run in here and climb in my bed."

"That's cool. Floor's fine."

Paige sat on the mattress edge and rubbed the bruise on her ankle. "Ow. The bed's big enough if it's not too, uhh, weird."

"Is it weird to you?" Emily pulled her sneakers off. "I don't want to impose."

*You've almost been killed by dark magic twice and you're worried about making me feel awkward? Geez, you* are *too nice.* Paige slid under the blankets. "I can't make you sleep on the floor." *That's where the spiders are.*

"Okay." Emily shut off the light and crawled in next to her.

Her room faded to black and white. Wavering branches danced in a patch of moonlight on the wall. Every owl noise or snap in the underbrush frayed her nerves a little more. Paige lay motionless, staring at the featureless slab of pale grey overhead. She tried not to think about the arachnid swarm, or about the possible backblast of interfering with the spell. Mackenzie had to be lying because she still wanted Cole. Could a ritual done by one girl overpower something they cast as a group?

*I wonder how long I'm going to stare at the ceiling tonight.*

## THE LAST GIRL

Wednesday October 21 - 2:06 p.m.

P aige squinted into a stiff breeze whipping between the school
buildings. The echoes of shouting grade-schoolers thrilled to be free
faded into the distance as they ran home or scrambled into buses. She
waited at the end of the L-shaped sidewalk connecting the high school's main
entrance to the parking lot. None of her friends had shown up today. She'd
sat alone before the first bell, ate lunch with Emily, and hadn't seen any of
them in the hall. No big surprise why Santana was out, but she worried about
Sofia. Renee too... she'd been afraid of her father last time they spoke.
Mackenzie's absence triggered suspicion more than concern.

She brushed windblown leaves from her black jeans and jacket, wondering
what Emily had in mind. The 'plz wait 4 me after school' text didn't explain
much, and the girl hadn't replied to anything she'd sent after.

"Come on..." Paige watched the elementary school entrance, waiting for
Melissa.

A metal *squeak* behind her announced the aluminum framed doors
opening. Emily emerged, dragging Cole by the arm. She gave him a worried
look, which seemed to erode his hesitation. The couple walked up to her and
stopped.

"Hey," said Emily. "This is Paige."

"Hi." Cole flashed a far more polite smile than he'd given Mackenzie.
"What's up? Emily said you wanted to tell me something?"

"I do?" Paige blinked. "Em? 'Splain."

Emily blushed. "Sorry, that was a little stretch. I didn't want to say anything without Paige here to back me up so you don't think I'm crazy."

"Welcome to the club." Paige chuckled, and glanced again at the elementary school. A smear of ginger hair caught her eye, but *he* looked like a fifth grader.

"Okay…" Emily took a deep breath, and gave Cole the cliff notes version of the spell trying to kill her so he'd love Mackenzie.

Cole hung his head. "You don't have anything to worry about, Em. I'm not sure what's got you so anxious all of a sudden, but I am *not* cheating on you."

"Do you remember yesterday afternoon?" asked Emily.

"A bit. We hung out at your place for a while, but you wanted to go to sleep early. Said you had a test or something, right?"

"You were acting all kinds of strange. I said that at nine, and you stayed outside my house until like ten-thirty, just staring at my window."

He shot her a suspicious look. "I don't remember that."

"Maybe it wasn't really him?" Paige puffed her cheeks up and let the air seep between her lips. "Could've been a dream or an apparition, or maybe it got into him like it got into Jared and made him rob the bank."

"Whoa." Cole raised a hand at Paige. "You're saying that scumbag was possessed or something?"

"More or less." Paige shivered. Her jacket seemed to have lost its wind-resistant qualities. The icy breeze bored through it to her skin. Another look at the grade school made her feel worse. "Uhh. I think I need to go."

"Em." Cole grabbed Emily's hands. "I love *you* and only you. I swear that if anything happens to you, I won't want any other girl. I wouldn't take Mackenzie Walsh if she was the last living girl on the planet. Sure, she's got a perfect body, but that's all she is. Inside, she's rotten. Selfish, spoiled, entitled." He drew Emily's hand up to his lips and kissed her knuckles. "You've got the whole package. You're beautiful inside and outside."

Emily hugged him, and sniffled into his chest. "Cole, please stay safe."

"How?" he asked.

Paige couldn't peel her eyes off the grade school. "Something's wrong. Uhh… how? You should look out for circumstantial dangers. Something that the spirit can nudge just a little to cause an accident. You see *Final Destination*?" Cole's eyes widened, but Paige ignored him and took a step for the school. "I really gotta go."

"Are you all right? You look white as a sheet." Emily grasped Paige's arm.

"That's normal for me." Paige flung Emily's hand away. "Sorry. Gotta go."

Her cell phone rang. Dad's ringtone.

Paige collapsed to her knees under a mountain of dread. She extracted the phone from her jacket and stared at it. Tears splattered on the touch screen, magnifying it to individual pixels. One finger swiped to answer, and her voice came out as a raspy croak.

"Hello? Dad?"

"Where are you?"

"I'm still at school."

"Is Melissa with you?" He cleared his throat.

Paige clutched her chest, face contorting as she cried harder. "No. I'm waiting for her."

"Damn. When was the last time you saw her?"

"Last night when she went to bed," wailed Paige like a three-year-old. "I slept right through my alarm." She sobbed. "She was gone when I woke up. Mom was too. I thought Mom drove her in so I just went to school alone."

"I want you home right now. The school called and asked why she never showed up today."

"Okay." Paige let her hand fall onto her thigh, and bawled.

Emily knelt beside her, arm around her shoulders. "What happened?"

Paige looked at her. "Melissa's gone." She sniveled and sobbed. "I gotta go home."

Cole took her arm. "You're not gonna walk like that. Come on."

The world seemed to glide by on its own as Emily and Cole pulled her to her feet and held her arms on the trip to an eight-or-nine-year-old Chevy Blazer. One of them pulled the door open. Cole picked her up and set her on the seat. Emily ran around and got in the back with her, holding her hand.

Paige fought the nagging feeling she'd saved Emily at the cost of her little sister's life. A trade? Or had the dark thing been vengeful. *I told it to take me and leave her alone!* Her mind ran away with scenario after scenario of demon-twisted fate. A serial killer chooses a different exit off the highway and winds up in her town. Melissa sleepwalks outside in the middle of the night and falls in a well or gets mauled by bears.

She sniffled back tears. *It's not as intense as when Amber died.*

"Positive thoughts," said Emily. "You get flashes right? What are you feeling?"

"Yeah." She hid her face in her hands for a few seconds before raking her fingers up and over her head through her hair. "Felt worse when that car was coming for us."

"Left up here?" asked Cole.

"Yeah," said the girls at the same time.

"That one." Paige pointed at her house.

Cole pulled up to the driveway and threw the truck in park.

"I'm okay." Paige opened the door. "You don't have to carry me. Thanks for the ride. You guys are awesome."

Emily grasped the amulet under her sweatshirt. "Thank you..." She gazed down, a hint of worry in her expression. "Go get her."

Paige stopped in her tracks at Amber's voice coming out of Emily. "What?"

"I said thank you." Emily tilted her head.

"You're uhh, welcome." Paige nodded at Cole. "Thanks."

Dad opened the front door. He looked scary-angry as well as terrified. She sprinted up the driveway, spraying rocks into the hubcaps of his car. He caught her at the door in an embrace teetering on painful, but she didn't make a sound. The Blazer drove off, pulling a U-turn to head back in the direction of downtown, toward Emily's street. She clung to her father until the sound of Cole's engine faded away to silence.

"Daddy," she mumbled. "I'll find her."

He ushered her into the house and closed the door. "I want you to stay inside until we know what's going on. This isn't your fault."

Her stomach felt like a block of stone. "Uhh." She bit her lip, but chickened out of saying anything more.

Dad stumbled over a few words, gave up, and pulled her into another hug.

Paige stared at the wall, sick with guilt. She felt like a murderer showing up at the funeral and getting hugged by the victim's parents. Mr. Ruiz, that poor screaming girl, the rest of Sofia's classmates, and even the two metalheads—all of it was her fault, at least in part. She held on to her father, unable to stand on her own. Todd and Peter weren't exactly model citizens, but the spell made them worse. They wouldn't have attacked her otherwise, the same way Jared wouldn't have robbed the bank, but he *had* tried to rape Renee... for that she didn't feel *too* bad about him, but the other two... Their deaths weren't justice.

And now it had Melissa.

# 25

# TOO LATE

Wednesday October 21 - 5:07 p.m.

Paige curled up on the living room sofa, holding the purple Xbox controller her little sister had used the day before. Mom whipped through the house like a dervish, calling Melissa's name over and over. The pain in her mother's voice raked down Paige's back with each repetition of the name, deepening the guilt. Dad's shoes clomped in the kitchen and the back door closed with a firm *thump.*

Mom cycled from calling her, to yelling 'come out right now. It's not funny' and finally to pitiful begging directed at no one in particular to 'give my baby back.' Paige cringed at the memory of all the faces Melissa had made whenever she'd screamed at her to 'go away' or 'get out of my room' or called her annoying, immature, 'twerp,' 'too girly' or any of a dozen taunting names. The simple act of not wanting to be around her little sister had elicited an expression as though Paige had ripped the head off one of her mermaid dolls right in front of her.

She hugged one of the maroon throw pillows to her chest and sniffled.

Dad walked up behind the couch and put a hand on her shoulder. "There's no sign of forced entry on either door or any of the ground floor windows, though the kitchen window had some animal scratches. Bear maybe. I couldn't find any footprints, but there was something strange."

"What?" Paige sat up, keeping the pillow in her lap.

"Some damage to the siding. All over, most of it too high to reach without a ladder... it looked like someone was throwing watermelons at our house."

"Or punching it." Paige shivered.

"Unless we got attacked by a drunk angel, or something else that could fly... There's nothing in the flowerbeds. That's soft dirt, hon. There'd be some kind of evidence."

Mom thundered down the stairs and walked in a circle through the living room as if she couldn't figure out where to go or what to do. Dad set his hands on Paige's shoulders and rubbed his thumbs up and down the back of her neck.

"She's gone," said Mom. "I checked all the closets. Under the beds and even on that little roof overhang."

"It doesn't look like anyone broke in. Did she go out?" Dad rushed over to the door and grabbed his State Police jacket and belt.

"You think our eight-year-old daughter ran away?" Mom scowled. "Are you serious? She hates being alone."

Dad took the Maglite off his belt and clicked it on for a second to test it. "That's not even close to what I said, Andrea. I'm going to walk around outside, see if I can find her."

"I thought Paige took her to school when she wasn't in her room. I haven't seen her all day." Mom whirled to face the couch. "How could you lose your sister?"

"I didn't!" Paige leapt up. "You were gone when I woke up. Both of you. The house was empty."

"Stop lying to me, Paige." Mom lunged and grabbed her arms. "I know your guilty look. What did you do?!"

"Nothing!" Paige screamed. "I overslept. I woke up at like twenty after seven."

"I was home then!" shouted Mom.

Paige pushed her away and backpedaled. "No you weren't!"

"Andrea!" Dad lunged forward, standing between them. "We don't even know anything happened yet. Maybe she went outside to play and got lost."

"Maybe she decided to walk to school alone since Paige couldn't be bothered to take her and someone grabbed her." Mom burst into tears.

"You're the one who's lying, Mom. These past couple days, acting like we're a family or some crap? Now I see... Melissa's the only one who matters, right?" Paige seethed. "I bet you wish it was me that got kidnapped instead."

Mom froze as if slapped. "You... you're jealous. What did you do?"

Paige sank to her knees, sobbing. "Nothing. I know I was a shit to her, but that's changed now."

"Easy for you to say."

"Andrea!" yelled Dad. "Will you back off? This is not Paige's fault."

*Yeah... it is.* Paige twisted around and slumped over the sofa cushion. She rested her head on crossed arms, crying. Mom was right about her guilty look, but not the reason for it.

"I was up and about at 5:45 this morning. I never left the house. What's she doing trying to say I wasn't here?"

Paige sniffled. "Mom?"

"What?" Mom yelled, red faced and seeming out of breath.

"When Amber died... uhh, I mean when I got through the worst parts of after, I realized how Melissa feels. I thought about how I'd have felt if Amber treated me like I treated Mel, and it killed me."

Mom kneaded her hands.

"I mean it. It's different for us now. I care more about her than I do myself."

Mom glanced at Dad, the floor, the wall. "I did notice you've been spending more time with her lately."

"Why didn't you drag me out of bed like you usually do?" Paige tried to keep her tone as non-accusatory as possible, and sat back on her heels. "As long as I've been going to school, you've *never* just let me sleep in on a school day. Not even once."

Mom pointed, mouth open.

"Did you see Paige leave for school if you were here?" asked Dad.

"Don't go throwing this at me, Drew." Mom backed up, staring at them both as though either one might whip out a gun and try to shoot her.

"Mom. Calm down. Please." Paige sniffled. "Why did you let me sleep in?"

"I... didn't. I guess I got absorbed in making those charm bracelets for Rhonda." Mom pulled at her hair, looking anywhere but at her family. "When I looked at the clock it was late. You and Mel were already gone. Sorry. I don't know why I suddenly wanted to blame you..."

*I ran through the dining room and I didn't see you. Damn spirit...* "I didn't see Mel upstairs and you didn't answer when I yelled, so I figured you drove her in. I skipped food and ran right out the door to school."

"She's gone. Someone's got our baby." Mom sank into the recliner, pulled her legs up, and sobbed.

Dad took a step toward Paige, but she waved him off.

"I'm okay. Mom needs you." She stood. "I'm... I gotta calm down. I'll be in my room."

Mom seemed out of it as Dad pulled her upright and held her. Paige lingered at the archway watching them embrace. Within seconds, Mom broke down and wept on his shoulder.

Paige trudged upstairs. She begged in her mind that the spell was only concealing Melissa the way it hid Mom from her that morning. *Maybe it'll let her go if Dad snaps out of it?* At the top of the stairs, she stopped with her hand on the wall for balance. She had asked for Dad to be free of his grief, but she was tired of being ignored. Had she *wanted* to be special to them instead of invisible? Did the spell pick up on that glimmer of desire like it latched on to Sofia's anger at the way she'd been treated? *No. I wanted Dad back. I didn't want to be an only child...*

Hand over her mouth, she stumbled down the hallway and went past her room to Melissa's. Pink walls and the fluffy white bed brought instant tears. She bumped a small desk, knocking over a bottle of 'pixie fart' nail polish on the way to the bed, and collapsed amid a bevy of stuffed animals. *Please let her come home. Please don't hurt my sister.* Cold washed down her back. *What if I'm wrong? What if the magic is twisting back on me for interfering?* Two steps later, she fell on the bed, her face buried in a comforter that still smelled like her sister.

Paige curled up and wailed as if she'd been the one to kill her.

Wednesday October 21 - 9:52 p.m.

HER GUILTY CRYING EVENTUALLY CALMED TO A SILENT, MOURNFUL STARE AT THE far wall and Melissa's two massive dollhouses. A flash of light caught her eye from the window. She sat up. The light flickered again.

Paige slid off the bed, pausing long enough to collect a couple plush mermaids back onto the pile from the floor. Another flash drew her up to the windowsill. Dad wandered the area around the house with his Maglite. A second State Police car and two local patrol units parked on the road in front.

*He thinks she's been kidnapped. I gotta tell him.* "Right. And then he'll have *no* kids left because I'll be in a padded cell."

An unsettling feeling that something watched her raised the hairs on the back of her neck. She retreated from the window in a slow turn, surveying the room. Unconscious fear of spiders had her on tiptoe three steps later, though nothing moved. An echoing giggle of a small girl seemed to come from far off at the end of a stone corridor.

"Melissa?" asked Paige. She peered at the darkness in the slatted doors of twin closets. "Mel?"

One after the next, she pulled the doors apart to reveal dozens of dresses, white, pink, peach, yellow. *Melissa hates pants.* The giggle happened again, from behind. Paige whirled.

"Mel?" Her heart sped up. "Melissa, please. If you're stuck somewhere, yell."

*It's too quiet in here.* Her eyes swiveled from left to right in a slow pan. One of the plush mermaids seemed to have crawled away from the pile—or did she just not notice it before? She stared at it, half expecting it to move or speak.

Giggle.

Paige snapped her head to the left, locking on to the mirror over Melissa's desk. Barbie clothes, colored pencils, and nail polish lay askew. She walked over. Bottles on the left fell to the left. A box of markers on the right had fallen to the right. *She crawled over the desk to the mirror.*

Paige splayed her fingers and touched the glass.

Her vision flashed like a camera; she stood before a rectangular portal leading to a black and white tunnel of trees. Melissa, red hair and pink nightgown, giggled and skipped barefoot into a forest of greyscale nightmares. Paige tried to shout, but couldn't make a noise amid the simple vision. Another bright flash blinded her and she found herself sitting on the floor, peering up at the dainty white desk. For two seconds, the eerie woods remained as if the mirror were a window to another place. Blur manifested in spots and turned white. Expanding patches touched until the reflection of the ceiling replaced it.

"No." Paige leapt to her feet and slapped the mirror. "No! You can't have her!"

A door in the hallway creaked. "Paige?"

"In here, Dad." She pressed her hand against the mirror, frustrated at its solidity.

He walked in, a grim look on his face. "I've got everyone out looking. Benton told me to 'go clear my head' since I'm too close." Dad sighed. "FBI will be here in the morning. I got ordered to sleep. Yeah right."

"They're not going to help." Paige tried to drill holes in the mirror with her eyes.

Dad wrapped her in his arms. "We'll find her. The first forty-eight hours are..." He choked up. "I'm not gonna lose another daughter. I'm so sorry I got so distant after Amber's accident. I... couldn't deal with it." He broke down and sobbed.

Paige squirmed around and held on. "Dad. Dad. Dad. Dad."

He finally looked up. "Yes?"

"She wasn't kidnapped by a psycho."

"What are you saying?" He grasped her shoulders. "You know something about this?"

*Screw it.* "Dad. A dark spirit took her to shock you out of your funk."

"Oh, Paige." He shook his head.

"Look at the desk. She crawled up and through her mirror."

"Enough." He pulled her close and patted her back.

Paige pressed her hands into his chest and pushed back enough to look him in the eye. "Dad. At the bank. You saw the black stuff, didn't you?"

"The FBI has been doing this for decades. They'll find her."

She narrowed her eyes. "Dad. You did. That's what I'm talking about. The same thing got Melissa."

"People see things under stress." He swooped her off her feet and carried her out into the hall. "You're going to bed now. If you want to stay home from school tomorrow, I'll call you out."

*Damn. He thinks I've cracked.* "Okay."

A moment later, he deposited her on her bed and kissed her on top of the head. "Try to get some sleep." He started for the door, but paused with a faint smile. "Meet up in the kitchen for snacks around two?"

"Yeah." Paige gazed down. Anger simmered below the surface, focused at Mackenzie, but she didn't let any show. *I have to get that book.* "Two sounds good."

# 26

# DOMESTIC DISTURBANCE

Wednesday October 21 - 10:39 p.m.

P aige's eyes popped open to a close up view of her pillow. The spot near her nose still held a trace of strawberry shampoo from Melissa's hair. Within seconds, her teeth chattered. She lay on her front atop her bed in her underwear. She vaguely recalled undressing, and not caring enough to go hunt down a nightshirt. The chill in the air brought instant regret; once her limbs decided to obey, she scrambled out of bed. After trading her bra for a black thigh-length shirt with a Foamy the Squirrel print, she crawled under the covers.

"Paige," said Amber.

"Amb!" She sat up.

Her older sister had come out of nowhere, standing two feet from the bed. Nothing about her looked different, same Penn State sweatshirt and blue jeans, no odd feeling or inexplicable sense of dread. Paige grabbed for her, but her hand passed right through.

"You should go to your friend Renee's house right away."

"Where's Melissa?" Paige again tried to grab Amber's hand. "Can you tell?"

"She is somewhere I can't see." Amber gestured at the mirror. "She is alive. Renee's life is in danger. You don't have time."

"Where have you been?" Paige sniffled.

"Go," said Amber, louder. "There's no time. That blonde bitch won't stop this; Santana is in no state to function; the little one can't help, and Renee is about to die."

Paige flung off her tee and ran to her dresser. She grabbed the first thing she got her hand on, a black brocade shirt with long sleeves, a lacy collar, and frilled cuffs, then jumped into her jeans and boots.

"Are you sure this is a good idea?" asked Paige.

Amber's mournful expression deepened. "Too many are dead. More will die to what you set loose."

"Okay, okay." Paige rushed from her room and down the stairs.

The instant her hand touched the knob, a spray of vomit shot out of her and hit the front door. Such severe nausea slammed into her stomach that it emptied before she had even felt sick. She gagged and wiped her mouth on her hand, coughed, and pulled the door open. Trembling made it difficult to walk, but she made it to the street before stopping.

"What the hell am I doing?" *I'm being stupid is what I'm doing.*

The punishing dread abated as soon as she decided to run back inside. A minute later, she found Dad in the kitchen.

"You're early. Our meeting's not for another three hours or so."

"Dad. We gotta go to Renee's."

"What?"

Paige leaned her weight on the back of a chair. "Renee. My friend from school. Can we please go do a wellness check on her?"

Dad flicked a finger at the handle of his coffee mug. "Where did that come from? Did she call you?"

*Lie detector vs. odds of him believing me.* "It would be easier to lie and say yes, but you always catch me lying... so you're going to have to believe truth that sounds like a lie."

"Oh boy." He rubbed his right eyebrow.

"I got a bad feeling. A really bad feeling."

His lip quivered, though his eyes looked angry. "The same kind of bad feeling as when Amber..."

"Yeah. Dad. Amber's ghost is here. She's been visiting me for months. She just appeared and told me to get to Renee's right away."

He stared at her.

"Okay, fine. You can think 'wow, my daughter's cracked,' but *please* take me there. You didn't believe me and Amber died... Don't make me go through that again... knowing and being unable to stop it." Warmth encircled her eyes. She covered her mouth. "Please. She said Renee's gonna die tonight."

Dad drained the mug and set it down. "Okay. One condition."

"What?"

"If nothing is going on, you're going to see a professional."

"Deal."

Already in uniform, Dad recovered his utility belt from the dining room table and put it on. Paige followed him outside to the car and hopped in as soon as the door locks clicked. A moment later, he backed out of the driveway and switched on the pod lights. Paige checked her phone.

"202 North Quaker Ave."

Dad tapped the address into the system and the GPS popped up. Red and blue lights flashed off the trees, painting the ordinary forest into an alien mass of shadows. Paige rubbed her hands up and down her thighs, chanting 'please be okay' over and over in her head.

"What kind of situation am I possibly walking into?" asked Dad a minute later.

"Renee's father left them when she was like three or something. He came back a couple days ago and she said her parents have been fighting bad. Amber said Renee's going to die. I think her dad's gone crazy."

He nodded.

"So you believe me?"

His fingers creaked from squeezing the wheel. "You freaked out the night Amber was killed. You sounded like you were having a similar episode right before that kid tried to rob the bank. I heard you throw up in the living room. I… Let's just say I don't *not* believe you."

"I'll take it." She fidgeted. "I barfed 'cause… I don't think it would've been good for me to go to 'Nee's alone. I'm sorry. I'll, uhh, clean it up when we get back. Mom shouldn't have to."

He slowed a little to roll through a red signal, and went right. "What for?"

"Uhh. I'll explain later. If Renee turns out to be just fine, I don't want you thinking I'm completely crazy."

"I don't think you're crazy." He took a left three blocks later. "I think you're under a lot of stress."

A bit of squelch filled the car a second before a woman's voice. "Thomas, this is dispatch, come back."

Dad grabbed the radio. "Go ahead, dispatch."

"Drew, locals are asking why you're running Code 3 in the middle of town."

He let his hand dangle for a second. "One of my kid's friends sent a panic text about a possible domestic. I'm going to check it out. Might be nothing. I'll call in if I need backup."

"Copy, please advise on status asap."

"Roger." He hung the mic on the dash and cornered right again onto a residential street.

The houses resembled Philadelphia suburbs, only with fifty or sixty yards of trees between them. He pulled half into a driveway behind a Conrail work truck and a little silver sedan, and killed the roof lights.

As soon as he opened the door, screams of a man and woman arguing from inside became clear. Dad raised a hand at her.

"Stay in the car."

"Okay." Paige leaned forward and looked at the neat two-story house. Moonlight made the siding glow cobalt blue, but the second story seemed filled with black smoke. "Whoa. Dad?"

Three paces away, her father stopped. "What?"

"Do you see anything weird on the second floor?"

"It's dark."

A loud woman's scream preceded a heavy crash and a sound like plates or dishes smashing. Renee's higher-pitched shriek followed. Dad sprinted to the car and grabbed the mic. The woman's tone changed from cries of fear to wails of agony.

"Dispatch, Thomas. Confirm domestic with violence. Need backup. 202 North Quaker Avenue."

He dropped the mic and ran before the response came.

"Copy, Thomas."

"No!" shouted Renee. "You killed Mom! Daddy, please, no!" A longer scream rang out.

Dad pulled his gun and rushed the house. Paige bolted from the car, chasing him to the front door, which he booted in as if it were made of balsa wood. He whipped through and aimed.

"Police! Drop the knife," yelled Dad.

Paige skidded to a stop in the foyer. Renee hovered on the opposite side of a dining room table from a tall dark-skinned man with a short afro. His blue button-down shirt hung open, stained red like the tank top under it. A woman lay on her back, arms twisted in the air like chicken wings, gasping for breath in a puddle of blood tracked in footprints around the table. Renee scooted side to side, emitting a high-pitched keening mixed with sobs. Her figure vanished amid a massive Eagles sweatshirt, also sprayed with blood.

"Put the knife down and back away," yelled Dad.

"Mama!" yelled Renee.

"I told Colleen ta shut her damn mouth," said the man. "Bitch don't listen. Bitch never listened." He lifted his head and faced the door with eyes like solid onyx orbs. A demonic grin spread across his lips. "I told that bitch to get an abortion. Now I gonna do it for her."

Paige screamed.

"Drop the damn knife," said Dad. "Last chance."

"What'chu gonna do about it cop man?" Renee's dad took a step, raising the weapon.

*Bang.*

Renee shrieked while hopping up and down, flapping her hands.

A small red hole appeared near his heart. The man glanced at it as casually as if a fly had landed on him. His grin faded to a blank, emotionless look. He took another step toward Dad.

*Bang. Bang.*

Two more bullet wounds appeared near the first, and a vase in a china cabinet behind him exploded. Paige screamed again. The man stomped toward Dad, emitting a low guttural laugh from his throat, though his expression showed only the grim nothingness of a corpse.

Paige exchanged a half-second stare with Renee before running into the front yard. Dad backpedaled, firing five more times. Renee's father lumbered onto the stoop; a bullet hole in his forehead and below his left eye leaked blood in gushing trails down his face, yet still he advanced.

"Uhh," said Dad, backing up. "Mother of God. What the hell?"

Renee's father let off a murderous wail, and charged. Dad ran to the side, leading the big man on a roundabout chase, weaving around sycamores and oaks in the front yard. Paige looked back and forth between them and Renee screaming at her mother to hold on. Her brain's gears finally caught; she sprinted to Dad's car and grabbed the mic.

"Dispatch? We need an ambulance at Quaker ASAP. Renee's mom's been stabbed. Shots fired."

"Who is this?" asked the same woman.

*Bang. Bang. Bang.*

"Paige Thomas... his daughter."

"Where's your father? What's going on? Why are you there?"

*Think fast.* "Uhh, Renee's father is high on something... Daddy shot him a couple times, but he's not going down. They're running around the yard. He's got a knife."

*Bang.* Dad yelled something unintelligible. *Bang.*

"Listen to me, honey. You lock the doors of that car and get down out of sight. Backup's on the way."

"Okay."

Dad swung around and fired four more shots into the man, which seemed to do nothing but make more holes in him. He ducked a sideways swing from a fourteen-inch carving knife, and smashed his Glock across the man's face. The hit staggered Renee's father, but only for an instant. The dead-but-not man lurched forward into an overextended stab, which gashed a patch of bark from one of the sycamores as Dad sidestepped. He grabbed the man's arm, trying to wrench the weapon loose.

Renee's father reached across and grabbed a fistful of uniform jacket. He lifted Dad off the ground with ease and hurled him fifteen feet in the air. Dad landed and rolled, managing to get to his feet before the knife came down again.

Paige screamed with each swing and dodge. Renee's father chased after him behind an endless series of rapid random slashes, each one accompanied with a zombie grunt. Dad fumbled to reload while running backwards. The man tried for another overhead chop. Dad ducked right and drove his shoulder into the man's side, knocking him flat. He jumped back two steps and unloaded his second magazine so fast the Glock sounded like a machinegun. Renee's father moaned and got right back up.

A tingle spread through her right hand. She glanced down, finding it empty but itchy. *A premonition?* She closed her eyes and tried to let whatever random thought knocked on her skull in the front door.

The Conrail logo appeared on a patch of moonlit metal. A truck. A toolbox. A narrow metal rod with a flat end and a point. *No... a spike. Iron.* Her eyes snapped open. Dad flew shoulder first into a tree and slid, hugging it, to the ground.

"Daddy!" Paige yelled and scrambled out of the car.

She wanted to run to him, but forced herself toward the railroad truck.

Dad rolled over, sitting up, and went for his second spare magazine. Five more bullets in the face reduced the man's gait to a sloppy drunken wobble, but he kept advancing with the same, deep chuckle reverberating in his throat. Paige ran to the truck's side panel, letting intuition or randomness guide her hands to the latch of a compartment. She twisted and tugged at the silver ring until she figured out which way to move it to open the hatch.

Inside, a shallow tray held a couple of hammers and other tools she didn't recognize. Beneath it sat a metal bucket with a few dozen railroad spikes. She grabbed one, and the tingling in her hand stopped.

"Paige, get in the damn car," yelled Dad. He caught the knife arm in both hands, twisted, and flung the man to the ground. "Now."

Renee's father grabbed Dad's leg and pulled him off his feet. A downward stab caught Dad in the left bicep, making him growl more out of anger than pain. He stomped the man in the face, knocking him flat, and rolled to his feet.

"Dad! Here!" Adrenaline shot trembles through her body. Paige ran *at* the knife-wielding impossibly alive *thing*. "Stab him with this!" She tossed the spike.

"What? Are you craz—"

"Do it!" she shrieked.

Renee's father let off a horrible, inhuman moan and bounded upright. Despite at least thirty bullet wounds, he showed no signs of slowing down.

"Hey!" yelled Paige. She focused on the feeling of *otherness* within the body. "Darkness summoned, darkness lost. I banish you now, too great the cost."

The man swiveled, raising the knife at Paige, seeming bewildered. Dad rushed. Renee's father brought his knife arm up and around, but Dad caught it at the elbow, holding it harmless and high while driving the spike into the largest cluster of bullet wounds near the heart.

Renee's father collapsed like a rag doll without so much as a moan.

Dad panted and grabbed his left arm. "What... the hell... was that?"

Thick black smoke exuded from the mouth, nose, and ears of the dead man. It swirled around in thin trails, weaving together in midair. Sirens emerged in the distance. Color drained from Dad's face as the mass of shadow took on a humanoid shape—the same face that showed itself above the pentacle. It glared at Paige, but only for an instant; the form dissipated as fast as it appeared.

Paige grabbed her father's arm. "You're hurt."

"It's not deep." He hurried to the front door and inside to the woman.

Renee sprawled at her side, holding her mother's hand in her lap and whispering 'stay with me' repeatedly. Dad took a knee and looked her over before grabbing his shoulder mic.

"Dispatch, I need an ambulance out here yesterday."

"Copy that, Thomas. They're already on the way. Good to hear your voice... what's going on?"

"Woman, thirties, multiple stab wounds to the torso and arms. One suspect down." He let off the mic and applied pressure to the largest wound.

Not quite a full minute later, sirens wailed to a halt outside and three local cops rushed in. After a quick look around, one escorted Paige outside while another tried to examine Dad's arm. He brushed him off and pointed to the woman. The front yard shimmered in red and blue, mixed lights making purple patches dance on the trees. Paige crossed the lawn to the State Police car while an ambulance pulled up. She leaned against the front fender, arms folded, gaze down.

Soon, she watched yet another person get wheeled off on a stretcher. Renee walked out in a daze, still wearing only a long sweatshirt, and got into the ambulance with her mom. Paige rubbed her hands up and down her sleeves, trying to make up for not having a coat. Black lace cuffs tickled her chin when she breathed heat into her fingers. It appalled her she didn't feel like crying. Her reaction to the sight of Renee's mother felt more like an *I told you so* than an *oh my God*. Compared to her missing sister, Renee's situation felt like she'd brought it on herself. Melissa was a complete innocent caught up in a crapstorm of bitchiness and greed.

An emotion broke through her numbness a few minutes later—guilt.

"Damn, Drew. How many mags you empty on this guy?" asked one of the locals, a way-tall white-haired man whose nametag read: Baker.

"Two full ones plus five rounds. Christ, Tony, this guy just wouldn't stop."

Officer Baker chuckled. "What's with the spike?"

Dad looked at him. "You put thirty-nine rounds in a guy with a knife and it doesn't put him down, you learn real quick how to improvise."

The Suburban pulled up. A different local officer grumbled about rubberneckers and started to stomp over, but halted when Dad yelled to him.

"My wife." He waved at Paige.

"What?" Paige ran to him. "Why is Mom here?"

"I gotta stick around for a couple hours yet. You go home and go to bed. Sleep or not. Stay safe."

Paige hugged him. She leaned up on tiptoe and whispered at his ear, "I'm not crazy."

He shook his head. "No. If you are, then I am too. Now get home."

Officer Baker took her hand and escorted her to the Suburban.

"Thanks."

He nodded and opened the door for her. Paige climbed up and in, and Baker eased the door shut behind her. At least Mom had set the heat on max.

Mom shivered in her seat, eyes red, snot dripping out of her nose. She had one of Dad's winter coats on over her nightgown. "Are you going to tell me what's going on?"

"My friend Renee from school. Her father went psycho and… probably killed her mom. Tried to kill Dad." Paige held her hands over the air vents, trying to warm numb fingers.

Mom gasped. "This was supposed to be a quiet town… Your father needed calm to deal with his grief and—"

"He's dealing." Paige put a hand on Mom's arm. "There's just a lot to deal with right now. Are you okay to drive, or do you want me to?"

"You don't have your permit yet and there's cops all over the lawn." Mom wiped her eyes with a tissue.

"Melissa's not hurt. Amber told me."

Mom stared. She started to shake her head and mutter a series of 'no's.

"I had a dream about… oh hell. You know Grandmom saw stuff. I had a feeling about Renee, and it was right. I have a feeling about Melissa too."

Mom closed her eyes and took a few calming breaths. "For years, I thought my mother was off her rocker. We'd been planning a trip to New Jersey when I was about nine… oh, 1984-ish. I'd been looking forward to it for a month." She checked the mirror and pulled out into a U-turn. "The day we were supposed to go, Mom decided she'd rather take me to Hershey. I threw such a tantrum we wound up not going anywhere at all."

"That sucks." Paige stared at the door mirror until no trace of emergency lights remained. *Good thing these houses are so far apart…*

"Do you know what happened at Great Adventure that day?"

"Mom, I'm sixteen. That was like forever ago."

"The haunted house burned down. Killed a number of teenagers. Fair bet I would've wanted to go through there. I used to love scary stuff."

Paige's eyes widened. "Grandmom saw it?"

They stopped at a red light. No cars came from the other direction on the deserted street.

"I don't know if she did or not. Maybe she didn't see exactly what was going to happen, but she had a feeling *something* bad would happen to me." Mom broke out in silent tears. "Maybe it was no one ever believing her, or maybe her mind went for some other reason. I'm terrified to think you might wind up like her… talking to walls."

Paige smiled. "I'm not nuts, and Grandmom was probably speaking to ghosts."

Mom exhaled. "You didn't just say that."

"Okay. I didn't just say that." She clunked her boots together. "If you want me to act like nothing's weird, I will. Leave you out of it and all."

"Do you see ghosts, Paige?"

"On a regular basis? Only one…" She shivered. "Okay two."

Mom nodded in slow motion.

"Maybe I'm dreaming it. You know. Product of grief."

"I'm too fried to think now." Mom turned right onto the street that led out of downtown up the hill to their house a mile and change away.

"Me too." She wanted to crawl in bed, but doubted she'd sleep much.

# 27

# BETRAYAL

Thursday October 22 - 5:26 p.m.

Paige paced a circle in her room, holding her cell to her ear while waiting for Renee to come back on the line. She kept glancing at her closet mirror, hoping it might turn into some kind of gate through which she could go after Melissa. Her shirt's lacy cuffs brushed her cheek as she nibbled on her fingernails.

"Come on..."

She swatted at her gauzy multi-layered miniskirt, momentarily amused by her failed attempt to get a rise out of Dad by showing so much leg three months ago. The fishnets didn't even get a crooked eyebrow from Mom. She reached out with her left hand and touched the mirror, *wanting* something to happen, but only managed to chill her fingertips. Her satin choker resembled a circlet of grape-sized black roses around her throat, a little more comfortable than leather.

"Back," said Renee. The creak of a leathery cushion came over the line. Stuttering breaths at the verge of full-on sobbing followed.

"Hey." Paige ground her toes into the rug. "Can I do anything to help?"

"I can't believe you showed up when you did." Renee sniffled. "He... would'a killed me too."

Paige dropped in place, sitting on the floor. "Oh, no... your mom."

"She's in surgery again. They... the doctor said she might not make it through the weekend." Renee cried.

"I'm so sorry." Paige tugged at her choker. "I don't understand why that happened... You didn't do anything to interfere with the spell."

Renee took a few minutes, sniffing and coughing. "I don't think so... Mom said they broke up because he was always smackin' her around and stuff. She wanted to get me away from that life and he didn't care she wanted to leave. When he came back, he said he'd cleaned himself up about six years ago. Had a little recording business on the side managing a couple up-and-coming artists. I checked it out online. He said it was almost big enough for him to quit the railroad job. Looked legit. I... don't know. Maybe being with Mom was like poison to his soul or something."

Paige scratched at the rug, making patterns in the pile. "The spell forced them to stay together."

"Yeah." Renee's voice slurred with grief. "What am I gonna do now? He had his life together and now he's dead because of me."

"It's not your fault... you wanted a whole family. You couldn't have known they were, like, so incompatible." Paige narrowed her eyes. "Mackenzie tainted the spell."

"What?"

"I'm not sure if it was what she asked for or putting corpse blood in the candles, but... whatever she did it made it dark." Paige started at a *creak* from her closet door. Nothing looked amiss, but it felt like something watched her. She crawled backwards away from it. "Uhh... I'm gonna stop this."

"How? You saw her attitude. She's not going to let you." Renee mumbled away from the phone, asking something to please protect her mother.

"This thing took Melissa. I can't just sit around and do nothing. Are you gonna be okay?"

"I dunno." Renee wept. "I feel like shit because I'm not upset enough over Dad. I... didn't really even know him. But, Mom"—she sniffled—"If your Dad hadn't gotten there when he did."

The closet door slammed.

Paige jumped to her feet. "Eep!"

"What was that?"

"Uhh, remember that whole interfering with the spell thing? I uhh, kinda pissed it off."

"What did you do?" Renee's voice got quiet.

Paige explained the protection ritual on Emily.

Clicking... Renee tapping a fingernail on her phone filled her ear for a few seconds. "Do you think that affected my family?"

"I don't think so." Paige closed her eyes, weathering a wave of guilt. "Everything I found online made it sound like it would only blow up in *my* face if I messed with it."

"Okay." Renee made a noise half sob half chuckle. "Sounds so weird to think about looking up magic on the internet, right?"

"Yeah." Paige stared at her toes. "I'm sorry. I never should've gone to the cabin."

Renee sniffled. "Don't take all the blame. Not like any of us really believed anything would happen."

"Paige," yelled Mom.

"I gotta go. If you need anything at all, call me."

"'Kay. Don't do anything stupid. Kenz isn't used to hearing the word 'no.'"

"I can handle Barbie. Want me to try a healing spell for your mom?"

Sniffle. "No. Please… no more voodoo. I'll take good vibes though."

"You got it. See ya."

"Bye."

Paige tossed the phone on her bed and went downstairs. She padded into the kitchen where Mom sat at the table, staring at the wood grain. "What's up?"

"Are you hungry?" Mom glanced at the clock on the range. "I should probably throw some dinner together."

Paige grasped the back of the chair opposite Mom and leaned on it. "Are you?"

"No… but I'll eat if you do."

"We should." Paige glanced at the empty living room. "Where's Dad?"

"Still at the State Police barracks. Paperwork from last night. His superiors are a little concerned that he's been involved in two fatal shootings so close together. They questioned his use of so many bullets on that man, but… it's a miracle his dash cam caught most of that."

Paige slipped around the chair and sat. "Is he gonna get in trouble?"

"It doesn't look like it… both incidents had witnesses and are on report as justified, but it's… two in a week. This was supposed to be a quiet little town."

"Yeah." Paige stared into her lap. "Want help with dinner?"

"Sure." Mom heaved a sigh and stood. "By the way, that skirt is too short and those stockings are slutty."

"They're not slutty, they're Goth." Paige spoke in a dry monotone, making light of a mother-daughter argument.

"Is that what they call it these days?" Mom's deadpan left her unsure if she meant it. She paused. "I'm not going to handle it if Melissa's gone."

Paige helped gather supplies for spaghetti and sausage. "Yeah. I'll mix up the arsenic for us both."

Mom shot her a hard glare. "You're not allowed to kill yourself."

"Back 'atcha."

After a ten-minute hug, Paige browned sausage while Mom put the sauce together. Before too long, they sat at the table with smallish portions. Paige couldn't deny her stomach called out for food, but her pet black cloud wasn't having it. She clung to hope in the form of her 'gift' not making her worry about her little sister, and forced herself to eat. Mom took her time, but had only made it about three-quarters through her food by the time Paige finished.

The phone rang, startling a yelp from them both.

Mom swiped the cordless off the table.

"Hello?" She listened to a male warble for a few seconds before deflating. "Okay. We just made some spaghetti. There's more than enough left for you. Yes. Okay. Nothing?" She caught her head in one hand and sniffled. "No. No one called or left any kind of ransom demands."

Dad's voice murmured.

"I know that, Drew. You don't have to tell me. Okay. See you in a bit."

Mom hung up. Tears brimmed in her eyes when she looked at Paige. "Did you know perverts don't leave ransom demands?"

Paige reached over and grabbed her mother's hand. "A perv doesn't have her. She's lost and can't find her way home. Trust me."

Mom set the phone down and squeezed her hand. "I'm trying."

*Wham.*

Paige looked up.

"What was that?" asked Mom.

"Either an angry spirit or the house shifting in the wind." She bit her lower lip. "Uhh, Mom? Can I borrow the truck? I wanna drive around the area near the school and look for Mel."

"Paige... you're still three months away from being old enough for a permit. Sixteen plus six months, remember?"

"You gotta stay here in case the FBI or a... kidnapper calls. Dad's a State Trooper and my little sister's missing. They won't give me a hard time."

Mom pushed a sausage chip around, plowing a trail of clean plate through a lake of sauce. "With everything that's been happening lately, I'm afraid you'll get hurt in an accident."

"I don't feel worried." Paige twirled her last bit of pasta on her fork. "I won't be out long and I'll come back before dark."

"The police have been scouring the area. Why do you think you can find her when they can't?"

"How many cops do you know like Grandmom?" She carried her plate to the sink and rinsed it. "Call it a hunch?" *Damn, I thought she'd say yes without thinking. I can't tell her I'm going to Kenzie's. Technically that is helping find Mel.*

"Okay. I suppose anything that'll help find Melissa. Are you sure you don't want me to drive?"

"What if someone calls?" Paige turned away from the sink, hands on her hips.

Mom pursed her lips. "Didn't you just say she wasn't kidnapped?"

"Hunches aren't an exact science."

"Okay. But if you're not back before it gets dark I'm going to..." Mom sighed. "You're going to make me sick with worry."

"Swear."

Paige ran upstairs to her room. She hurried into her boots and jacket, tucked her phone into the pocket, and ran back down. Mom met her at the landing with keys. Paige grasped the bundle, but Mom didn't let go.

"I don't know why I'm trusting you with this given how erratic you've been this past year, but..."

"Desperation." Paige exhaled. "I wanna find her as much as you do."

Mom let go of the keys. "Be careful."

Paige hugged her. "I will, Mom."

THE GPS ON HER PHONE LED HER THROUGH DOWNTOWN SHADESBORO AND OUT the long, winding path to Mackenzie's home. Set back from the unpaved road by a quarter-mile, the house seemed larger and more foreboding than the last time she'd been there. With the garage closed and the lights all out, she worried the trip had been a waste. *Should I break in if she's not home?* Worry for Melissa clashed with dread at getting caught doing something tangibly criminal. *No one would believe me if I said I needed a spellbook to save a life.*

She drove along the curving driveway, around a huge oak, and parked in front of the rightmost of the three garage doors. A glance at the rearview, and no police car following her, brought a weak smile. *Guess I did okay.*

Paige killed the engine and speed-walked to the stoop, not bothering to lock the truck. She pressed the doorbell and waited. Two minutes later, she hit it again. A whorl of freezing air rushed over her from behind, spiraling about as though she stood in the center of the world's tiniest tornado. She cringed as her hair whipped her in the face. The wind died down, and the door clicked open, sucked inward three inches by the breeze.

"Mackenzie?" yelled Paige.

Diana appeared inside the door, one eye lined up with the gap.

Paige leaned back and gasped. The spirit faded as the door pulled open the rest of the way, revealing an empty atrium. *Guess that's an invitation.* She crept inside. "Kenz?"

Loud music drew her deeper into the house. Mackenzie sat on the couch in a knee-length hot-pink tee shirt. An image of 'rabbit pimp' on the front had gleaming metallic silver sparkles on its sunglasses and an oversized baseball cap. Some reality TV show blared from the massive flat panel at the same time she listened to music over headphones.

Paige went down three steps to the sunken living room and approached the sofa. Faint marks in the ceiling indicated where the Ouija board had smacked upward. She suppressed a tremble at the eerie feeling of warning pervading the house.

Mackenzie started when Paige reached the end of the sofa, and whipped her headphones off. "What are you doing here? You ever hear of a doorbell?"

"I hit it twice. You didn't answer."

"So you break in?"

"The door opened on its own." Paige held her hands up. "Swear. I don't know how to pick locks."

"Oh." Mackenzie tossed the headphones on the couch. "Missed you at school today. I heard about Renee's mom. How's she doing?"

*Like you care.* "They don't know. Doctor said she might not make it."

"That's too bad." Mackenzie put one foot on the coffee table and splayed her cotton-separated toes. "How's your dad doing? He still broken?"

Paige rounded the corner of the sofa. "He's had to shoot two people because of what we did."

"But is he still all depressed?" Mackenzie waved her hand, fanning peach-hued polish. "I mean, that's what you wanted right?"

"He's not, but he's getting the third degree for being involved in two fatal incidents so soon."

Mackenzie put her other foot up and plucked the cotton away. "I wouldn't worry. The magic arranged everything to look plausible. And your request helped someone other than you, so I doubt it'll bite you in the ass."

"Like yours?" Paige glared. "Your 'ask' tried to kill Emily. Twice. I want to see that book. I'm going to stop this before it kills half the town."

"Oh, relax." Mackenzie collected cotton into a bowl and stretched her legs. "Everything will run its course. If you want to be a witch, you have to harden up. Bad things happen sometimes. It's all part of the cycle of life."

"You're not a witch. You're a... a... diabolist or something. Dead people's blood in the candles? Really? What did you think would happen?"

"It was a necessary component. Assyrian mysticism is big on blood magic." She glanced away, fussing with her hair. "I'm thinking of going for a feathered style, what do you think?"

"I *think* you're messing around with powers you don't understand. Necessary for what?"

Mackenzie's expression went dismissive. "Certain entities have more influence over the mortal world. I wanted to make sure the ritual worked."

"So you called a damn demon." Paige sighed at the ceiling. "*You* are why people got burned at stakes. This stops now. Where's the book?"

"I still don't have my Cole. Nothing's stopping. Everyone else got what they asked for and I'm still alone."

Paige narrowed her eyes. "Did you ever stop to think *how* you're going to get Cole? Renee wanted her dad back... and she got a dead body."

"I have more control than that." Mackenzie examined her fingernails.

"Goddamit Kenz, it's got my sister!" Paige stomped. "It took Melissa!"

"Sorry." Mackenzie muted the TV and stood. "You want some tea or something?"

*How many years would I get for choking her?* "I don't *believe* you. She's only eight."

"Maybe you should've thought about that before you interfered with Emily." Mackenzie flashed a dark smile on the way past her to the kitchen. "Green or normal?"

"Please." Paige whined. "I'll help you with a love potion or something, but this... this *thing* we set loose has got to be sent back."

"You worry too much. They'll find your sister. Super-cute missing white girl will be all over the news. The media loves that stuff. Not like it's Santana's little brother. He'd be lucky to get a write-up in the local paper."

"What is *wrong* with you?" Paige yelled. "Santana's father is *dead*, Kenz. *Dead!*"

Mackenzie disappeared into the kitchen. Seconds later came the squish of a refrigerator seal opening. "Since you didn't say anything, I'll grab normal tea. And Santana got her wish. She asked for financial security. It's her fault she didn't specify *how*. Most intelligent invokers ask for lottery winnings."

Paige snarled and drew her foot back to kick something, but decided against it. "Maybe it would have if you didn't call a friggin' demon! Did you hear that one kid screaming when they wheeled her out of the school? I *still* can't get that out of my mind."

Mackenzie paused in the kitchen doorway, a glass of iced tea in each hand and a sad look on her face. "Yeah... I *do* feel bad about those little kids. That's not right." She padded across the room, set Paige's tea on the coffee table, and sat on the couch. "Sofia focused on how angry she was with them. She *said* she wanted friends, but in her heart, she desired revenge."

"We have to send this thing back before it kills someone else."

Mackenzie sipped her drink. "Do you think Sofia is dark enough to want to kill one of her classmates?"

"Of course not." Paige glared.

"Then don't worry about it. It won't."

*She's going to keep me going in circles all damn day.* "You're not going to let me see the book are you?"

"Sure I will... after I have Cole. You're not going to cheat me out of my fair shake of the spell, which by the way I'd have already if you didn't block it off from Emily. By the way, I *love* that cute little skirt. You look like a vampire version of Tinkerbell."

Paige stuck her hands in her jacket pockets. She turned her back and pulled her phone out. A few taps started audio recording. *Okay. Let's play a game.* "Mom hasn't texted me yet... no word on Melissa."

"Sorry."

"You don't sound very sincere, but I guess you wouldn't. How sincere can someone be who poisoned their own mother?"

Mackenzie giggled. "Oh, now I see why you're acting so strange. You think *I* killed her."

"Didn't you? Isn't that why you got so freaked out whenever someone mentions her? She's here you know. I saw her when we messed with the Ouija. She knows."

Mackenzie pinged her fingernail at the rim of the glass. "I didn't kill her. I loved my mother. She was awesome." A trace of sadness lingered in her eyes. "Dad did it."

"What?" Paige sat on the edge of the sofa. Her throat dried out. She finally accepted the tea, but stared at it with suspicion.

"It's not poisoned." Mackenzie swiped it from her hands and took a sip before handing it back to her. "Jesus H. Relax."

Paige drank. *Ugh. Too much sugar.*

"Mom caught him cheating with two paralegals from his office. She was going to divorce him, and they had no pre-nup."

"You knew?"

"I found her dying." Mackenzie seemed to deflate. "It was too late to save her. She died like twenty seconds after I took her hand. She wheezed 'Dad killed me' and gave me this awful pleading look... then she went still."

Paige sniffled. "I'm so sorry. Guess I know why she's so pissed now, but... what happened? Didn't the police believe you?"

"I don't think they really did." Mackenzie smirked. "I told them Mom had been depressed for months and I saw her try to kill herself once before. You know, working the story Dad came up with."

"Uhh." Paige slouched forward, arms on her legs, tea suspended between her knees. "How could you do that? You've been living with a... murderer."

"He's still my father." Mackenzie's downcast gaze faded after a moment. "I didn't want to wind up in foster care."

"Kenz. That was your *mother.*"

"Yeah... so what? She's dead. Not like it would've brought her back to throw my father under the bus. I didn't want to ruin my life for 'justice.'"

Paige gawked, mouth open. "I... can't even..."

Diana Walsh appeared standing on the other side of the coffee table, a forlorn stare aimed at her daughter.

"M-Mom?" Mackenzie cringed into the sofa cushions. "P-Paige... how did you do that? What did you do?"

"Our spell opened a door." Paige looked up at the spirit. "You broke her heart."

Mackenzie trembled. "I'm… I'm sorry, Mother… I thought he'd kill me too."

Diana's sad eyes went cold. Her whisper seemed to come from everywhere at once. "Liar."

The spirit blurred into a smear of beige light that raced to the front door. For an instant, Mackenzie looked pissed, but when she made eye contact with Paige, tears started.

"I don't believe you either," said Paige. An icy spectral hand brushed its fingers around her heart. "Oh, shit. Something's about to—"

*Bam!* A heavy metallic crunch preceded the brief chirp of a car horn.

Light from outside painted the foyer in a harsh glare. Paige twisted to her left, one hand on her gut. "Don't go out there…"

Mackenzie jumped over the sofa back and ran to the door. Gripping the knob, she peered out the window. "Daddy! Oh, shit." She flung it open and sprinted barefoot across the porch.

Paige set her half-finished glass on the coffee table and followed at a cautious walk. Mackenzie screamed 'Daddy' every few seconds as she dashed across the sixty or so yards of grass between the porch and the giant oak tree, where a white Mercedes crumpled.

The left front tire spun, three feet off the ground. Blood spattered the smashed windshield and the headlights imparted a glow to clouds of smoke and fog swirling about the wreck. Diana Walsh stood on the dirt and gravel road leading down to the paved street, at the point where swerve marks gouged away from it into the lawn.

She looked back over her shoulder at Paige, smiled, and faded away.

28

## CLIQUE CLIQUE BOOM

Thursday October 22 - 6:32 p.m.

Paige crept to the end of the porch. Crickets screamed from the woods on three sides of the property. Strong lights on the front wall of the house bathed the scene of the crash in a harsh glare, and deepened the shadows among the trees. Mackenzie reached the car and struggled at the driver side door, banging her fist on the window and screaming. Head down, Paige tromped over, but stopped about twenty feet away at an angle where she had a good view. She didn't look long; one brief glimpse of brain matter oozing out from where the steering wheel broke through his eye sockets was enough.

*Of course the airbag would fail.* Paige buried her face in her hands and focused on Mom smiling, on Melissa giggling, on the feeling of Dad holding her. *Don't throw up. Don't throw up.*

The moment seemed to freeze in time, silent and still save for an unidentified hissing coming from the smashed Mercedes. Screams from the house preceded Linda, in a white robe and pink bunny slippers, running over to the wreck. Mackenzie backed away, looking more frightened than saddened.

Linda burst into tears and hyperventilated. "Don... Oh, my God, Don!"

"I'm sorry, Mrs. Walsh," muttered Paige.

With her stepmother resuming the battle with the bent door, Mackenzie whirled on Paige. "You want a war, bitch?"

"What?" Paige gasped. "Seriously?"

Mackenzie pointed. "You did that. I should've seen this coming. This is part of your plan, isn't it?"

Linda slumped in the lawn, staring at the sky.

"What plan? No, Kenz... this is karma sinking its fangs into both of your ass cheeks."

"*Karma*? Really? That's *so* not even funny." Mackenzie snarled. "You want to knock me down and take over the coven. Renee's in love with you and little Sofia thinks you're amazing, but not me. I see what you're really doing."

"Kenz... slow down. You're paranoid." Paige backed toward the house. "One. What we did... that's not a coven. We're just a bunch of stupid kids farting around with a book you never should've touched. Two, you never liked Sofia. You only treated her nice because she could get you pieces of dead people." She shuddered. "I saw the way she looked at you. She wanted a friend more than anything, but all you did was use her. She knew it too, but didn't care."

"You killed my goddamned father!" Mackenzie screamed and jumped.

Paige got her hands up in time, blocking a punch to the face. Mackenzie snagged her hair and pulled. The world spun around twice. Paige let off a growl, clawing at the blonde. One hand got hair, the other a breast.

"You *would* grab my tits." Mackenzie grunted and tried to pull her over sideways by a fistful of hair. "Renee said you two weren't."

Paige grunted. "We're not." She drove her knee into Mackenzie's gut, knocking the wind out of her, and swiveled her head to bite the other girl on the wrist.

Mackenzie abandoned her grip. Hair free, Paige disregarded an opportunity for a good nose punch and backed away.

"Don, honey. What do you want for dinner tonight?" asked Linda, sounding dazed.

"You're wrong, Kenz. I did *not* do anything to your father. All I ever asked the spirits for is help and protection. Never harm. If you had actually read anything, you'd understand the concept of threefold—"

"Shut up!" Mackenzie screeched and ran in again.

Paige ducked a punch and sidestepped another hair grab. Mackenzie caught her by the shirt, slipping fingers in the button seam between her breasts.

"Stop!" yelled Paige. She stomped her boot on bare toes. As Mackenzie faltered, Paige delivered a hard slap across the cheek that knocked the older girl to the grass. "What's wrong with you!?"

Mackenzie grabbed her foot, growling and cursing.

Diana Walsh's laughter rang over the front yard, as if on loudspeakers.

Linda screamed and darted straight out of her slippers on her way to the house.

"Listen to me." Paige took a step away, pointing. "We opened a door and your mother was pissed. She came through on her own when we did our ritual. She's not part of it. Yeah, we let her in, but we didn't call her. I did *not* ask anyone to hurt you. You either don't know anything about the forces you're messing with or you don't care what happens as long as you get what you want."

"She always was a selfish little thing." Diana manifested next to Paige. Her nightie no longer had any trace of puked chocolate shake. Mackenzie didn't react to her. "Please stop her."

"I'll try."

"What?" Mackenzie stopped rubbing her toes and looked up. "Try what?"

"Your mother just asked me to talk sense into you and stop this. Even after what you did to her, she doesn't want you to get hurt."

Mackenzie scoffed and got up. "If she didn't want me to get hurt, she shouldn't have killed him. What am I supposed to do now? My life is ruined. I'm gonna lose the house. Who's gonna pay for my car insurance or college?"

Paige's hands shook with adrenaline. "At least you're eighteen now. You won't get put in a home. What about Linda? You still sorta have a parent, even though she's like two years older than you."

"Bitch." Mackenzie breathed heavy, staring through a waterfall of disheveled blonde. "What are you anyway? Some kind of freak, talking to your dead sister? This is all your fault. *All* of it. Nothing worked until you showed up. Maybe you're a real witch, huh, Paige? You know the bad ones they used to light on fire for killing children. I bet all that stuff going on at the grade school is you collecting parts for the next conjuration."

"No!" Spaghetti churned in Paige's stomach. "Didn't you say it takes five to tango? You turned our spell dark. Dead blood. Selfish greed. That's no Wicca book."

"Oh, I hit a nerve." Mackenzie circled. "Step one: alienate me from my friends. Step two: summon my mother so I'm scared and off balance. Step three: collect the rendered fat of an innocent for whatever you're going to do next. *Missing* sister huh? Nice cover story. Step four: a blood sacrifice"—she gestured at the Mercedes—"Daddy. How convenient your little sister disappears. Did you at least put her to sleep in peace before you cut her heart out?"

Paige shrieked with incoherent rage and charged. The sudden attack landed a perfect overhand right into Mackenzie's cheek. The willowy blonde hit the ground and log-rolled. Paige's first kick caught her in the back, the second in the gut. Mackenzie scrambled upright and backed off.

"How could you even say that," shrieked Paige. "I did not hurt Melissa!"

Mackenzie coughed and cackled. Paige pounced, tackling her to the grass again. They grappled, grabbing each other's hair and tumbling over each other.

"Everyone else got what they wanted already." Mackenzie tried to bite Paige on the face, but she held her back. "I'm not doing a damn thing until I get Cole. I don't care who has to die to make that happen. He is mine."

"I'm taking the book. I won't let it hurt Melissa."

After trading a few weak body punches, Paige screamed when Mackenzie grabbed her skirt and pulled it up. She flung Mackenzie off and scrambled upright. Shrieking, the blonde came running at her again, grabbing for her throat. Paige drove her boot down on a bare foot for the second time and dug her fingers into Mackenzie's breast, gouging until the girl released her clothing and howled, limping away while cradling her chest.

"You evil bitch." Mackenzie glared.

"Pot. Kettle." Paige panted for breath. "Next time you decide to pick a fight, bring shoes."

Mackenzie roared in a rage and charged. Again, both girls got a double handful of each other's hair and yanked. Around and around they whirled, Paige trying to stomp on Mackenzie's vulnerable toes. A lance of pain rode up the left side of Paige's head from a vicious jerk on her hair. Shrieking, she switched her grip and pulled Mackenzie's tee shirt up—revealing her ex-friend's complete lack of underwear. Adrenaline overpowered mortification. Like a hockey player, she wrapped the blonde's head in fabric and punched her six or seven times before throwing her down.

Mackenzie struggled to cover her crotch with one hand while untangling her shirt with the other. Silver sparkle disks littered the grass.

"News flash, Princess." Paige spat blood from a cut lip to the side. "Cole doesn't want you. Even if that *thing* we called kills Emily, he will never want you."

"I know." Mackenzie's voice deepened, not quite male, but not quite Mackenzie either. A raspy chuckle came from her lips as she pushed her shirt down. Her gaze snapped up to lock Paige's, her eyes full black. "It told me."

Paige stumbled back. "Kenz... what the hell?"

Mackenzie's grin, broad and dark, seemed to stretch far too wide for a human face. Chuckling became laughter that echoed in the woods. She stood, coal-black stare drilling through Paige's heart.

"Get out of her," yelled Paige. "You are not welcome here. I'm sorry Kenz; are you still in there? It's making you say stuff."

"Oh, Paige... so caring." Mackenzie took a step closer. "The spell will run its course. I will have what is mine, and you will not take the coven from me. Crawl away and hide in your little bedroom, crying for your dead sister. Stay out of my way and maybe I'll give you the other one back alive." She laughed. "Sanity optional."

Paige glared, and took a step.

"Go right ahead. Kill me. That's what it wants." Mackenzie's grin shrank back to human size and her eyes returned to their normal blue. "Linda's calling the police now if she's done sucking her thumb. Run on home, Paige, and let me play the grieving daughter."

"I'm not going without the—"

"Melissa wants you to leave." Mackenzie stuck a finger in her mouth and sucked blood from a bent nail. "She doesn't wanna get hurt."

Paige glanced at the gaping door. *Maybe her mother will lead me to it.* She squeezed her fists. "I don't believe you."

"Oh?" Mackenzie grinned. "Me and the spirit... we're on a first name basis. Remember? My hair in the candles? He's mine."

Another glance at the house caused her body to shake and a chill to freeze through her limbs. The same feeling she'd had before the car nearly crushed Emily.

"Okay... fine. You win." Paige held her gut and took a step toward the Suburban.

The blonde swooped forward and grasped her on either side of the head. Paige tensed for a fight, but hesitated when the girl only smiled. "If you behave yourself, I might even let you stay in the coven and put this little misunderstanding past us. You have real power. I can't wait to tap more of it. Imagine the magic we could weave."

Mackenzie kissed her on the lips, thrusting her tongue inside.

Paige shoved her away, gagging and spitting, wiping her mouth off on the back of her arm while Mackenzie laughed.

"Run along home now, sweetie." Mackenzie waved.

"Ugh." Paige coughed. "What the hell is wrong with you?"

"My biggest flaw is impatience." Mackenzie brushed dirt and grass from her long tee while walking over to the crashed Mercedes. "You probably don't want to be here when the police arrive. They might get suspicious if you keep popping up where bad things happen."

Paige spat again and trudged on wobbly legs to the Suburban, nauseated by the crocodile tears sprouting from Mackenzie. She ran across the wide driveway and grabbed the door handle.

Diana Walsh appeared as a reflection in the window.

Paige yelped.

The woman gave her an apologetic look of resignation and faded away.

After waiting for her heart to resume beating, Paige climbed in and backed into a U-turn. Mackenzie knelt by the wreck, sobbing and asking the clouds 'why?' She drove away, a little faster than she felt comfortable with. *I gotta get outta here before the cops show up.*

Fading sun turned the western sky orange; patches of harsh glare filtered among the trees making her squint. A few minutes later, two local police cars shot by going in the direction of Mackenzie's house. A little under a quarter-mile from the start of downtown, Paige slowed to twenty-five as the road became difficult to make out due to the sun in her eyes.

She clenched the wheel with both hands, still shaking from post-fight adrenaline. Bruises all over her ached, hits she hadn't realized she'd taken in the moment. Squinting didn't help. The brilliant glare always seemed to find a gap in the wavering treetops to blind her.

A sudden dread made her slam on the brakes. The Suburban skidded to a stop in the part-dirt road a split second before a boy with darkish skin darted out of the woods. Paige screamed. He stopped in the beam of the headlights, looking terrified. Paige threw the shift in park and opened the door.

"Oh, my God, are you okay?"

The boy, who looked about twelve and rail thin, zoomed around and tried to get in the truck with her. "It's after me!"

"What is?"

"The shadow man."

Paige held on to him and peered into the woods. Nothing but trees. The kid trembled so hard she didn't doubt him. "It's gone now."

He gulped. "Y-you didn't say there's nothing there."

"You're Santana's brother, aren't you?"

"Yeah." He fidgeted. "Oh... you're her hot new friend. Uhh." He blushed. "I mean her..."

"I've never been called hot before... usually 'ghoul' or 'dead girl.'" She sighed. "I believe you about a shadow man."

He shivered. "It almost got me."

*It wanted to chase you into the road so I hit you. Either more money for Santana or my butt in jail.* "It's gone."

"Will you drive me home? I don't wanna be alone." Huge brown eyes devoured her willpower.

"Okay."

He climbed over her into the passenger seat.

Paige drove as if taking a road test. Everything by the book and at least five miles under the limit. She barely breathed until she'd dropped Michael off at his house. The place looked like it needed work. The sight of Mr. Ruiz's battered old Nissan Altima, both front quarter panels green on a tan body, choked her up.

Michael hesitated at the edge of the seat. For a second, she thought him afraid, but caught him checking out her legs. She made a playful growl and gave him a little push.

"Try again in like six years."

He sulked and got out. "Thanks for the ride."

She drove through downtown, hooked a right on the long rural street, and pulled into her driveway seven minutes later—right behind Dad getting out of the State Police car. "Oh, crap."

Dad gave the Suburban a quick noncommittal glance, but did a double take when he realized who was driving. His WTF look melted into a frown. He braced his fists on his hips and tapped his foot.

Paige parked, killed the engine, and got out. "Hey, Dad."

"Nice casual act." He curled his lips in.

"Mom said it was okay." She handed him the keys. "I was out trying to help Melissa, but I didn't find her."

He sighed. "Your mother's under a lot of stress right now. You caught her at a weak moment with a cheap shot."

"I really was trying to help Mel." Paige looked down.

"What happened to you?" Dad leaned close and traced a finger on her lip. "You got into a fight, didn't you?"

"Yeah."

"Anything you want to tell me about?"

She bit her lip. "Umm. Nothing you'd believe."

"You know if you get popped by one of the locals for driving without a permit, you won't be able to get one in January. *And* you'll make me look bad for allowing it."

Paige looked down. "I'd risk more than a license to get Melissa home safe."

Dad wrapped her in a tight hug, patting her back. "Yeah. Me too."

For a few fleeting seconds, Paige felt like nothing could hurt her, safe in her father's arms.

# 29

# PROMISE BROKEN

Thursday October 22 - 7:13 p.m.

Homework didn't provide much of a distraction. Flicking the corner of her textbook between her fingers, Paige replayed the day in her mind. Only Sofia had shown up of their group, and the poor girl couldn't stop crying. Two more boys in her class had been hurt. One fell off his bike the day before and broke his jaw. The other suffered an arrow in his shoulder while on a hunting trip with his father and older brothers, in the arm he'd used to dump pudding over her head.

She wasn't surprised at Mackenzie's absence. The school's gossip mill got to work, and it didn't take long before everyone heard that her father wrapped his $90,000 Mercedes around a three-century-old tree. A doughy woman with a massive orb of curly white atop her head took over Mr. Ruiz's class. Half the students amused themselves by trying to get tiny paper airplanes stuck in her hair without her noticing. After the accident, they'd shut down all lab work pending a thorough review of safety policy and procedure, so the first period she'd once looked forward to had become a snore.

Paige slumped over her desk, pulled her black hoodie over her head, and cried.

Mom poked in. "Aww, honey…" She walked over and rubbed her back. "I'm not giving up."

"I miss her, Mom." She sniffled. "I feel so helpless just sitting here."

"Have you..." Mom looked at the door and lowered her voice to a whisper. "Had any more visions?"

"I can't tell if you're serious or think I need help." Paige sat up and let her hands drop in her lap.

"Maybe some help isn't out of order. You've never worn pajama pants to school before."

"No one noticed." She smirked at the soft red plaid.

Mom patted her on the shoulder. "So nothing?"

"Nope." She sighed. "I think she crawled through the mirror on her desk."

"Paige... After the fire my mother seemed to sense coming, I can maybe accept visions... but now you're scaring me."

"Dad didn't find any evidence of a break in. How do you explain that neither one of us saw each other that morning despite us both being here?" Paige looked her mother in the eye. "I believed you when you said you were here. I know I was here... so how do you explain that?"

"I can't." Mom walked to the door. "Even if... Don't say the wrong thing to the wrong person. I couldn't handle them taking you away from me too."

A lump swelled up in her throat. *I got my wish.* "Okay, Mom."

She stared at the squiggles and diagrams in the chemistry book after Mom left. Her brain rejected all input as it did after Amber's death. She couldn't summon the tiniest shred of care about schoolwork. *What's Kenzie up to? She said she knew about Cole...* "Shit."

Paige jumped up and flung her pajama pants down. She grabbed her phone and tried to dial with one hand while pulling on jeans with the other. Emily picked up in six rings.

"Hi," said Emily. Lots of background noise made her hard to hear.

"Where are you? I think we need to do a protection spell on Cole. Something's going to happen soon and I don't want to wait for the last minute."

"What are you talking about?" yelled Emily.

"Cole," said Paige. "Mackenzie wants him. I think she's working on something that will *force* him to go to her."

"You think that's... possible? I haven't—" Her voice drowned under a crowd cheering. "I haven't had anything weird happen again."

"Good. Look, can you talk Cole into going along with a protection spell? Where are you?" Paige flipped the phone to speaker mode and dropped it on the bed so she could get her jeans on. "I'll bring all the stuff I'll need. It'll take like ten minutes tops."

"We're at the school. The Goats are playing. It's a close game." A wave of boos welled up. "Oh. That was a penalty and they didn't call it."

"Damn right it was a penalty," yelled another girl, likely right next to

Emily. She launched into a diatribe of profanities. Out of about fifteen words, the only one that wouldn't have made Mom blush was 'referee.'

"Sorry," said Emily. "Other team just got away with cheating."

The crowd launched into a repeating chant of 'bull-shit.'

"Okay. I'm coming. We'll do it after the game."

"If he goes for it." Emily seemed to hold the phone to her chest long enough to scream 'run' before coming back on the line. "I'll try to talk him into it, but he's stubborn. I tried to tell him about the ritual and the accident and the wire, and he thinks witchy stuff is for little girls. Will it work if he doesn't believe it?"

"I don't know." Paige stepped into her boots. "See you soon."

"Okay."

She stuffed the phone in her sweatshirt pocket, zipped her boots, and collected candles, the sage, the bowl, a couple incense cones, and some salt in her backpack after leaving all the schoolbooks on the desk.

Mom yelled her name the instant her hand touched the doorknob.

"Yeah?"

"You're going out?" Mom walked in from the dining room. "It's after seven."

"I won't be long. I'm going to the school to help a friend. As soon as the game's over, I want to do something to help protect him."

"You're going to a game when your little sister is out there with who knows what kind of maniac?" Mom covered her mouth and hyperventilated.

"I'm not 'going to a game' like that..." Paige put a hand on her arm. "I'm physically travelling to where a football game is going on, but you know I couldn't care less about sports. The person who's in danger is at the game."

"Your sister is in danger." Mom grabbed her shoulders. "How..."

"What's going on?" Dad came in from the living room.

"Our daughter wants to go watch football while Melissa is out there."

Paige stared up. "Geez Mom, that's not it at all."

Mom burst into tears and stormed off to the kitchen.

Dad raised an eyebrow. "Okay. What is it?"

Paige huffed, blowing her hair off her eyes. "I'm going to meet up with this girl Emily and her quarterback boyfriend to cast a protection spell on him so the demon we set loose doesn't force him to fall in love with this bitch Mackenzie." She held out her hand.

"You want a tip for the story?"

"No, I'm waiting for the cup to pee in." She lowered her arm. "I'm not on acid."

"You're really into that whole witchcraft thing huh?" He raised his hands. "I'm not judging... it's just nice to see you actually interested in something for once."

Paige clenched her jaw. "I'd prefer never to think about it again, but I don't think that's gonna happen... at least not for a little while."

"Demon, huh?"

"You saw it." Paige looked down. "Renee's dad."

"Going to catch the football game is a believable cover story." He patted her on the shoulder. "You need moral support from your friends. Just don't stay out late."

"Okay." She hugged him. "I'll be back in like an hour."

Paige jogged down the driveway to the street, hooked a left, and walked fast. At night, the tree-lined stretch of downhill road became a twisting knotwork of scraggly limbs and warped shadows. If not for having been two feet from nose-to-nose with a demon, the scene might've scared her. Random whispers and twig snaps did unsettle her, but no bizarre feelings of imminent doom came on, so she tuned the creepiness out.

Crinkles and crackles in the brush approached from the right. She glanced over her shoulder, but couldn't see anything moving in the dark. The noise got closer and faster, a distinct sound as though someone trampled fallen leaves. Paige ran from the invisible force, trying to stay on the road. *Forgot a flashlight. Crap.*

Something grabbed her right arm. On instinct, she drove her fist down and back, aiming for balls, and hit something soft.

A pitiful childish squeak broke the silence, followed by wheezing.

Paige whirled around. Sofia clutched her stomach, making faces like a fish out of water. Beneath a black lace choker, her voluminous dress hung in multiple layers of faux tatter to her shins. Puffy shoulders capped velvet sleeves that ran all the way down over the backs of her hands to rings around her middle fingers. Dark stockings and black shoes left only her fingers and face not covered in black.

Sofia whimpered and fell to her knees, gasping. The fist aimed for a man's testicles had caught her in the solar plexus.

"Sorry!" Paige took a knee and rubbed the girl's back. "I didn't see you."

A moment or two later, Sofia's face remained red, but she breathed. "Shoulda said something. Too scared."

"How long were you following me?"

Sofia coughed into her hands. "I've been sitting outside your house since five."

"Stalk much?" Paige smiled. "You could've come in."

"I dunno." Sofia looked down, fidgeted, and grimaced a smile.

"My dad won't bust you for stealing blood."

"It's not that..." Sofia stood and grasped her wrist. "I didn't wanna curse your house." Her calm lasted another three seconds before she burst into tears. "Chelsea broke her hand in a door today when Mrs. Hoffman slammed it without seeing her, and Tiffany almost drowned in the toilet."

Paige giggled before she caught herself. "Uhh, sorry. Drowned in a toilet? How..."

Sofia bawled. When she recovered enough to speak, she went on in a sniveling whine punctuated by random staccato breaths. "Sometimes, Tiffany and this other girl Beth-Ann would grab me in the bathroom and hold me upside down and try to put my face in the toilet. Tiffany slipped and fell, hit her head on the toilet, and passed out with her face in the water." She sobbed into her hands. "She almost drowned. Please make it stop. I don't wanna hurt anyone else. It doesn't matter what they do to me. Please... You have to help me."

Paige put an arm around her and patted her. "I'm trying. I can't get the book. Kenzie's playing for the other team now."

Sofia sniffled. "She likes girls?"

"That's... not what I meant. She's controlling the demon."

"Please!" Sofia whined like a six-year-old and bounced on her toes. "Someone's gonna die next and it'll be all my fault. Please help me before someone gets hurt real bad."

*Too late.* Paige glanced down the road toward the school. "Okay... let's try something." She took Sofia by the hand and walked off the road into the woods.

"Where are we going?" Sofia looked around. "It's dark and scary here."

"Says the Goth faerie."

Sofia frowned. "You should talk."

"Far enough off the road that no one bothers us."

"Are we gonna have to dance around a fire or something?"

Paige sighed. "No."

A minute or so of walking through underbrush and dried-out vines brought them to a small clearing with a few tree stumps. An old picnic table implied they'd strayed onto someone's property, but at that moment, Paige didn't much care.

"Okay this works."

"I don't like it here." Sofia turned in a slow circle. "Feels like someone's watching us."

Paige set the backpack down and sat. "Sit there."

Sofia dropped in place and tucked her legs to one side.

Paige pulled her gothic 'dagger' letter opener out of her backpack and used it to draw a pentacle in the dirt around Sofia. She wedged five of the standard white candles in at the points, and held the sixth, wagging it, while she thought about where to put it or if she should skip using it. An idea hit her and she held it out. "Hold that one."

Sofia took the candle. "You're making this up as you go, aren't you?"

"Method and words don't matter as much as intent." *I hope.* "This worked for Emily."

"What?"

Paige explained her protection spell on Emily while using the letter opener to carve symbols representing the five Elements: Earth, Fire, Water, Air, and Spirit inside the triangular points of the pentacle. She handed Sofia the bowl, sprinkled in a little sage, and dropped an incense cone on top. Next, she got to her feet and pointed the improvised athame down. *Oops.* She grabbed a lighter from the side pocket.

"Where'd you get a lighter? Do you smoke?" asked Sofia.

"Tried it once a couple years ago." Paige turned green. "Never again."

She pointed the letter opener at the circle and walked around. At each point, she paused to light the candle and beseeched the element for its protection. The candles struggled to stay lit in the wind, but none had blown out by the time she reached her starting point after the third orbit.

Paige closed her eyes, envisioning the boundary of the circle as a tangible barrier between the worlds of life and spirit. "Thrice I walk this circle 'round, to ward the spirits from this ground."

She lit the candle in Sofia's hand. "I call upon the Element of Fire, to represent magic."

All six candles ceased fluttering, their flames stretching two inches, pin straight despite the continuing breeze.

Sofia drew in a breath.

Paige pointed the athame at the symbol of water. "Element of Water, I call upon thee to purify Sofia of her anger and resentment. Help her cast aside this burden." She directed the knife at Air. "Element of Air, you represent freedom. I beseech thee to free her of this curse. Send back the energy she contributed to the summoning."

Sofia sniffled.

Paige squatted, speaking in a whisper. "Sofia. Think about how angry you were with those kids for how they treated you. Concentrate on that feeling you had inside your heart when we did the other spell. Visualize yourself letting go of that anger. Focus on how much you want to protect those kids from harm. Let go of your hate."

"Okay." She closed her eyes. "I'm sorry. Spirits, please stop the demon from hurting them. I never wanted that."

Paige eyed the incense cone. Sofia lit it with the candle.

"We give this smoke to the Element of Air. Let it consume the sage." She took a small plastic water bottle from the backpack and poured some in her hand. "Element of Water, purify her anger." She dribbled it over Sofia's head.

"You beseeched the spirits for friends. If you think of them as friends, the spell stops."

Sofia closed her eyes. Her lips mashed together in deep meditation.

Paige set her hands on Sofia's shoulders. That one girl's horrible screams replayed in her memory. She had little trouble gathering the desire for the spell to stop harming the eighth-graders. Rapid trampling in the trees ran around them, a sound like a dozen angry wild boars. Paige leapt to her feet, turning, staring into the dark.

"What was that?" Sofia shivered. "Kenz said if we tried to mess with the spell, it would hurt us."

Paige squinted at a moving shadow. *I see you.* "Do you want more people getting hurt?"

"No." Sofia looked down.

"Then focus on that. Let me worry about the backblast."

"Okay," whispered Sofia. She sucked in a breath. "Look out!"

Paige whirled at another streak of darkness. A force hit her full front, as if a moving wall had slammed into her at the speed of a man running. Pain spread across her face. She hit the ground on her back, rolling over three times.

"Paige!" yelled Sofia.

"Stay in the circle." Paige grabbed her left cheek, finding it sore and burning. She clambered to her feet, but hit the ground on her chest again when a 'hand' tightened around her ankle. "Crap!"

She clawed at the dirt, trying to pull herself forward. Kicking found only air, though solid pressure constricted around her leg. Two spots of white light appeared about where a man's eyes would be. Cold raced up the back of her left leg, over her butt, and five needlepoints pierced the small of her back.

Paige howled.

Sofia leapt up.

"Stay inside!" yelled Paige.

"But… but…"

Paige gave up trying to pull away, and flung herself over onto her back. The sense of claws in her flesh dissipated. She sat up and slashed the letter opener through the dark spot, striking nothing but air.

"I banish you back to wherever you came from!" yelled Paige. She swiped the athame back the other way. "You are not welcome here."

The shadow form reared up, twisted as if looking into the distance, and rushed off into the woods. Paige rolled up on all fours and crawled back to the circle.

"Your face…" Sofia went wide-eyed.

"What happened?"

Sofia traced her fingers over Paige's cheek. "Red lines, like a cat got you... but the skin's not cut."

"It's trying to stop me from doing this." Paige shifted to her knees. "Keep focusing on protecting your friends."

"Elements of Air, Earth, Fire, and Water, I thank you for granting us your presence. Helpful spirits, we are grateful for your aid."

Paige blew out the east candle, and made her way around the circle counterclockwise, repeating thanks to the individual elements as she extinguished the candle at each point. She concentrated on the idea of energy within the circle returning to the earth.

Sofia blew out the candle in her hand last. She opened her mouth, but closed it without speaking.

"If you believe it worked, it will." Paige brushed over a section of the line, envisioning a door opening in the circle. "Step out here."

Sofia did.

"I return this circle to the spirits and the earth." Paige smoothed out the rest of the pentacle.

"Is the magic gonna come after you now?"

"I'll never forget the way that girl screamed."

"Michelle." Sofia looked down.

Paige reached behind her, hissing as she touched the burning spot. Her hand came back with a little blood on it. She pressed her palm into the dirt where the circle had been. "I can fight it. Those kids can't. Leave them alone and bring it on, bastard."

"Don't tease it." Sofia shivered.

"I'm not teasing it. I want it to go away, not fight, but... Kenz." Paige grumbled.

Sofia lifted Paige's sweatshirt and tee to expose her back.

Paige cringed at the feeling of cloth peeling away from a wound. "Ow. How bad is it?"

"Looks like a love scratch from a tiger or something. Not that deep." Sofia pulled the shirt back down. "You should take a picture and post it on a paranormal site. You could be famous. Scratch manifestations are cool."

"Ugh." She gathered everything into the backpack. "I gotta get to the school."

"I'm going."

"You don't have to." Paige stood and slung her pack over one shoulder. "What are you doing outside alone at this hour anyway? Your parents are like super overprotective."

"Ugh. Don't remind me." Sofia looked down. "Please don't tell on me. I snuck out my window."

"You sure? There's a lot of people there."

Sofia shook her head. "I don't wanna be alone out here."

"Okay."

Paige returned to the road and quick-walked into the lights of downtown. Every window in every storefront seemed to breed sentience, as though the blackness inside watched her with malicious intentions. She refused to look, dreading what she might see. A few blocks in, she took the corner and the glaring lights of the school's football field came into view. For whatever reason, they'd put it some distance away from the building.

*They have that massive field there... why'd they build the stadium four blocks away?*

She slalomed among dozens of cars parked in a grassy patch, crossed a street, and strode among more cars in a paved lot. A tall fence to the left of the gate, below bleacher seats, blocked much of the view. Sofia followed her to the back end of a crowd gathered as close to the sidelines as the officials allowed.

Not being taller than the wall of senior and junior boys (and having zero interest in football), Paige didn't bother trying to look at the players running about and scanned the stands for Emily. Having no luck, she pulled out her phone and called.

"Hey," said Emily.

"I'm here... but I can't find you."

"I'm up top under the scoreboard. I'll stand."

Paige looked back at the bleachers. Emily waved at her from the topmost row, under the display of 21 to 24, in favor of the Goats. "Got it. How much time is left?"

"About six minutes, then one more period."

"'Kay." She hung up and climbed into the bleachers, intent on scaling the rows.

Sofia grabbed her hand. The girl's discomfort at being in so public a place showed clear as day on her face. *Guess she's more afraid of dark woods than crowds.* Fortunately, everyone paid more attention to the game, and the only reaction either of them got was someone leaning to the side to watch around them or a grumble at having to do so.

Tightness pressed on Paige's chest from all sides. Her lungs refused to take in air. Her heart slammed in her chest. Overwhelming dread caused her legs to lock. The crowd around her erupted in boos.

Every fiber of her soul said 'don't look,' but she turned anyway.

The world seemed to drag into slow motion as two huge players in green and yellow jerseys closed in on Cole. The Goats' play had gone south; their offensive line broke apart in shambles. Cole faded back a few yards, then a few more. One opposing player launched himself over the remnants of the wall of bodies in a flying tackle.

A faster defenseman rounded the near side of the line, sprinting into Cole from behind and right as the flying kid hit him like a missile. The Goats' quarterback flipped airborne in a sideways spin and crashed down on his helmet. The ball bounced away, and disappeared under a pile of players. The visiting fans went ballistic, cheering.

Boos resonated in a chorus from the home team fans. The ref dropped a yellow flag and waved at the player who went airborne. The boy who hit Cole from the side picked himself up and reached down to help Cole up, but he didn't move.

Paige collapsed onto the nearest bench, staring at him. Sound fell into a watery nothingness. Emily's desperate scream filtered through as a high note among the chaos. Sofia's face appeared in front of her. The younger girl shook her and seemed to be speaking, but the sound had no meaning.

Paige knew Cole wouldn't be getting up.

Not tonight... and not ever again.

# 30

# THE WRATHFUL DARK

Thursday October 22 - 9:24 p.m.

Paige lay face down on her bed and sobbed into her pillow. The ride home from the stadium felt like it'd happened days ago. She didn't remember Dad pulling off her boots or even carrying her upstairs. The memory of the downtown passing by a car window played on loop between long periods of watching Cole's neck snap. Over an hour after she lay down, she noticed her clothes were different. She hoped she'd been the one to change herself into her Foamy the Squirrel shirt and ditch her bra. Her pillow smelled like fabric softener, without a trace of strawberry. Its absence made her cry harder and she spent a few minutes sniffing after any sign of Melissa having existed, but found none.

She rolled on her side and curled up, bawling at the thought she'd let him die by stopping.

"I took too long getting there... Sofia wasn't in danger. Why am I so stupid?"

She cried herself numb, and lay quiet listening to the weak murmur of the television downstairs. Every now and then, Mom broke into tears as well. She yelled at Dad too, but more in the sense of 'why aren't they doing anything' rather than being angry with him.

A tiny voice echoed in her room, a single word too faint to make out.

She looked at the clock. *That kid's outside kinda late.*

"Paige." The voice again, louder, a girl, came from her closet. "Paige, where are you?"

*Melissa!* She shot upright. "Mel?"

"Paige, I can't find you. Where am I?"

She slid off the bed and gasped at the coldness of the carpet. Her socks perched at the top of her boots near the nightstand. Cold air blew out of the closet, hard enough to press her tee against her body.

"Paige? Can you hear me?" Melissa sounded as though she yelled from far away.

The closet door didn't want to move. Paige set her stance and grabbed it with both hands, grunting and whining; her muscles burned. Carpet gathered between her toes as she strained to pull it open, her feet sliding more than holding. She braced one leg against the wall and shoved. As if made of stone, the door begrudgingly gave way and creaked wide. Wind picked up strength, blowing out of the mirror.

Rather than a reflection of her room, the mirror presented a view into a creepy white-tiled hallway reminiscent of an abandoned asylum. A medical gurney lay empty against one wall, and a pair of double doors with translucent round windows stood at the end.

"Paige, please, you have to hurry," yelled Melissa. "This place is scary!"

She reached out and touched the glass. Her bedroom flashed to black and white and the wind ceased. Paige pressed on the glass, which no longer felt cold, but remained hard. When she pulled away, her fingers stuck for a second before peeling loose, sending ripples across the glass as though it had become water.

"Pay!" yelled Melissa. She sounded closer.

"I'm here," shouted Paige. "Melissa?"

"Amber says you gotta help your friend." Melissa's voice sounded tinier, farther away.

Paige raised her arm, feeling nothing where mirror had once been. "I shouldn't..."

Fear gripped her.

"Okay. Maybe I should." The unusual terror faded as soon as she decided to go through.

Grasping the sides of the mirror-door, she climbed through and set her foot down on pale linoleum tile neither cold nor warm. Two steps later, she turned. The hallway behind her ended in a black swirl where a narrow rectangular portal contained a view into her bedroom. She surrendered to curiosity and advanced, walking at an angle with her left side forward. Halfway between mirror and the end, she pulled open a plain white door on the right. Jars of chemicals lined the shelves of a closet almost as big as her dining room. She closed it and continued to the double doors.

"This is so weird." Paige looked at her palms, then the backs of her hands. "I really am in black and white." She remembered classmates teasing her with that line for being so pale. Now, a few years removed from sixth grade, it seemed funny.

She pushed the left door open and choked on a cloud of chemical fumes flooding her nostrils and burning into her throat. Two heavy-duty steel tables stood at the center of a large room with white tile walls. One held a body-shaped silhouette under a white sheet. A tray of tools waited nearby. Between the tables lurked a giant machine with two cylindrical tanks connected to hoses tipped with gargantuan needles. An opening on the right led to a darkened alcove. One look at it filled her with an instinctual urge to avoid it at all costs. Light filtered in from the round windows of a second set of double doors on the left. Along the wall on the opposite side of the room from where she entered, a long steel table held two sinks and an array of cabinets as well as boxes of makeup. Two steel procedure tables stood at the center of the room, one empty, one with a human shape under a sheet.

"Oh, shit." Paige shivered. "I'm in the morgue or something." She took a breath and yelled, "Mel where are you?" She eyed the body on the slab. "Uhh, hey. Sorry you died and stuff. I'm just gonna walk by, okay? No disrespect."

Gaze locked on the body, she crept to the other set of double doors. Her hip caught the end of the empty table. The giant steel construct didn't wobble in the slightest, bolted to the floor.

"Ow." She slumped over it. "Damn that hurt."

The body sat up. White sheet slipped down, exposing Cole's face. Dark bruising encircled his neck. He turned an emotionless expression toward her.

Paige screamed and backpedaled. "I'm sorry!"

Cole swung his legs off the table and pulled the huge embalming needle out of his arm. The sheet fell away as he stood. Paige's guts churned. She wanted to look away from the nude boy, but didn't dare take her eyes off the animated corpse.

He walked toward her.

"Cole... please... I'm sorry I took so long. Sofia was so scared. I had to help her." She backed up. "What do you want?"

He continued advancing, arms at his sides, no emotion in his eyes.

Paige shrieked when her back touched wall. She scrambled to her left and shoved the second set of doors open amid plastic clattering. Another white-tile corridor led about twenty yards to a black-painted metal door. An open archway on the left offered a view of a small locker room with three shower stalls.

The clap of her bare feet on the tile echoed louder than it should have as she ran to the black door. Her hands slipped around the brushed steel knob, which didn't move. Cole brushed the doors open, drawing nearer.

"What do you want?" Paige yelled. She thrashed at the knob, but it seemed strong enough that the entire Goats football team couldn't break it down. "Cole, please... I'm sorry."

Dead steps dragged across the floor in a steady, unrelenting rhythm.

Paige rolled her back against the door. The former quarterback ambled down the middle of the hallway. She hesitated, terrified at the thought of going near him. She tried to force her body to pass through the metal door when he reached six feet away. One step later, she faked left and darted to the right. He caught her by the arms. She leapt back as if burned, waving her hands and shrieking.

Again, she backed into the door that refused to open. She whirled to face it, pounding on it. Cole stopped behind her, so close his pectorals touched her shoulders.

Paige trembled against the painted steel. "I'm sorry. Please don't hurt me."

His hand settled on her arm.

She screamed and dropped to the floor, crossing her arms over her face, bawling.

"Paige," whispered Cole. He looked down at her, his head sagging at an inhuman angle to the right.

"I'm sorry." She managed to stop crying.

"Stand."

She pulled her knees up and hid her face behind them. "I..."

"There isn't time." He offered his hand.

*I don't wanna touch a dead person.* With nowhere to go, she reluctantly raised her arm.

Cole pulled her to her feet. A sickening grinding of bone came from his neck as he straightened his head. "Take Sofia out through the mirror. There isn't time." He backed up and turned flat against the side wall.

"But..."

He pointed at the shadowy room she shied away from.

"But..." Paige shivered, shaking her head. "No way. That's evil."

He took her hand. Goosebumps sprouted everywhere.

Paige shied to the left, not looking at him as he led her back through the prep room to the alcove. He stopped before the wavering shadow curtain.

"There isn't time." Cole put his hand on her back and shoved her forward.

Flailing, she broke a thick gauzy mass that broke apart like a dense spider web full of frantic scratching cats, and hit a thin-carpeted floor on all fours screaming. She shivered from the pain, gazing in disbelief at her intact arms, expecting to find shredded skin. To the right, four steps led up to yet another set of double doors without windows. Paige peered back at the archway.

Cole glared at her from the other side of the tattered shadow curtain. His eyes flashed blood red.

"Aaah!" Paige leapt up and ran for the stairs.

A switchback behind the doors led up a much longer stairway to a white-walled corridor decorated with somber landscape paintings and dainty tables bearing flowers in vases. Light fixtures in the shape of frosted glass seashells hung in facing pairs every fifteen feet. Three red-curtained archways sat behind black felt signs mounted on thin steel poles. Two were blank; one had white plastic letters set by hand that didn't quite line up in neat rows.

MRS. EDNA G. RUTH MAY 10, 1922—OCTOBER 14 2015
    First Viewing October 23: 9 a.m.—noon
    Second Viewing October 23: 6 p.m.—8 p.m.

*HOLY CRAP. THEY REALLY DO LIVE HERE.* PAIGE SHUDDERED. NO WONDER THOSE kids thought she was creepy. *That's kinda cool actually.* She ran past the viewing areas to a front room with waiting benches, a podium with a brass light, and a folding table set up with a white cloth and coffee makers on either side of a bowl containing various sweetener packets. Her gaze locked on to a white door with gold italic letters reading: Private.

Murmuring started behind her, as if forty friends and relatives appeared out of the blue in the farthest of the viewing rooms. Paige jumped and stared at the curtains. Nothing moved. One of the seashell lights faltered and buzzed. An elderly woman sobbed, but soon silenced herself.

Paige grabbed the knob on the private door and pulled it open. Stairs inside led up to a landing with a narrow window that looked out on a fenced-in parking lot with two hearses and four limousines. She turned a one-eighty and ran up the second set to another door. It opened without protest, letting her into a hallway that looked like an ordinary home. A shaggy grey dog on the floor in the living room to her right pedaled its legs and whined in its sleep. Left, the dining room and kitchen beyond looked empty. A closed door on the far side of the kitchen muted a man snoring.

Thickness gathered in the air straight ahead, as if the house itself did not want her going that way. She took it as the work of the entity and rushed across the multipurpose room at the top of the stairs into a claustrophobic corridor. A narrow wooden table, barely eight inches square, fell over with a *bang* behind her, breaking a tiny vase. Again, she jumped. Scratching ran down the walls on both sides, followed by the pounding of fists. Overhead, a yellowed smoke detector emitted a dire warble. As soon as she looked at it, the cover blew off and showered her with plastic fragments.

Paige ducked and guarded her head. She hurried by a narrow bathroom to the end of the hall and three doors. The one to the left stood open, revealing some kind of den set up with a giant blue velveteen wingback chair, a table, and hundreds of books on shelves. The door right in front of her turned out to be a closet. She left it open and barged through the other, into a bedroom full of dolls. Almost every iota of visible wall space held six-inch wooden shelves, packed to the brim with everything from Barbies to ragdolls to baby dolls to porcelain-faced antiques. Most of them moved to look at her. Some clapped.

"Daaaaamn," whispered Paige.

Sofia lay on the bed, curled on her side with her back to the door, her arm over a stuffed unicorn almost as big as her. The noise of thirty-odd plastic babies crying 'mama' woke her. She sat up, gazing around in horror at the cacophony of moving dolls, seeming about ready to scream herself hoarse. At the sight of Paige, she clamped her mouth closed and stared.

Paige ran over and grabbed her by the wrist. "No time to explain. You have to come with me."

Sofia let out a wail of protest as Paige hauled her out of bed. She tripped on her long-sleeved shin-length nightgown, but managed to grab the massive unicorn plush by its horn. The girl set her heels only for a second before deciding to run along after her. The bedroom door tried to close itself, but Paige thrust her hand into the doorjamb, screaming as it slammed her forearm against the wood. She snarled and dragged the door open with both hands.

"What's happening?" Sofia clutched the four-and-a-half-foot-tall unicorn to her chest. "Why is everything black and white?"

"No time." Paige held the door open.

Sofia ducked through. Paige battled the force trying to slam it and backed into the corridor. She grabbed the girl by the arm again and pulled her down the hall to the central room by the stairs. Four steps from the stairway, Sofia locked her legs.

"No. I don't wanna go down there at night. It's scary."

"Sofia… don't make me carry you." Paige attempted the same look Mom always gave her when negotiation didn't exist. "We have to."

Sofia's grip on her unicorn tightened as a battle of willpower seemed to rage inside her.

"… 'Kay."

Paige led the girl down the steps to the funeral parlor. Sofia let off a keening whimper/whine noise the whole way down the extra-wide corridor between the viewing rooms. Again, she resisted being dragged at the stairs to the basement.

"I'm not allowed down there."

*Like that stopped you before.* "No debate."

Paige pulled the sobbing, struggling thirteen-year-old down the stairs and into the prep room. Cole had vanished. Both tables gleamed, clean and empty.

The embalming machine stood against the wall to the right of the long table full of makeup equipment. She pondered the oddity of it for only an instant and ran for the corridor she'd come in from.

Sofia hid her face against the stuffed unicorn. "What's going on?"

Paige shoved the doors open hard enough to slap them into the walls. Sofia gasped at the portal. Her whimpery demeanor shifted to one of curiosity.

"Whoa. That's so cool."

"Come on." Paige put an arm around Sofia's back and rushed ahead.

The closet door burst open and a mass of yellowed writhing hoses flailed at the air, hissing like livid cobras. Sofia shrieked at the suddenness of it. Paige raised her arm and bore the brunt of the rubber serpents' whipping. One slapped down on the instep of her left foot with a *crack* that stung like ten bees. A rotting tube coiled around Sofia's left ankle, and pulled her off her feet.

The girl screamed and burst into tears, futilely clawing at the tile floor with nothing to grab hold of. "Mommy! Daddy!"

"Shit!" Paige yelled, hopping in pain.

Another hose lanced out and wound about Paige's neck. She forced herself to the side, stretching the leash, and grabbed the rubber cord dragging the screaming Sofia into the closet by the leg. An army of angry tubes whipped Paige across the back as she overpowered the tangle of rubber and freed her friend's foot.

Sofia let out a high-pitched shriek as more hoses lanced out to grab her. Paige threw herself in the way as her friend scrambled away and leapt upright, dragging the enormous stuffed unicorn with her. A handful of heavy-duty surgical tubing wrapped around Paige, pinning her arms to her sides, squeezing so tight she could barely breathe, trying to draw her backward into the closet.

"Go! Jump through," wheezed Paige, grunting and squirming.

Sofia ran to within arm's length of the hole before stopping to turn back.

"Go!" yelled Paige. She wrenched herself around, throwing her weight into the tubes to grind them against the edge of the doorjamb. She struggled to reach up at her throat, but her pinned arms couldn't move far enough. Desperation welled up with the clear thought she had seconds to spare before death. With a defiant roar, she surged toward the waiting exit, stretching rubber with a spine-tingling creak. Hoses snapped and she lurched forward to her knees. The one around her throat stretched taut as she rolled to face the closet and backed toward the mirror-portal, raising her freed arms to defend against the ceaseless tangle of whips.

Sofia ran up behind her and forced her fingers between the tube and the back of her neck. One by one, Paige caught the whips and tore them. Pressure

THE WRATHFUL DARK | 235

around her neck cut off blood to her brain. Reality began to fade to woozy darkness.

A second before she passed out, the old rubber cracked and snapped, dumping Sofia on her butt. The leash zoomed back into the closet with enough force to drag most of the mass of writhing tubes with it. Paige scooted away from three more hoses scrabbling at her feet. She flipped over on all fours and clambered up to a run, caught Sofia with one arm, and jumped into the mirror.

They landed in Paige's room, sliding over the carpet and crashing into the side of the bed, flung forward by a burst of energy. Ripples spread across the mirror. Color filled in; the reflection of her bedroom devoured the mortuary hall.

"That's so messed up." Sofia abandoned the unicorn (which now had a forest-green mane and yellow horn) to grab Paige. "Are we dreaming?"

"I don't think so." Paige shifted her weight and sat up with her back against the bed. "I saw Cole downstairs."

"No way. He *just* died today… they wouldn't have brought him to the home so fast." Sofia shivered. "Grim was barking his head off all day, like there was something in the house."

"You named your dog Grim?"

"Yeah." She looked down. "The Grim Pee-er. I thought it was funny when I was six."

"I guess it is kinda funny. Sorry if my sense of humor's on vacation right now." Paige combed her hair with her fingers.

"He's an Irish wolfhound." Sofia wrapped herself, arm and leg, around the unicorn. "How did I get to your house?"

"I don't know. I heard my sister in the mirror and it turned into a doorway and Cole said I had to bring you through… that there wasn't time?"

"Wasn't time for what?" asked Sofia.

A distant explosion went off with a brief flash of red-orange light reflected on near-skeletal trees.

"What the hell was that?" Paige ran to the window, giving the dark woods a cursory glance. "I don't see anything."

"It's mad at me." Sofia shivered. "I had a bad dream that all the kids at school found out it was me that hurt them. They were chasing me around with knives. Is it gonna kill me?"

Paige swallowed hard. *It just tried.* "Uhh… Uhh…" *How do I tell a kid her parents just died in an explosion?* She trudged over and sat on the bed. "I don't know. I thought the spell I did would protect you. Maybe it did."

"Huh?" Sofia glanced at something under the bed. "Wow. I didn't know you played with Barbies." She reached in and extracted a mermaid doll. "This is cute."

"It's my sister's."

"Uh huh. Sure." Sofia smirked.

"Seriously." Paige leaned forward, fighting back the urge to cry. "I used to scream at her for leaving her junk in my room all the time." Her eyes popped open. "That wasn't here this morning."

The house phone rang.

Paige gulped. The phone cut out on the third ring. A moment later, the heavy *thuds* of Dad walking the hallway went by. He thundered down the steps. The all too familiar rattle of his utility belt preceded the front door opening and closing.

"Guess he's not on desk duty yet… or they need him bad."

Sofia crawled up onto the bed. "I guess I'm sleeping over. Your room feels different."

Paige looked at her. "Different?"

"Safer." She shrugged. "My house always feels scary at night. That's why I have so many dolls. They watch me and chase away the bad spirits."

Paige shivered.

"Do you think Cole hurt?"

"I dunno. It looked quick."

Sofia stroked the unicorn's mane. "I read about when they used to cut people's heads off in England, the head would be alive for a little while after. Like, sometimes the eyes would move. Is a broken neck the same?"

Paige exhaled. "No idea. I guess living at a funeral home kinda makes a person fascinated with death."

"Not really. Everybody expects me to be like Wednesday Addams, so… I guess I just did it."

Paige chuckled. "Kinda why I dove into the Goth thing. This isn't white face paint."

Sofia overacted a gasp. "Really? I don't believe you." She rubbed Paige's cheek. "Wow."

"Very funny."

"So, uhh. What do you do for fun?"

Sofia shrugged. "Not much. I usually read all the time. Sometimes I play games on the computer, but my parents only let me use it for two hours a day… including school work."

"That's bogus." Paige smirked. "School stuff shouldn't count."

"They're overprotective." Sofia swung her one leg that dangled over the edge of the bed. "It's not so bad. They're not gonna enforce that next year when I'm in high school." She paused a moment. "If I'm still alive."

Paige fidgeted at her skirt. "I got picked on too in grade school."

"Why?"

"I don't know. I avoided people my own age. My whole world revolved around my older sister. Somewhere between looking Goth without trying and being antisocial I made an easy target."

"I'm not antisocial. I tried to be friends with them, but all they see is the 'funeral home girl' or 'creepy chan.'"

"People can be dicks."

"Yeah." Sofia nodded.

"Maybe stop wearing all black?"

"Maybe dye your hair blonde?"

Paige grinned. "Checkmate."

"I like black." Sofia frowned. "Not my fault it's morbid. I'm not morbid."

Sofia got comfortable on the bed. Paige reclined, but sleep was *way* far off. She rubbed the spot on her neck where the hose had grabbed her. They chatted for a while about music, but Paige's mind kept drifting back to what Sofia's house must have become. Was Dad looking at the charred remains of everything-every*one* this poor kid had ever loved? She managed to keep an outward calm despite the roiling guilt in her heart while discussing the strengths and weaknesses of several bands like Sisters of Mercy, Joy Division, Peter Murphy, Type-O, and Evanescence. Out of nowhere, Sofia laughed.

"You *are* a Goth."

Paige sputtered. "Yeah... guess."

Sofia liked a lot of the same music, but also confessed to the occasional boy band or rap-rock.

Paige groaned.

"What kind of movies do you like?"

"I don't watch much TV." Paige flicked at the blanket. "Whenever I do, it's a cartoon for Melissa... used to be whatever Amber watched. She liked this one show with some blonde girl chasing vampires... and we were all into those ghost-investigation-type shows."

"Oh." Sofia picked up on the sorrow in her voice and got quiet.

Paige stared at the ceiling for a while. "What?"

"Sorry for making you sad. Was your sister in my house too?"

She sat up. "I don't think so. She's... somewhere on the other side of the mirror."

Sofia hugged the giant unicorn. "Is it better knowing she's in there than worrying if some creeper's got her?"

Paige shivered. "I... can't answer that."

*Whump.* The front door closed.

"Hang on." Paige hopped out of bed and ran to her door.

Dad trudged up the stairs, looking like he could sleep for months.

"Hey," whispered Paige.

He paused. "Hey. Still can't sleep?"

"Nope. What happened?"

"The Anderson funeral home exploded."

Paige expected as much, but still gasped. "Oh, no. Did they, uhh...?"

"Mr. and Mrs. Anderson are banged up, but they're okay. Their daughter..." Dad choked up. "Her bedroom was directly above the room full of chemicals that exploded." He took a long breath. "We didn't even find a tiny piece of her."

Vomiting came from behind Paige.

"What the hell?" Dad tilted his head. "When did we get a cat?"

"Uhh, sorry, Dad. I guess I should've asked permission first. Sofia was sleeping over tonight." She backed away from the door, pulling it open.

Sofia sprawled on the floor by the desk, head over the wastebasket, coughing.

Dad about fainted.

Paige held on to him. Tears slipped down his cheeks as he reached up to his shoulder mic.

"Dispatch, Thomas here. Come back."

"Copy, Thomas," said a male voice.

"Do we have anyone near the Andersons still?"

"Standby." The radio chirped off with a hiss.

Sofia ran over and grabbed Paige, looking up at her dad. "What happened to my dog?"

Dad sucked in a breath and reined in his emotion. "We didn't find a dog... alive or dead."

Paige rubbed Sofia's back. "Animals are aware of stuff. He probably got out."

"Thomas, come back," crackled the radio.

"Go ahead, Dispatch."

"One of the locals is driving them to the Shady Oaks Motel. I can't do a direct patch, but I can relay via phone."

*Shady Oaks... Gee that sounds like the scene of a horror movie.*

"They're going to want to hear this." Dad took another breath. "Someone or something was looking out for them tonight. Their daughter's at my house... she's friends with my kid. The girls didn't bother telling anyone."

"Thank God," said Dispatch. "I'll let them know."

Relief that Sofia's parents survived fell on Paige like a lead blanket. Sleep now seemed possible. She leaned on her father to keep from falling over. Sofia fidgeted.

"Thomas, local relayed the news. They're eager to see her."

"Shady Oaks?" asked Dad.

"Copy that."

"I'll run her over there."

"Copy."

He looked at Sofia. "Sorry to interrupt your sleepover. There's been an accident at your home."

She nodded, still shivering. "Okay."

"Get dressed."

Sofia raised her arms and let them fall at her side. "I am dressed."

"You came over in your nightgown?" Dad blinked.

"It's a long story, Dad. Basically, she did." Paige rummaged her dresser for an older, smaller pair of blue jeans she didn't bother trying to fit into anymore as well as a faded green babydoll top. "Here… you can keep these if you want." She studied Sofia's dainty feet. "Can't do anything about shoes though. Mom's anal about donating old ones."

"Thanks." Sofia ran to the attached bathroom.

Paige flopped on her bed, handed the huge unicorn plush over when Sofia came for it, and braced her arm across her forehead after they left. Did her spell work? *It had to. Why else would the demon try to kill her?*

"I… should cast another one to protect her." As ready as she'd been to collapse a minute ago, her old friend the ceiling remained square in her view. "I'm gonna need to cast a spell to sleep."

# ONE LEFT

Thursday October 22 - 10:27 p.m.

Ten minutes after the front door closed, Paige gave up on sleep and paced. Seven orbits later, she got caught a whiff of half-digested Italian food and took the wastebasket into the bathroom to clean it before resuming her circular bedroom wandering.

"What can I do?" She paused at the window. Trees caught the moonlight, glowing like stark white-brown brushstrokes on the black canvas of the night sky. "Every time I try to help someone with magic it feels like I only make things worse."

Pacing.

"I can't fight that thing without a spell, but... what'll happen next time?" She held her stomach and continued walking around.

Circle. Figure eight. Square. She absentmindedly walked a pentacle.

"Should I break into Kenzie's place and take the book?"

Paige faced the closet mirror again. No portal, only a forlorn sixteen-year-old with smudged black lipstick in a long tee shirt. She pulled at her hair, almost down to her breasts. She'd never let it even touch her shoulders before... after Amber, she really did give up on caring.

*Hell with it. Mom always wanted me to grow it long.*

She stopped in the bathroom and wiped off the lipstick before pacing more.

"Maybe I could go to New Hope and find some old crone there who can tell me what to do?" She rolled her eyes. "No, they'll scam me... or think I'm some pothead. They'll never let me take the car that far away, and they won't make a trip like that with Melissa missing."

Paige sniffled. *Melissa.* She sank to the floor and hugged her knees to her chest, daydreaming that she clutched her little sister. Her tears still flowed freely when Dad came home about a half hour later. She let her legs slide forward and wiped her cheeks.

Dad tromped up the stairs and headed right to her bedroom door. "Hey."

"Hey."

He flopped on the rug next to her. After a moment of quiet, he broke down and sobbed into his hand.

Paige leaned against him.

"They were so happy to see her alive. Mrs. Anderson couldn't even talk." He let out an anguished gargle. "The Andersons only have one. I had three and I ignored two. I'm so sorry... I don't know what I can do to fix—"

"Dad..." Paige sniffled. "I forgive you."

"I've only got you left." He seemed to control his tears and held her close. "I swear if Melissa's still alive, you'll *both* have a father."

"Oh... crap." *This is exactly my wish coming true.* She thought back to that night she held Dad's duty weapon and thought about joining Amber on the other side. *If that thing kills Melissa...* "I'm not giving up on her."

"I will find the son of a bitch that took her, and when I find him... I don't care what the law says I can or can't do to him."

Mom, in a burgundy bathrobe, poked her head in. The sight of tears on Dad's face scared her white.

"It's okay, Mom." Paige waved her in.

"Andrea." Dad looked up at her. "It's not bad news."

Mom glided by and sat in the desk chair. "What's going on?"

Dad explained the funeral home explosion, thinking the Anderson's thirteen-year-old daughter had been vaporized by a freak detonation of chemicals plus a natural gas heating system, and then finding her right here in Paige's room without a scratch. The parents' reaction to seeing her had hit him like a ton of bricks.

Mom wiped her eyes. She seemed happy for them, but couldn't hide a tiny bit of jealousy.

Paige felt a cry building up inside her, but forced herself to detach. *I can't hold this in anymore.* "Mom, Dad... This is my fault. At least one-fifth."

"Don't go blaming yourself for what happened to Melissa." Dad squeezed her.

"I'm sorry for screaming at you the other day, Paige." Mom kneaded the seat cushion on either side of her legs. "I don't think you had anything to do with it."

"I did." Paige picked at the rug. "You might not believe me, but I did."

Amber peered out of the closet and walked up to the corner of the bed. Paige smiled at her.

"You've been through so much in this damn town that was supposed to be quiet." Dad frowned. "We should move back to the inner city for peace."

Mom scoffed.

"It's not the town's fault." Paige pulled her feet in and sat cross-legged. "Hear me out."

Her parents gave her expectant, but patronizing, looks.

"I met these girls at school the first day." She described Mackenzie, Renee, Santana, and Sofia. "I dropped Melissa off in the grade school, and on my way out, I hear this crying coming from a locker. Someone had shut Sofia inside and put a padlock on it. The girl who did it didn't even know the combination… she changed it with her eyes closed."

Dad shook his head. "Kids."

"I wanted to help her. I felt so bad. No idea why, but I grabbed the lock. As soon as I touched it, I like blacked out and saw the dial turning to the combination. I tried it and it worked."

Mom looked down. "Your Grandmother had stories like that too."

"Didn't you say your mother had dementia?"

"Maybe she did. Calling her eccentric was easier to swallow." Mom gathered her robe tighter.

"All these girls were really unhappy. Kenzie found this old book in her attic that she said had magic in it."

Dad rubbed his eyebrows.

Paige put a hand on his shoulder. "Don't zone out on me." She went through a description of the ritual, of what each girl asked the spirits for. "When it was my turn… I thought about wishing Amber back to life, but I had this crazy weird feeling that it would be a *very* bad idea."

Amber went wide-eyed. "Yeah… that wouldn't have ended well at all."

Her parents didn't react to the voice.

"Paige, you—"

She held a hand up, stalling Mom. "Instead, I asked the spirits to help Dad deal with his guilt. I asked them to help him break free of the funk he'd been in ever since Amber's accident."

He looked at her with an amused expression. "So you basically found a genie and used up your wish on someone else?"

Paige didn't smile. "That's why we're all still alive. Mackenzie tainted the ritual. She turned it dark with that stupid book. She basically bullied Sofia into…" *Shit.* "Dad. Turn off cop for now, please. I'll legitimately be angry with you if you report what I'm gonna say."

"Depends on what it is. Some things I can't ignore."

Paige bit her lip. "She took some blood from the funeral home that had been removed from a body."

Mom squirmed. "That's disgusting."

"Kenz bullied her into it." Paige raised her voice. "She's so desperate for friends, she'd do anything." She explained the candles, the hair, and the demon appearing. "Think about everything that's happened. The shooting at the bank. If her mother had been killed, life insurance or a lawsuit against the bank. We interfered and stopped that. The spell got pissed and went after Mr. Ruiz. Do you really believe a guy who's been teaching chemistry for twenty years is going to derp a simple experiment and kill himself? What about all those mishaps at the school with kids getting hurt? Doesn't *anyone* think it's odd that every single injured kid is in the eighth grade? Not one 'accident' happened to anyone younger or older. Sofia was hurt and angry inside, and the spell picked up on that. She asked for one thing but wanted another."

Mom and Dad exchanged a glance.

"My wish... The car that almost hit me. I still don't know if that was for Emily or meant as a near miss to scare you guys that I almost died to a car accident too. I *know* the entity took Melissa."

"Why?" Dad swallowed the croak in his voice. "Why would it do that? Get me out of one depression to start another?"

"I don't think it would kill her... it wanted to, uhh scare you. You know. That whole 'you don't know what you got till it's gone' thing? But, I dunno what's going on now. The spell's coming unwound. I interfered too much. I kept begging Kenzie to help me stop it, but she had her bitch blinders on and refused 'cause she hadn't got what she wanted yet. I tried to warn Cole and did a protection spell on Emily, and he said even if Em died, he'd never want a girl like Kenz." She closed her eyes, forcing out two tears. "Now he's dead. I don't know what to do."

Her parents remained quiet, perhaps practicing telepathic communication or some kind of semaphore involving facial expressions translating to deep, meaningful conversation. Dad broke the long silence first.

"Paige, I don't know what's caused you to internalize so much guilt. You blamed yourself for Amber's death... Maybe you did see it coming, maybe you had food poisoning that night."

*Damn. Here comes the shrinks.* "But, Dad."

"Paige, honey... do you really believe everything you just said?" Mom half hid her face behind her bathrobe's puffy sleeves. "I mean... some of those things do sound a bit too coincidental, but grief can do weird things. Make people see connections where there aren't."

Amber walked over. A brief puff of cold air wafted off her.

Dad startled and gasped.

Mom leaned back in her chair.

"Dad, listen to her." Amber reached toward him, offering a sad smile. "Mom..." She offered her other hand to Mom.

He tried to take her hand, but grasped at nothing. Mom stepped forward, but her attempt to hug her eldest passed right through her. With a regretful look, Amber lowered her gaze and walked to the closet, leaving Dad staring at the spot where she'd manifested. She hesitated at the door.

"Paige. The cabin."

"Wait." Paige twisted around and got up. "Amb, wait. Where are you going?"

"Watching Melissa." Amber touched the mirror and vanished.

Paige faced back to her parents. Dad and Mom both stared aghast.

She looked down. *Too late now. They think I've cracked.* "Yes. I can see her all the time when she's here. Amber said go to the cabin."

Dad cleared his throat and stood. She shrank in on herself as he approached, expecting worry and pity in varying degrees. He grasped her shoulders. "Paige."

She weathered his stare for a moment. Once the silence became unbearable, she forced herself to make eye contact. *I'm not crazy.*

"Go back to the beginning and tell me every little detail."

# 32

# DEAD INSIDE

Thursday October 22 - 11:38 p.m.

The pale eye of the moon gazed down from above a racing tangle of bare branches, stark black against a field of deep blue-violet. Paige huddled in the passenger seat of Dad's patrol car, her hands tented over her mouth and nose in a penitent's pose. Unnatural darkness settled in the woods, thickening the farther from downtown they drove. Even the patch of headlight on the dirt road up ahead seemed to fight to exist.

She tapped her boots together and rubbed her black jeans, trying to impart some degree of warmth to her thighs. The sense of the car hurtling through an infinite void chilled her to the bone. *As if going to* that *cabin in the middle of the night wasn't scary enough.* Clingy black sleeves itched her arms; the 'too-short-to-wear-without-pants' black dress she'd substituted for a shirt had no lace to grab in the middle of a fight, no button seam to get a fistful of. Paige wasn't sure what to expect at the cabin, other than violence of some form. Not that she could've walked there, as far as it was, but Dad insisted he come along. He seemed surprised when she readily agreed.

"Take that thing off your neck."

"It never bothered you before." She swallowed.

"You kept muttering about your fight with that other girl. Someone could grab it and strangle you."

"Oh." She took off the leather choker and stuffed it in her jacket pocket. "Right."

"Any idea what we're gonna see when we get there?"

Paige clutched her knees. "At best, a spastic psychotic blonde... at worst, probably some old-ass demon that isn't even solid unless it wants to be."

"I don't remember ancient evils being covered in training." He wrung his hands on the wheel. "That was really Amber."

"Yeah."

"How long has she been in the house?"

"She moved in when we did." Paige glanced to her right. Something tall and black appeared to be running at pace with the car a short distance into the woods. "Oh, shit. Dad... it's out there."

A thick tree flashed by and the silhouette vanished as if wiped away by it.

"I don't see anything but trees."

"Okay, maybe that one was my imagination." She bit her knuckle. "Dad. If it's gonna kill me to get Melissa back, let it."

"I'm not going to let it kill you, *or* her."

"I had one foot in the ground already." Paige looked at the floor.

Dad slowed, glancing back and forth from the GPS to the road as if the two didn't match. "What are you talking about?"

"You're not the only one who was depressed." Paige let her hands rest in her lap. "Like three months after the accident, I was pretty close to, uhh, like... umm. Hurting myself."

"Why didn't you say anything?"

It took a moment for guilt to release its strangle grip on her voice box. "Because I didn't want help... I wanted to be with her." She sniffled. "Amber talked me out of it. That's the night she showed up. Don't freak on me, Dad. I'm not standing on that cliff anymore. Not even close."

He reached over and held her hand. "She was so special. Everyone loved her."

"Yeah."

"You're special too, Paige. I know I haven't shown it much this past year, but... if anything happened to you, I'd be just as lost."

"It's my fault it took Melissa. If anything happens to her, I'm..." Paige shivered.

"Going to be put in a facility until you cope." He winked.

She laughed.

He squeezed her hand hard enough to hurt. "Paige. Promise me you'll work through it. Don't make us lose all three of our daughters."

She slumped forward and cried. "You're right... That's too easy. I should live with the guilt. Better punishment that way."

"Hey..." The car slowed. "Is that it?"

Paige lifted her head and pulled damp hair off her face, a macabre curtain exposing a haunted stage. The pale cabin perched at the top of a grass-covered clearing matched the image seared into her memory. Mackenzie's beige Kia Soul sat outside, parked askew at the end of tire gouges. Candle light flickered inside, making a pair of four-panel windows into glowing eyes.

A feeling of warning came over her, urging her forward instead of away.

"Yeah. We should hurry."

Dad pulled up behind the Kia, killed the engine, and got out. Paige scrambled around the passenger door, leaving it open, and ran past him to the cabin. Peeling paint flaked off all over her as she barged in and skidded to a halt a few feet past the entrance.

Mackenzie, still in the long pink night tee, knelt by the pentacle and flipped rapidly from page to page in the giant book. Six-inch flame needles of dark crimson sprouted from the nine corpse-blood candles, while the lone white one burned orange and normal. Small piles of crumbled herbs and orange, brown, and green powders sat on top of symbols painted in silver. The blonde's right palm dribbled blood from a small cut that seemed self-inflicted.

To her left, the frame mirror presented an exact reflection of the room with one difference—Melissa, in her nightie, lay unconscious in the middle of the pentacle. Paige stared at the real world floor. No Melissa, but the pattern of symbols and powders left an empty space where a small body might lay.

Dad entered and stood behind Paige.

"What are you doing?" She advanced. "Kenz. This is going to stop right now. *No* more. This is over!"

Mackenzie flipped backward through the book a little and smiled. "Hi, Paige. Hi Mr. Thomas. Thanks for giving her a ride. I could really use the help right now."

Dad gasped. He edged to the side, staring at the mirror.

"No, Kenz. I'm not helping you. What you're doing is blacker than black. I won't be a part of this anymore."

"That's too bad." Mackenzie leaned forward with a brush and traced a circle before adding small symbols around it. "I found a spell to bring Cole back."

"You're crazy. It'll never do what you want it to do. You'll get back some kind of horrible monster."

Dad grabbed his shoulder mic and squeezed it, but it didn't crackle or transmit. Worry spread over his face and he fussed with his belt.

"Oh, I'm sure this one will do exactly what I want." Mackenzie flashed a sultry smile. "The cost is high, so it doesn't have to play games." She glanced at the reflection. "All I need is the heart of an innocent. Ideally two, but that's hard to do on my own. People tend to get upset when children go missing."

"Where's my daughter," yelled Dad.

"Right next to you, Pops." Mackenzie laughed.

Paige snarled. "If he doesn't, I'm going to kill you if you don't let Melissa go."

Mackenzie sprinkled some loam-green powder in her cut hand and worked it into the blood before crumbling it over the new symbol she'd painted. "Kill me and she's gone. Unless you can work portal spells on your own." She laughed, a haughty sound that made Paige want to wring her neck without another word.

Her fists trembled with rage. "Kenz..."

"To complete the spell and get Cole back, I need the heart of an innocent, cut from the still living breast. We plant it in the ground and water it with six drops of my blood every day at midnight for one lunar cycle."

Paige shivered, barely containing the itch to pound Mackenzie into the dirt. "Then what. Eat it?"

Mackenzie laughed again. "No, silly. We dig Cole up and put the enchanted heart inside him. He'll wake up and be forever loyal to me." She twirled her hair around a finger. "He won't even get older."

"You're going to make him a zombie?"

Dad raised a hand. "Mackenzie... whatever you've done to Melissa, if she's still alive, it's not too late to work something out."

Mackenzie rolled her eyes. "I don't expect you to understand the subtleties of real magic. He's not going to be a zombie. The best translation I found so far called it a 'servitor.' He's not dead... He's closer to alive, but infused with power." She smiled up at Dad. "I don't *have* to use Melissa's heart. Paige is going to help me cast this spell, or I will. Do as I tell you, and your little sister goes home."

"Kenz!" shrieked Paige. "You saw what happened when you tried to make him like you. What do you think *this* is going to wind up doing? Stop! Your father is dead. You don't have to lie anymore. You can mourn your mother and move on."

The blonde giggled. "Oh... Mother's a little pissed at me. I can't even stay in that damn house right now. Stuff's flying around. Lights going on and off. Linda has some Chinese spiritualist coming over tomorrow. It's hilarious."

"You're surprised? You betrayed her... your own mother. *That's* why the thing we summoned has its hooks in you. You're all innocent on the outside, like everyone's poster girl for sweet middle America, but you're withered inside. No wonder Cole wanted nothing to do with you."

Mackenzie hissed. "You ruined everything when you warded that sugary bitch." Her voice turned sarcastic. "Oh, Emily's so sweet. Everyone loves her. She's so kind and pretty and loveable." She spat. "You killed Cole. You killed my father! Now you're going to help me get him back or I'm going to tear the heart out of your precious little sister."

"You're such a selfish bitch even a re-animated Cole wouldn't want anything to do with you."

"It's your fault!" Mackenzie let off a keening roar and sprang to her feet. She lunged at Paige with the athame.

Paige caught the arm in both hands, holding the dagger-point away from her chest. Dad pulled his gun, but didn't fire. She stomped on Mackenzie's bare toes, but the girl ignored the pain.

"You're still gonna help me, bitch." Mackenzie's eyes flared. "You're innocent enough. I bet you've never even kissed a boy. I'll use your heart too. One for Cole, and one to give to the Fire."

Paige grunted and twisted. Mackenzie grabbed her jacket and pulled. Another stomp failed to affect the enraged girl. "Kenz! Stop! It's possessed you. This isn't you!"

Mackenzie pressed forward until their bodies touched, squeezing Paige against the back wall. Dad holstered his weapon and grabbed Mackenzie by the shoulders, pulling her off. She whirled to stab him, but Paige held on to her arm. She shrieked and screamed, frothing at the mouth. Dad attempted to gather her other arm. A grab at his face distracted him from a kick to the groin that lifted him on tiptoe.

Dad swayed to the side. Paige hurled herself forward, tackling Mackenzie to the floor on her chest. The blonde laughed when Paige chicken-winged her arm up behind her back as if about to handcuff her. Dad's face reddened. He wheezed and fumbled at his belt.

Mackenzie jumped up, smashing the top of her head into Paige's face. Stars danced about. Paige grabbed at a shadow, but caught only air. Mackenzie threw her to the floor and leapt on top of her, straddling her hips. She raised the knife over her head in both hands, a manic look in her eyes.

*Bang.* A thunderous gunshot echoed in the small cabin, seeming to pause the world.

A spurt of black blood and silver sparkles burst from Mackenzie's chest, erupting from the forehead of the rabbit pimp. Mackenzie looked down at herself. She lowered the knife to one hand, and picked at the bullet hole with her left index finger.

Keening scrapes, worse than fingernails down a chalkboard came from the mirror. Paige risked a quick peek. A spiral web of cracks spread across the surface from where Dad's shot had broken it a few inches left and down from center. *Oh, no... the mirror! Melissa!*

Paige screamed and flung Mackenzie off. She jumped up and ran to the mirror, feeling helpless as the cracks spread and deepened. Dozens of little Paiges stared back at her from the smashed surface.

Mackenzie stood. Her arms dangled lax at her sides, the knife still clutched in her right hand. She thrust out her bottom lip and gave Dad a pathetic stare. "You shot me. I'm just a little high-school girl. How could you?"

His gun shook in his hand. He kept it trained on her, but his brain seemed to have jammed up. Paige shied away from touching a spatter of black blood running down the broken mirror. A matching spread seeped into the pink cotton over Mackenzie's back.

"Mr. Thomas… I'm only a child. How could you shoot me? Please tell me you didn't really mean that? If you say sorry, I'll forgive you."

He blinked. "Uhh…"

"Don't trust it!" yelled Paige. "She's trying to trick you. Stay away from her!"

Paige looked around the room for anything that seemed useful. The satchel of supplies, ancient book, candles, broken mirror, pentacle… *Yes.*

She focused her desire on breaking the ritual. "I call upon the Lady and the Horned God to protect me and reject this tainted offering. I banish the dark energy from this place. Evil spirits and evil hearts have no purchase here!"

Paige scraped her boot across the line of powder circumscribing the pentacle, brushing it aside. She concentrated on the feeling of breaking the circle and opening the wall. All ten candle flames flared up and snuffed out to fluttering black trails. Piles of reagents burst into clouds of smoke like old-time photographic flash powder.

Mackenzie's calm evaporated. She whirled, screaming, "No!"

The mirror twitched and exploded in a blast of energy and silvery glass that knocked Paige and her father to the ground and sent them sliding to the back end of the cabin. Two small paintings fell off the wall from the force of their impact. The entire structure shuddered, threatening to come down in a pile of matchsticks. Ghastly stench similar to rotten eggs and feces devoured the air, and a deafening roar howled from the mirror frame, which had become a rectangle of infinite black.

Mackenzie screamed and swatted at the glinting shards spiraling around her. The cyclone of fragments sped up and constricted. She slashed about with the athame. Two bits of mirror bounced away from the blade with faint *clinks.* Tiny cuts appeared on her legs and arms. A thin line of black crossed her forehead before it seeped a drop of ichor. Paige scooted over and grabbed on to Dad, unable to look away.

The knife slipped free of Mackenzie's fingers. She writhed on her feet, trying to guard her face with her arms, all the while shrieking 'no' repeatedly. Slice by slice, the whirling mirror fragments shredded her shirt. Scraps of pink cotton joined the cyclone. Mackenzie stood nude for mere seconds before the shards dug into her skin, flaying her alive. A finger broke off and joined the maelstrom. A glint of silver, and one breast split in half through the nipple. An ear went sailing. Larger pieces of mirror took her arm at the elbow. Mackenzie sucked in a huge breath to scream, but never released it.

Dozens of sword-like shards lanced from the tempest and jammed into her back and chest. The glistening red horror that had once been Mackenzie gurgled; black blood poured from her mouth. She started to slump to her knees, but invisible energy swept her into the air and drew her backwards through the empty frame. Bloody hands smeared black on the wooden edges; Mackenzie grunted and wailed, trying to hold on, but her grip failed as the torrent of swirling, black-stained glass hit the onyx slab with a rain of delicate twinkling, re-forming into the mirror. A skinless hand reached out from the point where the bullet had struck as if asking for help, slipping away a second later.

One black droplet crept down the seamless glass.

Paige leaned away from Dad and threw up on a pile of old leaf mulch.

He rubbed her back and squeezed her shoulder until the vomiting spell passed.

She sat back on her heels. Unable to reconcile the smiling, friendly girl she'd met on her first day at school with the *thing* that got sucked through a portal to oblivion, she wept.

"Paige..."

"Yeah." She plucked a strip of pink fabric off her arm and flung it away, not wanting to touch it.

"Where's Melissa?"

Her tears dried up. She clamped her right hand over her heart and pointed at the mirror. "In there."

# 33

# THE TENTH CANDLE

Thursday October 22 - 11:51 p.m.

The mirror presented a normal reflection of the room around it. Aside from black fingerprints on the worn pale wood of the frame, it offered no clues anything unusual had occurred. Paige pressed her hand into the glass, crying out with every ounce of wanting she could summon to pull Melissa back. Her touch left smears, but did little else.

Dad staggered to his feet and walked around, favoring his groin. He tried the radio again, but it remained dead. "What are we going to do?"

"Stop it." Paige whirled to face him. "I hate it when you sound scared. You're supposed to be the dad. You're supposed to have the answers and stuff."

He cleared his throat. "That girl was a lot stronger than she looked."

"Dad…"

"Uhh." He frowned at the pentacle. "I don't have these answers, sweetie. I never believed I'd see anything like this ever."

"Magic." Paige sighed. "Maybe I can open it again."

"That sounds like a bad idea, but…"

"I got nothing else."

Paige brushed the disrupted line back into place to close the circle. She spent a few minutes leafing through the book, but every page held descriptions of dark deeds or symbols that referenced specific demons. Most of the writing was in a language so foreign she couldn't make out individual letters. Some English translation scribbled in the margins hinted at demon summoning, influencing the minds of others, invisibility, rituals to obtain wealth, power, and one even claimed to be a path to immortality. At the description of drinking a baby's blood, Paige slammed the book closed.

"What's that?"

"Uhh... it's *not* Wicca." She cringed. "I have no idea, but I know I don't want to touch it."

"What should I do?" asked Dad.

"Try not to laugh at me. Maybe believe whatever I try is gonna do something?"

"Mmm."

She retrieved the athame and poured water over the blade, envisioning the act purifying it from Mackenzie's dark intentions. Next, she wiped away the symbols Mackenzie had added to the basic pentacle. With that done, she set up a bowl of incense and found a large bundle of sage in the satchel, which she rested on the floor at her knees. *Air is associated with travel spells...* She took some feathers from the satchel and made a little pile. *Water for purification and love.* Paige poured some water from a plastic bottle into a wooden bowl and set it down. She tried to get rid of the black candles, but they stood like iron posts jammed into the ground. No amount of grunting and pulling moved them in the slightest. Dad even tried, but after a minute of red-faced straining, he gave up and gasped for air.

*I gotta use them... Hope this doesn't turn it dark again, but... maybe I need them for the counterspell.*

She knelt in silence for several minutes, hands upturned against her knees, and meditated on her desire to bridge a connection between the world Melissa wandered in, and reality. She desired the entity they'd summoned to be cast out of this realm, banished back to where it came from.

Dad fidgeted at the apparent nothingness going on, but remained quiet.

With her focus clear in mind, Paige rested the dagger over the bowl of incense and lit it. White smoke rippled and peeled around the blade, filling the room with the scent of sandalwood and myrrh. "I cleanse and consecrate this circle and this athame. Element of Air, may your presence bring clarity to my purpose, so mote it be."

She held the knife in the path of the smoke for a few seconds longer, tilting it around so the aromatic wisp touched every inch of it. Paige stood and pointed the blade at the circle before starting a methodical walk clockwise.

"Element of Air, I welcome you to this circle." She tossed some feathers over the pentacle and lit the black candle at the tip. "Blessed be."

Paige walked to the next point.

"Spirits, I beseech thee to lend me your power and welcome you into this circle." She channeled her innermost belief that she *was* capable of doing this. "Blessed be."

She lit the candle at the top point and moved on.

"Element of Water, I welcome you to this circle." Paige sprinkled water from the bowl over the pentacle, and herself. "Blessed be."

Another candle lit, she walked around to the next point.

"Element of Fire, I welcome you to this circle." She lit the red stubby candle as well as the black one, and sprinkled incense flakes into the flame. "Blessed be."

Three steps.

"Element of Earth, I ask for your protection as I welcome you to this circle." She stuck another acorn into a bowl of dirt as Renee had done, and buried it. "Blessed be."

Once all the outer candles glowed, she took the athame in both hands and pictured a stream of energy flowing out of her, focused by the blade, boring into the ground along the circumscribing line.

Twice more, she walked the circle before stopping at the spirit point. She knelt and reached forward to light the remaining four black candles at the inside corners, the white one last.

Dad fidgeted. He seemed ready to cart her off to a hospital, though a glimmer of hope showed through his skeptical expression.

Paige waved the knife, tracing a pentacle in the air. All ten candles burned bright and high.

"I speak to The Lady and to Cernunnos with utmost respect and love. I humbly ask that you guide my sister back to us. May the lone white candle burn as a symbol of her innocence and purity. Protect us from that which we unknowingly set free upon this world."

She took the Barbie-mermaid out of her jacket pocket and set it in the middle of the pentacle. Anger and determination hardened her voice.

"Evil spirit, this is not your place. It is time for you to go back where you came from. As we beckoned, so I release. Shadow to shadow, dark to dark." The candles fluttered and spat. "I charge you to do no further harm. I forbid you from this world. I command you to release Melissa *now*. So mote it be."

Her body shook with conviction, every fiber of her soul crying out to send that thing home. Paige reached forward and put her hand on the plastic mermaid.

"At my right, The Lady, the Goddess. At my left, The Horned God, Cernunnos. Guide me into the place beyond; I beseech thee to be a beacon in the night."

Paige concentrated a moment more.

"I thank the elements, the Lady, and the Horned God." She rose to her feet and walked counterclockwise, snuffing the black candles one by one. Three orbits later, she knelt at the spirit point and extinguished the remaining four crimson flames before holding her hands near the white candle. "The pure flame I let burn. Let it be the beacon that guides Melissa to us, out of the realm of shade."

Paige envisioned the circle opening, releasing the spirits back to whence they came. She concentrated on her desire for a portal to connect to the otherworld, so her little sister could come home.

A subdued crunch came from behind her, like glass broken under a pillow.

"It... My God." Dad pointed.

She peered back over her shoulder. The mirror looked like a doorway into an unfamiliar house from long ago. An intricate repeating pattern in a diagonal grid spread over peeling wallpaper the color of coffee-stained paper above dark wood wainscoting. Small tables and cushioned wooden chairs made the hall look over a century old, or more.

Melissa's voice shouted from far away. "Paige?"

"I'm here," yelled Paige. "Come to us."

Distant soft thuds of a running child got louder and faded. "I can't find you!"

Paige got up. "I'm going in."

"Not alone, you're not." Dad put a hand on her shoulder.

She stepped over the bottom edge of the mirror. The instant her head passed the portal, the cloying stink of mold made her gag. Classical music, scratchy and monaural, emanated from nowhere in particular. Behind her, the rectangular shape of the mirror frame hovered a foot above rotting red carpet.

Dad climbed in and looked around. "This place looks like it's from the 1800s."

Paige glanced at wall-mounted candleholders and a conspicuous lack of electric fixtures. "Yeah."

"Where are you?" yelled Melissa.

"Here." Paige shouted and tromped down the hall.

She checked every door she found, roaming a ballroom devoid of furnishings, a library where all the chairs had white sheets over them, and a bedroom with a huge four-poster bed. Only the ballroom seemed promising, as the bare footprints of a child crisscrossed the dusty floor. Paige followed the trail, but it led straight into the wall between two of eight white tall-backed chairs with ornate carved trim painted gold.

"Melissa?" yelled Paige, her voice echoing in the cavernous room.

A rolling groan of settling wood rippled overhead. Paige stepped back from the wall and put her foot through the floor up to the knee. Decaying boards gave out as she struggled. She dropped on her butt. "Dad! Help!"

Silence.

Paige looked back and found herself alone.

"Dad?" She shivered. Her hands smeared clean trails in thick dust, but she pulled her leg free. "Daddy?"

Melissa let off a terrified shriek that sounded miles away.

The hole in the floor widened, sending a racing crack straight toward her. Paige yelped and rolled to her feet, sprinting away from it to the hallway. The trail of destruction stopped at the end of the room, striking the walls with a loud *bang* that lofted a rectangle of silt from the doorjamb. Heart slamming in her chest, she backed into the facing wall.

A spider as large as a dinner plate crept onto the top of her head and down over her face. She screamed and swatted it aside. It landed upright six feet away, and glared at her with a wrinkled, stark white old-man face. Paige shrieked and raised her boot, but it scurried out from under her stomp. Floorboards cracked. The horror charged into the baseboard and exploded in a cloud of shadowy smoke.

Melissa's scream repeated from around a ninety-degree right turn at the end of the corridor. Paige ran toward it, ripping up the rug as she passed. A door on the left opened itself as she approached, causing the tinny music to get louder. Paige tried to stop, but her boots peeled the carpet from the floor and her legs flew out from under her.

A plume of dust billowed up around her when she landed flat on her back. The wood crunched like eggshell. She whimpered, grabbing at dry rotted fabric, fearing a fall through to who-knows-what. Gingerly, she rolled to her right out of a Paige-sized depression.

"Holy crap..." After a few breaths, she got up and peered in the door.

White spectral flames flickered in a fireplace on the far side of a pair of maroon wingback chairs. A box of cigars and two tumbler glasses occupied a brittle wood table between them. On the left, a brass-horned Victrola ground out Mozart or Beethoven or whatever, the handle cranking on its own.

"Mel? Dad?"

A closet door at the right inner corner creaked open. Paige's heart paused, hoping beyond hope to see Melissa emerging from a hiding place. The hand that curled around the edge of the door wasn't a little girl's, or even human. Black-taloned fingers grasped wood about six feet up from the floor. It didn't look at all ethereal anymore.

Paige screamed and ran.

Her boots left small carpet-filled craters in the floor; fear of breaking through collided with her panic, slowing her all out terror-fueled dash to an ungainly rapid tiptoeing. She headed for the first door she saw, ducked in, and slammed it.

Water sloshing behind her made her turn.

A woman about Mom's age with long, straight blonde hair and skin that made even Paige feel like she had color sat nude in a bathtub, looking shocked and mortified. The surface met her skin a few inches beneath her breasts, but wherever she existed below the waterline appeared skeletal and dry. Glops of former internal organs wavered in a suspension of purplish muck at the bottom of the tub. Some pieces seemed to slither about as if alive on their own.

Paige flattened herself against the door.

Hard foot stomps grew louder outside. The small bathing chamber had no way out beside a square window too small for her to use as an escape.

"Are you the new servant?" asked the woman. Her voice floated whispery and melodic. She reached out to grasp her arm. "Bathe me."

Paige whipped the door open and bolted into the hall, shrieking as black fingers swiped close enough to snag her jacket. A tall humanoid form of onyx black, larger than Dad, waited right outside. It grabbed at her again. She swerved into the wall to duck, and pushed off into a full sprint.

"Where are you going?" shouted the woman. "Attend to me this instant!"

She ran ahead, not looking back; pounding footsteps drove her forward. Paige hooked a left at a four-way intersection, sliding into the wall as the carpet peeled up. Plaster and fragments of wallpaper rained down all over her. Something ceramic fell and shattered. She bounced away and ran to a pair of white double doors that opened by sliding apart. As soon as she slipped past, she slammed them hard enough to crack the paint. The floor ceased shaking.

They locked with a flip hook, which she secured so fast it felt like a reflex. She eyed the feeble bit of brass, not trusting it to weather the onslaught of an angry demon. *It's not gone. It's waiting.* A little girl giggle echoed behind her.

Paige whirled. "Mel?"

Pea-green wallpaper covered with a swirly pattern of darker green velvet surrounded her. Four dressmaker's mannequins stood on posts to the right, one bearing a withered wedding gown. A dollhouse at the far-left corner showed signs of recent use, small handprints in the dust.

Soft tapping rippled along inside the wall, a noise like a hammer or wrench dragged across slats. Whispering came from the area around the mannequins, chattering about measurements and size. Dry air laced with the smell of rotting fabric sucked the moisture out of her throat. She coughed on a tickle at the back of her mouth.

Her cough became a gagging gasp when unseen forces tugged and poked at her clothes. A chilly strip of thin material pulled taut around her throat; she clutched her neck, grasping nothing but skin. She squealed at the sensation of a hand sliding up the inside of her thigh, and grabbed her crotch. That time, she felt something under her jeans that shouldn't be there, and screamed. Frantic fingers fumbled with her zipper for a few seconds until she remembered how to work it. She opened her fly and fished around, finding a thin strip of cloth.

Paige stared dumbfounded as she extracted an antique tailor's measuring tape, shivering from the feeling of it sliding along the entire length of her left leg. One of the empty mannequins twitched and wobbled, as though someone worked on a nonexistent garment. Similar tapes littered the ground in the corner, among skeins of fabric and dust-covered thread spools.

"Paige!" screamed Melissa. Her voice echoed up from beneath the floor. "Help!"

"Melissa?" yelled Dad, also from below. "Paige? Where are you?"

Invisible hands continued to tug and prod at her jacket. She walked forward despite it, heading toward a narrow white door opposite the entry, arms reflexively raised to shield her face. The delicate crystal knob turned without resistance, and she stepped into another ballroom-sized chamber with massive sections of floor missing. Dust glimmered in beams of strong moonlight shining in through breaks in the ceiling. The dry tickle in her throat faded after two breaths of humid air filled with the taste of earth and moss. A narrow path of solid ground connected from the doorway to another corridor on the far side, weaving around irregular openings fringed with splintered floorboards jutting out at jagged angles.

"Oh, no way." Paige backed up.

"Paige," yelled Melissa.

She sounded directly below.

Paige stared at the ceiling. "Figures." She gulped and crept out onto the dangerous looking pathway.

About ten paces from the door, Paige leaned ever so slightly to the left and peered over the edge of the first gap. One story down, a charcoal-grey room glimmered with thousands of shards of smashed mirror. Wine bottles lay scattered about amid the ruin of an old wooden rack. Random dark smears and globs on the walls made her look away.

*I hope that's not Mackenzie.*

"Melissa? Dad?" yelled Paige.

"Here!" screamed the girl.

"Paige?" Dad shouted. "Where are you?"

Her body stiff from fear, she edged farther out along the narrow walkway, expecting the entire thing to give out at any second. Every creak or groan of protest from the wood made her freeze for the span of several breaths before taking another step.

Melissa shrieked in pure terror.

Dad let off a few rapid obscenities.

She forced herself to advance at a normal speed and looked down into the next breach on the right. The wine cellar floor also had holes, though they looked to be deliberate pits rather than the effect of time and neglect. Thick roots covered the outer walls, grown through the mortar of a haphazard foundation of irregular-shaped stones. At the far-right edge of the cellar, Dad stood at the bottom of one of the wells, his head not even as high as the midway point. He backed away from an advancing cloud of darkness. The front edge shifted into the shapes of hundreds of cat-sized black spiders.

Melissa huddled in the corner of another sunken chamber at the far-left corner, a good twenty yards away from Dad and separated by earthen walls. Black gunk and grime smeared her legs and nightgown; she clung to an antique doll, holding it up as if it would somehow protect her from another mass of spiders that inched toward her.

Paige stared at the wine cellar floor below; flakes of smashed mirror on the dark stone tiles glittered in the moonlight like a field of stars. Disregarding her fear, she squatted and searched for a handhold on the old wood. She lowered her legs, intending to hang for a second before dropping, but the board came away in her hands and she fell. She landed on her boots and spilled forward. Her leg throbbed, but didn't feel broken.

"Paige?" yelled Dad.

A splinter tugged out of her hand as she tossed the board aside and stood. Two thin points of mirror protruded from her left forearm. She pulled them loose and dropped them, advancing along a four-foot-wide strip of solid floor between the rows of oubliettes.

"I'm here," yelled Paige. *Who the hell has a dungeon in their basement?*

"Help!" Melissa burst into tears. She pressed herself into the brambles covering the corner of her pit.

Roots blackened and whipped around her, holding her helpless in the face of the advancing spiders. One jet-black vine circled through her mouth, winding around her head three times; another length tightened about her chest, pinning her arms at her sides. Melissa squirmed and shrieked with blind panic.

Shadows swelled forward from the wall at the end of the path, closest to Melissa's pit. The entity from the summoning ritual stepped forward from the darkness; nine feet tall, its skin glistened with the sheen of a wet chitinous shell. Horns protruded from its elbows, shoulders, and around the ridges of its eyes. Dark-red blood leaked from gaps in its plating, running down armored plates to the next seam where some unknown force drew it back inside. The not-quite-human jaw opened, exposing two rows of three-inch teeth like transparent icicles.

"I told you to go away," yelled Paige. Melissa's horrified screaming fueled her determination and destroyed any sense of fear. "You cannot strike at me for disrupting the spell. You didn't do what was asked. You're evil."

It stopped a few paces away, staring down at her, arms still at its sides. Oversized eyes of inky black glass held no discernible emotion.

Her little sister howled, unable to form words with roots in her mouth.

"Melissa!" shouted Dad. His gun discharged, followed by three rapid pings and a spray of dust and splinters from the ceiling. "Shit. Melissa!"

She replied with an incoherent wail that broke into sobs.

Paige pointed at the entity. "I wanted Dad to be set free of his depression over Amber. That doesn't mean kill him. Your task is done."

The demon took a step closer, snarling. Black ichor dripped from needlepoint teeth. Its breath washed over her with the scent of rotting meat. It radiated the overwhelming want to harm her, saturated with the frustration at being forbidden to do so.

She backed up.

"Paige," whispered Amber.

Her older sister approached from behind. Solid arms encircled her in a warm hug.

Tears slid down Paige's face.

"Your selfless desire shielded you from backlash. As much as it wants to, it cannot hurt you directly."

One of the cat-sized spiders climbed over the ridge of Dad's pit. It darted at Paige, but the instant it crossed into a beam of moonlight, it evaporated.

"Let them go," said Paige. "If you send them home alive, I'll let you have me."

"Not an option," yelled Dad.

Melissa gave up on screaming and sobbed. She tried to kick at the spiders, but could barely move. Whipping roots flailed at Dad, trying to grab and pull him to the wall.

"Don't be afraid of it." Amber squeezed her and let go. "It can't harm you."

Paige squatted and grabbed a large hunk of mirror. She held it out to the moonbeam and directed the light at Melissa. The roots holding her disintegrated under the ray, as did the front edge of the mass of spiders.

The demon roared and swiped at her. Paige cringed, but held her ground. The demon's claws passed over her head. She angled the moonlight into Dad's pit, searing away several feet worth of spiders, but they kept coming. Melissa screamed; she burned away more spiders, going back and forth from Melissa to Dad, but the encroaching creatures did not cease.

The demon leaned back with a soft, phlegmatic laugh. Dark fluid dribbled from its needle fangs, joining the sheets of blood rolling down its chest. It gestured at Dad, then Melissa.

"It doesn't want you," said Amber.

Paige shivered. "No... I can't choose." *It wants to kill me but it can't... so it's going to hurt me worse.*

She stared at the jagged sliver of mirror in her hands and raised it to her throat. *I'm sorry, Mel.*

# 34

# INTO THE ARMS OF REGRET

Thursday October 22 - 88:88 p.m.

P aige closed her eyes and took a deep breath. Giving herself to the otherworld in trade for her sister and father seemed the only way to save them. It couldn't make her choose between them. If someone *was* going to die, if she had any control at all, it wouldn't be them. At least Melissa would be alive to suffer the emotional destruction of losing her favorite sibling. The scrape of glass at her neck brought a whimper, louder in her mind than Melissa's desperate screams about spiders.

Amber's hands clenched around Paige's wrists. "No!"

"I have to." Paige struggled, but her older sister overpowered her and pulled her arms down.

"No!" Amber shouted. "It won't take you!"

She whirled on her, sobbing. "I can't keep the light on both of them *and* get them out. It wants to hurt me by making me pick who dies."

Paige wrenched her arms away from Amber and reflected moonlight at Melissa, clearing her of several mammoth spiders. Dad put up more of a fight, seeming able to hurl them away. She scoured one pit then the other. "I can't keep up. They're both gonna die."

"White for innocence," said Amber.

*I'm a dumbass!*

"Dad," yelled Paige. "Light kills them!" *One candle burns.* "Candle of white, part the night." She chanted the phrase again and again, picturing the white candle back in the cabin far off in another world. *The white candle, a symbol of Melissa's innocence.*

Her little sister's screaming ebbed. She made an odd noise of confusion.

"Take that you ugly little bastards," yelled Dad. "Hah!"

Paige looked.

Dad wielded his Maglite like a death ray, clearing spiders as though he'd turned a flamethrower on a snowbank. Glistening black bodies burst into clouds of dark smoke, drawn away on a slight breeze.

Melissa glowed with searing radiance, her body projecting a shimmering orb of pure light. The nimbus held back the mass of flailing arachnid limbs and seared away the shade brambles behind her, exposing clean rock. The surging horde of spiders kept her trapped in the corner, but seemed unable to tolerate coming within a foot of her luminous form. *Yes!* Paige pivoted the mirror, directing the moonlight into the demon's face. It let off a wail of anguish and blurred to the side.

She sprinted forward and leapt into the chamber containing her sister. Hundreds of spiders as big as basketballs splattered under her landing. Legs like icepicks raked down her back and scratched at her face. Paige swatted and flailed, propelled to her feet by utter revulsion and panic. She pounced on Melissa, who clamped on and burst into tears. She hugged her little sister in a desperate embrace, never wanting to let go again.

A scratching leg on the back of her calf ruined the moment.

Paige whirled, holding her sister up like a cross at vampires. The sublime light radiating from the girl kept the spiders at bay. "Get on my back, kiddo."

She set Melissa down on her feet and turned to face the wall. Melissa climbed on as Paige grabbed the roots. Once her sister had a good, solid grip, Paige climbed, stomping her boots into the dead thorny wood wherever she could. Thorns bit her hands, but she growled and pressed on. Still-living vines attempted to ensnare them, but withered to crusty charcoal as soon as they entered the shimmering radiance. The wall seemed much taller than the fifteen feet or so she'd fallen. Her sister screamed in her ear, dangling by her arms around Paige's neck while kicking at spiders racing up the wall after them. Whenever her foot touched a spider, she shrieked in revulsion, but kept on punting them.

One pounced on her back, but exploded in a puff of smoke on contact.

*Candle of white, destroy the night.* Paige kept chanting in her head.

Melissa let out an ear-piercing shriek, and shuddered in a panic. Paige glanced down at a tiny growling voice. Half the toes on her sister's right foot vanished into the mouth of one of the creatures. The little wrinkled face wagged its eyebrows at her. Paige let go of the roots long enough to punch it in the forehead, but it didn't let go. She drew her arm back again, but the glimmering aura around Melissa disintegrated the miniature horror before it could do much more than leave a cat scratch above her big toe.

A fistful of root came away in Paige's hand, causing a near fall. She dropped an F bomb and flailed for a second before finding a good grip and clinging. Neither girl moved more than necessary to breathe for a moment.

"You said a bad," whispered Melissa.

Laughing despite being ready to ruin her underpants, Paige pulled them up another fifteen feet or so to where moonlight lit the walls of what had become a long shaft. Eerie shadows filtered among the tangle of twisting roots. Dead flowers the size of grapefruits broke off and fell, flaking to dust. Old mortared stone behind the rotting vines glistened with moisture and moss. Once she'd climbed fully into moonlight, Paige looked down. The writhing mass of spiders gathered at the boundary between dark and light, miniature wrinkled human faces curled in hateful sneers.

Feeling momentarily safe, she clung in place to catch her breath.

"Why am I glowing?"

Paige removed her hand from a thorn and grasped a smooth section. "Don't worry about it. Think about wanting Dad to be okay. Can you do that?"

Melissa hooked her legs around Paige. "Yeah."

*We need to get out of here.* She dragged herself upward, gazing at the square of darkened sky. Hand over hand, she pulled them up until at long last, she grasped a tuft of... cool grass.

*Whoa.*

Grunting, Paige dragged them up and over the edge of a well so deep she couldn't see the bottom, and slithered onto damp forest floor. Melissa crawled off and knelt beside her.

"I'm still glowing." Melissa pulled the cotton away from her body and peered down inside, eyes wide with awe.

Eerie noises reverberated among the trees—howls, grunts, and heavy snuffles a few degrees removed from normal animals. Melissa looked around, her fascination with the light fading to terror.

"I don't like it here."

Paige examined her perforated hands. "Neither do I."

She stood, turning in a slow rotation to take in their surroundings. Autumnal trees, painted in various tones of grey, hemmed them in on all sides. Every so often, a hulking shape appeared for an instant and vanished. On her third spin, a tiny point of yellow light caught her eye in the darkness. She stopped. It resembled the window of a distant, tiny cabin.

"There..."

"What?" Melissa jumped up and grabbed her.

"I think I see the way out." Paige grabbed her sister's arm. "Come on."

Something heavy crashed through the underbrush, growling.

Melissa went rigid, too terrified to even scream.

Paige didn't bother looking, and bolted, yanking Melissa into a stumbling run straight off her feet. Heavy thuds rocked the earth behind them. The child screamed and tripped. Snarling and gnashing teeth close behind kept Paige running, dragging her sister along the ground.

"Look out!" screamed Melissa.

Paige dove to the dirt. An enormous mass of black leapt over her, accompanied by the sharp *clack* of a huge jaw snapping shut. A four-legged creature, huge, furry, and heavy, bounded off into the trees, trailed by a nine-foot-long tail tipped with barbs.

Not waiting to see if it returned, Paige hauled Melissa upright and ran again. The girl stumbled and fell within five steps.

"Ow." She bawled. "The ground is pointy."

Paige stared at her sister's bare feet, one bleeding from a thorn prick. She pulled her on like a backpack, held her by both wrists, and sprinted. Vines and runners crunched under her boots, splintering. It didn't matter how many thorns got stuck in her inch-thick soles. Nightmare forest streaked by on both sides. She lost track of the yellow for a few dreadful seconds, but caught sight of it again and diverted left a little.

Melissa's whimpery voice hummed the theme song to *Mermaid's Journey*.

Lupine howls, far too deep to be ordinary wolves gathered behind her. Paige's lungs burned, but her muscles didn't hurt—nor did she notice the thorn wounds in her hands. Nothing mattered but getting to the cabin.

A pair of black-furred creatures resembling foxes with shark's teeth and huge lime-green eyes gazed at her from atop a fallen tree, only half visible in Melissa's glow. They scampered to the side at her charge, vanishing into the dark seconds before she vaulted over the trunk. Melissa let off an 'oof' as the landing crushed her into Paige's back.

Her boots ate the ground. *Thump thump thump thump* in time with her heartbeat. "If any of the elemental spirits are listening… Lady, Cernunnos… please. I don't care what happens to me; protect Melissa. Please get her home safe."

"No," yelled Melissa. "I don't want you to stay here. This is a bad place."

The yellow window seemed closer, larger, as welcoming as it was frightful. Paige jumped across a tiny burbling creek and scrambled up an incline on the other side. Branches smacked her in the face, but she refused to let go of Melissa's arms. After a painful few minutes, the forest split apart to circle the edges of a massive lake of perfect calm. The brilliant shimmering glow along the surface made it look as though made of pure moonlight. Its overall shape seemed more like a fat river, being about two hundred yards across, but almost six times that in width.

A squarish bridge of rock about three feet thick spanned the lake. Widest where it met the midnight-black bank, the arch narrowed as it stretched to the center before widening again nearer the far side. It looked like a treacherous journey, barely as wide as a sidewalk with no railings at the narrow middle point.

Unseen creatures trampled through the woods behind them, drawing near. Paige looked left and right. Since the lake went so far to the side in either direction, not taking the bridge would force a run along a woodline filled with scary noises. *Something'll get us.*

The prospect of running across a narrow stone bridge caused a flutter in her heartbeat, but bothered her less than shadowy teeth and claws. The cabin she needed to reach sat a ways up a hill on the other side, eerie orange light in the windows beckoning her toward freedom.

"Hold on. We have to go across."

Paige ran ahead, bounding up the steep stone curve. It leveled off after about six yards, allowing her to sprint at full speed. She kept her gaze down, hoping whatever chased them found this bridge as terrifying as she did. No, *more* terrifying than she did... *I'm still crossing it.*

*Thank you for your protec—*

Stone crumbled out from under her. A twenty-foot section disintegrated into fist-sized chunks. Paige's shriek lasted two seconds before she plunged into the water. Melissa's fingernails raked over her throat as an unseen force tore her away with too much strength for a person. Paige swung her arms, rolling over as she sank. The glowing spot of Melissa's aura raced off into the inky depths. She reached for Paige, futilely trying to claw at the water. Scream-filled bubbles flew from her mouth. In seconds, the light had gone too far away to see.

*No!* Paige tried to swim after her, but felt like a snail watching a bullet train vanish into the horizon. No matter how hard she tried to kick or pull herself up, she sank. Wavering moonlight overhead filtered in bands through the murky water, dimming.

Points of yellow light glimmered in the darkness beneath her. Gravity and resignation pulled her over to face down. Beneath a deep-indigo haze, the lake bottom seemed made of thousands upon thousands of humanoid figures shaped from black tar, each embedded to the waist in muck. They all reached for her, baleful yellow eyes widening. Whispers echoed in her head.

"Welcome home, Paige."

"You belong with us..."

"This is what you deserve."

"Your fight is over, child."

"So long denied, it is time to sleep."

Glossy darkness appeared on her forearms, spreading in a creep toward shoulders and fingers.

*Melissa's gone... I lost her.* Paige stopped trying to swim. *I'm sorry, Mom.*

*Dad's gone...* She stopped fearing the shadow people reaching up to her.

*Mr. Ruiz... Jared... those two boys... Renee's Dad. Everything that happened is my fault.*

Paige stopped trying to hold her breath, and sank.

Slimy hands grasped her arms and pulled her close. More clutched her legs, a cocoon of limbs wrapped around her in a welcoming embrace.

## THE SUNDERED PORTAL

Thursday October 22 - 88:88 p.m.

P aige drifted in a void of darkness. She waited for the panic of
drowning, but floated in placid quiet. Acceptance offered peace she
never imagined possible. Not since she stared into the barrel of her
father's Glock did she feel so at ease with who she was.

A faint voice broke the quiet, female, far away, an indecipherable warble.

*Go away. I'm dead.*

"Paige," yelled Amber.

She squirmed in the wrap of gelatinous arms, as if rolling on her side
in bed.

"It's still here. You have to stop the demon. Send it back where it came
from. You have to do it since you opened the door."

*Amber...*

Paige opened her eyes, peering through someone else's black fingers at the
murky lake bottom. Another hand rubbed her hair in loving strokes.

"I'll never forgive you if you give up and pull that trigger," yelled Amber.
"Think about Melissa."

She jolted as if snapping out of a foggy dream. The urgent need for air
overwhelmed her with panic. Paige thrashed and kicked. Her boots sank into
spongy ground. She grabbed at the shroud of arms, pulling and pushing as she
twisted.

*Help me, Amber. I'm drowning!*

"Paige!" yelled Amber. "Swim up."

Fingers slimed over her back, hooking the waist of her jeans. She grabbed the arm and pulled it away before kicking at the bottom to launch herself upward. Hands slid down both legs, failing to gain purchase. Her head pounded. Paige *wanted* to surface; she wanted to survive; she wanted her family. Again and again, she clawed at the inky water, dragging herself up from the depths in a lake made of despair. Silvery shimmer drew closer, every inch felt as if it took hours. After an eternity, she thrust her hand out into cold air. Breaking the surface, she gagged and gasped. Spots danced in her vision as she coughed to the point of throwing up water.

Amber stood at the tip of the break in the bridge, smiling at her.

"Where's Melissa?"

Her older sister pointed at the cabin.

*I'm already wet.* She sputtered and choked as she swam, heading for the bank nearest the cabin. The bridge was out of reach anyway, too high over the surface. She stared at the weeds at the water's edge. *Please don't be full of hands.* Before long, her boots found mucky earth; swimming became trudging. Nothing grabbed her, and ten paces from the lake, she collapsed and puked up another wave of brackish water.

She collected herself and fought her way to her feet while wiping her mouth on the back of her arm. The thorn marks on her palms and fingers stung. Clenching her hands into fists dulled the pain only a little. Paige took one more deep breath and stomped over a field of black grass to the cabin. Neither car existed in this shadow realm. The rickety wooden structure had shifted colors; its 'otherworld' counterpart appeared photonegative.

Inside, the room looked as it had in the real world. Unlike this place, the reflection in the mirror had color. Small bare footprints in water traced a path from the door to the mirror. Paige ducked her head and sprinted. She jumped the gap between the bottom of the mirror and the floor and landed in a cabin filled with chilly October air, made colder by her soaked clothes. The wind tore through the small one-room structure, though the white candle flame stood tall in defiance of it at the inner base of the pentacle. Paige's heart sank at the lack of Melissa's footprints on this side of reality.

She whirled and leapt at the mirror, but hit solid glass. "Bastard! You tricked me!"

Rage and fatalistic sorrow warred in her head. She swooned to her knees, forehead pressed against the frigid pane. Minutes passed in silence before she gazed at the reflection of the athame, lying on the floor behind her.

"Amber... You're right. I have to close this thing."

She crawled to the blade. The instant her palm touched the handle, claws seized her by the shoulders from behind, pinpricks piercing her jacket. The demon hurled her into the air and threw her to the far end of the cabin before she could even scream.

Paige hit the wall sideways about halfway between floor and ceiling, bounced away, and landed on her chest. By some miracle, she'd managed to close her fingers around the knife. The creature's head scraped at the roof as it stalked after her. Here, in the realm of mortals, its body seemed at once solid and ethereal. Patches of chitin glistened before fading to smoke in an endless cycle.

The creature took another step toward her, shaking the cabin.

"I'm not afraid of you." Paige rolled to her feet, woozy from the hit. She pointed the knife at it. "I know I have the power to send you back."

It roared and rushed at her.

She stabbed it in the chest, though her arm vanished amid an intangible cloud of vapor. Solid hands grabbed her at the shoulder and side, lifting her. She swiped the athame through it without effect as it spun her around and flung her into the back wall. Paige screamed, managing to get one arm in front of her face before impact.

Flight became lying on the floor in an instant.

She scrambled around, dizzy. The room spun as she pulled herself upright with some help from the wall. Her shoulder ached, her head pounded. Blood dripped from her nose over her lips. "I guess I don't want it bad enough." She held up the blade. "If I want this to kill you, it will."

The demon let off a low, grating chuckle that gave her goosebumps.

Paige raised the knife at the creature, which widened its arms as if to say 'bring it.'

She charged two steps before darting left. The demon caught the ruse too late to grab her. She jumped over the boundary circle and landed in the middle of the pentacle. Enraged, the creature sprinted at her. When it reached the edge, it exploded into a torrent of black smoke that wrapped around an invisible cylinder. Stunned, the demon re-formed on the other side and whirled about in a rage. It raked at the air, its body turning to smoke wherever it tried to cross the circle.

Paige's mind raced. Elation from an unexpected sense of safety made her giggle. "Wow... That really worked. Now what?"

The demon roared and burst into shadows, surrounding her.

"Paige, help!" yelled Melissa. "I'm drowning!"

She looked at the door as the shout seemed to come from outside, and narrowed her eyes. "Nice try." *What... what... what... Unbinding the spell. Mackenzie... the candles!*

Paige dropped to her knees at the center of the pentacle. The demon tore its claws at the air, creating bone-jarring screeches as if its talons scraped on glass.

"Paige?" yelled Dad. "There's too many spiders. Where are you? I need you."

"Lies," yelled Paige.

She plucked the black candle from the north point, cringing at touching something made with a dead person's blood. The sinister wax absorbed light, having no luster at all. A thread of singed blonde hair protruded from the wick.

The demon roared, slamming its face into the 'wall' as close as it could to her.

Melissa shrieked and shrieked, sounding much like the girl who'd been crushed by the falling light, screams that stopped only long enough to gulp another lungful of air. Paige shuddered. *It's lying. It's trying to trick me out of the circle. That's not really Melissa.*

She raised the candle up to eye level.

"Magic cast with dark intent, your time is now in total spent."

Paige held the athame's edge to the middle of the candle. A slow downward pull severed it. Blood welled out of the wax, spraying into the air from each half, far more than could've fit inside. She dropped the pieces and picked up the second candle.

Dad's voice screamed as if he boiled alive.

"This spell of ours, I unmake. Darkness' hold on this world break."

Paige sliced the second candle. Thicker, darker blood oozed from it, running hot between her fingers. She dropped the halves and picked up the third candle.

"I have the power to close this gate. No more will you touch my fate."

The third candle crumbled to bleeding fragments as soon as the edge gouged the wax.

Melissa begged Paige to come outside before the spiders ate her.

Paige snagged the fourth black candle. "Darkness' end is drawing nearer; I banish you now back through the mirror."

Arterial spurts gushed from the candle when she sliced it and let the pieces spill out of her hand. The severed bits bled onto the floor, though rather than form a puddle, wisps of crimson trailed a spiral into the air. Dark red fluid formed a latticework of thin threads, twisting over and around each other in an intricate weave before plunging into the demon's chest.

"Your time now is at an end. To this world, your link I rend." Candle number five melted to blood jelly in her hands within seconds of the knife slicing in. She threw the glop on the floor with the rest, but it soon rose to join the pulsating threads in the air.

The demon writhed and twisted. Spiraling winds filled the cabin, collecting leaves, twigs, and dirt. Within the pentacle, no trace of a breeze stirred. Toe claws ripped gouges in the floor as spectral force drew the demon toward the mirror. Her shoulder throbbed where she'd smashed into the wall, but she tuned it out.

Melissa screamed in a voice as high and clear as a bell. "Paige, no! If you close the gate, I'll be stuck here. I wanna go home!"

Paige hesitated for a second. *Lies. Please be lies.* She grabbed the sixth candle.

"Spirits and Elements, I beseech. Hear my voice and seal this breach."

She cut the wax in half. Black blood oozed forth, hot enough to burn. She flung the pieces down and wiped her hand on her jeans.

The walls rattled, separating here and there from the roof. Paige looked up, unsure if this pentacle could protect against a collapsing building. In a hurried rush, she grabbed the seventh candle.

"I unbind this spell at this hour. No more souls shall you devour."

Candle seven threw out a geyser of icy blood when she cut it. Thick fluid twisted upward and joined the thickening stream siphoning into the demon's heart. The entity sank into the mirror, but hooked its hands and feet at the sides, holding on.

"What goes out returns times three. Your magic ends. Blessed be."

Bloody fragments slid among her fingers. Paige grasped the eighth candle, but it refused to unstick from the ground. She strained, but couldn't budge it.

Paige set the knife's edge across the top of the candle by the wick. She stared at the demon.

"Shadows spinning, draining through, demon of black, I banish you."

She forced the blade down, splitting the eighth candle lengthwise. Hot blood sprayed in her face; she closed her eyes and mouth, pushing on the knife until her knuckles touched the floor.

"Candle, candle, number nine. This gate I close; the power's mine."

She grasped the athame in both hands and swung it like a sword, cutting the last black candle in half where it stood. It spat a stream of blood straight up into the rising sanguine serpent. The force of the fluid pushed the demon into the mirror until only eight claws hooked four to each side of the frame remained visible.

"I have the power to close this gate." Paige held the knife up.

Nothing happened.

"No, no, come on! There has to be something—" She grabbed the satchel and rummaged through bottle after bottle of various colored powders and herbs. As soon as she saw the salt, she *knew* she needed it. She bit the cork and spat it to the side before pouring a thin line of white crystals around the circle and then over the pentacle. The wooden mirror frame creaked beneath the demon's weight as its claws dug in and trembled.

Spiraling threads of blood formed a ropey writhing mass. Seconds after she finished tracing salt over every line of the pentacle, the candles ceased bleeding and the end of the bloody cord detached from the floor and disappeared into the mirror, which had become a yawning vortex swirling with red and black.

Paige set down the athame and cradled her hands around the white candle's flame. *I don't care what happens to me. Please protect my little sister.*

"I seal this gate forever."

She blew out the candle.

A keening scrape emanated from the mirror, which flashed to a solid slab of opaque silver.

Paige exhaled with relief. "Well—"

The world erupted in chaos with a deafening explosion. Paige felt the air leave her lungs, but heard no scream over the roar. Small fragments buffeted her. Star-speckled sky flashed by, trading places with the darkness of the forest floor again and again.

*Wham.*

Paige gasped, unable to move from the shock of pain through her body. It took her brain a second to restart and absorb her surroundings. She lay flat on her back, spread eagle on the hood of Dad's patrol car. The cabin had vanished, including the floorboards. Only a scorch mark gave any indication something had been there. Bits of wood debris rained, clattering and clunking over the police car and the Kia. She shielded her eyes until the pelting ceased.

"Dad?" Paige sat up. "Mel?"

Only crickets answered.

"Dad!" Paige screamed. "Melissa!"

Her voice echoed back from the tree line. The crickets quieted for three seconds before resuming their song.

*What did I do?*

Lip quivering, Paige curled on her side atop the hood, and sobbed. She cry-yelled for her father and sister a few more times before grief took over and she succumbed to incoherent bawling. It didn't matter how long she lay there. She'd let herself starve if no one found her.

Paige closed her eyes and buried her face in her knees.

---

# 36

## SISTER DEPARTED

Friday October 23 - 1:18 a.m.

Paige stopped crying some time later, all out of tears or the urge to care about anything. She stared at the strange patterns of reflected moonlight on the hood, not believing anything she'd witnessed over the past hour. When they had first told her of Amber's death, she'd refused to accept it. She closed her eyes, willing reality away. *No. This isn't happening. I didn't just trap them both in the other place.* Perhaps in a few hours, maybe after the sun came up, she'd find enough care to get up and see if Dad kept a shotgun in the trunk. She wouldn't feel that, but right now, getting up would take too much effort.

Cricket song numbed her mind. Melissa's desperate cries while she unmade the ritual replayed in her mind. What if it had really been her little sister? Perhaps she'd saved more lives by sending the creature back, but she didn't feel noble about it.

*Thump.*

Something landed on the roof.

Paige pushed herself up enough to peer over the top of the windshield. A few inches in front of the light pods lay the plastic mermaid doll, slightly scorched. She reached up to grasp it and fell onto the hood in a ball, clutching the toy to her chest. Sobs came heavy and unrelenting. Within moments, she wailed like a mother who'd watched her child killed before her eyes.

Only crippling grief kept her from moving, searching for an escape from the pain.

She closed her eyes and begged anything that would listen to take her away.

Paige started awake. The fog of interrupted sleep clouded her head and proved she'd lapsed from exhaustion. Pressure squeezed at her shoulder.

"Paige?" asked Dad.

She rolled toward him onto her back.

Her father stood by the left front tire, Melissa clinging to his side with her arms around his neck. Both looked as though they'd gone for a long run in the woods. Her sister's waist-length mop of dense ginger hair had more leaves in it than most of the trees.

"Pay..." Melissa grinned.

"Daddy!" Paige sat up and grabbed him. "I thought you were gone."

He held her. Melissa squirmed down and climbed onto the hood. Paige crushed her in a hug she never wanted to let go. After a moment of happy crying, she looked up through a blur of tears at her smiling father.

"What happened?"

He scooped both girls up at once and carried them around to the passenger door. "Well... as soon as you said light, I felt like a moron. The flashlight melted them as good as the moonbeam. I thought it required magic or something, never expected an ordinary bulb would work. You're a bloody mess. Are you hurt?"

Paige sniffled into a giggle. She climbed in when he opened the door and pulled Melissa into her lap. "It's like the spells I guess. The words don't matter as much as what you want. Most of this blood isn't mine." She held her hands up. "Thorns... and a couple pieces of glass in my leg and arm."

Dad jogged around and got in. "I'm going to guess it's probably wise not to be seen here. They'll cart us both off to the looney farm. As far as we're concerned, we were home all night."

"I got a better idea." Paige kissed Melissa on the head. "We spent the night driving around looking for her, and found where she'd fallen in a hole in the woods. That way we don't have to come up with any bogus kidnapping story."

"That works." Dad started the car.

"So... what happened with the spiders?"

"Well." Dad accelerated along the dirt road, driving a little faster than Paige felt comfortable with. "The Maglite burned those little bastards up good. I saw you go up the wall and disappear into the ceiling. Eventually they stopped coming after me and I climbed out. Like that crazy place lost interest in me once the two of you had gotten far enough away. I found a cave opening at the other end of the wine cellar and it led to the woods. I tried to find my way back to the cabin, but I heard Melissa crying."

"After we fell in the water, a hand grabbed my leg," whispered Melissa. "It pulled me backwards through the water and into the forest. I got scared being alone and cried."

Paige grinned. "I asked them to protect you." She closed her eyes, meditating on feelings of gratitude. "I thought something bad got you." The receding clearing in the rearview mirror gave her a strange feeling of calm. "Dad... I have the strangest feeling Amber's not coming back. And you might wanna slow down." She gestured at Melissa in her lap. "This isn't safe."

He eased off the gas. "Perhaps I'm not the only one who had to move on. I hope she's at peace now."

"Yeah." Paige teared up. "Sorry for being a snot."

"Forgiven," said Dad. "Sorry for acting like Frankenstein's monster."

"Huh?" Paige glanced at him.

"Bolts in my neck." He winked.

Paige winced. "Sorry... and forgiven." She grasped Melissa's face in both hands and stared into her emerald eyes. "Can you forgive me for all the mean things I've ever said to you?"

"It's okay." Melissa laid her head on Paige's shoulder. "You were sad." She kept quiet for a moment. "Sorry for fallin' inna hole and scarin' you."

Paige squeezed her sister tight, laughing into her hair.

Dad flicked on the extra spotlights to help navigate the woods. "Call your Mom. We shouldn't keep her waiting any longer."

Paige reached into her jacket and pulled out a rather wet—and rather dead—cell phone. "Umm. I think I'm gonna need a new one."

"What happened?"

"I fell into a giant lake of pure sorrow. Almost drowned."

"Oh, so basically not in the warranty."

She smirked.

Dad handed over his phone. It took Paige a few attempts to dial between still-numb fingers and her refusal to maintain at least a one-armed hug of Melissa.

"Hello? Drew, where the hell are you?"

"Hi, Mom. Dad's driving."

Paige held the phone out as Mom blew up screaming at them for scaring seven shades of Hell out of her. "You done?"

"I can't believe you two!" Mom breathed hard.

"Mom, we're on the way home now. Hang on a sec, 'kay?" She handed the phone to Melissa and winked.

"Mommy!" Melissa cringed at the roar coming from the earpiece. "I got lost in the woods."

A wail came over the phone.

"You should tell Mom the truth," said Dad. "But no one else, okay? They won't believe us."

Melissa nodded.

Paige leaned back in the seat, holding her little sister, while the girl relayed a story no sane person would believe to her sobbing mother.

# 37

# AN ACCORD OF NOTHING

Wednesday October 28 - 5:11 p.m.

H appy shouts from elementary students carried from the far side of the field where a group of fifth-to-seventh-graders played touch nerf football. Black ribbons adorned a few trees and railings around the school, in honor of both Mr. Ruiz and Cole Harris. Paige huddled on a bench, regretting her choice of frilly short skirt and fishnets on a blustery day. Sofia seemed glum, stuck in a plain blue dress, white stockings, and black satin ballet flats. Despite bristling at the Wednesday Addams thing, she still preferred black, but her entire wardrobe had gone up in smoke.

Santana slouched forward, arms folded across her knees, face hidden behind long brown hair, her body lost in an olive-drab army jacket way too big for her. Renee appeared at the end of the school building and scraped her sneakers on the way over. She'd taken over Santana's place as the flannel-wearer that day, in a red and black shirt over jeans. A quarter-inch of black hair showed at the base of her violet frizz.

"Hey," said Paige.

Renee sat next to her. "Hey."

Sofia slurped the last of her soda through a straw and looked up. "Halloween's in three days. What are you guys going as?"

Silence.

"It's good you, umm, closed that door before the thirty-first." Sofia shivered.

Renee grumbled. "I don't wanna know what that thing would've done."

"Yeah," said Paige.

"So…" Sofia tapped her feet. "I'm thinking of dressing up as Wednesday. Pigtails and all."

Paige giggled. "That would be adorable."

"Don't you hate that shit?" asked Renee.

"Paige hated being called a Goth, but she is one. I wanna own it."

"Fair enough," said Renee. "I don't think I'm gonna dress up."

"How's your mom?" Paige took her hand.

"She woke up from the coma, but the doctor says it's still up in the air. She might recover or she might not wake up one day. If she makes it another week, her odds get a lot better."

Santana tucked her hair behind her ear.

"Sucks about your house," said Renee.

Sofia frowned. "Thanks. I hate the stupid hotel. It's gonna take them months to rebuild the place. Can I come over? I wanna see Grim."

Paige smiled. "Of course."

"Your dog's at Paige's?" asked Renee.

"Hotel wouldn't let us have him. My mother was gonna leave him at a shelter." Sofia got worked up, red eyed.

"Mom's not too thrilled with having a dog around, but she understands." Paige chuckled.

"Whatever you did, it worked." Renee glanced at the football game. "Haven't been any more kids getting hurt."

"They still giving you trouble?" asked Paige.

"Not really." Sofia looked down. "Brittany's kinda my friend now… sorta. The others are nicer since everyone thinks I almost died in the explosion." She shivered. "I would have if Paige didn't pull me through the mirror world when Kenz tried to kill me."

"You both got your hands on some grade-A weed." Santana shook her head. "Through the mirror?"

"I don't think it was Kenz. At least not the 'trying to kill Sofia' part." Paige's teeth chattered under a cold gust. She ignored Renee calling her a dumbass for wearing a short skirt, and sighed at Sofia. "I think that was the magic blowing back for breaking the covenant."

Sofia stared into space. "I don't care. We had to stop it from hurting anyone else. Paige did a spell and it worked."

Paige repeated the explanation she'd given them before class a few days ago, about how Mackenzie's book seemed to be something far darker than simple 'witchcraft,' and between the corpse blood and her 'get what I want and damn the cost' attitude, it tainted everything. "Without that, it probably would've done what you asked instead of grabbing on to that little nugget of anger."

Renee, Sofia, and Santana nodded.

"Can I still hang with you guys even though we're not doing spells anymore?" asked Sofia.

"Of course," said Paige.

Santana shrugged.

Renee patted her on the head. "Sure. Every group needs a runt."

Sofia stuck her tongue out.

"I hope your mom gets better." Sofia flashed a hopeful smile to Renee.

"Thanks."

Santana's mood seemed to darken.

"Sant?" asked Paige. "You haven't said much. I'm *really* sorry about your dad. He was like the best teacher in the world. I... I wish I never moved here. None of this would've happened."

Santana lifted her head and stared at Paige for an uncomfortable moment in silence. "That bitch would've found some way to make it work. It ain't your fault... least not all of it."

"It's on all of us," whispered Renee.

"Mostly Kenz." Santana's voice came flat, devoid of emotion.

Paige's lip quivered.

Santana looked away. "No, I ain't gonna kill myself."

"I've been where you are. When Amber died, it was like nothing mattered anymore. I just wanted be with her again. If you ever wanna talk... If I can do anything to help..."

"Mom's still a mess, and Michael ain't much better. He's havin' nightmares of big-ass wolves chasing him in the woods and he thinks if he goes near the high school it'll blow him up." Santana leaned back and stuck her hands in the pockets of her army coat. "My grandparents are flying in from PR Friday to help."

Paige nodded. "That's nice."

Santana scowled. "The insurance company is driving my mom over the edge. At first, they were going through with the paperwork, but outta nowhere they said it was a 'suicide' since all the teachers said Dad was always super careful. Now they think he wanted to kill himself."

"Probably the spell smoothing it over and when she closed the gate it stopped," said Renee.

"Sorry." Paige looked down.

Santana swatted her on the shoulder. "Don't say sorry. You had to do that. Grandpa said they can't refuse to pay out 'cause o' some two-year suicide clause... thinks they're just being dicks to see if we're dumb enough to give up. I don't really care." She wiped at her eyes. "Money won't bring him back."

"Damn," said Renee. "Hey, you could argue he was murdered... a demon did it."

"That might work if the judge is on acid," said Santana.

Sofia cleared her throat. "We should probably never tell anyone what happened. Not like they'd believe it anyway."

"Yeah," said Paige.

Renee's eyes tracked a flying nerf football. "Yup."

"True," said Santana, silent tears running down her face.

Paige held out her hand. Sofia took it, followed by Santana and Renee. "A pact then. We agree to say nothing happened."

Everyone nodded.

"What'd you do with the book?" asked Sofia.

"Nothing." Paige spun her empty coffee cup in her hand, frowning at the chill. *Ugh. My cup ran out of warm.* "Everything blew up. The biggest piece of that cabin was about the size of my pinky."

Santana mumbled something in Spanish. "Maybe it went back where it came from."

"Yeah, maybe." Sofia slurped on her straw again and frowned, as if forgetting her drink had run out.

"Good." Paige threw her coffee cup at the trash, cringing as soon as it became obvious it would overshoot. A random gust caught it and sent it through the hole at the top of the container. She looked away. *No one saw that.*

"I'm gonna go to the hospital." Renee stood. "See you guys tomorrow."

Paige got up and hugged her. "Melissa's making a card for your Mom. We'll stop by tomorrow."

Renee smiled. "Okay."

"Bye," said Santana. "Guess I should go home too."

"You gonna be all right?" asked Paige.

"Yeah. Hardest part is not tellin' Mom what really happened." Santana stood. "She'd never believe me and she couldn't handle it if she did. I can barely look her in the eye without fallin' to pieces. It's a bitch wanting to confess and knowing it'll only make it worse."

Paige grabbed her hand. "Maybe you could deal with guilt by being there for them. You had no way to know what Kenz was planning."

"Easier said..." Santana squinted into the wind. "S'pose I should at least try."

"You hear from Emily at all?" asked Renee.

"She's a wreck, but I think she'll deal. Still freaked out. I think she's avoiding me right now. I dunno if she blames me for what happened, or I just remind her of it all. I dunno." Paige looked down. "Maybe she feels guilty that it killed Cole because I protected her."

"Rough." Renee shook her head. She nodded in the direction of the parking lot. "You two want a ride?"

Paige shivered. "Yeah. It's a little cold out."

Santana wandered off to her dad's car, now hers. Renee stuck her hand in her pocket. Seconds later, a white Lexus SUV flashed its lights.

"Holy cow," said Sofia. "Nice. Hang on, I gotta text my parents I'm goin' to Paige's."

Paige smirked. "Congrats. You paid triple the price for a Toyota."

"It ain't mine. It's Mom's."

Paige winced. "Sorry. I could try a healing spell?"

"I'll kick your ass." Renee laughed.

"It might be okay without a demon book and candles full of dead blood." Sofia looked up.

"Nah. I've had a damn 'nuff of magic for a lifetime." Renee hopped in behind the wheel. "Please, let whatever happens naturally happen."

Paige choked up. "Okay."

Sofia climbed in the back seat.

Renee pushed the starter button with a trembling hand. She made no attempt to put the SUV in gear or drive for three minutes. Tears rolled from her eyes. "You think it'll be clean? I... can't lose my mama."

"If you want me to try, I will." Paige held up her hands in surrender. "Totally white magic."

"Can I help?" asked Sofia.

"'Kay," said Paige.

"Me too." Renee grabbed the wheel.

Paige shook her head. "No, 'Nee. You're too close. Your emotion might throw it off. Hell, I'm guilty enough for all three of us."

"When you gonna do it?" asked Renee.

"Day or two." Paige pursed her lips. "Let me try to talk my Dad into a trip to New Hope first."

# 38

# MOVING ON

Wednesday October 28 - 7:40 p.m.

Paige padded down the stairs, awkward in her frilly nightgown. She felt like a huge doll, and debated how long she'd stay hidden under her bed if anyone at school saw her wearing such a girly thing. Mom caught a glimpse of her from the kitchen as she crossed from the stairs through the hall, and nearly dropped a box of popcorn. Her gaping mouth morphed to a semi-teasing grin.

She sped up and ducked into the living room where Melissa waited on the sofa, covered to the neck in a hot pink blanket. Her little sister's smile became a gawk. Grim, looking much like a grey throw rug someone had kicked into a lump in the middle of the room, perked up. He regarded her for a few seconds before laying his head down again and emitting a contented grunt.

"You wore it!" Melissa squealed and bounced. She lifted the blanket so Paige could get under it next to her.

"Yeah." Paige snuggled in. *Ugh. So much pink.*

Melissa leaned into her, grinning. "Where's Dad?"

"On the phone out front."

"Is it gone?" whispered Melissa.

She looked around. "Is what gone?"

Melissa pulled the comforter up to her eyes and shrank into the cushions. "*It.*"

"Yeah." Paige grasped her sister's hand under the blanket. "It's gone."

The child relaxed. "Did it hurt Amber? I don't see her anymore."

*Uhh...* "How long have you seen her?"

"Since before we moved. She told me you didn't really hate me and said mean stuff 'cause you were hurting." Melissa sounded sad, but looked up with a smile.

Paige hugged her. "I think I somehow brought her back from wherever ghosts go. I guess I needed her too much. Maybe I'm okay now."

Melissa gave her a serious look. "Don't summon another demon or I'm telling Mom."

Paige coughed, and started a tickle fight.

Mom walked in at the height of giggles and set two large plastic bowls of popcorn on the coffee table. Paige held Melissa by the wrists to end the battle.

"That nightie looks cute on you." Mom sat at Paige's left.

She grumbled and made a playful-sour face, while Melissa kept struggling to force fingers into armpits. "Enough, I give up. You win."

Melissa slumped back, out of breath and laughing.

The front door opened and closed. Dad entered with an unreadable expression and flopped on the sofa to Melissa's right, sandwiching her between him and Paige.

"How'd it go?" asked Mom.

"Captain Hourihan had some questions no one could answer about the bank incident. Lieutenant Benton has apparently decided none of this ever happened. I'm in the clear, but that Sweeney kid didn't show up on any of the security cameras. Only a vaguely human-shaped shadow. They're blaming the software. We had enough witnesses that the cameras weren't that important anyway."

Melissa snuggled at Paige's side.

"Do they still wanna interview me?" asked Paige.

"Nope. Everyone's more or less assumed the kid was high, even though the toxicology screen came back only showing low levels of pot. His hair tested positive for LSD and methamphetamine use, but he didn't have detectable levels in his system at the time. When no one could explain anything, it's like all the doctors looked at each other, said 'flashback,' and closed the file."

Paige held Melissa like a living teddy bear. Things weren't perfect; her little sister had wicked nightmares, and couldn't sleep alone. That didn't much bother her though, Paige found herself fond of sharing the bed. Being able to sleep through the night would take getting used to. Dad struggled to deal with the aftereffect of killing two people. He seemed to have trouble sleeping; the undying knife-wielding man left a mark. *Guess that's why he got a bigger gun.* Mom had gone clingy with both of them. Paige wasn't sure how much of Mom treating her like a nine-year-old she'd take before snapping, but for now, a doting mother proved a whole lot easier to deal with than demons running loose in Shadesboro.

She exhaled.

Paige's new iPhone erupted with The Cure's *Burn*. She jumped, stuffed her hand into the side pocket of the nightie and fumbled the phone to her ear. "Hello?"

Dad and Mom both gawked at her.

"She didn't just say 'speak,'" whispered Mom. "Maybe we should take her to a professional."

Paige rolled her eyes, but smiled.

"Paige?" asked Emily. She sounded mousier than usual.

"Em…" Paige sat up. "How are you? I'm so so so sorry…"

"I… not too good." She sniffled. "Umm. I think Cole is here, trying to talk to me. I'm still trying cope with everything that happened. I'm freaked out, but I'm not mad at you."

Melissa snuggled tighter.

"I…" Paige sighed.

"Renee talked to me. I know it was Mackenzie. Hey, do you think you could come over sometime and maybe do like a séance or something?" She seemed to be working hard to hold back tears. "If he's trying to communicate, I need to know."

"Uhh, sure. I can do that. Friday after school?"

"Thanks. See you then."

Paige let the phone slip back in her pocket. "Emily wants to know if Cole's haunting her."

Dad pursed his lips. "Guess this is the new normal."

"That poor girl." Mom rubbed Paige's back.

They sat in quiet for a few minutes, Mom looking like she couldn't come up with anything to say, Melissa content to snuggle, and Dad lost in thought.

Mom grabbed the remote. "So, what do you girls want to watch?"

Melissa and Paige exchanged a glance, and answered at the same time.

"Nothing scary."

*fin*

# ACKNOWLEDGMENTS

Thank you for reading!

Nine Candles of Deepest Black is so far the first book I've written where I had a title picked out before I had any inkling of story. I was at a Barnes and Noble signing copies of The Summer the World Ended, and something in sight must have snagged on my subconscious. Out of nowhere, the title came to me and I knew I *had* to write a story to go with it.

I'd recently read *Malus Domestica* by S.A. Hunt, and I'm quite sure that put the whole 'witchy' thing in my head. Within a week of that signing I had an outline, and not too long after that the first draft.

So to that end, I'd like to thank Sam for the inspiration.

Many thanks go out to Kate Bystrova for her excellent advice while editing and Eugene Teplitsky for a most excellent, creepy cover design!

# ABOUT THE AUTHOR

Originally from South Amboy NJ, Matthew has been creating science fiction and fantasy worlds for most of his reasoning life. Since 1996, he has developed the "Divergent Fates" world, in which *Division Zero, Virtual Immortality, The Awakened Series, The Harmony Paradox, and the Daughter of Mars series* take place. Along with being an editor at Curiosity Quills press, he has worked in IT and technical support.

Matthew is an avid gamer, a recovered WoW addict, Gamemaster for two custom RPG systems, and a fan of anime, British humour, and intellectual science fiction that questions the nature of reality, life, and what happens after it.

He is also fond of cats.

Visit me online at:
   Facebook: https://www.facebook.com/MatthewSCoxAuthor
   Pinterest: https://www.pinterest.com/matthewcox10420/
   Goodreads:                           https://www.goodreads.com/author/show/
7712730.Matthew_S_Cox
   Email: mcox2112@gmail.com

# OTHER BOOKS BY MATTHEW S. COX

### Divergent Fates Universe Novels
### Division Zero series

- Division Zero
- Lex De Mortuis
- Thrall
- Guardian
- Harbinger

### The Awakened series

- Prophet of the Badlands
- Archon's Queen
- Grey Ronin
- Daughter of Ash
- Zero Rogue
- Angel Descended

### Daughter of Mars series

- The Hand of Raziel
- Araphel
- Ghost Black

### Virtual Immortality series

- Virtual Immortality
- The Harmony Paradox

### Prophet of the Badlands Series

- Prophet's Journey

### Divergent Fates Anthology

- Containment
- Catalyst

Alexis Silver series (with J.R. Rain)

- Silver Light
- Deep Silver
- Silver Quarrel

Samantha Moon Origins series (with J.R. Rain)

- New Moon Rising
- Moon Mourning

Vampire For Hire series (with J.R. Rain)

- Moon Master
- Dead Moon

Maddy Wimsey series (with J.R. Rain)

- The Devil's Eye
- The Drifting Gloom

Samantha Moon Case Files series (with J.R. Rain)

- Blood Moon

Immortal Operative series (with J.R. Rain)

- Broken Ice

Young Adult Novels

The Eldritch Heart Series

- The Eldritch Heart
- The Cursed Crown

Evergreen Series

- Evergreen
- The World That Remains

Middle Grade Novels

The Adventures of Ubergirl series

Tales of Widowswood series

Standalones